# My

# Nemesis

## MIRROR OF DECEPTION

MY NEMESIS, SPECIAL COLLECTORS EDITION

PAPERBACK

ISBN-13: 978-0615947051
ISBN-10: 0615947050

Cover Design by Aija M. Butler
Cover Design: AMB Branding
ambbranding@gmail.com
**http://mynemesisthebkseries.blogspot.com**
Facebook: www.facebook.com/ambaijamonique
Instagram: @ambmonique
Twitter: @AMBBRANDING

# ~THE MIND'S EYE~

## WEATHER THE STORM

## ~1~

# Conscious

Joy gasped as the inhalation of the open air hit her seemingly virgin lungs. Abruptly she awoke buried deep into an abyss of darkness. She feared she was abducted. Joy was unable to open her eyes. She began to panic tussling around, moving her fingers in search of clues to her surroundings. Joy's arms and legs burned as she tried to free herself. Her eyes moved rapidly under her lids. She was afraid, but fought to calm herself as she called her attention to the footsteps approaching.

Joy swallowed hard and braced herself as best she could as the quickening steps moved closer to her.

"Good morning Mrs. Anderson, we are elated that you are awake."

"Where am I?" Joy was groggy and in desperate need of water. Her body ached, she moaned and groaned trying to adjust herself to a comfortable position.

"Mrs. Anderson, are you ok?"

I am scared. I feel as if I am crushed between two walls." Joy's eyes were badly bruised and swollen. Her face arms and legs were bandaged. "I can't move or open my eyes. What has happened to me? Where is my family?"

"Don't try to move too suddenly, you are just feeling fatigued and sore. You were in a coma for 3 weeks. I am Dr. Swartz. I was the doctor that operated on you after your accident."

"Wait… what?" Joy tried to move but she was sadly mistaken. She could barely wiggle her fingers. Her pain was minimal, but somehow she knew her injuries were serious. It hurt for Joy to speak. Her forehead creased as she swallowed under her bandaged skull. Her throat felt as if she had swallowed glass. She began to gasp for air.

Dr. Swartz quickly dropped his clipboard onto the bedside table and fetched the cup of ice-cold water and a straw. "Here Drink this."

Joy sipped slowly flinching as the cold water wet her palate. Even the cool liquid burned her throat, its pain was different, as though sores on her tonsils were being burnt away.

"Slow." Dr. Swartz directed. "Take your time. Your throat is very sensitive as we just removed the tubes from your throat less than 48 hours ago. I can only imagine how thirsty you must be. I want to talk to you a bit about your case."

Joy slowly wiggled her fingers, indicating that she understood the Dr.'s words.

"Joy you were in a terrible car accident. Your car sped off the road and into the river just below the hill. It is a miracle that you are alive. The impact of the water broke the windshield of the car. You suffered some blows to your head. You slammed into the steering wheel of the automobile, which caused some neurological damage, to your optic nerve."

"What are you saying?"

"More simply put, the occipital lobe is where sight is processed which comes from the cranial nerve II, the optic nerve." Dr. Swartz was using hand motions to convey his message. Feeling odd at the silence in the room, he realized that Joy was unable to see his hand gestures. Dr. Swartz called out to Joy to make sure she had not fallen to sleep as he explained his prognosis.

"Joy, your visual perception has been severely damaged. As I'm sure you are aware, that **Visual perception** is the ability to interpret information and surroundings from the effects of light reaching the eye." Dr. Swartz paused to try and get some form of response from Joy, indicating she understood his words.

"Wait! What is all this? Is there someone that can come and explain all this in English?"

Dr. Swartz pinched his lips and folded his arms, grateful of Joy's inability to witness his growing irritation. He was slightly aggravated having read Joy's file. Her level of intelligence was way above average.

Dr. Swartz placed a puzzling hand under his chin and as if hit with compassion he softened his aggressive tone. Pulling the visitors chair up to the side of Joy's bed, he cleared his throat and began again. "Mrs. Anderson, due to the severity of your injury's your retina's were singed. Which means you may regain some of your sight but not all. Our team of Ophthalmologist's and I performed an extensive amount of tests to evaluate your sight.

The neurological damage in relation to the brain that allows for vision is severe. We have concluded that you are in fact, legally blind. I know this may be a lot to take in, but I need you to understand what type of life you will lead after sustaining such an injury."

Joy began to black out. None of what the doctor was saying made any sense. She could not recall the moments leading or following the accident. She had no interest in discussing them either. She wanted to know where her family was.

"Excuse me. I don't mean to interrupt." Joy tried to clear her raspy voice unsuccessfully. "I don't understand. Will I regain my sight?"

"We are not sure Mrs. Anderson. Many people diagnosed with blindness, have experienced periods where they can see clear as day, as if they were never blind.

Others see light, shadows, or just can't see in color. We are however optimistic about your situation. You have surpassed all of our expectations."

"Where is my family?"

"Your husband is out with your children waiting for the results of my evaluation. I did not tell your husband about your issue with sight. You just woke up and I did not want to overwhelm them with science and medical jargon. I wanted to talk with you to determine how lucid you were. I see that you are a literary agent and hold a degree in psychology yourself, so you understand the functions of the brain and mind.

However, being a victim of such tragic events can alter the most intelligent person. I would like you to seek counseling. I would also like you to take the time to just recover, this means, NO WORK." Dr. Swartz tilted his glasses to get a better look at his patient. He could not tell by way of facial expression, her attitude towards the matter, but the silence spoke for itself.

"Joy, it will take you some time to get used to the new you, but I see no reason why you will not be able to continue in your life's work. You will just have to be patient. I am setting you up with some rehabilitation as your wounds heal. "

"I understand." Joy commented without emotion or the slightest interest to continue the conversation. "This is some new me." Joy whispered sarcastically.

"Mrs. Anderson, with today's technology you can use the voice command system on your computer to write and correspond with your clients. You will be fine. The rehab will help you learn how to live with your disability. Many learn to read within a year. I have great confidence in you. I will leave you now to visit with your family. I am sure they are very anxious to speak with you."

"Wait! Joy took all that she could muster to get the

docs attention before he whisked out of the room. Please, do not tell my family about my blindness. I don't want them to know."

"I wouldn't advise you to be silent in a matter as serious as this. You will need all the support you can get."

"I understand, but if I am going to live with this I need to deal with it in my own way. My family isn't used to my not being able to carry the world and tend to their needs. I think that they are devastated enough. I will tell them, but in my own way and on my own watch. Please just extend me this courtesy."

"I have no choice. It is against policy for me to divulge information without consent. I will, however advise you to tell your husband right away. It is important that he understands the extent of your injuries. He seems like a very good man. He hasn't left this hospital in the three weeks you have been here."

"Really?" Joy smiled and tried to adjust her position in bed. "Patrice is a Godsend." Joy spoke in an elevated gesture as the annoying twinge continued to aggravate her. Her narcotics must have shut off midsentence. She moaned at the flame of pain that flowed through her torn flesh and broken bones.

"Are you ok, Mrs. Anderson?"

"I think the meds just wore off."

"Ok, I will get a nurse to get you something for pain right away. In the meantime I will send in your family so that you can see them."

"Thank you." Joy was exhausted. She squinted because her eyelids were itching. She grimaced at the agony as she squeezed her eyes shut in an attempt to relieve the itchiness.

Dr. Swartz was gone in a flash. His long white jacket flew in the wind as the revolving door closed slowly. Just before the door clicked into its sill, she heard a familiar voice. It was Justin. She tried to pry her eyes open to test the severity of her injuries, but they were glued shut by crusted pus.

Joy began to panic. Her breathing grew rapid and her heart felt as if it were fluttering about in her chest. "What's happening to me she thought?" Trying to regain her composure she began to tell her self that things were going to be okay. The pain and loss of sight would just be temporary.

Joy was beginning to use her breathing technique to regain control of her mental capacity. Until, suddenly, a woman's voice uttered words of discouragement. They were so loud and clear she could have sworn the strange woman was standing just over her head.

"You are blind, you idiot. You will never see the faces of your husband and children again. Now look at you. Once again lost and taken into a vulnerable depressive state. Are you trying to kill me? I would just assume so."

"Hello!" Joy called out frightened by the woman's words of discouragement. Her pupils moved rapidly under her badly bruised eyelids. "Is anyone there? Who are you? What are you talking about?" Her presence was gone as quick as she came. She whispered into Joy's ear, leaving behind a cool breeze that frosted the tip of her nose. The sensation was an awakening of her sixth sense.

Joy heard her words, but quickly let them go. She was excited to see her family. Realizing that she would not be able to see their beautiful faces, a tear strolled down the sides of her eye. Her tears began to pool and be soaked up by the gauze that covered the remainder of her face. They were quickly absorbed. Joy heard the door of her room open and then the soft scuffs of little feet. She knew then that her boys were in the room. Lagging behind dragging was her daughter. "How frightened she must be." Joy thought to herself. She did not want any of her children to see her like this.

Justin stepped forward. She could smell him

instantly. Again, the tears wet the dried pus on her eyes. Justin leaned in and touched her dry and cut lips. "I am so sorry." Justin whispered unable to hold back the emotion that had cut off his breathing. He began to sob hard like a baby and fell into the seat, next to Joy's bed. Joy wiggled her fingers, as she tried to reach for Justin's deep shining waves. She longed to touch is soft mane. She wanted to touch him, to comfort him.

It was not his fault as she led him often to believe. He was her muse and the only one she knew would care enough to listen and take heed to her feelings. Burdened often with the dysfunctions of her family, she held her tongue.

Tired and frustrated with their obvious lack of respect for her and her own livelihood she took out her anger on Justin often. It was a fight she had not planned. Her anger flowed from deep within her pores. She could not stop her mouth from moving and slaying his very being. She was so angry, so rude and horrifically nasty she herself could not believe it.

Memories prior to her accident started to flow as she calmed the worry from Justin's brow. She was guilty of tearing him to shreds because of her need for acceptance, now she could hardly stand the feel of her own skin.

Her mother showed up at her place of business after years of very little contact to ask her for help. Joy's mind scattered angrily, but still in need of the comfort and closeness a daughter longs to have with her mother, she let go of the past. Gullible Joy fell for her Mother's plea and gave her five thousand dollars from their joint account.

Justin was furious when he found out. It was not the money he kept stating to a confused belligerent Joy. It was the fact that she had kept it from him and lied when the bank statement rang true of her deception. Joy grabbed her purse and threatened to leave him as she always did, when she did not have the answers or when conflict arose.

~ 10 ~

Justin called her bluff, an unusual stance from his normal reaction to Joy's threats. He tossed Joy, her keys and blew her a kiss goodbye sarcastically as he knew her better than anyone. Joy shook her thoughts back into reality and managed to abandon her thoughts of guilt.

"It's okay." Joy finally managed to speak. She did not want Justin to feel responsible for her accident. It was neither one of their faults. A driver was careless and lost control.

Joy called her attention to her children. The boys were afraid and stayed towards the back of the room. Joy could feel the tension. She could not see them, but she could hear Jr. asking Ashley if it was their mother under the bandages. He thought that perhaps she was a mummy or ghost.

"Shh!" Ashley whispered loudly, pulling Jr. close by her side. She jerked him so hard, Joy could hear him grunt and his shoes scuff the tile floor.

"Don't pull on your brother like that Ash." Joy scolded. "Come to mommy. The three of you, come here. I need to tell you all something."

Ashley and the two boys inched slowly towards Joy's bed. Justin gathered himself and picked up his head from his slumped stance. Justin encouraged them to come closer to their mother. Jr. took his small hand and placed it on Joy's swollen fingers.

"Mom!" he yelled "You in there? What happened to you?"

"Mommy had a little accident, but I am going to be alright. I am glad you are here. Where is your little brother?"

"Right here, open your eyes!"

Justin looked up and took hold of Jr. He placed his hand on the small of his back and began to coach Justin Jr., about his mother's condition. "Son she can't open her eyes right now. They are sore and bruised. Its better if she keeps them closed."

Ashley was quiet. She didn't know what to say and she was afraid to come any closer to her mother. Worried that her mother would be angry or sad that she refused to engage in the visit, she forced herself to ask her mother if she was in any pain. "Mom, I hope you feel better. Are you in any pain? I could get the nurse." Ashley felt so uncomfortable she would have given anything to get out of the room. Joy could sense that she wasn't interested in staying in the room, but decided that she couldn't give her a pass. Her presence made her feel alive and she needed her children to be close.

"No honey, I feel as good as can be expected. It looks much worse than it is. I can't see you, but I can tell that you are far away. Could you come closer? Your voice is a mere echo. Why are you so distant?"

"Mom you know I hate hospitals. I hate being here. I hate that you are here. Dad can we go, please?"

Justin looked up with a look on his face that could have killed. Ashley stifled herself abruptly.

"What's wrong?" Joy said softly. Her throat was hurting and her arms and legs felt crushed. She didn't want to alarm Justin and the kids, so she pushed the nurse call button discreetly. Justin noticed how quiet Joy had become and that her nurse call button was on.

"Are you ok Joy?"

"Yes, fine."

"Babe, it's me you are talking to. If there is something I can do I would like to know?"

"Just a little pain that's all. I alerted the nurse. The doctor said that he was going to let the nurse know that I needed some medication for my pain, but she has yet to come."

"How long ago was that Joy?"

"Justin its ok, calm down. The pain just got a little

worse. I went ahead and sounded my alarm to remind the nurse's station is all. Please calm down. I don't want you to get all worked up for nothing. You should take the kids home. I am sure they have had a long day. I don't want them to see me like this for too long. Besides the boys could have nightmares. I don't want them to get this image of me locked into their minds."

Joy tried to smile, but the sores on her lips cracked and started to bleed. She licked her wounds and could taste the salted blood. Justin grabbed a napkin and wiped her lips softly.

"Justin." Joy said softly.

"What is it?"

"My lips hurt like hell."

Justin fiddled around in the drawers next to the bed and retrieved the complimentary Chap Stick from the top drawer, to soothe the burn of his wife's torn lips.

Joy was filled with a soothing sensation a mist the pain, as her husband touched her lips. Joy smiled, "So, how bad do I look? I mean from what you can see. My face feels so swollen under these bandages. What if I don't look the same? What if my face is deformed or scarred?"

"All that doesn't matter, I love you. The important thing is that you are alive. I want you to concentrate on getting better, so that you can come home, Ok?"

"Ok." Joy was weak with pain. The pain had become so unbearable she was nearing her breaking point. She wanted badly to call out for help, but she didn't want to alarm her children. "J...." Joy paused as the pain stifled her breathing. "Please take the kids home. I need to get some rest."

Justin could take a hint. He could tell that Joy was in pain and didn't want the kids to bear witness to her suffering. "Ok babe, we are going to go home. Get some rest." Justin coached the kids to come close to their mother and say good-bye. They each gave her a kiss on her lips. Jr.

was playing with his mother's fingers. He didn't want to leave. He was very protective of his mother.

"Jr., it is time to go. We will come back and visit mom soon." Jr. stood his ground for a moment later. He retreated when Justin lowered his eyes. Jr. knew he had better do what he was told. Ashley came close to her mother and kissed her softly. She whispered I love you and ran from the room. She was on the verge of tears and in her preteen years it was against the rules to show signs of emotion.

Justin looked down at Joy one last time before grabbing up the boys and retreating from the room. "I love you babe." he whispered as he opened the door to leave. Coming into the room was the nurse, bearing the gift of narcotics.

"It's about time." Justin scolded. He couldn't help himself. It angered him that the doctors and nurses weren't taking care of Joy. He looked back at Joy, smiled and bolted down the hallway to get Ashley.

Joy's veins warmed as the medicine seeped into her blood stream. In mere moments her mind drifted and asleep she went numb to the pain, but hurt for her family, as she so longed to be with them.

# ~2~

## HOME SWEET HOME

The next two weeks of rehab went by in a blur. Joy recovered from most of her injuries with flying colors. Her sight was the most disabling issue from the accident. Joy blew a frustrated hand gesture towards the nurse asking her to perform a few more leg lifts. "I know you mean well but I'm pooped. I just want to walk without a cane, maybe run a few laps around my living room and kitchen. I need to keep up with my two little rug rats. I am in no way interested in running a marathon, Nurse Betty."

"You could have fooled me." Nurse Betty chuckled. "You have been G.I. Jane to most of the nurses in this wing. I am motivated to get on a treadmill myself for a spell."

Joy laughed hard. As she wiped the sweat from her arms and neck. Opening her drawers to retrieve her belongings she froze as if lost in time and smiled for just a moment. She loved the sound and the way it felt to have some normality and happiness in her life. She was so excited about her recovery. The nursing staff showed very little concern for her recovery, except for Nurse Betty.

Nurse Betty always pushed her to fight just a little harder. Joy grew quiet as her mind drifted. Leaving the hospital after such a long stay was frightful. She was filled with mixed emotions. She found herself becoming quite teary eyed as she continued to pack the remainder of her things.

"Joy, it's ok? You will be fine." Nurse Betty comforted, as she too felt the lump settling in her throat. "I am going to leave you to get the rest of your things in order. Justin already phoned. He and the kids are on their way to pick you up."

Joy managed to smile through her confused state. "Ok Thanks. I will be ready shortly."

Joy squeezed her eyes tight before she made an attempt to open them. Her deep brown eyes lightened to a soft hazel after the accident. They blended perfectly with her cappuccino colored skin and natural spiral mane that danced just below the nap of her neck.

Joy opened her were eyes greeted by a blinding white light. Literally, shocked by the painful blow, she shuddered at the thought of a second attempt to open her eyes. Taking in a deep breath she bravely opened her eyes for the second time slowly. Her vision was blurred. She could make out shadows at best. Everything was in black and white. She was now, a character in a 1950's drama. All she needed was a stick of ruby red lipstick and finger waves.

Joy closed her eyes and continued to pack her things. She had become quite used to the dark. She could feel when others were near and her sense of smell heightened. Joy became overwhelmed with fear when she thought about reuniting with her family. Her biggest hope in recovery was to regain her sight.

"Mrs. Anderson? Are you all set to go home today?" The discharge nurse on duty came by with her clipboard to run through her list, standard protocol for patients being discharged.

Joy laughed to herself at how serious the nurse sounded. She was quite interested in what she thought she could steal from the hospital, some towels, a gown, maybe some slipper socks. She sure as hell didn't want the watered down lotion and shampoo. Joy smirked and let out a loud chuckle at her thoughts, "Now, Dove and Caress, is cause for worry." she spoke with an arched eyebrow while gathering her belongings from the side table drawers.

"Yes I am quite excited. A bit worried, but I am very excited to see my family." Joy looked down when she realized that she wasn't going to be able to see anyone, not the same anyway. She had in fact been dreading going home. She was going to be faced with yet another challenge. She was fearful of going back to her life as a mother, let alone her business.

The voice command program she had set-up on her laptop was an intelligent invention. However it had quite a few quirks to work out. Most of her dictation was poorly imputed. The playback was both hilarious and illiterate. She would be sure to forfeit her license if she published works relying on the good sense of her computer alone.

"Don't worry about it Joy. Your family is ready and waiting for you to come home. The kids are very excited. Justin was telling the staff how much they were doing to help you get settled in. The kids are making you a welcome home dinner and cleaning the entire house for you. What a treat? I wish my kids would volunteer to do the laundry, take out the trash or maybe wash a dish or two."

"Oh Girl don't worry." Joy chuckled as she stood slowly to put her things in her bag. "This is all just temporary. They will be back to their normal destructive selves the moment they get wind I can scramble an egg. I will be sure to milk this for what its worth. I'll have an update for you by the time my next check-up rolls around." Joy turned towards the air blowing in slightly through her 5th floor window. "The air feels good." Joy smiled at the thought of the wind blowing into her hair.

"Good luck to you." The discharge nurse scratched on her board and left with a satisfactory spin.

"Yeah thanks." Joy reached down to retrieve her bag. She heard the door opening and her heart skipped a beat, "Justin is that you?"

"No, just me, I just wanted to make sure I said

goodbye before I left for the day. You know I'm happy you are better, but sure sad to see you go. I am going to miss our late night chats. It made my nights go by fast. Oh and the laughs. Thanks for listening to my ranting about the other nurses. This wing has some rather funny characters. I often wonder where they got their credentials."

"You will be surprised." Joy laughed. "I will miss you too."

"I know you are worried about regaining your eye sight. There are plenty of success stories that you can derive some motivation from. You may only be able to make out shadows for now, but who knows in a year's time. If you continue your rehabilitation you may make a full recovery. Don't always listen to what these doctors say. You and I both know that there is a higher power working in our favor."

"Yes. I know Betty thanks. Sometimes I have to be reminded about God and his grace and mercy. Even though he is always showing us his goodness, we forget about the blessings he has bestowed upon us. I will take this one day at a time." Joy zipped her bag and sat on the edge of the bed. Her lunch had arrived. She could smell the chicken and potatoes.

"Well eat your lunch. Justin and the kids should be here any minute. I wouldn't want him to tear the place down if he found out we didn't feed you."

Joy smiled, "Who Justin?" Joy commented sarcastically as if she didn't know her husband could cause a stir.

"Yeah, him." Nurse Betty sashayed from the room leaving Joy to enjoy the comforts of peace and solidarity for one last time. She was soon to be greeted by a tribe of overly excited children and a husband that would drive her crazy with questions and pampering. Not that she minded it much.

# ONE YEAR LATER

# ~3~

## MRS. JOY ANDERSON

"Honey, do you have everything you need?"

"Yeah, I think so. I wish you were coming with me."

"I know sweetie, but you will be fine. Just give your father a chance. He and his family are very excited to meet you. You have a grandmother and grandfather you've never met. Many people should be so lucky to have two sets of living grandparents." Joy looked down at Ashley's floral printed bedspread. Her mind drifted away to a far away land. "Ever since my father died, I've seen things a lot differently. I know Justin has been your father since you were 2 years old, but you should know your biological father as well. Justin and I have had our disagreements about this from time to time. However, we both agreed that up until now, you were too young to be bounced around. We just wanted to protect you. So please don't blame your father, he has made a number of mistakes. Although I can't say that he doesn't love you, he does so very much. Both of your fathers do."

"Mom all that is well and good and I know that you guys were protecting me. That's what parents do. I get it. I also get that I have a father. I don't care about visiting those people. If they knew about me and where we lived, why haven't they come to see me? I don't want to go?"

"You're going!"

"Why? What is this really about Mom? Is this because of the house and the stress you have been under? I can help. I know the boys can be a handful."

"No Ash, you don't have to. I want you to go and enjoy yourself. I need you to. It's not the house, it's me."

"Are you sick? Ashley began to get worried. She started to shake immediately, as the tears began to stream down her face. She always had a hard time with stress and anxiety. It was as if she went into panic mood at the slightest notion that something was wrong.

"No!" Joy smiled crookedly as her lips quivered visibly. She was lying and she couldn't hide the emotional effects that stormed upon her. She hated lying to her family about her recent battle with illness. Her physical health was deteriorating. As a result, her mental state of mind was flawed. She became delirious at times, with a vicious rage that she could not explain. Her actions were murderous. Her memory was short, just like her temper. The family knew as much. The tension so thick, often you could cut it with a knife.

Justin was close to breaking down himself. She thought for sure he'd file for divorce. Joy couldn't bring herself to tell the family that she was dying. She knew Justin well. He and the children would waste the time she had left pitying her. Sending them away while she went through treatment was best.

Joy and her sister Samantha spent countless hours researching possible treatment centers and trial studies, for her rare lung disease. Ever since the doctor called with the news, Joy was on edge. Sam begged Joy to just tell her family what was going on so that they could support her. Her change in mood was obviously unsettling to the children, because she was usually such a fun loving, easy going spirit, a workaholic, but clearly devoted to her family.

Sam and Joy did stumble upon a small research project that involved some heavy duty consent forms and cash. Joy didn't care she had to try something before giving in to informing her family of the news. The treatment would cost $10,000. Ten thousand Joy couldn't afford at the time. Justin and Joy had just bought a home. Her business loan was excessive and tutoring for Ashley was an arm and leg. Although Justin's business flourished she couldn't go to him for the money, without explaining the need for such a large amount of cash. So she was forced to take her business elsewhere, a place she'd rather not expose. It was almost as bad as going to a loan shark for the money.

Darin, Joy's ex, supplied the funds. His cocky throwback swag was from something out of the old gangster film, "New Jack City." He sat at the head of the table unnecessarily far from reach, as he discussed the terms of the loan. Joy nearly threw up as he whistled with his teeth and his tongue. He always wore this nasty, gritty, sex face, when he talked to her. His nose was turned up and his brow creased as if something smelled.

Joy knew the game already she knew exactly what he wanted. In exchange she would finally agree to send Ashley down to visit for a few months. Joy swallowed hard as she agreed. She didn't have an excuse not to send her since her preteen years arrived. Her main excuse had always been that Ashley was much too young to be traveling alone, or visiting strangers without her presence.

"Mom, are you ok?"

"What I'm fine? I just drifted off for a moment."

"Yeah, I know. You were squeezing my hand. Is everything                                                                      ok?

"Yes of course. I'm just going to miss you, is all."

"I am too. That's why I should stay home." Ashley cheesed with her bright overly exaggerated smile she used when she was trying to get her way.

"Nice try! Grab your things the train is always early when we are running late."

"Mom, you always do that."

"Yeah, but this time you really have a train to catch. So let's go. Let's go." Joy threw her hands in the air shooing Ashley to grab her bags.

Justin was already heading for the car with the boys in tow.

"Hey were you going to say goodbye?"

Justin turned around with a glare in his eyes that burned Joy's face. She could literally feel the heat as she touched her reddening cheeks.

"I wasn't aware you cared, with the way you are shoo flying us about the house. One would think you were deliberately trying to get rid of us for some odd reason."

"Justin stop, you are being ridiculous. I am going on my book tour. I have a ton of research to do, meetings..." Joy shook her head and raised her arms, as she pinched her lips tightly together. "This trip will be good for you and the boys. I will drive up next week. It makes no sense to postpone the trip, waiting around for me. Go! Take the boy's they are going to love the snow." Joy smiled and bit her bottom lip at Justin seductively.

"Whatever Joy." Justin couldn't help but smile at his lover and best friend.

"I just wish you would put this book tour aside. You can go and sign books anytime."

Joy looked down at the ground solemnly and kicked a few pebbles from her garden back into its bed. Realizing that she may be giving away the possibility that something was in fact wrong, she perked up as if a switch was turned on and off. "Yeah you say that now, but when the publishing company refuses to pay my advance, you will be singing an entirely different tune."

"Funny Joy, real cute, you better have your ass in Yellow Brook by noon Sunday morning. Remember we are taking the boys for their Jr., ski lesson."

"Ok, Big Daddy. I will be there with bells on. I can't wait for you to see my night in the snow lingerie."

"Yeah me either." Justin grinned. "I doubt you'll be wearing it long. Justin winked at Joy and got into the car. The boys were fastened tightly in their seats and screaming, "Daddy let's go." They were anxious to get on the road. "I love you Joy." Justin screamed out the window as he began to back out of the driveway.

"Oh Yeah." Joy replied smiling generously. "For how long, just for today?"

"No Babe, *Always Infinitely*."

Joy waved her last goodbye and ran into the home to recover, from the cold on her bare soles. She slammed the front door and ran to her soft shaggy rug to warm her chilling feet. "Wow, I'm really going to do this. What if it doesn't work?" Joy blew a tendril from her eye. It was itching and irritating her eyebrow. She plopped down on the couch and sighed. "I hate that I lied about this whole treatment business, but I just couldn't bear to get Justin's hopes up. I hadn't even told him I was sick and if he thought there were some chance at a cure he would be sure to stress himself. I couldn't risk him worrying about me. We have the kids to worry about. I do hope this works." Joy was pacing the living room floor, until she found herself in the kitchen searching for her Hagen Daz ice cream and a huge spoon. "I hope and pray I can just make this nightmare go away." Joy said as she gulped down a huge spoon full of ice cream and looked into her reflection peering through the spoon.

Joy gathered her thoughts and took the tour around her home. She hadn't been home alone in such a long time. She didn't know what she was going to do with herself. Joy locked the doors and windows of her home and made her way to the upstairs bedroom. She had a plan to soak in the tub and review a couple of chapters, of her life's work before going to bed. She was shaky about how her book would end. So she decided to use her time soaking in a tub of bubbles to perhaps brainstorm some fresh ideas.

Joy couldn't help but think of Justin and the kids. Ashley should have been half way to Los Angeles by now. Joy thought to give them a couple more hours before she phoned to check on them.

As the water filled the tub, her mind raced. She really had no interest in reviewing her notes on the book. Her stomach was hurting. She felt nervous and uneasy. Stress and anxiety were two of Joy's major setbacks that threatened her sanity. She wasn't comfortable being alone in the home. Nor had she been away from her children or Justin longer than a day at work, or temporary stay, at the hospital, since the accident. The home was too quiet and dark.

Joy turned off the water to her bath and ventured off into her master suite, to let the water cool before she took a dip. She had her own, "cleansing system" she liked to call it. She would run the bath as hot as the temperature allowed and wait for the water to cool to her liking. Lightly skipping about the room, Joy located her remote and flipped through the channels. As she turned she noticed that all the channels were blue. "Damn It." an irritated Joy threw her arms in the air and rolled her eyes. Blowing her hair from her brow she smacked the side of the television. "I hate this TV. I knew we should've switched services." Joy shut off the receiver and hit the power button to reset the device. As she waited for the television to reset, she scurried into the bathroom to check her bath.

As Joy tipped into the bathroom, the winds blew wildly rattling the glass and shudders. Joy's stomach dropped, but she quickly gained composure. She leaned over the tubs edge to check the temperature of her bath, when suddenly, the glass window of the bathroom shattered, falling inches from her head. More than shaken, Joy ran from the bathroom to search for her tennis shoes and gun. She thought for sure there was an intruder afoot. Boldly shuffling through her drawers and boxes, she cursed

Justin and thanked him just the same. The gun was a plus in this particular situation, however to find it she was sure as dead.

Justin thought it best to protect themselves and their property. The neighborhood was very nice and quiet, however his motto was, "Better safe than sorry." Justin bought his and her guns in case of an emergency. Joy sighed as she grabbed her 22 and unhooked the safety. She moved quickly to the hidden door of her bedroom closet.

The bedroom closet led to the basement. It was the perfect hideaway in case of an emergency. Joy grabbed her purse and cell phone, as she ran down the stairway towards the basement. She quickly powered on her phone and dialed 911, as she bolted the trap door.

"911, what is your emergency?"

"I think someone is trying to break into my home." Joy's heart beat fast and her blood pressure elevated from the adrenaline pumping in her veins.

"Ma'am, get to a safe place. There is a terrible storm coming, she is the most horrific our parts has seen. The Reports from the Natural Disaster Bureau predict her to touch ground in approximately ten minutes."

"Oh My God." Joy's mind drifted. Her thoughts ran together and showed flashes of her life, as though they were scenes from an old movie.

"Ma'am...did you see the intruder?"

"No, the window broke in my bathroom. I thought someone was trying to get in."

"Get to a safe place. It may have just been the winds from the storm. It's coming down pretty hard out there."

Joy swallowed hard, as the worry began to burn her cheeks and ears. Her skin was incredibly hot and her stomach felt sick. "I am in a safe place." Joy mumbled as it was becoming hard for her to speak. "I locked myself in the basement."

"Good Ma'am. Stay put."

~ 26 ~

Joy was delirious. Her thoughts ran wild. She couldn't help but think about her family. She wondered incessantly if they had traveled out of range of the storm, dodging the horrible twister.

"Ma'am."

Joy was standing with the phone glued to her ear. Hanging up the phone, she quickly switched her psyche into survival mode and hung up and called her attention to the beeping sounds from her television. The emergency broadcast system had just chimed in, protocol for natural disasters and safety guidelines were unconceivable. Joy listened and stood so still it was as though she were paralyzed. Her mind locked somewhere between la, la land and earth. She had completely blacked out just as quick, as her natural instincts rang. She couldn't hear or see a thing.

Joy was filled with odd feelings. She was nervous. Quickly, as if being pulled by a force outside her grasp of understanding, Joy searched the basement pantry for safety equipment and emergency supplies, another one of Justin's plans of action. He was serious about emergency procedures. He had the kids practice fire drills and earthquake precautions monthly.

As Joy rumbled around the pantry gathering supplies, she felt an enormous amount of fear hovering over her clouded mind. She had been in many storms, but none as gruesome as a tornado. Trying to get her water supply into the deep freezer, she winced with pain, as she tried to hike the 5 gallon jug of life just over the freezers edge. Just as she was able to get the jug into the freezer, the lights went out. "Shh...! That's just great." Joy slapped her hands on the side of her jeans and sunk to the floor just in front of the freezer. She buried her head in her hands and began to sob softly.

# ~4~

## PRINCESS ASH

Ashley, stared blankly into the window of the train, as the country hills blew by. Passing through the San Joaquin Valley was peaceful and a great time to think things through. She was only twelve, but an old soul, much like her father. Ash was nervous about meeting him. She didn't quite know how she was going to address the situation.

She wasn't exactly honest about her feelings. She wanted to get to know him and her new sister. She was just worried about hurting her stepfather's feelings. She knew her mother wanted her to get along with both sets of parents. She expressed how lucky she was to be blessed with such a loving and accepting family, often.

Although Ashley was excited about seeing her biological father, she still had a number of questions she needed to have answered. As a new thought lit the memory bank in her mind, she looked down at her paper of scribbled pros and cons to jot down some of her most recent thoughts. She was very much like her mother. The pen and pad were her most treasured tools. They were also the most powerful. Ashley was great with creative writing and had received a number of awards for her writing.

Deep in thought Ashley began journaling, the exciting adventures of her trip home. She called the adventure, "Home" because she was traveling to a place where she would meet the other half of her creator. Finally, the pieces of her soul would be united and she would be able to fully understand who she was and where she had come from. She wrote of her past meetings with her father. They were vague, but she remembered bits and pieces of their encounters. It was important to her to write, the description of him as she remembered. She wanted to fill in the blanks, when she saw him again.

Ashley was beginning to get sleepy. The Hot Chocolate was a Godsend. It calmed her nerves and enabled her to write freely, but it relaxed her muscles so much she felt extremely exhausted. Suddenly, the lights went out overhead and the train shook violently.

Ashley unbuckled herself to get a better look at what was happening. She flew from her seat. Concerned and out of touch with the seriousness of the situation, she swayed with the trains vibrations, sliding from seat to seat as the train danced on and off the tracks.

A woman was slumped over in her seat and bleeding. She was sitting next to a small girl who was in tears and screaming. Ashley was shaken herself. She rushed to help her sit up in her seat and grabbed a pillow. The woman was unconscious and the little girl seemed to be crushed by the seatbelt buckle lodged in her bulky parka. Ashley tugged at her belt to loosen the girl's belt and adjust the woman seated next to her in an upright position.

"You are going to be ok, is this your mother?" Ashley consoled the little girl whose eyes were beginning to well with tears.

"Yes." the little girl responded filled with fear and uncertainty. Her mother warned her about strangers, but she felt safe speaking to Ash.

Ashley rubbed the girls arm and gave her a reassuring smile. "Sit tight and keep an eye on your mom, ok."

The little girl nodded to confirm she understood Ashley's instructions just before the trains lights began to flash on and off.

Ashley made her way back to her assigned seat as the attendants flowed through the aisles to help passengers stay calm. There was a loud chatter thundering down the small wing of train cars. Ash began to get alarmed. She reached for her phone, but it had fallen from her coat pocket and was on to the floor of the train. She caught sight of it just before it slid across the floor as she plopped back into her seat. Ash grabbed her journal, but her gloves were too thick for her fingers to grab hold of the flimsy pages. The Journal soared across the train car as the beverage cart flew past her cheek. She could feel the burn, as it scratched her, much like the rug burns, her older cousins gave her at family functions.

Ashley began to panic fumbling about her seat she grabbed her seatbelt as the train began to sway out of control. Her hands were shaking so badly that she could hardly buckle herself in. The bell rang just above Ashley's head as she grabbed her armrests. Her heart was beating out of her chest.

"Ladies and Gentlemen, please get to your seats and take refuge."

"Refuge?" Ashley whispered to herself. "Could we use 12 year old language here? What the Fuck is going on?" Ashley quickly stifled herself, as she could hear her mother's voice in her head telling her to remain calm and watch the language. Ashley swallowed hard as the panic button resounded just overhead. The Conductor mumbled on incoherently. All she could hear were muffled sounds of panic and distress. It was in that moment Ashley let go of her cocky attitude and prayed that her Mom and Dad would come to her rescue.

Ash closed her eyes tightly as the loud sounds of wind and rain hit against the metal of the train. The trains Plexiglas windows shattered and the body of the train melted into thin air. Ashley felt lifted into the heavens as the wind whipped her and the other passengers in her car up into the air. The spinning made her nauseous. She hated rollercoaster's. Wind and dust entered her lungs as her napkin mask, she held tight around her nose and mouth ripped from her face. She never opened her eyes. She dreamed as if she were a ballerina dancing at an opera. She was without fear gliding upon the stage. She was gone without a trace, a peaceful trip that she happened to chance upon.

## ~5~

## NO EXCEPTIONS

"This trip is long over-due boys." Justin ranted on, as he drove up the winding hills. The sky had turned dark and the winds blew furiously. Traffic was so backed up he could see lines of cars for what seemed like miles ahead. "Hold on Boys, I am going to see what the hold-up is, around here." Justin jolted with a dash as he jumped from his truck to take a look at the scene. The wind was cold and chilling to his bones, his muscle tee blew in the wind like a sheer scarf.

Justin thought about his coat that was in the trunk section of his Suburban and ran against the wind to grab it. As the winds velocity began to pick up, Justin threw on his coat anxiously in an attempt to shield himself from the blows of the wind and rain.

As the showers began to pour, he took notice of the other drivers looking high towards the east of them. A large cloud was swirling in place and growing larger by the second. Justin ran towards his car, after slamming the trunk of his Suburban. "Boy's!" Justin screamed afraid more than ever. The Boys were sleeping soundly. The sounds of rain patted the windows of the truck, rocking the boys to sleep. Justin's eyes began to swell with tears. Others around slowly got into their cars to take cover. Some stood and embraced their loved ones bravely to face the inevitable.

Justin was lost in thought and in emotion. He was scared for the lives of his children. Joy was at home alone, he couldn't bear to think of the thoughts running through her mind. Justin's breathing grew shallow in his over-sized puff coat. He pulled himself from under the smothering fabric and began to pray.

Frightfully, he grabbed his steering wheel and locked eyes on his two boys sleeping in the back seat. Tears began to stream down his cheeks. Unable to tear his gaze from his children, he buckled his seatbelt slowly. Justin commanded his On Star to phone Joy. He was worried about her and wanted to make sure she was ok. The phone rang once and went straight to voice mail. Justin was so disappointed he wanted to break down and cry.

Clearing his voice he waited for the sound of the beep. "Joy, honey its Justin. I just wanted to check in on you. I love you, Honey. Talk to you soon." Justin knew in his heart that it may be the last call he would place. He was saddened at the thought that he wasn't with Joy during this disastrous time.

The last thing he wanted her to know was that he loved her. As he hung up the phone, via his blue tooth he removed it from his ear. It was coming down pretty hard. The other drivers were beginning to panic. Noticing the winds picking up speed and velocity he took precautions to lock the doors and make sure all the windows were up in his Suburban.

As the spiraling Queen of winds sang, Justin curled tight in the backseat with his two boys shielding them from the possibility of broken glass.

The howling wind danced, to her tune of destruction as she captured the lives of men, women and children, all looking with shocked helpless eyes, as there were no exceptions. After the winds treacherous vengeance on Mother Nature the roads were left with a soft whistle. Debris scattered the roads, bodies of all kind lay badly battered and bruised. The rings in their ears were the last sounds of life.

Justin closed his eyes as his shelter was swallowed into the wind. He went peacefully at the thought of his children dreaming serenely in the fold of his arms.

## ~6~

## AFTER THE STORM

Joy came from under her wooden shelter. The whistle of the wind dissipated scampering behind was a soft whisper. Joy was so afraid she had never experienced such an event. When the tornado hit it was like the wind was screaming. The blustery weather was calling out murderous vengeance against the wrongs humans did upon their natural resources. She was stunned at the damage the tornado left behind. She was underground and still felt its wrath.

Joy winced as she pulled herself up from under the wreckage. Her wooden shelter gave way about half way through the storm. She was lucky to have recovered without medical attention, after suffering such a blow to the head.

During the storm, a can of half empty paint, fell from the edge of one of the wooden storage shelves above her haven and hit her in the head.

Joy's arm however, was in worse shape. It had suffered the blunt of the shelves demise. She used her shoulder to shield herself, as she was knocked to the ground. After the blow to the head all the strength she could muster was to simply, ball up into the fetal position. Leaving her arm fully exposed her head and face protected.

Joy was crushed by the wood. With her arm in such pain it took some time to free herself. Joy threw herself into survival mode and limped from the wooden pile. She couldn't believe her eyes. The glass of the basement windows was broken and the curtains blew slightly as if breathing faintly. There was a shadow of light that streamed into the basement exposing some of the damage that lay upon the basement floor.

Joy stood in the middle of the lighted path and gazed out the window. She was slightly hunched over. The pain was excruciating. It was starting to cloud her judgment. For a moment she could have sworn she saw her husband Justin, standing just outside among the fallen debris, holding the hands of their three children.

Joy blinked anxiously trying to clear her mind and vision, as the warm blood from her battered head, dripped into her right eye. She hadn't realized she was bleeding. Joy frantically wiped the blood from her eye and forehead and blinked again limping towards the window as fast as she could. She nearly stumbled over her own feet, as her mind was moving faster than her body could carry her. She blinked again and grabbed hold to the windows edge. The glass from the shattered window pierced the raw flesh of her hands. She didn't take notice.

"Justin....Ash... Jr., Josh!" she called out to the winds. They were whispering something. All she could see clearly were the remnants of the rose bushes she and the kids planted, when she and Justin first bought their home.

The petals were scattered on the ground and along the cement path which led to the backyard. Joy could see clear through the fence that once separated her and her neighbors. It was destroyed and taken by the tornado. Joy called out to her children once more.

"Ashley Josh, are you ok? Can you hear me?" Still nothing but the dim whisper of the wind, she couldn't even hear a small cry for help. It was like the town had been abandoned and she was its only resident.
Joy looked down at her hands. She was squeezing the window sill so tightly she hadn't noticed the blood oozing from her pinched fingers.

"Oh my God," Joy realized that she was hurt and looked out the window for one last glance, before she sought medical treatment. There was nothing but the wind remorsefully praying its apologies.

Joy retreated from the window and went to look for her emergency backpack she managed to pack just before the storm hit. She had found the first aid kit, Justin purchased in case of a natural disaster. It was in perfect condition, never opened.

Justin was funny like that. Over protective and well prepared. It was almost as if he was waiting for his chance to cast for the next season of, "Survivor."

Joy remembered how she used to tease him about his, "MacGyver," concoctions. He was always inventing some type of gadget out of little to nothing, to either protect himself or use for survival. Now she loved that very trait about him. Some of the, "Go, Go Gadget," monstrosity's were high on her list to help find, food and shelter.

"I don't think you planned on a tornado hitting good ole sunny California, did you baby?" Joy was smiling as she talked to herself. She was busy climbing her way back towards the entrance of the basement.

"I sure hope we have something left to climb out to." Joy sighed.

# ~7~

## THE SHADOW

Joy thought about her relationship with Justin. They were more than lovers, they had become best friends. The Anderson pact was a vow to handle the decisions of home and family jointly. It was hard to believe that they had been together for almost ten years. With every season's passing their love grew stronger. Loosing Justin would be unimaginable.

The Anderson's had only bought their home a year ago. It was their first official purchase together. They had rented and financed cars separately, but they had never actually purchased something of long term that they shared name and title. After they finally decided to get married it became official. They were going to walk the walk and truly trust one another with their lives and the lives of their children.

Justin and Joy had both suffered from the trials and tribulations of a dysfunctional home and family. So they took their devotion to one another quite seriously. Joy had some stability after she was removed from her mother's care. However, she never got over trying to make sense of what had occurred in her youth. She was still trying to gain love and acceptance from both her mother and father.

On the other hand, her father was trying to gain forgiveness from her. He blamed himself for the abuse Joy suffered at the hands of her mother's new boyfriend, at the tender age of 6. It would take Joy years to reveal her abuse.

She had suppressed the memories of her nightmares to survive the harsh realities of the world.

As if her mother choosing a man over her wasn't enough. During her years of adolescence the dreams began. She was tortured nightly by the visits of the, "*Shadow.*" The "*Shadow*" was the name assigned to her assailant. He'd appear after dark, when the house was quiet. He grew tired of her mother and would venture to other parts of the home to seek comfort.

His ritual became frequent as he stood in the lighted path just outside her door. Standing there breathing, she could see his chest rise and fall. The smell of beer on his breath stung her eyes, as if he were standing just over her.

After the abuse became a ritual, Joy often awoke with unexplained scratches and bruises on her arms and legs. Cuts that were so deep it looked as if she were cut with a knife. It was clear the markings were from fingernails, hers to be exact. She was fighting to free herself from the man. "*The Shadow*" a demonic plague, a horrific reality that began to invade her dreams salting her innocence.

**\*\*\*\***

Joy's mind drifted into a distant place. She sat on the staircase of the basement, reliving her demons. The counseling sessions after her accident had gone far beyond the scope of her expectations.

Depression came along for the ride when she was released from the hospital. Joy was argumentative in sessions and often refused to participate in discussion. The truths that she would just as easily bury along with her were challenged and sought.

After weeks of pulling teeth Joy finally opened up, enough to share her story. She was nearing a breakthrough, but for some reason she shut down when the dreams came back to life. It was like a force from the devil and his advocates that were insistently, trying to keep her in their realm. Once the dreams came so did the voices, she was just as bad as the Shadow's wrath. It was as if she encouraged her demise. She as in the other woman that plagued her mind, a soul, both Joy and her Doctor debated upon existing. She was damaged goods. She'd spent the better half of her adolescent life hiding her dark side. She was taunted when sparks of this revelation were revealed. There was someone else that lay dormant in the corners of Joy's mind.

# ~8~

## MEET LILIAN ANDREW'S

*I am the Angel of Night, the demon prince of conception. My gift is of vanguard invention. I can bring forth both good and evil, for my mind controls both quarry and praise. Andras is my other half, a killer of men by way of conjuring magic. I am one that has many faces, I am hard to detect. Deception is my game. Malice is my true claim to fame.*

"Joy would you like to talk about your childhood, the abuse to be exact?"

Joy cleared her throat. There was never a good time, to speak of such horrific acts, acts that should never have happened to an innocent child. Her legs grew weak. Her throat began to burn. It was hard to swallow, as her mouth went suddenly dry. The palms of her hands shook, tipping over the glass of water she attempted to grab. Giving up on wetting her parched lungs, she adjusted herself on the couch and folded her arms, as if to comfort herself.

Joy's forehead began to fold and bead with sweat. She sat very still, remotely focused on the black and white oak table that sat just in front of the couch. Dr. Zimmerman was nothing but a mere shadow, of light. Her only clue as to the good in him, as opposed to the dark shadows, that lurked in her consciousness. Joy swallowed hard as she began.

I was 17, when the dreams resurfaced. They originated when I was 12. I quickly suppressed them and continued living in darkness. My caramel complexion was bright and glowed in the sun. The outside seemed bright and anew. Just beneath the first layer of skin was meat, tainted and rotting. My soul was dark and dismal. The joy of life was gone. My reflection was a distorted, mirror of broken glass.

I was only 6 when it happened. I remember like it was yesterday, the wind in the trees, the darkness and quiet of the night. I could smell him from a mile away. My door was always left open at night in case I had a nightmare. However, the nightmares weren't happening in my sleep. There were living breathing, torturous moments of my childhood. I would just rather forget it ever happened. I'm not sure that it did. At least I don't remember much of the abuse. I don't reckon anyone would want to, unless they were planning some sort of revenge. 14 years old was my time of awakening. The dreams began. So did my bout with the troubling, "Teen Opera" of adolescence.

I was short, awkward, the times were changing and I was lagging behind. I decided that my hair would look grand in one of those jerry curls, television commercials were advertising. The hair do turned out to be a hair do gone wrong. I was so excited to get to school, to showcase my makeover, only to realize that my new style was the hot topic of last year's fashion trend.

8th grade happened to be the year of A-symmetrical haircuts, short one side long on the other. I still can't understand the concept of cutting one side of your hair short and leaving the other long. What if I wanted to where a ponytail. I don't know, it seemed like a good idea at the time, so I joined in. I have this need…this need to be different, but the same equivalently. I share what is meant to be sacred to us as individuals."

"Is this going anywhere?" Dr. Zimmerman purposely queried, trying to egg Joy on towards a break into her maladjusted past.

"I don't know, you tell me. You're the professional. I don't have an identity. I still question my own judgment."

"Last time I checked you wanted to be me. A counselor that is, Brain Doc."

"I did until I found out that my head was much too screwed up to remotely assist in someone else's problems. My cup has been full since I can remember. My mind has always raced, raced in many directions. Maybe that's why I have never been able to decide on a for sure career. I am an unstable victim of circumstance. I think I could use that excuse for the rest of my days. Many say you shouldn't over use your sob stories for sympathy. However, it has worked for me. Why fix what is not broken? I have been broken so many times and in so many ways it really doesn't matter to me if I am evidentially readable. It hasn't caused too much of a set-back. Brains and Beauty has some advantage you know.

Honestly, the thoughts in my brow are often not of my own will. I act on emotion where this invasion, acts on rage. I am plagued daily with thoughts of suicide simply to end my torment. Is this open and clean cut enough for you?"

"So what do you do? How do you deal with this invasive woman?"

"Whatever sounds good enough to believe? I have no defense against this inhabitant. She is my curse. One that I propose I have been punished with, in another life."

Dr. Zimmerman was not, satisfied with Joy's use of her alternate psychosis. He tapped his pencil on his pad to a beat thumping about in his head, again looking to aggravate Joy's alternate ego. "You seem to enjoy using this new found addition to your personality to fall upon when you have clearly made a slip in judgment. It must be nice. So, how long do you plan on keeping up this act?"

"What act? I'm serious about my new practice."

"I'm not talking about your writing."

"Is any of this supposed to go anywhere? What does this have to do with my dreams? They're back. I haven't had one for about 4 years now. About the time, Darrin and I broke up. What do think this could mean? My relationships go to shit, when the Shadow returns. It doesn't help that more often than not all I can envision are the shadows of my life, the good and the bad. It's hard to decipher what is what. I get scared."

"We went over this. You need to get past the issues you have with your father. It's time to grow up. You have to be the adult in this. I know it's hard to swallow, but it is what it is."

"That's rich. How in the hell and I supposed to get over the fact, that my father wasn't there to protect me when I needed him. He let that man molest me over and over again. He left my mother to be beaten while he went on his creative ventures. I hate him."

"I don't think this is at all true. I think that you were a child, left in a horrific situation, but you were taken by family and well taken care of might I add."

"Is that supposed to make everything better, Dr. Seuss? I mean these riddles you are throwing at me are great. Sure wish this information was of some use to me."

"We are out of time. The good doctor has clients waiting, other clients with real issues."

Dr. Zimmerman was anxious to get rid of Joy he had a date with some files that could be very insightful to the origin of Joy's mental state.

"I don't know what to do ok? I need help, more meds, something."

"No doctor in their right mind will give you a prescription." Dr. Zimmerman didn't want to prescribe Joy any more medications that would add on to her possible hallucinogenic traits. She appeared lucid at the present time. He noted that her mind could possibly remain uncompromised in the absence of therapeutic drugs. He knew full well that he could not prevent her from seeking counsel elsewhere, but he would try and keep her within his practice as long as he could. He was so close it became evident that the dreams and flashes started when she started taking the drugs. Without the hefty side effects, Joy would be forced to deal with her inner demons.

"Just forget it. What was this anyway? We spend an hour rehashing my indifference. I reopen the secrets of Pandora's Box every time I come to you. I leave feeling just as broken and confused as when I came in. What is this? None of my family seems to give a shit about what I am going through. Or whether they truly believe me, is still a mystery. Tell me what to do? I can't keep coming back here and leaving empty handed. It's not fair. This talking to you about nothing is exhausting. Things aren't going to change. I at least need the meds to calm me. Don't do this. I need the medication."

"No you don't. You need to deal with your real issues. If you keep masking them with drugs you are going to lose everything. You are not alone, in this."

"Yes I am doc. Yes I am." Joy grabbed her purse and slung it onto her shoulder violently. She was dangerously close to brushing the Doc's face, with her leather hobo. She secretly, pondered upon knocking his glasses off his face. He looked so brave and bold. Not a care in the world. He held all the cards. Joy didn't want to play his games any longer. She needed a new way to get her hands on medical supplies. Her usual fight with prescription drugs wasn't as bad. Lately, it's all she seemed to care about.

Joy ran down the hall to make the elevator. She was angry. Her plans were falling apart. If she didn't have the meds to fall back on, there was no way she would ever get sleep. Her mood swings were erupting far less sporadically. She was shaky at best and her work was suffering severely.

"I want out of this mess of a life." Joy sunk to the bottom of the floor of the elevator and threw her head into her hands. "I just can't take this anymore. I can't go home."

"You must. You have children."

"How did you get here? I don't want to hear any more of your stupid ideas about me. I'm sick, sick in the head, ok. I need professional help."

"No you don't. You are sick, but not in the head. If you weren't so busy, feeling sorry for yourself you may be able to accomplish something."

"Well I don't need you. It's not the first time someone has abandoned me. Even, I don't believe in me. I don't expect you to stay. Why are you here anyway? All the confessions you made about my so called evil spirit. I just love how you showed the doctor a thing or two. I can't even get my prescriptions filled."

"Begging for them sure wasn't going to get the job done. Maybe it is time for old Sammy, to come and plead your case. You should start using your resources. They sure haven't hesitated in using your services for the greater good, when they need something done."

"Maybe right now, I just want to get the hell out of here, before I have a nervous breakdown."

"Nervous breakdown." Lillian shook Joy's head in amazement of how co-operative her brain was working towards deceit. "That may not be such a bad idea. You are thinking a little more along my lines of deception."

****

Joy shook the thoughts, visions and haunting spirits, to cause her attention to the whereabouts of her family. If she could manage to find her phone charger, she would be able to get some juice on her phone. She was saving her battery to call Darrin. She was sure Ashley should have made the station by now. Justin she knew would have taken refuge with the boys, if he had the foresight to do so, before the storm hit.

Recovering from her slighted loss of focus, she

continued up the barricaded staircase to make way through to her home. She was nervous, but hoped for a miracle.

# ~9~

## SAMANTHA, "SAM I AM"

Sam awoke from her nap confused and discombobulated. She was shocked that she could sleep through such a tragic event. The tornado passed through her calm streets like a hovering cloud. After it touched ground miles away it lifted like a plane taking off. The evening news showed spectators reporting their sightings of the great tornado and its wrath.

"Wow!" Sam chuckled as she threw back the covers on her bed. That was some nap. She was well rested after her long snooze. She was so exhausted, but couldn't get to sleep so she took a sleeping pill to help calm her nerves. She had slept so soundly, if the house had been air lifted into another state, she wouldn't have even known it.

Sam got up and scooted to the edge of the bed to find out just where the tornado had touched ground. She was laughing out loud at some of the idiots broadcasting how scared they were of the whirlwind torpedo, but stood dangerously close to its angry winds.

"It had to be one of us." she said to herself as she shook off her restless state, to regain full conscious awareness. Sam turned her attention to the news broadcast.

"Disaster has struck in our otherwise sunny state. California has never seen such a storm. The angry winds of the great tornado have past. All we have left are remnants of our homes and precious belongings. There are shelters opening in nearby cities. If you need shelter, please do not attempt to stay in your home. The foundation of your homes may be very unstable. After suffering such a storm there are several problematic issues that can cause further horrific fatalities.

The American Red Cross is asking that you be careful around electric wiring and gas stoves. There could be a leak somewhere in your home or business. The American Red Cross is also asking that if you are a Dr., Nurse, or Health Care Provider and you are not injured, please look to find a shelter to volunteer your services. The county hospital was hit hard. The local clinic is open and is being prepared for emergency patients only. Patients with minor injuries will have to be looked after in their local shelters."

Sam sat down and as she began to worry. "Oh my God, I hope everyone is okay.' I better find my phone."

Sam ran about the room tossing her covers and pillows here and there to uncover her buried phone. She was beginning to get nervous the way she did when she wasn't in control. Diving onto the floor to retrieve her phone as it toppled out from under the crumbled bedspread. She fell to the floor as if rescuing a live grenade.

Sam dialed Joy's number without looking and paced the floor impatiently. "Damn it, Joy pick-up the damn phone." Sam had begun to get frustrated with Joy and her stupid electronic devices. She prized herself on having the latest of everything known to man, in technology. Yet she failed to answer or respond to any of her messages.

"God I hope you are ok." Sam grabbed her shoes and slung them onto her feet. For the last two years it was only she and her older sister, Joy, left in the family. The others were gone, gone on to bigger and better things. Sam was both envious and angry with her siblings for abandoning one another. She was stuck on family and believed in strength in numbers. With six other brothers and sisters she was confident that if they had vowed to stick together, nothing could break them.

Sadly, there closeness is what ultimately caused a need for separation. The others were the reason for most of the disputes in the family. The ones they loved couldn't understand why they had to be so close. Why they called one another when the other was in trouble or in harm's way. Quite often they were teased individually by their companions about who would be called to rescue them from their burning eyes.

Joy was the peacemaker. She believed in family and she held on for as long as she could. She tried to foster and nurture the importance of family and education. Some of them listened. Some felt as if to feel the burn, was the essence of life. Joy believed in risks and taking those that would amount to something. "Selfish endeavors would only end in defeat." She whispered those words every time one of lucky 7 got into trouble.

"The lucky 7," is what she called them. Lucky she said they were, lucky to have such a task force of support. Even in times of indifference, if there was a knock on the door, which threatened to bring harm to one of their flock, there would be a wage of war. No questions asked.

Sam paused as she grabbed her purse. The aftermath of the storm, showed reports of the damage done in the city where Joy lived. Sam dropped her purse and keys to the floor when pictures of the city were flashed upon her large 64 inch flat screen. She was so shocked and dismayed that she couldn't move. Her legs felt like stone. She was frozen. Her hand covered her open mouth and her eyes were wide with surprise. Sam's thoughts were spinning out of control. She didn't know what to do next. She quickly grabbed her purse and keys and headed for the door. Fumbling to get her jacket on her arms she dropped her phone onto the kitchen floor. It didn't shatter as it hit the tile flooring. Her case was like magic. It finally did its job. Her phone remained in mint condition. The shell was now trash, but her battery could easily be put back into her phone without complication.

"Calm down Sam everything will be fine." Sam tried to calm her frantic spirit as she dove for the floor to pick up the pieces to her phone. Her arm was half way in her leather blazer and her hair was thrown towards her face blocking her view of the phone. "You have got to get a hold of yourself. Oh My God, the boys, Charles. I hope they weren't in the middle of the storm?"

Charles and her children worked and attended school in downtown San Francisco. He and Justin were in business together and worked out of offices in Oakland Hills as well as the San Francisco Bay Area. Sam was anxious to get in touch with Charles. She knew he had meetings during the afternoon, but had no idea where they were located.

Sam finished gathering the necessities for her trip and mapped out the quickest route to get to Joy. Since most of the roads would be closed she would have to go around. She could only imagine the traffic. She had no choice but to go and find out if she was ok. Oakland was hit the hardest. The number of causality's grew by the minute. Sam changed the battery in her phone and sprinted to her car. She wanted to try Charles one last time before she got on the road.

Sam got into her car quickly and followed her safety precautions, before dialing Charles again. "Come on Charles pick up." Sam wanted, needed to hear his voice. Even though she knew now that Charles and the kids didn't feel the brunt of the storm, she needed to know that they were ok. The most Charles and the boys experienced were some heavy rains for about a half hour. Sam breathed in deeply and exhaled as she heard Charles clear his throat in an effort to say hello.

"Hey Sam. You ok? I have been trying to call you for at least an hour now. My phone has been going in and out since the power outage."

"Oh my God. I am so happy to hear your voice." Sam sighed with a sense of relief. "I didn't realize the power went out where you were, as well."

"Yeah it's out, in blocks all over the city. We are having some sort of rolling blackout. The tornado took out some power lines in Oakland, power lines which we all happen to share. I'm just happy to hear that you are okay. I checked with the boy's school already. They are fine. All the students were ushered into the auditorium. The principle is holding all of the students there until the parents arrive to pick them up."

"Okay great. I am so glad to hear that."

"Where are you?" Charles noticed the quieting winds hitting the phones receiver. "Are you outside?" Charles asked with a hint of aggravation in his voice. "What are you doing outside? I heard the highway patrol discouraging anyone without an immediate need, to stay inside. You aren't going where I think you're going, are you Sam?"

"I have to Charles. She is all alone. Her book tour was this week. The children and Justin left this morning. She has to be worried sick. Plus what if she's hurt? If you heard the news, then you know?"

"Then I know what Sam? That you are running out to save a grown woman with a family of her own. She has a husband that loves her just as I love you. You can't be everywhere all the time."

"You know what, that was an awful thing to say. You can be really harsh at times. I love you Charles. I will see you soon. Thank you, for picking up the kids." Sam hung up the phone. She turned on her blue tooth and put her earpiece on. She started on her way.

\*\*\*\*

Charles reluctantly hung upend disconnected his phone from his car charger. He was fed-up with the club rules of sisterhood. Trying to shake the thoughts of envy from his brow, he was reminded that a member of his team was not accounted for.

Justin, friend, family and business partner, had yet to check in with him either. Justin had phoned Charles about a meeting with a client that he needed him to head up in light of his family trip. He was so caught up with chasing his secretary and hiding his gambling debts he simply forgot. Charles was often preoccupied with Sam and the kids, finding out about his secret obsessions with cards, horses and sport bets. He could handle his indiscretions it was Sam he couldn't deal with and her meddling sister, Joy.

Charles worried that without Justin, he would become lost in his own mind. Without Justin to calm his nerves, the straight and narrow path he fought hard to emulate, would be lost in the winds. After all, Justin had become the big brother he never wanted, but realized he needed.

# ~10~

## THE INVISIBLE WALL

Joy came from within her shell and decided to shake herself back into reality. She had drifted into a cocoon of worry and destitution, afraid to come to the realization of the inevitable. Sounds of unfamiliarity came from what was left of her living room. Without a second thought she pulled herself up from her knees and dusted her fears to the wind. Stepping high and fast over the debris she flew from her den and ransacked the gentleman from behind like a 300 pound full back. Wrestling the man down to the ground, her hair clouded her vision. Beating him about the head and shoulders she yelled murderous, threats and obscenities as the man begged for his life.

"Please, I am not an intruder. I'm here to help."

Joy ignored his plight. "Get the hell out of my house, you thief."

"Please lady I can't find my wife. I am looking for her and other survivors." Joy stood up slowly still holding tightly to the man's worn sweatshirt. She wasn't sure that she could trust him. Joy could admit that she did seem a bit deranged. She was screaming and howling like some crazed animal that managed to escape its cage.

"Cut the crap! I seriously doubt your wife would be in my home."

"Oh really?" The strange man straightened his stance and wrinkled his brow. He folded his arms across his chest and prepared to be enlightened by her ideas on the matter. "I didn't know that the tornado had designated quadrants in which they threw people. I don't know where she is. I have scoured the entire neighborhood for more than 5 miles from here. Still, there is no sign of her."

"I'm sorry." Joy looked down at her hands that were still trembling with fear and rage. "I don't know what came over me." Joy looked down at her hands as her heart softened. "I didn't mean to hurt you. I just didn't expect anyone to be snooping around in my home. It's amazing how people become so helpful during times of trouble. Instead of trying to help others most are too busy trying to help themselves. What is your name anyway?"

"It's Mike." He smirked scooping out the room. Mike traced his hands along Joy's mantle and picked up one of the figurines. He tossed it in the air as if to toy with Joy. He knew she was concerned about his presence and beyond agitated. He smiled her way and placed it gently where he found it.

Mike was a mysterious rogue. He continued his investigation looking high and low around the perimeters of Joy's living space. Joy felt uneasy about Mike and his infatuation with her home and personal belongings. She began to conduct a plan of escape in her mind.

Mike became intrigued at a vase that sat unharmed on an end table beside the couch. He recognized the design. His eyes lit up as he knew that the vase collection was very rare and over a hundred years old. Not paying attention to Joy's growing agitation and worry about his true motivations, he picked up the vase to admire its beauty more closely.

"So I guess you are all alone, huh? My wife isn't here, I don't see your husband or any rug rats running about." Mike whistled through his teeth and dusted his hands as if preparing to eat a hearty meal.

Joy cleared her throat, "Get the Hell out of my home." Joy pointed her finger praying to God that she could hold her hand and finger still, hiding the tremors of fear overcoming her cognizance.

"Sure lady, I meant no harm. You got yourself a nice piece of art here. Lucky she didn't break. I wasn't looking to steal. I just complimented you on a fine piece of artifact you have here." The surprisingly cocky man looked around the open room and smiled a crooked smile. "I sure as hell wouldn't call this a home." The man said as he looked around the remains of Joy's beautiful 5 bcd room home. He stared at Joy for a moment longer and put his hands down to his side. "Hey let me know if you see my wife, will ya, she owes me money?"

Joy was frightened more than ever, he surely had a different agenda. Joy clutched her cell tightly in her palm searching discreetly for her power button. With one push ICE would be on alert. The "In Case of an Emergency." application on her phone was a Godsend. This Mike character was obviously no stranger to the family, but none of which she had, had dealings with. It was her only hope that Justin hadn't either. The fact that he had her home address is what stifled her with fear.

Mike pointed his finger at Joy immolating a gun and pulled the trigger. "See you soon." Mike scurried out the new exit to Joy's home and was gone with the wind. Joy's entire left side of the living room was completely gone. It was like they were standing in the middle of the twilight zone. Privacy and their rights now exposed to the public.

Joy looked out into the open space and remembered how close she came to finally feeling safe and comfortable. Her home was destroyed. Her vision blurred and filled with tears, as she walked among the destroyed pieces of her most treasured items. Joy called out to God for help. She was becoming weak with emotion.

Joy's home phone began to ring. Just hearing a sign from the civilized world gave her strength. She was weak with emotion, but filled with the yearning to survive and bring her family home. Joy wiped her face and fled about the rubbish on a search to recover her phone.

"Come on Damn it." Joy was frantically throwing around the fallen pictures, lampstand cushions. "Ring...Come on, I'm here I just need you to ring again damn it." Joy was so frustrated. It was lost among the rubbish.

She fell down to her knees and began to scream. She began to cry hysterically. "I've got to get out of here. I need to get to my family."

After a few moments alone with her break down she recovered with a new found passion to rescue her children. She looked up suddenly as if she could hear their voices calling out to her. Joy cleared a path, so she could put some things she would need for her trip to the side. "Where the hell is my purse?" Joy quickly thought aloud as her memory was jogged. "I need to phone Darrin."

# ~11~

## GONE WITH THE WIND

"Hello?"

"Yeah, where the hell have you been? I have been trying to reach you for the last hour. What's going on?"

Joy looked down at her receiver to realize that he hadn't been in touch with Ashley either, "Darrin!"

Darrin was still ranting on as he had yet to learn the news about the terrible storm that had hit the Northern parts of California.

"SHUT UP, for God Sakes." Joy began to sob slightly as she quickly recovered to see if she could get some answers to the mystery. "Darrin where is Ashley? Is she ok? Did you get to her in time?"

"What are you talking about? You're kidding me, right? Joy I was calling you to see if you had in fact really put her on the damn train. I haven't heard a thing and the people here at the train station are saying that they don't even have her train number listed as one of the trains operating today."

Joy sighed at the sign of some hope. "Oh ok." hoping he just got her train numbers confused she ran for her purse to pull out the itinerary for Ashley's trip, "Darrin?"

"Yeah I'm here."

"Her train number, what do you have? I have train number 913."

"It's 923." Joy said plainly.

"Well that figures. I guess I heard something else."

"Ok! Darrin hurry up and see what you can find out. I will hold the line. I am so nervous. I am praying that the train is just running late. Please hurry. I have to make sure she is ok so I can try and get a hold of Justin and the boys."

"Wait Joy what's going on? Has something happened are you ok?"

"Yes I'm fine." Joy's break in speech was clearly a sign that she wasn't fine at all. She was quite fragile at the present time and she still melted when Darrin asked her about her personal comforts.

"There was a terrible storm, it touched down just a few hours after Ash's train left. Justin and the boys were headed towards Yosemite. My home is in complete shambles. I'm worried I haven't heard anything on the news. There have been reports about all kinds of tragic accidents and fatalities. I still however haven't heard anything about Ashley I just recovered my phone and purse from all the rubbish. I got hit in the head with a shelf down in the basement. I don't even know exactly how long I was out before I came too."

"Joy I am going to find Ashley. Then I am coming to get you. We can find the boys together."

"What about Justin?"

"What about him?"

Joy didn't bother to argue Darrin's immaturity at the present time. She needed to find her family. Her heart and chest were hurting so badly, she could barely catch her breath. Joy paused for more than a minute. The anxiety was becoming far too much for her lungs to bear.

"Joy you there? Are you ok?"

"Yes, Yes. I'm here. Just see what you can find out. I need to make a few more phone calls. I am just a little light headed from the blow."

"Joy maybe you should get to the hospital and get yourself checked out. I can take over the search from here. I am sure Ashley is fine."

"No! The county hospital has been shut down. It sustained far too much damage to take on any emergency victims from the storm. I would have to travel way across town or to the shelter either way is about an hour drive. I don't have that kind of time. The fatality rate is climbing by the minute. I need to get a hold of Justin and the boys. You handle Ash. I have tried her cell a number of times, but it's more than likely out of reach or has lost its signal if it's not damaged."

"Will do, but Joy?"

"Yes."

"Please slow down. You need to stay as calm as possible. Your health is at stake as well."

"Ok I will. Now go find Ash. Please. I will call you again in about an hour."

"K, bye." Darrin hung up hurriedly and ran to the customer service desk. He grimaced at his parting words to Joy. "K," Darrin remarked as he took his place in line. "That was beyond weak bro, way to hide your true feelings." Darrin lectured himself as he moved slowly through the line. He waited in line impatiently. Darrin pulled the wrinkled paper from his pocket. Shaking vigorously, he unfolded the paper in his sweating palms and read the numbers to the clerk.

"Sir, how may I help you?"

"Yes um, I am looking for this train. Train number…" Darrin paused as he tried to read the blurring numbers off of the small crumbled piece of gum wrapper. He was nervous and scared and suddenly felt as if he were going to throw up.

"Uh…yes train number 923. I am looking for my daughter she was coming in from the Martinez Amtrak Station. Is the train late? I understand there was a storm down that way."

The clerk looked off to her right and appeared to get uncomfortable. Darrin immediately picked up her discomfort and grew agitated. "Ma'am is there something wrong? Where is the train?" Darrin's voice grew louder as he failed to keep his composure. When the clerk didn't respond he grew angry. She placed her hand over her microphone and exchanged a few words with her colleague. Darrin angrily slammed his fist into the Plexiglas-glass window to grab the attention of the attendant.

"What the hell is going on?"

"Sir, Please. We are checking out that train number. The train 923 was involved in an accident we lost all communication with the train about an hour ago. Technicians have gone out to see what they can find out about the train and its passengers. We have yet to receive any information, but if you would take a seat we will let you know of any updates on the matter. I am truly sorry that we cannot be of more assistance at this time."

Darrin began to sob immediately. "Do you have any idea of the severity of the accident?"

"No sir, not at this time."

Darrin's stomach dropped to his feet. He slowly crumbled the paper in his hand and walked over to the waiting area. His hands were shaking violently. Darrin sunk into one of the metal chairs, as his phones vibration rattled his pocket. Startled by his phones panic ring he shook and scooted to a standing position, almost as if bugs were crawling all over him. Slightly embarrassed he regained his equanimity and answered the phone.

"Damn it Joy." he muttered as he began to speak. He left room for very little response on Joy's end. Darrin was fully aware of how Joy loved control. She would stop at nothing to monopolize the entire conversation. Dictating to him his next move, Darrin was sure to state his case before she could demolish him with her questions and blame.

Still, even years after their relationship ended Darrin felt obligated in rescuing Joy and seeing to her happiness. Darrin rubbed his eyes trying to focus. She was needy, but he couldn't blame her after all the hurt and pain she endured during her childhood. He just broke, Darrin knew his love for Joy would never dissipate, but he couldn't heal her wounds. He awoke one day to realize that perhaps his devotion to Joy was out of guilt. Though he loved her it would be impossible to mend the fences torn apart if she couldn't first learn to love herself. She would never let him in, not completely. She harvested her fear of abandonment and it ultimately destroyed the both of them.

Darrin swallowed hard and answered the phone call. Straightening his stance he coached himself to act like a man, "Hey Joy, I haven't received word yet on Ash's train. The attendant asked me to have a seat in the holding area, while they checked the status of the train. All lines of communication were lost when the storm hit so they don't know what the location is on the train. They sent out an emergency car with tech. support. I am nervous." Darrin's voice was beginning to crack as the emotion overwhelmed him. He was finding it very hard to keep from breaking down on the phone with his first love. However he didn't want to alarm Joy, since she was dealing with the missing boys as well.

Joy was quiet. She was stunned at the horror in Darrin's voice. He hadn't done a very good job of holding in his emotions. She realized that he was merely trying to shield her from possible devastation, but she couldn't rest until she knew the exact whereabouts of her family. She could tell that he was keeping something from her. All she could think about was getting off of the phone with him so she could call the train station herself and get some definite answers about the whereabouts of the train and her daughter. "Ok well just stay put and let me know the minute you find out something. I am getting ready to head out."

"Head out, where?"

"I am going to drive up the mountain. I want to see if I can spot Justin's car. Maybe go up and help the highway patrol find survivors."

"Joy, I don't think that is the safest thing to do. I think you should stay put and stay near a phone. Let the police and emergency personnel handle this. Have you tried to get in contact with Jakes mom? Perhaps she has heard from him. Is she ok? Was she caught in the storm as well?"

"No." Joy didn't seem too much concerned either way. She couldn't believe that Darrin suggested she sit tight while her husband and children were missing. "No. Justin's mom is out of town she and her sister went back home for their annual family reunion. We weren't able to attend. I had the book tour and Justin had the camping trip reserved since last year. There was no way he was going to let all that money, go to waste."

"I see. But I still don't think it's a good idea for you to go out on some vigilante rescue mission alone. We need to start an organized search party, with the help of the police. Contact the police and file a missing persons report. Then check with the highway patrol to see if Justin's car has been seen or found."

Joy sighed as her stomach began to fill with worry. She didn't want to accept that something horrible could have happened to her family, but she needed to at least prepare herself for the worst. Somehow contacting the police made things seem too real for her, as if she were sure that they were in trouble.

"Ok. I will contact them right away."

"What about Sam, have you heard from your sister? Is she ok?"

Joy blacked out for a slight second. She was going

into panic mode. "No I haven't as soon as I powered my phone back on I called you."

Darrin smiled at the thought that Joy's first instinct was to phone him. He was still very much in love with Joy, but she had moved on and was quite happy. Because of that he too, was happy for her and would never do anything to destroy her happiness. "Call them to let them know what has happened. Maybe they can be of some help."

"Ok." Joy hung up quickly and began to dial Sam's number. As Joy began to dial Sam's number she thought that she should first phone Justin's mom to see had she heard from him. Hanging up on the second ring she tried to get a hold of Justin's mom, Patrice.

Patrice answered the phone on the first ring. "Joy, are you alright? I heard about the storm we are trying to catch the next plane out. Where is Justin? How are the boys?"

Joy's stomach fell to the floor just like her hopes. She was sure that Justin had called and checked in with Patrice. Joy didn't know how to respond to Justin's frantic mom. She would be sure to blame her for sending them away in the first place. Instead of answering Patrice's questions she began to explain her side of the story before Patrice could accuse her of being careless.

"I'm sick. I didn't want Justin and the kids to know. I was going to be undergoing treatment during the next few days to see if this aggressive new medicine could in fact give me a chance, at a somewhat normal life. I wanted to tell Justin. I just didn't want him to worry. I was going to meet him in Yosemite this weekend."

Patrice cut Joy's explanation short. She didn't care to hear Joy's excuses after the fact. She merely wanted to know where her son was located. "Joy do you know where Justin and the kids are, are they ok?

Joy grew agitated as she noticed Patrice's disregard for her acknowledgements. Joy realized that Patrice was concerned for her son, but it was also obvious that she was to blame for the whole business as always. In Patrice's eyes she had caused the storm and therefore was responsible for her son's whereabouts. "No. I haven't heard from Justin." Joy finally answered. "I called you in hopes that he had contacted you."

Patrice covered her mouth in an attempt to stifle her horrific screams, she feared the worst. "I will be there by tonight. In the meantime call the police and keep trying his cell. He was in the hills so maybe he is just outside of the call area."

Joy sighed with a calming sigh of relief. She had forgotten that the signal was extremely bad in the hills. Perhaps he and the children were still alive, but couldn't call out for help.

"I am going to drive out there." Joy blurted out in the midst of her thoughts of Justin and the children cold and hungry. "There is no other way to find them. I know where the cabin is and if they managed to get half way up the hill to Yosemite, he and the boys more than likely have hiked up to take refuge in the cabin."

"Joy, Justin is a strong man, but in the eye of a tornado, it just doesn't seem feasible. Please, call the highway patrol and see if they can get a copter out to scour the area."

"You're right. I just can't sit here and wait around. I am driving myself crazy."

"You are crazy alright." A voice from behind Joy's ear whispered into her ear. Joy fought to shake the thought. "This is all your fault. She knows it and so do you." The voice continued to taunt Joy and her senses. Joy shook herself back into reality as she tuned in to Justin's mother calling her name for the third time.

"Joy, are you there? What's going on? Call the police. I am sure they are out looking for survivors in the storm. Maybe they have already found some individuals and are waiting for family to contact them."

"Okay, ok. I will."

Joy hung up and noticed the red light blinking on her phone. Scrolling down her missed calls, she noticed Justin's number. Joy nearly dropped the phone from her hands as she hit her voicemail command in hopes for a miracle.

# ~12~

## LOST AND FOUND

Darrin plopped down into a seat in the waiting area, he twiddled his thumbs as he waited for the train station clerk to come and speak with him. Darrin was startled at the phones ring, he was afraid that it was Joy. He was still waiting to find out some information on Ashley and knew how irate and upset she could get. Darrin fought hard to keep Joy in the best of spirits. She had been good not to report him to the child support agency, or hassle him for cash tediously.

"Yeah."

"Hey son, let me speak to my grand baby. I want to make her a special dinner tonight. I am at the grocery and want to get an idea of some of her favorite foods." Darrin's mom was so excited she hadn't noticed Darrin's solemn voice. She had ranted on for an entire minute before checking to see if Darrin was still on the line.

"Honey you there?"

"Yeah Mom." Darrin sighed and breathed in deeply before continuing.

"Mom, Ashley's train hasn't come in yet. They say the train was caught in the storm."

"Storm?"

"Yeah, it's bad. I don't know…" Darrin's voice trailed off as he fought back tears. His hands and voice were so shaky his mother could barely understand.

"Now Darrin listen to me." Darrin's mother Linda was from deep in the south much like Justin's family. The only difference is they seemed to be somewhat California grown where as Justin's mom sounded as if she had just flown into town the night before. Her accent was just as prominent as if she were fresh from the cotton fields. "Darrin calm down. Has anyone reported on the status of the train?"

"Not yet. I'm afraid. I know Joy is going to blame me. I was always worrying her about sending Ashley down. The second she decides to compromise this shit happens."

"Darrin, Ashley is your child too. You have every right to see her and participate in her life. You cannot beat yourself up about this. You don't even know if Joy is thinking along these lines."

"No! I know Joy and honestly if it were me, I'd be thinking the same thing. She is scared and hurt. I am just praying that I can report good news that would set both our hearts and minds at ease to some extent. At least if Ash is ok, she can focus on finding Justin and the boys."

"Justin and the boys are missing too? Oh my God. I will start praying."

"Once I find Ash, I am going to fly out to help the search party."

"Well son, that is commendable. Are you sure you will be welcomed? I'm sure his family will question your interest in helping."

"Mom I love her and if finding Justin will make her happy, then that is what I will do? The children are my main concern. His family should be able to get past any pettiness in regards to my past involvement with Joy. Family is family and now is the time we should all pull together."

Darrin was so busy with his speech to his mom that he hadn't noticed the station clerk approaching.

"Hi, Mr. Lang is it?"

"Oh Mom it's the train teller. He is here to give me some information. I will give you a call back as soon as I know something."

"Alright son, just be patient and try to remain calm. I will be praying."

Darrin hung up nervously and addressed the man standing just in front of his path, rather close for his comfort. The attendant adjusted his pants and shook his leg as if to unravel his boxers. Darrin became instantly aggravated.

"Yes, call me Darrin." Darrin stood to shake the man's hand. He wiped the sweat on the front of his hooded sweatshirt and cleared his throat. "Is everything alright? Were you able to find my daughter?" Darrin starred deep into the man's hazel eyes to see if he could get a reading on the man's demeanor. It was obvious that he too was unsure how to answer Darrin's questions. He appeared to be slightly nervous and shaken as well.

"Sir if you would come with me?"

Darrin nervously nodded and gave a hand gesture to lead the way. Darrin dug his hands deep into his worn jeans as he took the walk down the corridor, which seemed to grow thin as walls passed. The walk was quiet and long. At the end of what seemed to be about an hour walk they were greeted by a suit just in front of a large door.

"Hello Mr. Lang. I am sorry to meet under these circumstances, but I would like to ask you a couple of questions."

Darrin's heart sunk almost immediately as his knees buckled from beneath him. Darrin breathed in deep trying to regain his self-possession. "Yes of course anything you need."

"Well I understand you were inquiring about your little girl. Was she traveling on a train today?"

"Yes."

"I see. Sir was that train number 923."

"Yes it was. I had to call her mother to verify the train number. I was so nervous about seeing Ashley, I wrote the train number down wrong. I'm sorry, Um

Mr....."

"It's Detective."

"Detective...."

"Just Detective"

"Ok, is everything alright? Have you found my daughter?"

The Detective shifted his feet as he adjusted his tie. "Mr. Lang if you would take a seat?"

"I'd rather stand." Darrin clinched his jaw and planted his feet firmly onto the floor, in an effort to prepare for the news.

"Please Mr. Lang, you should really sit down."

Darrin reluctantly took a seat and folded his hands onto the metal table. The fear on his brow peered back at him as he starred at his distorted reflection in the mirrored metal surface.

"I am sorry to tell you this, but train 923 was taken by the storm. Our rescue crew went out to the tracks where the train lost communication. The train was completely taken apart by the winds of the tornado. Our men are making every effort to comb the area for survivors we have recovered several bodies from the wreckage. We have two young girls among those that were recovered. We would like to see if you could identify either one of these victims as your daughter."

Darrin began to cry violently as he pulled his wallet from his back pocket. The detective instructed the attendant to take the photo and match it up against the photo in the file. The attendant didn't speak but made an affirmative head gesture to the Detective.

"Sir is she your daughter." The Detective laid an opened manila folder in front of Darrin with a Polaroid picture of a girl, with the words Jane Doe written on the bottom. Darrin afraid to look at the photo raised his eyes slowly to view the body of the little girl. He knew as soon as he saw her hands. She was wearing her birthstone ring he had purchased for her on her last birthday. Darrin began to scream as he fell to the floor of the interrogation room. He sobbed pulling his legs close to his chest he made a tight ball to comfort himself. He wept like a child. The Detective excused himself from the room.

"Take as much time as you need. I am sorry for your loss."

"How am I supposed to tell her mother that her little girl is gone?" Darrin got to his feet with his hands out stretched towards the heavens. He was visibly shaking and looked as if he were going to pass out at any given moment.

"Sir. Sir. Mr. Lang I think you should sit down." The attendant noticed Darrin shifting from right to left. He was unsteady and mentally unstable. "Mr. Lang I am going to call an ambulance and get you some water. You don't look so good."

"I'm fine." Darrin fell back into the metal chair nearly toppling to the floor.

"I will be right back with that water. Stay put!" No sooner had the attendant sped from the room, Darrin wasn't two steps behind him venturing into the opposite direction. Darrin had to get to Joy and tell her the news before she heard it in a broadcast on television. They were sure to be releasing the photos of recovered passengers on the train soon. He needed to get on the first thing smoking towards Northern Cali.

Darrin blew past the waiting room with blurred vision. He caught a distorted glimpse of a little girl standing with a worn doll and a torn journal with the words, "Ash," printed in jewels on the front.

Darrin's chest tightened as if his heart were being squeezed. He smiled slightly and slowed his pace as he began his walk towards the journal. Darrin was nervous and his hands began to perspire. In such a tragic event the last thing he wanted to do was approach this small child only to find that she wasn't the finder of his daughter's journal and traumatize her more.

"Excuse me I don't mean to bother you." Darrin rubbed his hands like a shy kid.

The little girl's mom recognized the resemblance of the girl that saved her little girls life. "Your daughter saved me and my daughter's life. She was very brave. My daughter kept her journal in hopes to give it to her, but…" The little girl's mother hung her head. She couldn't bring herself to utter the words.

Darrin nodded with agreement and smiled a shaky smile. It took everything in him not to break down and cry. His heart was broken and to see a little girl survive the incident he was both envious and elated that his daughter traded her life for another. She died a hero.

"Here Mister." The little girl stepped forward and took Mr. Lang's hand. "I couldn't find Ashley, but I found her journal. I hope she is ok." The little girl handed Darrin the rugged journal and bowed her head.

Darrin smiled as he took the journal from the girl's hand. "Thank you so much. I am sure she is ok." Darrin bowed to thank the girl's mother and shook the little ladies hand. He strutted away without a second glance afraid the tears would give away his sadness.

# ~13~

## THE RAT RACE

Darrin took a cab to the Los Angeles Airport. He was too shaken to drive. He paid a parking fee to leave his car at the train station and left with just the clothes on his back. Good thing he was now the owner of the security firm he once worked for. His job was the only thing that kept him out of trouble. The street life was a hard thing to ditch and frankly all he knew how to do was hustle.

The traffic to LAX was gruesome as usual. The nervousness settled into Darrin's stomach when they finally got about three blocks from the drop off. Eager to get to Joy's side he decided that to wait for the traffic to let up, would be wasting entirely too much time. Instead he paid the cab driver and jumped out.

Darrin ran through traffic sprinting like a track-star, high-knees and all. He got half way up to the ticket booth when his phone rang once again.

"Yeah." an out of breath Darrin answered.

"Darrin is everything ok?"

It was Sam, calling to see had Ashley made it to Los Angeles. She was in traffic herself.

"I'm on my way to Joy. I can't get her on the line. I am so worried. Did you pick up Ash? Have you talked with Joy this evening?"

"No!" Darrin's speech broke. He didn't want to alarm Sam or tell her that Ashley was a victim of the storm. He hadn't even talked with Joy yet. However, he was finding it hard to keep it together, as if the reality of the situation was just hitting him.

"I am on my way to her now. I want to help." Darrin hung up to avoid any further questioning. Sam was good at interrogating individuals and he couldn't stand her either. She was such a, "Bug a Boo." His entire relationship with Joy involved Sam and her needs as well. Sam was full of it and always doing something she had no business. It didn't help that they shared the same face. Genes were a questionable fact. Darrin couldn't understand how someone with the same genetic make-up could be so different.

Darrin ignored the vibration of his phone for the second time. He was sure it was Sam wondering why he hung up so abruptly. He had no answers for her. She would soon know, but not before Joy if he could help it.

Darrin managed to snag a seat on the next flight that was leaving less than 15 minutes. He was excited about being able to get to Joy in such a short time, but his chest hurt in that he was going to be the bearer of bad news.

Stumbling onto the plane, as he nearly tripped over his own shaky feet, he quickly sat and flagged for an attendant. Darrin whipped out his identification and asked for the strongest thing available along with an icy cold beer.

"Sir is that all?"

"No, I'd like some of those complimentary honey coated peanuts and a miracle if you don't mind."

The attendant chuckled. "That bad huh? I think I can manage the peanuts. The miracle is another story. However, I have heard a number of beautiful stories about the beauty of flying and prayer. Something about being closer to God that makes things a little better."

"Thanks, I think I will try my hands at that. It's been awhile since me and The Ole Guy spoke."

Darrin closed his eyes for a few minutes to see if he could focus on putting the pieces of the last hour together. He couldn't begin to think of a way to tell Joy about Ashley. The drinks weren't much help either. The reality was heart wrenching. The numbness he was looking for, to at least calm his feeling of guilt and helplessness, had abandoned him.

**\*\*\*\***

Sam slammed her fists into her steering wheel. She was so frustrated about the traffic situation she thought about just turning around. She hated when Charles was right about something. He would never let her live it down. She wanted so much to rescue Joy. She could care less about the argument her and Charles would be sure to have upon her return.

"The kids are fine." Sam noted to herself. "Charles can handle picking them up and getting them fed."

Sam's thoughts quickly shifted back to Joy and the kids. She smiled slightly, finally the hero. Sam wondered why Darrin was in such a hurry to get to Joy himself. Was he trying to win back her love, after all these years? He hadn't dropped his careless, loose living ways, since Ash was born. Guilt can be a silent killer. Perhaps it was time for him to show face.

Sam reset her phone to see if she could get a signal. She hadn't talked with Charles since she left. A simple one hour drive had turned into three. She was sure he was worried. The phone rang several times and still she got no answer. She hung up and phoned again. Perhaps he was driving? He should be wearing his blue tooth at any rate. Sam didn't truly trust Charles as far as she could throw him. There were a number of indiscretions in their marriage that surfaced. It seemed like every year there was a misc. chick coming out the woodwork, to let Sam know of Charles and his extra-curricular activities.

Sam wasn't at all innocent. At least two of their children were in question. She was easily persuaded to seek counsel in other men when Charles was out and about. Sam was in a vulnerable state often and men tend to take advantage of women in these states. She used that fact to her advantage as well. She wasn't always the victim. She learned how to use those same men to get what she needed financially. Most were married themselves and couldn't risk losing their families over a one night stand.

Sam cleared her head. As much as she wanted to make it to Joy before the rest of her family she knew that would be against all odds. Traffic was heavy. Ciaos was afoot and her tank was a little on the empty side.

"Damn it!" Sam cursed when her red light came on, if that wasn't a sign? Charles had yet to return her phone calls. Sam and her car troubles would add fuel to the fire already enraging Charles. Sam thought if she could just make it to the next exit, she would be able to get off the highway and pull into a rest stop. Otherwise she was sure to be a victim to quite a few drivers and their smoldering road rage.

**\*\*\*\***

Charles' phone was ringing off the hook. He looked at the caller ID and flipped it over. The kids were safe and sound and in their room, so there was nothing to discuss with Sam. His biggest worry was Justin and the gang that he could have sworn was following him on his drive to pick the kids up from school. Charles was fuming with anger to think that Mike had administered goons to follow him, around as if he weren't good for the money. Charles had to admit that his gambling had gotten beyond out of hand. He was borderline bankrupt. Justin was not only his backbone, but his financier. He knew he could call Justin and he would bail him out. Although Justin didn't know why Charles needed the funds Justin would up the money, because of the kids.

The last portion of loaned money was truly to pay the loan sharks before they broke both his legs and torched his 2011 Land Rover. Justin paid the money because he thought Sam was spending frivolously and because of her carelessness the mortgage suffered. Without Justin, Charles was sure to feel the blunt of his misappropriation of funds.

His gambling problems and free for all dating would bury him alive. He had to find Justin. He was his lifesaver.

Besides that, he was happy to say that his meeting with a lucrative granting agency went extremely well. He was excited to report the good news. Charles took a sigh of relief that he was at least listed as one of the beneficiary's to Justin's estate, he frowned upon his jealousy however, because he actually had something to leave to his wife and children. If Charles passed in a freak accident that very moment he would leave nothing but a bunch of debts that his wife would surely have to tend to, or be next on the hit list.

Charles' phone rang once more. He slammed the remote to the television down and huffed as he answered with a frustrated greeting.

"What's up?"

"Charles it's me Sam."

"Yeah I got that, from the caller ID. What's up? Is everything ok?" Charles was not at all interested in Sam's whereabouts or the issues of her day. His voice was dry and lacked emotion or remorse.

Sam began to cry immediately. She was so fragile. The traffic was frustrating, but more so than that she was upset about the fact that Darrin would get to Joy first and therefore become her hero for the day. It pained her greatly that she couldn't win for losing in every effort she made to one up Joy, or at least prove to her that she needed help as well.

"I get it, you are angry with me, but you have to

understand that I needed to go and make sure Joy was ok. She is all alone."

"I get it and please Sam spare me the drama of you wanting to help. You forget I know you well. You want to play captain save a hoe, go right ahead. I mean that in the best way possible. We both know I am the one that married the hoe." Charles was nasty in his remarks and looked for the go ahead to continue in his spitefulness. He was irritated himself, worried about the possibility of being followed. His kids were heavy on his mind. He dare not blink too long for fear someone would enter his home unannounced.

"You know Sam? We just may have issues in our own home we need to tend to. It would be nice if I could count on my wife for a change. I realize Joy is your sister. I also realize that she is about the only person you can count on when you are in need of help. But I think you tend to forget that you can't be of any assistance to others if you can't help yourself. I need to go. I want to get the kid's bath going before the movie comes on. I don't presume you will be joining us for our family night will you?"

"Charles."

"Never mind. I am sure you have better things to do."

Sam just hung up the phone as she thought about the truths of Charles' argument. "It is AJ's world, always has been. We are just living in it." Sam cursed as she remembered Joy's break down of her prize possessions. AJ's world was simple. It was the initials to her name, Justin her husband and her 3 children all beginning with either the letter A or J. She proclaimed that all her actions were to secure the needs and safety of her family. That was why she worked so hard, went back to school, started her own business, etc., etc. Sam shook her head and put her blinker on to signal her desire to get into the exit lane of the freeway. Sam was going home to her family. They needed her far more than Joy did. She would call her later to make sure she was ok.

# ~14~

## WAKE UP!

Joy floated up to her bedroom to change into some warm clothes. Her new air conditioning system worked far too well, the mirrors and pictures that hung throughout the first floor of her home were cold and foggy. As she neared her bedroom door her stomach began to quiver. The thought of having to sleep in their bed alone was frightening. Joy ventured into her walk in closet, her favorite part of the home. She carefully slid her hands along Justin's side of the closet caressing his garments. She smelled them to see if his scent still lingered within them.

As she drifted off she began to pull the shirts and jackets from their hangers and put them on, she warmed as she wrapped the overgrown sleeves around her small frame and smiled at the thought of him holding her in his arms. Joy thought about her counsel with Dr. Zimmerman, as a voice from behind threatened her wavering sanity.

"You know you should have kept up with the counseling. I know I could use a tall cold drink and maybe a Demerol. Let's not forget that cute little orange pill of yours Fluvoxamine."

Joy began to shake rather violently, as she shut her eyes tightly. "Go away. Please. Now is not the time."

"Awe, poor baby. I didn't know you had scheduled times for your psychotic breaks. How is the medicine treating you? You know the ten thousand dollar treatment you traded your family for? What was that drug called?

Oxycodone was it?"

"No! It was Voriconazole. What can I do for you?"

"Oh nothing I just came to see how ghastly you have managed to louse things up this time."

Joy's head began to hurt so bad she heard sirens and the room went completely dark. She could no longer see shadows or flashes of objects that helped her identify her way around. Scared that the bump of her head had caused actual neurological damage she scrambled from beneath Justin's clothing, to locate her migraine medication."

"Looking for these?" The splitting image of Joy stepped into the light and tossed a bottle of pills onto the floor just in front of her. "You should really take those things regularly. I hate how people misuse medication. They never follow the regime and wonder why the symptoms worsen, or the drug stops working all together. Pick up the pills and take one, or two. Why are you doing this to yourself, Mrs. Anderson?"

Joy crawled towards where she heard the pills fall onto the rug, reaching helplessly she grabbed the pills, only to grab a handful of shaggy carpet. Joy's face hit the floor hard as she was exhausted and out of breath. She had only moved inches, but the adrenaline she used to keep panic away from the pain she endured exhausted her.

Joy's mind went blank as she drifted into a coma of uncomfortable memories. She found herself on the couch of her most dreaded place. At Dr. Zimmerman's office along with his prying beady eyes and his psychological speeches.

****

"I heard about your thesis. I thought your synopsis on stress, had entirely too much medical jargon. I mean you did want those of different backgrounds to get the just of your argument. I paid close attention to your theories of the mind and stress. I found it hard to put together. How can one thought be hypothetical and a proven theory at the same time?"

"Well my friend that is because it wasn't a theory. It was a hypothetical question I posed in order for individuals to ponder their responses to the situation. As you have and proposed that it didn't make sense."

"It was preposterous, inhumane."

"Inhumane? How can you categorize a human emotion as one that is inhumane? It may not be socially acceptable, but it is certainly not inhuman. It is quite popular might I add, no matter how frowned upon the notion."

"I see."

"What, are you immune to the realities of the world?"

"No. Just don't feel as if this is my area of expertise, nor my problem. I was hoping to discuss my personal issues. Not your thesis on the mind. I merely mentioned that I had some recollection of the piece, which I found to be distasteful."

"Well while I am sure you have a well-developed analysis in regards to my work. I too, have a report to expose."

"You know that I wish I could tell you something that would be exciting to talk about amongst your colleagues, but I can't. My spiritual inhabitant doesn't appear with some mystical cloud of smoke, or theme song. She is ruthless. She takes control of my mind and leads me to believe that I am in control. She ignores my thoughts."

"I find that quite hard to believe. I believe you are in complete control of this 'so called personality'. She is a part of you, you know. She simply acts out all those suppressed emotions you try so hard to hide. She doesn't hold back those emotions, because she doesn't have that type of control. You should be prepared to answer to those she comes in contact with. Maybe, just maybe, she is your way of exposing those truths that may be keeping you locked in a box. She needs you just as much as you need her. Regardless of how out of the ordinary this may seem to you. The two of you must come to some sort of understanding and compromise. How do you think we as humans normally work out the good and the bad? Do you honestly think all of us are not faced with this issue? I fight the torment each day or stresses simply may just push me over the edge. It may be time for me to sit in your seat and tell all. I am plagued with thoughts of hurting those who have hurt me. I too, think that I am entitled to fairness and at times wouldn't mind taking the law into my own hands to cool my britches."

Joy's nose flared. She was enraged at the Doctor's analysis of her multiple personality. She all of a sudden grew hot and sweaty. "If you don't mind, I need a drink of water." Joy excused herself to visit the ladies room. She bolted down the long hall she could hardly stand enclosing walls of the psychiatric office and Dr. Zimmerman's beady eyes judging her. Joy locked the doors of the bathroom and let out a loud sigh of relief. She rushed to the bathroom sink and turned on the faucet. Joy rinsed her face vigorously, as she peered into the vanity mirror.

"Keep it together Joy. Can't you do anything right? You are shaking like a leaf."

"The shaking is just a simple side effect of the medicine. I don't feel a thing." Joy stood speaking into the mirrors reflection motioning her hands to add clarity to her argument. "I'm just lingering around. I hear nothing. The children look like they are laughing and playing, but I don't know why. I have no desire to entertain. I am just here. Wishing I weren't, or at least wishing I had some reason to be here. Like my presence is needed. These pills make me feel sober, solemn and slow. I don't have the spunk of my usual personality, when I am around my husband. I don't stress about the children and their wellbeing, eating, shelter. Things that matter, don't you think it's important for me to at least care? I understand my issue with stress. But at least I cared. I worried. I had empathy for those wronged or harmed. Is this really your idea of healing, my mind is in more disarray than it was before. I feel like my brain is scrambled."

"I'm tired, sleepy." Joy's reflection replied, dismissing her entire speech on the matter. "I don't think I want to talk about this right now. You are under a lot of medication and you yourself have no idea what you are talking about. Why don't we revisit this some other time, shall we? I mean really. You seriously think you have no need for meds? You are talking to me for God sakes. Isn't that enough of a reason? I asked you to get help. Doctors ordered you to sleep. He ordered you to change your diet. You decided to take a pill, the quick fix. I think the meds will work, if you stop abusing them.

"Abusing them, you are the one who showed me how. I guess that was when the actions of drugs benefited your desires. Now that I can't think straight, you abandon me. Just like everyone else. I don't have the steady hand to do your dirty work any longer. You are just like everyone else. How could even you abandon me?"

"How can I abandon you Joy? I am you."
Joy slammed her fists into the mirror. The pain of the blow shook her into reality as she realized she had been gone for quite some time.

****

A shaken Joy awoke and looked around at her surroundings. She seemed shocked that she was in her closet back at home. Joy tried to regain her composure, but her thoughts ran continuously wild. She sat upright into a pile of Justin's clothes in their walk in closet.

She was going crazy thinking about all of the things that could have happened to her children and husband. Joy began to rock slowly and whisper words of comfort, when there was a knock on her front door. In addition to the heavy knocking, they rang the doorbell in an alarming frenzy.

Joy staggered to a standing position, as she danced and jiggled her way out of Justin's over-sized clothing. She quickly grabbed a sweatshirt and headed towards the front door. Jogging down the stairs she grabbed her flashlight just in case she were about to be confronted by another so called drifter looking for survivors of the storm.

"Hold on! I'm coming."

Joy unbolted the front door as if the left side of her living room was still intact. She opened the door slowly to preview her guest. It was the police. Joy's stomach dropped and a huge lump formed in her throat. She was having troubles breathing as she slowly opened the door. The police officer had a small leather bound note pad and when he realized he was about to address a woman he immediately removed his hat.

"Mrs. Anderson?"

"Yes? What can I do for you?"

Joy could barely breathe. She placed her hand over her chest and placed her other hand on the sill of the door to hold herself up.

"Ma'am may I come in? I would like to talk to you about Mr. Anderson. Is he your husband? We traced the license plate numbers of some of the vehicles that were found in the storm and this address came up in our system. Do you happen to own a 2011 GMC Suburban?"

"Yes. Is everything ok? You found my husband and children?" Joy was ecstatic. "Well are they ok?" Joy buckled through the door and shoved past the decorated officer to peer out at the cop car in hopes to see her missing family members wrapped in blankets. Nothing was there.

Joy solemnly pulled herself back into the inside of her doors frame and starred into the eyes of the officer.

"I am so sorry." The officer began. He was having a bit of trouble explaining his visit, as if he were a rookie. The officer cleared his throat and began. "Your car was found halfway down the cliffs of the mountain. Most of the cars found had been thrown off of the road and into the forest. They were killed instantly by the impact of the winds. You will be happy to know that your husband and two children didn't feel a thing."

Joy looked at the officer more puzzled than ever. She was clearly lost and had transposed into something demonic in a matter of mere seconds.

"What the hell do you mean? Pleased to hear? Is that the best you can do? Oh your husband and children were killed in a tragic tornado. They were blown off a damn cliff pummeling to their death, but not to worry they felt nothing. Did you recover any bodies? Will I be able to identify them, to make sure, I mean?" Joy was deranged and slipping out of control. She was yelling at the top of her lungs. Residents that were still in their homes, stepped out onto their porches in wonder of the matter.

Joy turned her attention to her nosing neighbors and stepped out onto her porch to give the spectators an accurate view of the show. "Hey everyone, this nice gentleman, compliments of Oakland police department has come to inform me that my children and husband were killed in the storm, but I should thank my lucky stars that they didn't feel anything. Well, guess what? I feel it. I feel the pain. I feel the wrath of the storm. Why didn't it take me too? What point are you trying to prove, God?"

The officer looked nervous and pulled his walkie from his side pocket to call for back up. He was in no way prepared to deal with the emotional tirade Joy and her multiple personalities had unleashed.

Joy turned around and stumbled back into the home.

The yelling and screaming exhausted her and she suddenly felt the urge to lie down. "If you don't mind Mr., whoever you are?" Joy backed slightly from the front of the door and blacked out almost instantly.

Falling back as she nearly fainted. Darrin caught her mid-air. During the ruckus she hadn't noticed his cab pulling in. He went around to the side of the home and invited himself in. It wasn't hard the entire wall was missing.

Joy both stunned and amazed, spun around without hesitation to greet who she thought to be Justin.

"Justin is that you? Oh my God I was so worried."

"Sir, may I ask you who are and how you are related to Mrs. Anderson?" The officer butted in to make sure that Mrs. Anderson's guest was a welcomed one.

Darrin stood still, unable to move or respond, he couldn't understand Joy's state of mind since he was standing in plain view. Darrin had no idea of Joy's disability. She could see flashes of black and white rarely in color. The migraines made her sight that much worse.

"Joy it's me Darrin." Darrin finally managed to speak when he noticed Joy was staring straight through him. He ignored the police officer's line of questioning and continued to console Joy, "Are you ok?" Darrin figured she had just gone into complete shock.

Joy was stumbling into a breaking point close to the edge and fast. The entire room began to darken. "Darrin..." Joy's lips began to quiver as she used her hands to search for a place to sit down. She was sure she would faint. There could only be one reason why he would come to see her.

"Here, let me help you."

"Ma'am do you know this man?"

Joy threw her hands up immediately. "No, I can do it myself. What on earth are you doing here? I thought you were going to call me? What's happened? Where is Ashley?"

"Yes officer, he is my daughter's father. He was supposed to be picking up our daughter from the train station this evening, but we lost communication during the storm."

Darrin was silent and sure he was dreaming as he couldn't believe he was standing in the same room as Joy. His mind was racing and he couldn't pull himself to reality.

The officer lowered his eyes at Darrin and excused himself from the couple. "Ma'am, here is my card. We will be in touch. Any items we can salvage will be returned to you when the construction and clean-up begins. Here is a bag of the belongings we recovered from the car. There is no need for us to keep them since this is obviously ruled out as a death by natural disaster. I will leave you two to catch up." With that the officer departed and jogged to his patrol car. Joy stood with her back turned to the door as she didn't bother to acknowledge the officer and his gesture of sentiment. She was in shock to see Darrin standing in her living room. He didn't have to say a word, his presence said it all.

Joy fell into Darrin's arms. She cried violently. Enraged with fury she pummeled her fists into Darrin's chiseled chest. Darrin didn't say a word all he could muster was his grip. He held onto the small of Joy's back as he caressed her hair.

Darrin closed his eyes wishing he could take the pain away. He cursed his thoughts. They were traveling at high speeds, towards his overwhelming passion to reclaim his first love. Joy's mind raced. Her heart sunk and for a moment she lingered on towards a quick escape from the hurt and pain that was sure to suffocate her. Joy lifted her head. Her brow met his full lips. Darrin kissed her softly on her forehead.

Joy fully aware of her growing vulnerability feared she could not be responsible for her actions. Her alter ego lingered near and her overactive libido was sure to indulge in such pleasantries.

Joy's sudden urge to rekindle the spark was unsettling. Quickly, she gathered her senses and tore herself away from Darrin's advances. Joy apologetically tapped her hands upon Darrin's chest and walked over to the brown paper bag. Darrin was disappointed, but adjusted the bulge of his pants as he stood to help Joy.

Joy could smell him approaching. She focused on the bag. The room was black. Sitting in the center of blackness was a grayish white bag. Joy could see nothing else. She feared what was inside. She prayed for the strength to search its contents. Darrin made a few steps towards Joy. She was standing still as if she had been confronted by a ghost.

"Joy…"

"I'm fine. I just…I…" Suddenly Joy recalled her conversation with the police officer. "He never said whether their bodies were recovered did he?"

Darrin placed his hand gently on Joy's shoulder praying he didn't startle her. He was so confused. He didn't know what to say, for fear he would upset her further. "No, he didn't." Darrin calmly spoke.

"No he didn't, did he?"

# ~15~

## THE TRUTH HURTS

Patrice landed at the San Francisco airport just two hours of speaking with Joy. She was anxious to get to Justin and the children. Joy had yet to phone on the status of the search, so she was unnerved. Flagging down a cab she threw her overnight bag into the back seat and asked the driver to take the quickest route to Oakland. The cab driver looked concerned and asked if she knew about the big storm that had hit the city. Patrice, a bit agitated ignored the cab drivers small chatter. She advised him to pay attention to the road, especially in light of the storm and the high traffic of police and pedestrians.

Patrice tried Justin's phone once more, she had phoned him over 20 times since her plane touched ground. She was horrible at sending text messages so she didn't attempt. However, it was unlike Justin to ignore and neglect to return her phone calls. Patrice's chest grew tight as she listened for the phones ring and a familiar voice to greet her on the other end. Instead the answering machine chimed in. Patrice smiled at the sound of Justin's voice. It was the only thing that seemed to keep her hopes afloat.

Patrice laid her head back onto the cab drivers shabby leather seat and drifted off. She was exhausted from the flight and experiencing jetlag. Swerving in and out of lanes the cab driver sped through the back roads of the city to avoid the traffic and blocked areas of the storms greatest destruction. Shaken by the turbulence of the cab's stunt driving, Patrice was shaken out of her sleep to catch her cell phone ringing for the second time.

Patrice fumbled through her black snakeskin satchel in search of her phone. The phone silenced. Patrice was so emotional her desperation to get to her son drew tears to her eyes. She finally managed to find her phone and looked at her missed call list. Her heart sunk when she saw Justin's name and number appear as the last call she had missed just moments ago. Patrice began to scream with cheer startling the cab driver to nearly hit the car just in front of him.

"Oops I'm sorry. Chile' I didn't mean to scare you." Patrice apologized with a huge smile. Her nausea subsided within that very moment, as she realized her son was ok. Coming down from her celebration she decided that she had better return his call, as he too could be worried about her and her whereabouts. Patrice hit her call back button and awaited to greet her son with a warm welcoming, "Hello and Thank God you are ok."

Patrice sat anxiously on the phone as it rang for the third time. When she didn't get an answer she started to worry again. Just as she were about to hang up and call again she heard an answer on the other line.

"Hello."

Patrice nearly dropped her cell phone in her lap alarmed and taken aback at the voice on the other line. It was not the voice of her son Justin. It was Joy. Patrice couldn't even imagine why she would have his phone at such an hour. Her only excuse to even answer his business line was if Justin had specifically instructed her to, if he were expecting an important phone call and needed a message taken.

"Yes, Joy. It's Patrice. Where is Justin? I see you have his cell phone, so he and the kids must be alright?" Patrice sat waiting on Joy's response on pens and needles hoping that her assumptions were correct.

"Uh, Mom, I think you should come home as soon

as possible. The police just left our home about twenty minutes ago. Darrin flew in. They're gone, Patrice. They're all gone."

Joy broke down in tears as she hung up the phone. She couldn't bear to hear Patrice scream for her son. Nor could she take the mental and emotional beating she would be sure to give her. It was obvious that Patrice blamed her for Justin and the children leaving town in the first place. Joy just couldn't take dealing with the bad mouthing and scrutiny of her decision making process.

Patrice was stunned to hear the news of her son and grandchildren. She held the phone to her ears and zoned completely out. Patrice's eyes were as still and clear as glass and her body was as if made of stone. Her skin paled and her knuckles turned white.

"Ma'am you okay?" The cab driver inquired as he pulled up, to the front of Joy's home. "From the looks of it you can't even tell that there was a tornado, from the frontal view of the home." The cab driver chuckled, trying to make light of the situation. He noticed an entire wall was missing from the side of her home. "You don't think any of your family members are still here do you? You sure this is the right address? Surely they have gone to the shelter. It's just not safe around here after something like this happens. The freaks come out at night. There is looting and violent crimes are high on the rise. I don't want to leave you here if your family has gone to a nearby shelter. I will take you there free of charge if you like?"

Patrice stared at the Anderson home now in shambles. It was a work of art. A home both Joy and Justin designed and paid for together. Now after a storm the foundation was a mess, but nothing their insurance couldn't handle. Joy would surely have to move into something a little more conventional until the home was repaired. Patrice handed the cab driver a fifty dollar bill and grabbed her bag from the back seat.

"I'll be fine. Thank you for the offer." Patrice closed the door of the cab and stood on the walkway before taking her walk to the inevitable. She didn't know what to say to Joy. She had just lost all three of her small children and like her she'd lost her son, but he had already lived. She couldn't imagine having to deal with burying her babies. Still, Patrice straightened her stance and walked confidently up the walkway and onto the porch to ring the doorbell. Thinking about who Joy said was in the home with her she thought she'd better just walk right in. She trusted Joy, but she didn't trust this mystery man. Patrice always identified Ashley's biological father as the mystery man, because he was in and out. He never stayed long, if he showed face at all. It was in fact a mystery why Darrin would be down in their parts in the first place.

Patrice used her spare key to the home and casually unlocked the front door. The spare key was Justin's idea, just in case of emergencies. According to Patrice it was for her to check things out from time to time to make sure everything was copasetic.

Patrice threw her satchel and overnight bag onto the bar stool in the kitchen and looked around for something to drink. She almost never drank unless on special occasions, but she felt as if she needed something to ease her anxieties. Scouring the kitchen cabinets and small wine pantry she found a half empty bottle of wine. Patrice pinched her lips tightly together as she peered around the corner of the kitchen, which led to the hall leading to the den and second floor.

The damage to the home was pretty extensive. There was a gaping hole in the living room wall. The housing and construction department did a pretty good job of putting up some type of tent contraption to separate the outdoors from shelter, but it wasn't at all livable in Patrice's eyes.

Patrice grabbed her satchel and headed towards the

den to take a look around before venturing upstairs to the guest bedroom. It was her favorite part of the home, since Justin designated the peach room for her visits. It was also a master suite. Patrice loved the peace and quiet of the night and the fact that she could easily get to and from the bathroom without hassle during the night. She was getting old and the trips to the potty were far more frequent than she'd like to admit.

Patrice peered into the den to find Darrin sprawled out on the sectional. He was wrapped in one of the good down comforters Patrice picked out and had the nerve to be lying under a blazing fire. Patrice could have ripped the blanket from off him and tore him from limb to limb, but she was tired herself. She simply went upstairs to check on Joy and go on to bed.

# ~16~

## BLIND FOOL

Joy tossed and turned as her counseling sessions with Dr. Zimmerman haunted her emotional stability. Joy could feel the cold air hitting her bones as if she were naked. She sunk further beneath her bedspread and grabbed hold to Justin's full size pillow. She couldn't sleep. Flashes of Justin and the children danced in her head. The memories were clouded by visions of their faces that she could see so clear before her accident.

****

"Joy wake up." Dr. Zimmerman clapped his hands in an effort to awaken Joy from her hypnotized state. He was exhausting every avenue known to man to get her to open up and discuss the issues regarding Joy and her abusive childhood. It was evident in prior meetings that Joy harvested anger and resentment.

Joy sat up on the couch and grabbed her head. It was pounding again. "What happened? How long was I out?"

Dr. Zimmerman blinked at Joy, but didn't respond verbally. "How is your eyesight? Have you had any visual hallucinations? What about voices?"

"I can see clear as day, while on medication. I can't explain how she can see and I can't."

"I see. I took a look at your file." The Doctor looked over the brim of his glasses and focused on Joy's face.

Joy was agitated at his lack of response to what she

thought was a major issue. "Well then, we have no reason to talk today do we?"

"Not if you don't want to, but I think we should."

"Well I will pass if you don't mind? Don't worry I will be sure to cut you a check for the hour of power. I'm beat and I would like to go home and get some sleep."

"That's wonderful. However, you and I both know that you don't sleep. So why don't you and I just cut the Bullshit." Dr. Zimmerman crossed his legs and folded his hands.

"WOW, such language doc? Now you're talking. I better sit down. Do you have one of those long rulers too?"

Dr. Zimmerman smiled at Joy's new quirky attitude. It became immediately evident that the woman he was speaking to was not Joy. Her demeanor was raw and sexy. Dr. Zimmerman's client stared him down and blew a kiss his way. She sat close to the edge of her seat and opened her legs wide and undid the top button of her blouse, fanning her chest as if it were hot in the well ventilated room. Dr. Zimmerman noted her change in persona and gave the woman his undivided attention.

"So, why don't we start with your name? It's clear I am not speaking with Joy any longer."

"It's Lillian, Lillian Andrews, but you can call me Lilly for short. I am named after our mother."

"Lillian." Dr. Zimmerman's eyes lit up.

"Yes, Lillian. I am the third child left to rot in our Mother's womb. Joy has become a great success. She is a bit on the weak side, but she is very smart. Sam on the other hand is a mess. It's embarrassing that we share the same traits, physical traits." Lillian looked up at Dr. Zimmerman to make sure he made note of their conversation. She wanted to be sure he knew the differences between Joy and herself.

Dr. Zimmerman looked puzzled as he flipped through Mrs. Anderson's chart. There wasn't a third baby listed on any of the medical charts.

"Don't bother," Lillian interrupted the doctor's concentration. "You won't find anything. I was absorbed into Joy's tissues during the second trimester. So I guess you could say that Joy is essentially two different people."

Dr. Zimmerman's mouth was wide open with surprise. He was intrigued by such a case. He could almost see his name printed on the cover of the next issue of the American Psychology Journal.

"I am a demon child." Lilly fluttered her fingers as if she were a monster. She enjoyed toying with the doc.

Dr. Zimmerman adjusted his glasses and wiped his brow.

Lilly closed her eyes briefly and paused as if Joy was resending into her rightful place. She then opened her eyes suddenly and wide, as she began to laugh at the doctor's facial expression. "This is going to be so much fun." Lillian smiled generously and took off her heels. "I have been waiting for a long time to come out and play. There was no way I was going to continue to let you or anyone else intimidate fragile Joy any longer. She has done her time. I think it's time some people get a taste of their own medicine. Fight their damn battles if you know what I mean? From now on, I'd like you to deal with me entirely. Those pills you gave Joy are doing her well. She sleeps. That is something she rarely does."

"Who are you?" The doctor never looked up from his pen and pad as he began to write anxiously, his thoughts.

"I am named after Leliel Andras, angel of night, ruler of deception and quarrel, death to be exact. I am the true angel of Death," Lilly stood embracing her glory and expanded her arms as if allowing her wings to spread. Dr. Zimmerman's eyes bucked with a sarcastic gesture and wrote vigorously.

"Really?" Dr. Zimmerman excitably interjected. He

bit his lip in shamefully as he hurried about adjusting his seat and clearing his throat, desperately trying to regain his composure.

"Uh, no. Sounded good though didn't it? I am Joy, her true personality, one in which she has fought so hard to keep a secret from others. However I think it's time that Joy sit back and let me handle things. Don't you think? I mean she has been run straight into the ground. She has her own husband and family to deal with. She can't keep tending to others and their individual trials and tribulations. It is one thing to be there for others, but it's simply unfair to carry the entire load. My back hurts from all the piggy back rides, Joy has been issuing. This accident with her eyes, made room for me. After the car accident, her mind was open to new things, people and areas of her brain that she had yet to use. Don't get me wrong Joy is brilliant. She just isn't a fighter, no matter how hard she wants or tries to get others to believe. It's always been me." Lilly looked into the Doctors face.

"If I didn't know any better, it sounds as if you are suggesting that Joy is expendable? Would you care to enlighten me? Mind manipulation is one thing, but entire body inhabitance..." Dr. Zimmerman closed his eyes. He was both confused and growing angry.

Dr. Zimmerman began to feel as if Joy was merely playing games to avoid talking about the issues regarding her family. Inventing this no nonsense character was just a defense mechanism, a poor way of dealing with the matters of her troubled heart and mind. "How are you going to get Joy to surrender her soul? She would never leave her family."

"She will if she has no reason to stay. Joy is going to be so miserable. She is going to feel her skin tearing. Her life dissipating as the foundation of her home crumbled around her. She will be disheveled filled with uncertainty and disdain. I will be there to comfort her. I will tell her that it was her family that facilitated her demise. I came to ask for help, hoping to gain restitution for my evil deeds. I worked for her betterment, not to destroy her.

She will say that things are fine, but we both know that they aren't. They haven't been for quite some time. It's time for Joy to grow some balls. Stand up to people, stop being the red carpet under other's feet. Her heart will be black as coal, eyes cold as ice. Much like the persons she has helped over the years." Lillian smiled as she sat back to ponder her plan briefly. Even she was concerned about Joy's ability to withstand and overcome her advances.

"So you think Joy would be better off if you were the dominating personality?"

Lilly's lips curled frightfully thin, as she was angered by the Doctors probing questions. "I have no intention of hurting Joy. I'm here to help her. She needs me." Lilly tried her best to sound soft and sincere.

Joy's doctor simply stared at Lilly from over the brim of his bifocals. "If this isn't the biggest load of bull I have ever heard? Do you seriously think that you could just waltz into a professional Psychiatrists office, feed me a few lines of bullshit to see if you can manipulate me to do what you want? Well I'm sorry, Lillian. I am Mrs. Joy Anderson's Doctor. If you are in need of counseling services, I am afraid you are going to have to schedule an appointment, or find yourself a Doctor."

"Well isn't that sweet. Creative even, but I think the two of us know that it's not going to be that easy."

The doc just stared for a while and decided to play along. "So how can I help, can I offer you a cup of coffee, some water perhaps? Your hour is just about up."

"Cute how very cute. Joy is here, she just can't come to the phone right now, if you know what I mean?

Dr. Zimmerman cleared his throat and interjected Lilly and Joy's thoughts. He sat upright in his chair and scooted to the edge of his seat. It was no doubt in his mind that during her brief silence Joy was communicating and desperately trying to force her way out. Lilly closed her eyes and let out a frustrated cuss. Dr. Zimmerman noticed Lilly's discomfort. He began to speak low, saying the same things over and over again. It was if he were chanting to conjure up spirits. Lilly turned away from the Dr.'s wrath to gather herself. Joy was returning and Lillian couldn't stop her. Dr. Zimmerman used words and conversation topics that he and Joy shared to gain the attention of Joy.

When questioned about certain subjects, Joy usually spoke as if her confidence had been ripped to shreds. Her heart began to beat rapidly and her knuckles turned white. She was gripping the edges of the leather couch, in hopes of regaining control of her mind and body.

Joy tried to focus, but she was still quite confused. Her eyes opened as they were shut tight. They were now hazel, although moments before they were darkest of browns Dr. Zimmerman had ever seen, almost black. Dr. Zimmerman made a note in his small leather pad and refocused his attention on Joy and her transformation.

"Joy we need to speak." Dr. Zimmerman finally managed to find words. He was in awe of what had just occurred. He sat witness to quite a few things in his time, but nothing as sci-fi as this.

"I need to speak with you fast." Dr. Zimmerman, put his hands in the air to signify how important it was to get through to Joy. "Joy, can you hear me? How long can you keep Lillian at bay?"

Joy was shocked when Dr. Zimmerman said Lillian's name. "You saw her? So now you believe me?"

Dr. Zimmerman, put his head down and began to twiddle his fingers. Joy didn't have to ask what Dr. Zimmerman was thinking. The silence spoke for itself. Joy's head began to hurt once more. The bright lights were causing her damaged eyes great pain. "Are we done here? I think I need to get to a quiet and dark place. The migraines are beginning to take their toll on me."

****

Joy's pupils moved rapidly under her forcibly closed eyelids as she fell in and out of a drug induced sleep. She had managed to find a few Trazadone pills swimming in an old pill bottle at the bottom of her medicine bag, anything to numb her pain and perhaps rid her of the nightmares.

Patrice peeked in on Joy before she went down the hall to the guest room. She didn't want to disturb Joy. She knew it had been a troubling day for her and she was not in the proper state to discuss the next steps in preparing to say goodbye to Justin and the children.

Patrice was surprisingly calm. She lost her parents at a young age and had spent most of her life caring for others. She hid her emotions mostly to protect herself from vulnerability. She would have a good cry in the confines of her room, but never in front of her children. She didn't want to alarm them. Raising Justin alone was a frightful circumstance being that she had him quite young and her husband was killed in the war. She had no childcare and she was still too young to work in many industries of the work force.

Joy was quite lucky to be in a place where both she and Justin were established career wise and having children wasn't much of a burden except for the actual labor. She smiled at how she'd always teased them about having a few more. She would be glad to move in and play nanny for the first year or so, so that their work wouldn't be affected. Justin Jr. and Josh were thirteen months apart. Rambunctious four and five year olds that by her definition, were already grown. Jr. was out and about playing with kids twice his age and Josh was an electronic geek. He loved gaming, cell phones and computers.

Dear Ashley, Patrice started to get choked up thinking about how much she had grown. Twelve years of age going on twenty-one. She was a fashion diva and sports fanatic. How she juggled the two was still a mystery to Pat, but she loved the fact that she was a force to be reckoned with.

Patrice's lips began to tremble as she thought about her childhood and the loss of her parents. She was saddened about the loss of her grandchildren. She didn't know how or what to do for Joy, but she would start with a word of Prayer. Patrice quietly closed the door to Joy's room and floated down the hall to the guest room. She needed to get her mind in order. It was sure to be a busy day in the morning. Joy needed to first find a new place to reside and Darrin's services were no longer needed. If she had too, she would make sure to escort him to the front door.

Settling into her large suite, she tossed back the peach colored iliac spread and jumped into the fluff of the pillows. She was safe in her room, the room that her beloved son designed just for her. She felt closer to Justin than ever. She thought if only she could see him one last time, she would be sure to express how proud and how much she loved him.

# ~17~

## WHISPERS

Joy woke up in a bed full of Justin's clothing. She had tossed and turned all night before drifting off to sleep. Finding the pills was a great help. She hadn't heard Patrice come in, but as soon as she woke up she could smell breakfast cooking. For a moment she got excited in hopes that Justin and the kids had miraculously found their way home.

Joy jumped from her bed and sluggishly dragged herself to her master bathroom to take a hot shower. She was in a hurry to wash the stink of the storm off her body. Her arms and legs were badly bruised and the scratches from the wood on her arm stung.

Joy tossed on her robe and slippers and walked out of her bathroom to find Darrin sitting in the middle of her bed.

"Darrin what are you doing in my room?" Joy was startled by her guest, but she felt no discomfort or embarrassment as she slowly closed her robe.

Darrin swallowed hard and wiped the sweat from his hands. "I was just coming in to check on you. Your mother-n-law is here. She got here last night. Apparently, she has her own key." Darrin pinched his lips tight, holding back a sarcastic remark. "You know she, woke me up at the crack of dawn with that singing and cooking. I didn't know where I was for a moment. Who could eat at a time like this anyway?"

Joy hunched her shoulders and blew past Darrin.

"Yeah, well she isn't cooking for our benefit. She is

upset. She either cleans or cooks. I hope you brought your appetite." Joy was nervous, she didn't want to get caught talking to Darrin in her bedroom, while wearing a bathrobe. "Darrin if you would excuse me, I'd like to get dressed."

"Sure." Darrin wore a confused and uncomfortable look on his face. He knew he was being oddly curious and borderline inappropriate, but he continued anyway. "What's wrong? You act as if I have never seen you naked?"

"Darrin please, you can't be serious right now. Now is most definitely not the right time to discuss our past, a past long over. I just want to get dressed. I don't want to even think about all the things I have to get done today. I need to contact the police to see if they have found my family. Darrin just go please."

Darrin stared at Joy as he began to realize how out of touch to reality she was. "Joy?" Darrin began, but Joy quickly put her hand up to ward off his advances. She didn't want to hear him speak of her husband and children. She just wanted him to see himself out.

Darrin shook his head as he turned and walked out of the bedroom door. Joy continued to get dressed. Her mind was wandering and spinning in circles. She became frustrated, looking for a pair of tennis shoes and her sweatshirt to her sweat pants. Joy took all her clothes from her drawers and tore down the garments hanging in her room size walk in closet. Slamming her boxes of shoes to the floor from her shelving she began to scream. She wore nothing, but her sweat pants and a floral printed bra.

Joy's head was pounding so hard the vision she had left became blurry and filled with spots. Joy fell to the floor in her closet and grabbed her head. The pain became so extreme she let out another curdling scream.

Patrice heard the sounds from downstairs, alarmed she dropped her glass of orange juice. Darrin ran upstairs to Joy's bedroom to make sure she was ok, Patrice followed.

"Joy you ok?" Patrice yelled up the stairs as she climbed the long winding staircase as fast as her legs could carry her.

Darrin busted the door to Joy's room down tearing the bolted lock from its frame. "Joy you okay?" Darrin scurried around the room in search of Joy. She was laid out in the closet. The pain of her migraines caused her to faint. Darrin quickly scooped Joy from out of the closet and placed her onto her bed. Patrice jolted into the bathroom to retrieve a glass of water, some pain meds and a cold compress.

Joy was coming to, slightly, but she appeared confused. She didn't know who or where she was. Patrice placed the cold compress onto Joy's forehead and asked her if she'd like a drink of water.

"Honey here, sit up and have a sip of this water. I have a few Tylenol to help with the pain."

"No thanks." Joy looked straight ahead, she felt the heat from Patrice's hands on her shoulder and she could smell Darrin's cologne to the left of her, but she didn't look either way. "I just want to be left alone if the two of you don't mind."

Joy's attitude was cold and nasty. She felt weird and as if she couldn't control her emotions or her actions. Joy managed to smile slightly to lighten the mood. Darrin didn't buy her sudden change in disposition. Patrice gave Darrin a nudge and asked him to leave the two of them alone. Darrin wasn't at all interested in leaving Joy's side, but he left willingly.

Patrice took hold to Joy's hand. It was cold. She folded her brow with worry and looked to comfort her daughter-in-law. "Joy, I am so sorry. I know this is especially hard for you loosing small children. I am also in so much pain. I don't know what I am going to do without my son. I want you to know that I am still here for you. We need to decide what we are going to do about the funeral arrangements. I don't want us to have to drag this out for weeks. I was thinking that we could have something as early as next week."

"What! What are you talking about? Joy jumped from her bed and began pacing the perimeter of her huge master bedroom. "What the hell is your problem?" Joy was stumbling around as the room was spinning. She was delirious. My husband and children are out in the woods lost. They are looking for help and you are here planning their funeral. Damn it!" Joy yelled as she stubbed her toe on her leather ottoman, in the sitting area of her master suite. "Who are we burying, Pat? There were no bodies in the damn car. The police brought a bag full of belongings that were left in his truck. Nothing Justin or the boys were wearing was in the bag."

Patrice stared at a very deranged Joy as the tears streamed down her face. Joy had completely lost her mind as she knew for a fact that at least one of her children's bodies had been identified.

"Joy Honey? Did you look in the bag that was given to you by the police officer that came by last night?"

"His phone was handed to me when the police officer came to tell me the news. Nothing substantial, my husband is alive." Joy's voice trailed off suddenly. She looked in Patrice's direction, but it wasn't Patrice she was looking at. She could see a shadow standing just behind Patrice. It was there one minute then abruptly she could hear a small whisper behind her ear. Joy turned her attention to the words she heard whispering softly. She stood like a stoned statue as if she could see a ghost. Again the shadow positioned it's self behind Patrice.

The shadow moved from behind Patrice and stepped in front of her and came closer, within reach. Joy could see clearly now, that it was Justin. His black and white image came so close it was as if she could feel him standing inside her. She felt her heart jump and warm. Her knees grew weak and the air around the room froze.

"We are ok." The whispers came again as she could feel something brush gently against her cheek.

"Mom did you see that?"

Patrice was still in shock from Joy's outburst. She didn't know how to approach the situation. "Joy I think you should get some rest. We can talk about the funeral arrangements tomorrow. I am going to look into some condos. We cannot have you staying here. Nadine called this morning from the office to send her condolences and she says that she can handle everything at work for the rest of the week. She says she will call you if there is something she needs your assistance with. We are going to have to find a way to get through this, Joy. Justin would want you to. You have a flourishing business with great promise."

Joy sat on her bed. She didn't have anything further to say to Pat. She felt alone. She couldn't understand why no one was interested in finding Justin and the children. They were in such a hurry to write them off as if they were dead.

Joy turned her attention to the brown paper bag that sat on the coffee table in Justin and Joy's sitting area of their bedroom. Her eyes began to well with tears as she wondered what the contents of the bag may be. Could his wedding ring be in the bag, his wallet, something more personable than his cell phone that he could have just left behind in a sudden rush for survival? Surely, they couldn't base his death upon finding his cell phone in the car. That would only help to identify that it was his vehicle.

Joy continued to ignore Patrice's presence. She decided that perhaps maybe, Patrice hadn't gotten the hint that she wanted to be left alone so she laid down and took refuge underneath her covers. Joy could hear Patrice sigh as she collected the wet towel from the side table to take it to the bathroom area.

"Mom could you close the door on your way out,

please?"

Patrice, no longer feeling the need to force the situation obliged Joy's request without a word. Closing the door behind her she decided to put Darrin to work. They were going to need to start packing up the home. Anything that was damaged would have to be thrown out and anything else worth saving put in storage. Patrice thought it best to start fresh and anew. Joy would do better in a completely new setting. Constantly hovering and burying herself in the confines of Justin's things would send her into an emotional tirade of dysfunction.

A change of scenery helped when she lost her husband to the war. Patrice picked up a phone book and got a realtor on the line. She didn't want to fool around long, she needed to get Joy settled into a new place by nightfall. Patrice was uncomfortable herself, staying in a place where loved ones had once lived. It was as if she could hear small whispers in the wind, as she floated about the home.

Whispers of death and anguish, it was horrific the cold breeze that chilled her bones.

# ~18~
## LOST

Sam's alarm went off early morning, but she was too tired to get up and get the kids ready for school. Darrin called with the news of Justin and the kids. She wasn't up for much of anything. Charles left late night after the news and had yet to return home. He hadn't answered any of her phone calls, so she was equally worried about him and his whereabouts.

Charles didn't take bad news of any kind very well. News of this caliber could be devastating. Justin was more than a business partner to him. They were like brothers, blood cousins in reality.

Sam forced her way out of bed. She could hear her tribe wrestling in their room. The arguing and bickering had already begun. It was time for a referee to step in.

Sam jumped from bed and marched down the hall to her son's room. Her three boys were in action, bickering over whose turn it was on the video game. Sam stepped just in front of the television to get their attention.

"You boy's get this room cleaned up. It's my turn." and with that she snatched the controllers from each of the boys and turned the television off.

"Not a word, until this room is spotless."

Sam left the room and made sure that the door was open so she could hear if any ruckus were started. She sprinted back to her room to get dressed. Today was the day to move Joy into her new condo and she didn't want to be late. Charles was M.I.A., she was sure he would come home to help her out, but he had been so distant it was any wonder where his thoughts were.

****

Charles pulled up to the Anderson home in a blur. He had been sitting out in the car for at least an hour when he spotted Darrin coming out the front door. He was hauling some boxes out into the rental truck. Charles lowered his eyes stunned that he had, had the nerve to show up after so many years of absence.

Charles fought to pull himself together. He turned off his CD and locked up. Bouncing from his car, he strolled up the walk way and caught Darrin's eye.

"So what brings you by the Anderson estate, my cousin ain't even cold yet and here you are pushing up on his girl."

Darrin turned around and flexed the muscles in his jawbone, "You here to help or talk. If you here to talk we can set up some other time to do that. I don't get down like that anyway. I am here for moral support. I lost my child too, Chuck."

Charles gripped his belt buckle, animating how he felt about Darrin's little speech, "Moral support? We don't need your moral support brother. Joy would have liked a little child support."

Darrin threw his hands up and drew them close to Charles' neck. "I'm warning you Charles. Now is not the time to discuss any quarrels you and Justin may have resting on your scrawny chests. I am here to help Joy. So do what you need too?"

Charles walked closer to Darrin in every effort to egg, Darrin on. He wanted him to make the first move. He was willing and waiting to finish it.

"What's going on out here?" Patrice stepped just outside the front door. She was wondering what was taking Darrin so long, "There is work to be done." Patrice directed her attention to Charles. "Hey Chuck, so glad you could make it. Where is Sam? We can use all the help we can get."

Charles ignored Darrin's quiet snares and greeted his aunt. "Yes Ma'am, show me the way. I'm sure Sam will be here shortly. I came straight from work. I pulled an all nighter. How is Joy holding up?" Charles walked past Darrin purposely knocking him off balance as he walked by. He could see in Darrin's eyes that he wanted to react, but he wouldn't dare in the presence of Justin's mother.

"She is doing as well as to be expected. She hasn't come out of her room all day, but she soon will have to. I plan to have her in her new place by tonight. The contractors will be here in the morn to figure some estimates and get started on rebuilding. I am not sure if she is going to want to sell this place, rent it, or move back in."

Charles' eyes lit up as he walked back inside the Anderson home with Aunt Patty. He was wide awake now. He was going to have to keep his eyes peeled for things that may be of some value. It wasn't going to be too long before Mike and his bandits found out where he had been hiding. It was best not to give Sam the details or accept any of her phone calls. He couldn't risk putting his family in danger over his gambling debts. She couldn't lie about what she didn't know.

**** 

Joy busied herself in her room packing her things. She awoke from her nap with a sudden burst of energy. She needed to keep busy. The brown paper bag the officer left continued to haunt her. She wanted so badly to see the contents of the bag, but she couldn't bring herself to open it. Instead she listened to the voice mail Justin left on her phone over and over. She tried to decipher his tone of voice. To see if she could detect some sign of distress. A clue of some sort, instead she heard him saying that he loved her and that he would see her soon.

~ 111 ~

Joy packed all of Justin's things in his suitcases. She folded them carefully. His suits were placed in his garment bag and toiletries in their designated area. She then did the same for her own belongings. Joy saw this as her chance to get rid of some old rags she had been holding on to. She knew it was long overdue. With the new agency and her magazine she barely had time for routine choirs. Justin was busy with the company as well as the business with the home.

Carefully Joy wrapped all of her African masks and figurines. She was anxious to move into her new condo, only to remove herself from the confines of a home that was once so beautiful. She didn't want the reminder of the storm lingering on.

Joy opened the door of her domain and entered the hall. She was shocked to find Charles there working on the paintings that were hung out on the balcony. She didn't speak. Joy simply put the boxes she had packed and labeled onto the floor and went back into her cave to retrieve more.

**\*\*\*\***

Sam sped into the driveway of Joy's home. She became infuriated when she saw Charles' car already there. She had been worried sick. Sam slammed on the brakes and turned off the ignition when she saw both Darrin and Charles prancing shirtless out to the moving van. Sam fell from her Toyota with one motion. She left the kids at a colleagues, she had no choice since her husband had failed to come home the night before. She had spent the last four hours combing the city, hoping that she wouldn't find his car abandoned or get a phone call from the police.

Sam high kneed her way up the driveway stepping over the beds of flower and rock to get to Charles.

"Where in the hell have you been?" Sam ignored

the fact that Darrin was front and center in all his masculine glory. She laid into Charles without shame.

"Samantha, why don't you run up and check on your sister? Grab a box or something." Charles was in no mood to argue with Sam, he turned up his nose, snubbing her very presence.

Sam rolled her eyes and stomped inside. He was right. Right now was not the time or place. The lump in Sam's throat began to dissipate. Although, the empty feeling in her stomach lingered on, she was trying to find the words to say to Joy. She had been in a daze most of the ride to Joy's home. Still there was nothing she felt she could say that would remotely help Joy through this tragic occurrence.

Sam felt as if she had lost her own children in many ways. The pain was far more than she could bear at times. The night was long, she tossed and turned. When she managed to get a few hours of sleep, she awoke soaking wet from night sweats. She wasn't able to shake the images of her niece and nephews.

Sam ran upstairs to Joy's room. She waved a dismissing wave at Patrice. Patrice was busy packing up the kitchen. Sam was sure she was getting rid of whatever items she didn't find fitting to her taste.

To Sam's surprise Joy was busy herself. She was afraid of what she may find behind the doors of Joy's sanctuary. The room was nearly empty. The boxes were well stacked and labeled.

"I guess you didn't need me after all."

"Sam is that you?" Joy spun around and spotted Sam's shadow in the light. She ran to her and hugged her long and hard. She was so happy to see her other half. She was lost and didn't know what to do or how to get through.

"I see you are up. I was afraid I would have to drag you out of bed. How are you feeling this morning?"

"I'm having those God awful headaches again, but

other than that, I am just anxious to get into this new place. I need to get settled so I can get out there and help the search party locate Justin and the kids. I know they are out there. I need to find them before it's too late. I have already lost my daughter. I don't want to just give up looking for Justin and my boys." Joy grabbed, squatted and lifted two boxes at once and hauled ass outside her door where she had stacked the others for pick-up.

Sam was in shock at Joy's analysis of the situation. Her forehead began to bead with sweat as her palms grew wet. She didn't know how to attack the situation so she excused herself quickly to gain some insight on where Joy's thoughts were. "Hey, I am going to go down and grab us a couple of drinks. I know you must be working up a thirst, be right back."

Sam didn't give Joy a chance to respond she needed to leave the room before she put her foot in her mouth. Joy was the psychology major in school and she counseled youth through her literary group. That was the very point of her developing the "Blog Diaries."

Her agency gave youth a chance and know how by way of effective written communication to openly share feelings they found difficult to express. Journaling had proved to be a very good way of self-counsel and reflection. Sam was in no way credentialed to discuss Joy's mental state. She would be sure to monopolize and challenge Sam's knowledge of the mind and how it worked.

Sam went downstairs into the kitchen to visit with Pat she was interested to know what she thought about Joy and how she was holding up. Pat was making sandwiches on the built in grill of Joy's stove. She seemed to be enjoying herself. The table was filled with cut fruit, green salad, lemonade and fresh baked cookies.

"How can I help you Sam? Lunch will be in about 30 minutes. I don't want the boys to think we are trying to starve them. That Charles is nothing but skin and bones, you feeding him?"

Sam rolled her eyes at Patrice's sarcasm. "He's eating." Sam kept her response short. She wasn't interested in conjuring any drama about Charles at the moment. She wanted to get some feedback on Joy. "What's your take on Joy?" Sam pulled up a chair at the bar and sat down to get a closer look at the sandwiches Patrice prepared.

"The girl has lost her mind if you ask me." Pat let out a laugh that scared Sam nearly to the point of falling from her bar stool. She couldn't understand what was so funny about Joy having a mental breakdown. She had responsibilities.

Responsibility's that needed to be handled. Patrice noticed Sam's nose flaring. "Chile, Joy is grieving. What on earth do you expect?"

"Tears, tantrums, depression, but shear dismissal of the loss will do no good. She can't even admit that they are gone."

"Would you?" Patrice slapped the last sandwich onto her serving tray. She cut them in nice triangular portions and added a few parsley leaves for garnish. "Look the best thing for Joy right now is to first get out of this place. Next, love and support. As long as we are there for Joy, she will come out of this. Just you wait and see. I know that you are worried about your sister, but this is all normal in the stages of grief. I went through some of the same things when I lost Paul. He was my best friend and my lover. Much like Justin was to Joy. I will admit to my ranting about the girl's unorthodox views, but the truth of the matter is that we need to give her space, room to breathe and let her know that we are there for her whenever she wants to talk. I would recommend that once she comes out of this she seek counseling. Other than that, let's just take this one day at a time."

Pat knew full well that Joy was delusional. She

couldn't stand Sam. It would be a cold day in hell before she would publically agree to her opinion on things.

"What about the funeral arrangements, the insurance for the home." Sam was getting worried about Joy's finances. "Not to mention her business."

Pat wrinkled her head at Sam's obvious deep concern about monetary issues. "Well I'm here and believe it or not she got a place without any problem. The insurance company's contractor will be here in the morning to handle the estimate and get the work done on the home. Nadine phoned this morning and is on her job. Things will be, "A," ok. We will have to just do what we can in reference to the wake or memorial service rather." Pat washed her hands vigorously, as she explained the plan. She hoped that she made it clear that her services were not needed. If it were up to her, she wouldn't have been contacted at all, her loyalty to Joy as always a question in Pat's eyes.

Sam wiped her hands on the lap of her jeans and scooted down from off her bar stool. "I see." Sam didn't at all understand, but she wasn't going to continue wasting time with Patrice as she cooked Joy's food. Sam couldn't really put her finger on why she didn't like the fact that Patrice was in Joy's kitchen cooking, but it bothered her more than she would like to admit.

Sam grabbed a few boxes to take out to the boys. They had managed to find a way around their issues. Outside the two of them were laughing and joking over a cigarette. "Hey, didn't know we had time for cigarette breaks, but I guess." Sam slammed the boxes down onto the grass next to the moving truck. She strolled by the two men as they starred her down. She looked at Charles and rolled her eyes and extended her middle finger to add to her display of disgust. Charles flicked the butt of the cigarette into the dirt and smashed the remaining burn under his feet.

# ~19~

## FACES

Joy unpacked her home quietly and slowly. Her new furniture was already in her new condo before she got there. She thanked Patrice for handling all of the arrangements, but the furniture was in complete disarray. Joy took some time to set up her home to resemble something suitable to her liking. She hung up some art work and cleaned the counters and mirrors of the home.

Joy pulled the boxes around the floor of her condo. She had labeled the boxes according to what the contents were and which room they should go. Joy found a big box labeled misc. She sat down in the middle of the floor to take a gander at what was inside.

She was looking for the files that contained the deed on the house and other possessions Justin owned. Justin and Joy made a point of outlining their lives to reflect what they had accomplished, what goals were still on the list of to do's and in the event that they were brutally killed in some jealous rage, who all of their worldly possessions would go to.

Joy pulled out Justin's file, along with a few pictures that were tucked away in between a few of the files. They were pictures of both Justin and Darrin. Joy looked at the facial characteristics of both men. She smiled at how different they were physically, but the same in that they had both endured such troubling childhoods.

Both men were so very head strong and stubborn. Their priorities however, were worlds apart. While one became a victim of environmental circumstance, the other used his misfortunes to abandon them.

Darrin born and bred in the streets of Los Angeles, fought against the urge to kill, follow and possess as he wished for a life of purity and honest work. Often harassed by the demons of the streets he was tested daily. Failing to beat the rap of his destined way of life, he became one of the people he detested. The hustle became his lifestyle. He'd fallen prey to the land of drugs, sex, and money. He traded the love for humanity for the love of the streets. His child suffered from the lack of attention.

However, he provided materials that he could not otherwise afford had he left his unlawful ways. It wasn't until his own brother's addiction that Darrin began to think about his future. The very drugs he sold were those that his flesh and blood drowned in. Darrin found himself in a deep depression. Guilt overwhelmed him. He too, ended up in rehab. Later, after graduating he landed a job in security. The same security firm 5 years later he now owned.

Justin on the other hand born in the Southlands was accustomed to gang violence and the like. Though after his brother was tragically killed, he opted out to take care of his mother. His first instinct was to go out and seek revenge upon his brethren, but he quickly changed course when his brother visited his dreams.

Joy was the first to believe the story of Justin's divine intervention. She too, had had some visitors of her own. Joy had a gift that she'd rather suppress. She could see things, despite her sight deficiency. She often had premonitions of happenings, or an awkward feeling when something was about to happen. Joy cursed her gift especially now that her family had gone missing. Her sightings of the future never involved her, just others. She hated to be the bearer of bad news. So she kept quiet and fled without warning others of the frightful terrors to come. She tried to caution others of the sightings, but more often she was crucified for exploiting such nonsense. She gained a few negative reviews from the public eye. Her mental state was questioned, so she quickly denounced her gift and concentrated on her writing and literary group.

Justin had come along in a time of Joy's life that appeared to be the end. She had been hospitalized for just under a year, for a disease that threatened her life. Daily she had to take medication for the disease that seemed to continue on in its rampage. Justin accepted her for who she was. The scars from the illness meant nothing to him. It was as if he didn't see them. She was beautiful, even when she was so thin he could see her skeleton.

Strangely, he loved her when she was at her lowest of times, all the way through her gaining complete conscious awareness and meat upon her frail bones. They encouraged one another and because of that they had become quite successful. Justin became an owner of a big name construction company that designed office buildings, luxury homes and art museums. He had always wanted to work in construction, but he was a victim of a stabbing in his early 20's. It had left him with some permanent nerve damage to his back and his lungs weren't fully functional.

Justin was her hero. He saved her life. She was going to do the same. Joy scooped up her files and placed the other items back where she found them. She covered the box full of files and slid them back into her hall closet. She was warming up to her new condo. It was a spacious three bedroom tri-floor home. The first floor opened up to a large living room and bathroom. From the first floor the stairs led to second floor, which was a huge kitchen with stainless steel appliances and cherry wood cabinets, adjacent to a beautiful den. Justin had designed the entire complex. Joy took great pride, in the fact that she was blessed to have a husband with such great talents. He designed the first home they bought together, her office building, as well as his own.

Joy was falling into a deep depression, she could feel her bones ache. She didn't want to get out of bed at times. It was hard for her to look at the kid's rooms and their belongings. Patrice and Sam were upset that Joy wanted to decorate the other room for the boys. She used the third room as a home office. She missed Ashley so much. Every time she saw a picture of her, her stomach got sick. Joy shook her way to reality and grabbed her purse, she was going to go and see the doctor about getting some medication for her issues. She was smart enough to know that she needed to tackle the situation before the voices returned.

A week had passed in such a blur the days seemed to run together. The messages on Joy's phone were countless as the mail, was saturated with condolence letters from Justin's clients and business partners. The front entrance to Joy's condo was filled with floral arrangements sent by friends and family. She simply ignored them. Joy couldn't understand what all the fuss was about. Folk were acting as if someone had died. Joy was in and out of reality. She told herself often that Ashley was away with her father. She took comfort in her safety, because then she could devote her energy into finding Justin and the boy's without causing Ashley great worry.

# ~20~

## SOMEONE TO LISTEN

Joy dragged her feet up the walkway of the Doctors office. She was not at all excited about her visit. Dr. Zimmerman was full of shit in her eyes. He simply refused to hear her desire to be left alone. It was just too much pressure. His continuous bantering on the issues of her past frustrated her and caused feelings of deep discomfort. Things, she would just rather put behind her.

Joy checked in and took her seat in the waiting room. She hadn't bothered to comb her hair. She just threw it up into her famous sloppy bun and went on with her day, a pair of clean sweats, an oversized t-shirt and sneakers. Fumbling threw the closet, she found a t-shirt of Justin's he had worn once or twice. She needed something to make her feel close to him. The pictures only made her sick to her stomach. She ached for his touch. She feared that her memories of him would fade as the days grew since he had gone.

"Ms. Anderson, the Doctor will see you now."

Joy looked up, shaken from her thoughts. "It's Mrs. Anderson."

"Yes of course. Right this way." The nurse assistant pinched her lips and motioned for Joy to follow her to the back office.

"Joy! Come in. How have you been?" Dr. Zimmerman's enthusiastic smile and tone drifted slowly as he observed Joy's outer appearance.

"Fine I suppose just want to get this meeting over with, I have things to do. I pick up the kids early today."

"Sure, sure have a seat." The nurse assistant paused at the door waiting to catch the Doctor's eye. Dr. Zimmerman was much obliged to notice her and looked downward with his eyes still fixated on her. The nurse responded quickly with a wide-eyed signal, one they used many times before and made her exit. Joy was crazy as they both agreed.

Joy looked at the Doctor inquisitively and decided to let him know that she was fully aware of the doctor and his assistant's side-note. "I know what you are thinking."

"Oh yeah and what is that Mrs. Anderson?"

"Oh, that I am crazy, that I am confused and completely out of touch with reality."

"Well, are you? I can't say that you are or you aren't. I think that with the set of circumstances I would be out of my mind, right about now."

"The over the counter sleeping pills aren't working anymore. I was hoping you could prescribe something a little stronger." Joy started in ignoring the Doctor's comments on the matters of her mental state.

"Well I don't know Joy. I am a little leery about prescribing something stronger. I understand that you are having troubles sleeping, however this is normal behavior during your time of mourning and bereavement. With the depression, adding on a medication for sleep can become both addictive and life threatening. I can't in good conscience prescribe you anything else."

"Fine." Joy stormed out of her doctor's office without a goodbye. She was so desperate for help she didn't know what else to do. The nights were long and painstaking. She was spiraling into a deep depression. Her eyes grew heavy, but her mind wouldn't let her rest. It was if she had passed out during the night hours, when she was able to calm down, her sleep was restless and filled with nightmares.

Joy could feel her husband and children around her.

At times she took comfort in the warmth of their presence and other times she felt as if they were haunting her and blamed her for sending them away. She felt guilty for lying to them about her health issues. She wished she could just turn back the hands of time. Now she was alone. Alone to face her fears and the demons that took over her mind and body. As much as she wanted to save the good natures of her heart, the pain that followed the loss of her family changed her.

Joy bombarded her way into the elevator nearly running over Nurse Betty.

"Hey! Mrs. Anderson? Is that you?"

Joy kept her head down. She wasn't interested in small talk. "Yeah it's me."

"Joy, its Betty, nurse Betty. How are you? Are you feeling alright? You don't look too good."

"I'm not. My family is missing and no one believes that they are still alive. I am so frustrated by this. My family has been busy doing nothing, but planning a funeral for bodies that haven't been found. My daughter's body was the only body recovered after the storm. She died in a train accident when the tornado hit."

"Oh my God, I am so sorry to hear that. Joy if you don't mind, I'd like you to take a walk with me down to my office. I am the nurse practitioner here now. I'd like to hear a little bit more about your symptoms. Its sounds like you may be suffering from Dissociative Identity and perhaps even Multiple Personality Disorder.

I know this may sound strange, but after you left the hospital after your accident, I took on a study about the mind, how it is altered after neurological incidence and eye sight. You would be amazed at all the findings. How the senses become heightened in other areas. How the brain begins to work much differently than it did before." Nurse Betty was fascinated by her case studies. Joy was equally enthused and confused. She knew that if she played her cards right she could score some drugs to help her get through her long nights. She also knew a great deal about the mind as well. After all she was a psychology major. Joy squinted, her eyes as the blinking light of the hall irritated her spotty vision.

Nurse Betty noticed and quickly made a mental note of Joy's symptoms. "Have you been suffering from migraines long?"

"Almost 10 years now. They started my freshman year in college and progressed since then. I didn't start taking anything for them until shortly after my accident. I started seeing Dr. Zimmerman and he prescribed Propranolol, it worked for a spell, but it didn't stop the migraines or the pain."

"They weren't supposed to. They were supposed to slow the progression and incidence of the occurrences. They aren't for pain. They are beta-blockers." Nurse Betty opened the door to her office and ushered Joy to a seat. "Where is the pain located predominately when you have these headaches and have you noticed a certain time when they occur? Is there some type of trigger associated with these headaches?"

Joy took a seat as she sipped the tea, Nurse Betty set before her. Her taste buds nudged when she smelled the tangy sweet of lemon and honey.

"I'm not really sure if there is a trigger, except stress and light. I only figure it to be light because there is a sensitive area in my right eye that tends to pain me when a bright image of light hits it in a certain way."

Nurse Betty dropped her pen and pad onto her desk. She was shocked and dismayed that someone issued Joy an actual license to drive. "Joy you do realize that you are legally blind. How and why on earth would you be driving? I am surprised you would even get behind the wheel of a car after such a horrific accident."

"Don't remind me. Who else was going to drive me

around? I have a life, job, family to take care of." Joy took another sip of her tea. She was growing agitated with Nurse Betty. Her counseling session was drawing them no closer to what her true desires were, which was to get her hands on some medication. "I can see perfectly fine Nurse Betty. My blindness has changed considerably since the accident. I believe the migraines attribute to my sudden spells in blindness and incoherence. I have been able to see quite well for the last 6 months."

"Really?"

"Yes Really! For the most part my blindness is in color. At times I cannot decipher the color of things and at others when the migraines come I grow completely blind. Everything goes black. I can see shadows, as my sight restores."

"What else has been going on?"

Joy relaxed a bit. She sat her cup of tea on the table and began. "I have auditory hallucinations. I can hear them laughing at me. They are taunting me. When I can manage to block out the sounds and screams the visions begin. I try to run and hide in a well-lit room, hoping the demons will stay at bay. The movies have it all wrong." Joy laughed a bit slapping her knee.

"What do you mean?" Nurse Betty wondered.

"Portrayal of the super natural is highly unrealistic. I guess everyone is different. I was a fool to think light and a clove of garlic and a cross around my neck would suffice, that's for sure. The yelling screams were so horrific my eardrums began to burn. The only thing I could do was try to relax my mind and listen to what and whomever they had to say."

Nurse Betty wrote in her journal her eyes were squinted as she concentrated on the words she was trying to note. "I was wondering if you would mind coming to see me for a while. I am not as credentialed as Dr. Zimmerman, but I think I can be of some assistance to you. I want to go over my notes and see if I can prescribe a few medications I feel will help us to target the origin of these migraine headaches as well as isolate the incidence when the hallucinations occur.

Call this a hunch, but I am not sure that you necessarily have a mental disorder. The side effects of certain medications that you have been previously prescribed may be the cause. I want you to discontinue the use of any current medication you are presently taking for the next couple of days. You may experience some issues with night sweats, as you will be go through a period of slight withdrawal. I am going to give you something to take the edge off today. However, I would like to see in a couple of days. I need to monitor you. I want to access your mental state before I issue you the medication I have in mind for you. Does this sound like something you can commit to doing?"

Joy sat upright in her seat. She was a bit worried about having to go through withdrawals. "I suppose. The night sweats couldn't be any worse than what I am already suffering through. I will give it a try, if we can find a cure to these hallucinations that would be a blessing."

"I would also like to get you set up with some grief counseling, for your daughter that is." Nurse Betty meant for her entire family, but if she was going to treat Joy she needed to first gain her trust. She knew Joy suffered from some sort of delusional separation from reality. She just didn't know how serious it was.

"Sounds good." Joy had no intention of attending. She casually grabbed her purse as she accepted the prescription from Nurse Betty. "Thank you." Joy smiled a shaky smile at the nurse. It had been a long time since she was able to do that.

"For what?" Nurse Betty reached out her hand to Joy. "I am only doing my job. I am glad I ran into you today. You have been on my mind ever since I started the study. I hope that my findings will help you."

"Me too." Joy guided her way out of the hospital and to her car. She was anxious to get home. She didn't do so well in public these days. The air felt different. The sun was out, but the days still seemed strange and unwelcoming. She took refuge in her three-bedroom home, a safe haven from the world's wrath.

Joy drove home cautiously running every red light she came across. She couldn't understand her own urgency. Joy had been taking pills from every source she could find. She was no longer able to get emergency medication from the mental health department in the county building, but she had gained some use out of her trips to the emergency rooms around the North Bay area. Although she was not welcome to the facilities near her house she had been fortunate enough to get a few pills from the Walnut Creek and Concord locations.

However, grateful for the pills, the medication made her nervous and fidgety. The side effects alone were reason enough to discontinue its use. Joy was much more concerned with her sleepless nights than her days full of solidarity. Her writing suffered and her business was beginning to feel the blunt of her clouded judgment.

Joy thought about her plans for the rest of the evening as she quickly pulled into the parking area of her new three-bedroom condo. Joy kept the door to the room of her missing children's bedroom closed. She didn't want anyone to ruin the surprise for them when they were found.

Joy was convinced that her children were still missing in the storm and that it was a matter of time before they were found. Anything she could salvage from the storm she kept, but all other things that had perished from the storms wrath she had to let go.

Family photos were damaged beyond repair. The water and mud had soiled them and disfigured the images of her family. She cried softly as she wiped away the water which smeared the faces of her loved ones. Patrice and Sam had to take over the job of packing and throwing things out. She did manage to salvage a number of family photos, photos that pained her to look at.

# ~21~

## A MATTER OF LIFE AND DEATH

Joy walked around her quiet apartment searching for answers. She didn't understand her recent bout with illness. She seemed forever plagued with the fear of death and dying. It had been almost three years since her cancer entered its dormant state, but she'd lived each day fearing that symptoms of her illness would resurrect, up until they did. Her chest hurt often and breathing was a chore.

Since the storm, Joy frequently visited the emergency room. She was paranoid and banned from the hospital in close proximity to her home. She was saddened by all the pictures of her missing family, so she busied herself removing them from their frames. She didn't want them to see her suffering. Most days she spent her time wallowing in self-pity. Work was the farthest thing from her mind. The housework suffered as well. Since the tragic storm, Joy had lost nearly thirty pounds. She was dangerously floating near skin and bones. Her sister thought she may have been starving herself to death. Sam was always looking for weakness in Joy something she was perhaps better at.

Sam felt as if things came too easy for Joy, that she had to work a little bit harder to get attention or become successful. Joy was also the big sister everyone depended on. She could do no wrong. She always came running when others were in trouble going well beyond the call of duty. She could be difficult to read.

Motherly, of course, but the true aspects of Joy's

personality was her desire to be loved and accepted. She wasn't interested in respect, at least it wasn't at the top of her list. She yearned for recognition. Although as of late, the horrible disease plaguing her caused her emotions to spin out of control.

Joy fell to her knees just beside the bed and began to pray. She was so lost she didn't know where else to turn. God was now her only friend. He was the one and only person she could rely on. She could vent without ridicule and repent for her sins. She worried constantly about others judging her. Even though in her heart she knew that only God could judge her, she still feared the eyes of the world.

Joy stood at bay when important decisions were to be made. She didn't want to be perceived as the heavy. Her business suffered slightly because of it. Good thing, those things that needed a stern hand were written and electronically submitted. She wasn't good with face-to-face confrontation. Still, she was vociferous and had a way with words, in the developmental stages of profitable ventures. Slightly shy, she commented on political views only when summoned. She never raised her hand to take charge of things that she herself didn't breed. She worked alone. It was as if pulling teeth if she were forced to ask for help. She would just rather suffer from sleepless nights and poor hygiene in order to get the job done personally. She was afraid that her ideas would be stolen. She couldn't bear to fall into the shadow of another knowing full well the ideas were her own.

Protecting her reputation was just as important as her family. She would fly off the handle and into a murderous rage when her judgments were questioned. Joy's prayers always consisted of one of two things, clarity and wonder.

Joy quickly ended her prayer session when she heard a knock on her door. She was slightly aggravated, but was curious to know who could be interested in her life as a mole. She was literally suffocating to death and had no desire for rescue.

Sam was yelling at the top of her lungs, just in front of Joy's town home. Joy scurried to her feet and made her way to the living room. Tossing on her robe, she grabbed her pen and pad and threw it over to the couch. She had to set the scene. Joy opened the door slowly and with little excitement.

"Oh Heeeeyy!" Joy dragged her voice sarcastically and threw on her fake smile. "It's so nice of you to drop by and so out of your way, what's going on?"

"Nothing much can I come in?"

"Sure, why not, would you leave if I told you No?"

Sam pushed her way in with a slight bump into Joy's hip and began to investigate her apartment. "So, how are you doing?" Sam threw her coat and purse onto the chair just next to one of the end tables and picked up Joy's writing pad. "Are you working on anything special?"

"Um not really I guess I have been going through a slight spell of writers block, but I'm sure it will pass."

The meds aren't making you sick are they?"

"I'm not on medication."

"Wait! Excuse me." Sam closed her eyes with disbelief. I'm not following. That medication is to cure your disease. The doctor said that you HAVE to take this medication, possibly for the rest of your life. How could you not be taking it? Have you lost your mind?" Sam stood with her hands on her hips with both irritation and disgust. "After what this treatment cost you. Forget the shame of going to your ex for the money, but the literal loss of your family."

"Sam, I understand your concern, but please watch it. You have no right mentioning my family in this. You know why I sent them on the trip. Don't you dare try to insinuate that this whole ordeal is my fault, I didn't want them to go, but what was I supposed to do?"

"So does this mean you give up? I get it okay?" Sam put her hand over her heart to show both her sincerity and fear. "You are depressed and you may have thoughts of just giving up, but suicide is not the answer."

"Suicide?" Joy began to laugh so hard she surprised herself.

"Sam I'm not suicidal. I just don't want to be numb. You and I both know those pills do nothing for the disease. It can come back, whenever it pleases. I am not going to wait around for its return. I am going to live."

"You have got to be kidding me. Is this really what you call living? You haven't stepped foot out of this house for weeks. I am surprised you still have a job. Where is the book you were supposed to finish? All I see are papers tossed about your office, blank pages at that, some with one or two words, others with a bunch of incoherent gibberish."

"Thanks Sam, for all of your concern. I really appreciate your coming by, but if you will excuse me I would like to get back to doing absolutely nothing, in peace. I have money to survive on. My company is doing just fine without me. Nadine is a total life saver." Joy was nonchalant and showed little emotion as her voice dragged on. She didn't bother to even look up from her empty notepad. She peeked out from under her bathrobe, which now swarmed her. She was thinning tragically. The bones in her face were prominent. She just didn't look well.

Sam ignored Joy's request and continued on to the next order of business. "The Wake is tomorrow have you changed your mind about attending?"

Joy looked up from her solidarity and rolled her eyes with disgust. She was becoming irritated with her sister's presence and her refusal to leave peacefully.

"No I haven't. I will not be a participant in a lie."

"Joy!"

"Sam."

"Joy, listen I know that this is very hard to accept,

but you have got to come to terms with the death of your children and husband. I loved them too, Joy, but the search was called off over a week ago. We need to honor their memory."

"There is no honor in forgetting that they may still be out there waiting to be rescued. I will not simply give up because others are tired and need an excuse to explain the disappearance of my family. My husband called me, Sam. I picked up the phone and he was there breathing faintly, hoping that I could trace his call. I'm pretty sure someone dead couldn't manage to call me on the phone."

"I understand what you are going through, Joy."

"No the hell you don't! I do believe your children and husband are alive and well, correct? I never should have sent them away. If I had only been honest about my illness I would have been able to save the lives of my family. We would all be here safe and sound."

"Joy you need to mourn the loss of your family. Hanging on to these hopes is not healthy at all. I mean look at this place. People would think that you have literally lost your mind."

"What are you talking about Sam?"

"Joy the damn table is set for a family of five. You look like you have been up since the crack of dawn making breakfast, eggs, pancakes, bacon, sausage, fruit, who is all this for?"

"My family" Joy looked at Sam with such terror in her eyes.

Sam shifted her feet and took a few paces back from Joy. "You know what Joy?" Sam said as she lifted her hands in an attempt to surrender. "I think we need to slow down and have a talk. Come on sis. I just want to help. I think it's time you went to see somebody about this."

"I don't need to speak to anyone. I am a damn psychologist."

"Just because you can counsel others, doesn't mean

that you know how to treat yourself. You are an emotional wreck. It's best you try and get your life in order. How can you feasibly carry on in your professional career if you are suffering from such turmoil? There is no way you can hide the issues of your life from your work. Your mind is clouded. You are out of touch with reality and you refuse to talk about what's really going on with you Joy."

Sam pushed Joy towards the master bedroom to see about tidying her up.

Joy broke from Sam's grasp and yelled as if she were being attacked by some unknown stranger. "I'm not going anywhere with you, Sam. You have the nerve, the gall, the audacity to stand there with your bare face hanging out and try to analyze me and my issue. You think losing my family in a freak accident is a fucking walk on the beach. You think waking up every morning only to realize that your family isn't nestled safely in their beds is easy. Just wake-up Joy. Move on Joy, say good-bye Joy. Fuck you, Sam.

Oh and wait, the family, his side of the family as well mind you. Have no problem at all just calling off the search and throwing flowers on a grave. Tell me, Sam how in the hell did they just get you to roll over and accept the fact that your niece and nephews were just blown with the wind? Tell me how Charles, his blood cousin, just in case you all forgot we married into the same family, could just overlook the fact that they had recovered some pieces of our luggage and our car, but there were no bodies in the damn thing, now were there? What did the oceans tide sweep their bodies away? Away Sam, off of a crowded expressway in the middle of a traffic jam?

Sam, Justin called me." Joy looked almost demonic. She was beyond irate. "He called me, I need to find him. I'm not crazy. I am just frustrated that you people are so quick to just give up on your loved ones. Just carve their names in a cemented plaque." Joy looked down at the floor as the room began to spin. She had been getting severe migraines for the last week almost daily. The pain was horrific. At times she could barely see and her right side of her face just shut down. She couldn't wait to return to see Nurse Betty.

"Joy, are you alright? Sam noticed that Joy didn't look so good. The color in her face turned almost grayish blue. She was shaking slightly and stopped dead in the middle of her sentence as if frozen in time.

"Joy!" Sam called out to her sister a second time to see if she could conjure her out of her trance. Joy looked up at Sam, but she wasn't looking at her. She was looking directly through her. Sam was frightened by Joy's behavior. Joy this isn't funny. Are you alright? Joy moved her index finger slightly as if it hurt for her to move a muscle. She couldn't speak as she tried to utter the words, "Help!" Again Sam asked if she was okay.

Joy was pointing at the bag on her counter. Sam finally got the picture and grabbed the bag. As she poured out its contents she couldn't decide what she needed from her med bag that would help her with her current state of paralysis. "Joy I don't know what medication to give you. I am going to call 911. I think you need to get to the hospital. We can always explain to them why you were unable to attend the wake. I want some answers Joy. I want to know how long you have been having these migraines. You may not be able to move, but I know you can speak. You must not forget that I was the one with you when you suffered your first bout with this disease."

Joy gritted her teeth loudly. "It will pass Sam. I have been getting headaches all week. It's just the stress. I am a little worked up is all? The fact that you and Justin's mom keep pressing the issue about this memorial service isn't helping either. I can't take it. I would just appreciate it if you all would just leave me be. You want to say goodbye then go right ahead. I will say goodbye when they have actually gone." Joy winced with pain as she struggled to finish her sentence.

"We are done here Sam. Don't worry about me. If I stand still for a few more moments the pain will let up. I have been suffering from back and neck spasm. They occur whenever a migraine hits. I'm already undergoing treatment to resolve this issue."

"Joy I'm not leaving you like this. You are standing in the middle of your living room like a statue for God sakes. You need help."

"Yeah you are. I don't want to talk to you about this any longer. You are the reason I am stressed now. So if you leave I will be fine. Please go! I can't take any more stress right now. You go and play your part. I don't have time for games. I am going to find my family."

"Your family is dead Joy! They're dead and there is not a damn thing you can do about it. You can't bring them back. Joy, if you ever want to see my children again you will get help for yourself. I can't have you around with your hallucinations and narcissistic views about the family, my family. So get over yourself Joy. You are not the only one who has suffered a loss. We all loved your children and Justin. How do you think Justin's mom feels? She too has lost a child. Just think about it for a minute will you, stop being so damn selfish."

"Yeah Sam, I am sure you have an abundance of love for my husband. You tend to float in forbidden directions, but selfish? You think I'm being selfish?" Joy couldn't believe her ears. She put her hand up against her chest as if she were short of breath.

"How dare you say shit to me about being selfish? There is no way in hell you can call me selfish, after I gave up my entire life for all of you."

Joy forced her leg to move an inch towards Sam's shadow. Sam flinched warding against Joy's advance. She feared Joy's paralyzed state had passed. She would surely tear her from limb to limb.

"Selfish. You really should be going now? Thanks for your time and rude comments. If I had the strength I would walk over there and slap the taste from your mouth. You are one piece of work. Let's see just how well you do when dear ole hubby finds out that you have been dishonest almost your whole damn life. Wait until he finds out about your indiscretions. You know what? If I weren't so damn sure that you weren't completely heartless. I would detect just a little bit of satisfaction coming from your end. Could you be happy that I have lost everything? Maybe now you won't have to continuously live in my shadow."

"Joy that's enough, I can understand that you are upset and going through something, but I won't be disrespected."

Joy laughed at Sam's articulation with words. "You know where the door is. Its high time you use it." Joy could hardly contain herself after Sam's choice of words. "HA!" Joy busted out with an over exaggerated laugh of disdain. "I won't be disrespected either. With my most recent issue honey, you would do good to see your way out of here. Sister or not I may start in on you and forget who you are. Don't mistake your blood to make me any difference at this point. Your face and its likeness to my own couldn't save you, because right now I hate myself. I am asking you to leave Samantha there won't be a second warning."

"Alright, I will leave you be. Today! I think I may have to pay that doctor of yours a visit. This makes absolutely no sense. If I have to find another care provider for you then so be it. I am not just going to sit by and watch you rot away in this hell whole. You think you could find the time to clean up, during your busy schedule? Since you have all this money, you don't even need to lift a finger. Hire someone."

"Thanks but no thanks I don't need help with the daily tasks of my home. My children will be home from school soon and I will have the home spotless and their afternoon snack waiting for them. So if you don't mind, I'd like to get back to work and another thing, don't you dare talk to me as though I am your homecare client. I run the affairs of my home and business."

Sam simply stared at her sister with disbelief. She looked down at the floor, before turning on her heel and leaving the apartment. She didn't say a word. Slamming the door behind her Sam looked out onto the road before making her way to her car. "Not for long Sis, not for long."

# ~VOLUME 2~

# VENGEANCE IS MINE

# ~22~

# TOWARDS THE LIGHT

Joy locked the door behind her and nearly ran to the kitchen in search for a cold stiff drink. She wanted nothing more than to drink herself into a deep coma. Nearly pulling her arm out of socket, Joy grabbed the fridge door and confiscated the half empty bottle of Arbor Mist and placed the bottled seductively and hungrily to her lips. She didn't bother to retrieve a cup from her bare cabinets, as they were scattered about the kitchen amongst the other soiled dishes. "Damn it! Where are you?" Joy began to speak aloud the thoughts probing her brow. She had summoned her conscience to reveal the secrets of her mind. She realized that she could not yet be honest with herself, sober.

Joy's thoughts ran wild she was ranting and raving on about her sightings. She almost had to narrate her illustrations aloud to prove to herself that they were actually occurring. "I can see their images, happily smiling engaged in normal everyday activity. In the seconds to come I see those same faces before me lifeless. I relive death each time. I am saddened and drawn back into such a depression I wonder how I will go on. Their bodies lay cold. They haunt me. I can see their eyes. They call to me. I rarely sleep because in my dreams they are calling my name and whispering in my ear. It has gotten so bad that the happenings occur when I am awake. I know that they are not truly there but it feels so real. As if there is a sign I am supposed to follow. Damn it how am I supposed to deal with these dreams and hallucinations? Even if I open my eyes to get clarity that nothing is there the images still play. I am no longer comforted by my absence of sight.

Where are you?"

Joy screamed frantically stomping around her home demanding her to show face. "Answer me." Joy fought to calm herself as she staggered down the hall to her bathroom. Setting the empty bottle of booze into the sink she peered into her reflection. Joy starred at her image as if she couldn't recognize her own likeness.

Convinced that her twin had abandoned her just as so many others had she fought to gain some sort of normality by taking a stand towards sobriety. Joy gripped the empty bottle of booze and tossed it up into the air. She stared blankly looking into the colors reflecting into the light as it fell into the trashcan below. It was a beautiful sight as she seldom caught a glimpse of color. Joy snapped back into her reality and bolted from the bathroom flicking the light switch on her way out.

Joy plopped down on her love seat in the living room. It was an early dark Sunday morning. Joy's heart was heavy. She just couldn't understand why God had forsaken her. Hadn't she tried to live her life right? Justin would often scold Joy for going far beyond the call of duty. He was saddened by the way her family treated her, often showing very little support, or gratitude.

As Joy flipped back and forth channel to channel looking for a, "Law and Order," marathon she heard a voice blaring from the television. It was Joyce Myer, she was hollering into a screen that was black as night. The satellite had yet to view the televisions picture. Joyce was speaking stern and loudly. Joy could have sworn she heard Joyce say her full name.

"Joy Anderson honey you have got to stop feeling sorry for yourself. You to have stop thinking that your life is of no value, wallowing in self- pity will only bury you alive and drown you in tears of misery. Remember, God is your savior. He is a comforter in times of need. You must trust and have faith. He died so that you can live. Joy, when are you going to wake up?"

Joy rose from her slumped position, her mouth was wide open and her eyes were glued to the black screen of her television.

"God has a plan for you. He may have to drag you to hell and back before you can see his plan, but he has a plan for you. Stand up! Claim your victory. You are a child of God, a woman of value. Your talents are needed to win the war. You are one of the His chosen few."

Joy was both honored and angered by Joyce's convincing, but unrealistic sermon. The horrific natures of this world continue to terrorize the good nature of those that believe in God and his promise. Joy was up and at her feet. She began to yell at Joyce, "Show yourself and these truths you so profess."

Joy demanded to see her employer and beckoned for God to show his face. Joy needed affirmation that God was in fact real and if so why had he refused to explain his actions? No matter how angry Joy was with God she did know that his will would be served. She just had to trust him. She couldn't understand, but she wanted to know why. Her understanding of God's mercy could not fathom how the loss of her family could be justified nor warranted.

Joy tried to pull herself together as she ventured off into the master bedroom. A nice warm bath would do her body well, it was sure to help ease her mind. Joy battled with her heart and mind about God and his hidden messages through Joyce and her televised sermon on God and his will.

Unable to ignore her need to speak to God any longer she fell to her knees just beside the bed and began to pray. She was so lost she didn't know where else to turn. God was now her only friend. He was the one and only person she could rely on. She could vent without ridicule and repent for her many sins. She worried constantly about others judging her. Although, she knew that only God could judge her; she still feared the eyes of the world. She herself hated that about her personality.

Joy stepped into her bathroom and stared into the dark. She walked slowly to the tubs edge and looked into the deep oval ceramic surface and sat on its edge.

The room seemed to expand as if the walls were no longer there. All she could see was a bright light that appeared from just beyond the tub. A calming glow that moved her to sway softly, as the luminosity calmed her soul. Tuning into her consciousness she turned on the water to the tub. The golden handles with pearl tips seemed to reflect small sparkles of gold onto the water, as it filled the bathtub. The room was well lit by the golden highlights. Joy watched the waters flow as if hypnotized by the clear crystals falling from its spout.

As the water surfaced towards the tubs edge, she could visibly see the steam hovering over its top. She could feel the soft warmth of the clouds steam and in it she calmed her weeping heart. She felt a great sense of peace.

Though the chill of the bathroom flowed from her feet against the tile floor, she was warmed by the presence of something. Curious with the urge to feel the closeness of her husband's spirit, she called out to him. Joy prayed that her lack paranormal belief would not hinder her possibility of experience. She quieted herself and looked into the empty space filled with light and steam from her hot bath. In it he stood quietly. She was fearful at first, at this presumed presence of someone that had passed on. She nearly fell from the tub. She could have easily hit her head and knocked unconscious.

Joy held on to her chest frightfully aware of her close walk with death and inhaled slowly. Grabbing onto the flesh of her chest she grabbed both the garment of her oversized shirt and the thin tissue between her breasts purposely to test her conscious awareness. Pain was definite and her eyes were focused even in the dark of the night. Slowly releasing her shirt, she placed her hands toward the illuminating light in an attempt to touch just the hem of his garment. Unable to feel the cloth she retreated and shook her head solemnly, then violently, as she realized her disbelief caused her to lose touch.

Just in that moment the peace that had culminated her mind, body and spirit dissipated. She was tired and worn. Her back slumped over and depression quickly settled. Moving from the tubs edge she turned her back towards the door and the light was gone. She slowly crumbled to the floor and fell into a tantrum of unexplained volatile convulsions, as she cried for mercy and understanding.

"Dear God, Why has Thou forsaken me? Why must I stay to die alone in the hellish ways of this world? What am I to do with this life, now that all that I have loved and cherished has perished?"

"You live."

Joy peered from between the small cracks in her hands. Slowly she uncovered her face. She could have sworn to have heard Justin's voice, but nothing was there.

"Hello!" she called out, making sure that her mind was in fact playing tricks on her. She was even fearful that the voice would again answer her. She too thought that she may be losing her sanity. Things that were happening were not of this world. She couldn't explain her thoughts or actions. Her mind raced and the outbreaks of sudden amnesia puzzled not only her, but her family.

"I'm here." the voice interrupted.

Joy this time was afraid to speak aloud. "What do you want?" she asked as if she wanted to know the answer.

"I want you to live." was his only response.

Joy's eyes widened with surprise but the voices request only seemed to add fuel to the fire burning within Joy's chest. She was angry. She wanted an explanation.

"What for?" she screamed.

"What for?" Again she called at the empty space just beyond her tub and demanded an answer. "How dare you leave?" she yelled begging for his return.

Still, the water drifted amongst the soft winds that crept in from the bathroom window. Soft drips of water hit the pool before her, but nothing more. Not even a whisper of apology and farewell came from the golden light that had lit her bathroom just moments before.

Joy's mind seemed to burst her brain was scrambled. She had bits and pieces of reality playing in her mind. She wasn't delusional as she was before. She was psychotic. She screamed at the top of her lungs beckoning Lillian to show her face.

She tore down the towel rack, slammed her fists on the sink and jolted open the medicine cabinet in search for relief. When she couldn't find the pills she stopped suddenly as if her breakdown were calming and just stared down into the drain of the sink. The small metal circle lit up brightly and reflected a small razor that had fallen from the shelf of the medicine cabinet. In that moment Joy felt relief. She felt as if her answer had arrived. That if only she could die, she could live passing on the horrors of this life to be resurrected anew, born into a new place and time a chance to start over.

Joy slumped over the sinks edge as if her head and shoulders were too heavy to bear. Her thoughts swarmed in circles.

"What are you waiting for? Here is your chance to be one again with your husband and children. They have gone to a much better place. You can go along with them."

"Why are you here? You have done nothing, but make me out to be a bad person, deranged even. You tiptoe around in your make-up and perfectly curled hair, ordering me around. I have no control over my thoughts and feelings. My husband said otherwise to what you are suggesting."

Joy could feel her hands warming as her hand glided towards the sink. She retrieved the blade from the bottom of the ivory marble and white surface and gazed at her reflection. Her skin warmed as if the blood were coming to a boil and excited to spill from her flesh. Joy's hands were shaking. She was forcibly trying to drop the blade but; she was not strong enough.

"I dare you to do something for yourself." I dare you to end these feelings of loneness and pain. How long has it been?"

"What do you mean?" Joy spoke through clenched teeth trying with all her might to regain control of her judgment and kinetics.

"How long has it been, since you have done something good for yourself, tended to your own needs, spent lavishly on something you didn't necessarily need but desired?"

"I don't know. Why does this even matter? I don't have any desires anymore. The only thing I want is to find my family. If that isn't up for grabs, then I'd just as well, spend the rest of my days rotting away?"

"It isn't fair you know."

"What do you mean?"

"The way you choose to live. Your illness has very little to do with the matters of your heart you know. Sure, you feel as if you are living your last days over and over once you have to visit the doc about his most recent findings, but really. You know what your problem is Joy? You are pathetic. You spend most of your time feeling sorry for yourself. You would much rather tend to others lawns than manicure the one you own. You have a good front for a life, but tell me are you happy? I bet if you had spent less time caring for others you would be way ahead of the game. You know it's your fault you lost them. You didn't have to send them off. You sure as hell didn't need to borrow money from that scum bag ex-boyfriend of yours. You are no better than a drug addict trading your daughter for money like that."

"How dare you? It wasn't like that at all. I needed the money to find a cure. I couldn't let my family see me in such a vulnerable state. I needed to know that they were ok. If my treatment didn't work out they would become filled with depression and loss of hope. Justin would have been fixated on healing me. I don't expect you to understand. It is obvious that you do not care about anyone."

"I care about you. I know that you have been stuck in this rut for far too long. I am here to put a stop to this madness. Your family died Joy. They died tragically in a storm. A tornado touched ground without warning and claimed the lives of over 1500 people. You and those other families suffered a horrible loss. I am here because you brought me here. I am the one that has the power to heal you. I am here to provide an escape from this lifelong disease of need you have been so plagued with. It's disgusting, this need you harbor to be liked, loved and accepted the need to be successful and looked up to. This need to please others at any cost is embarrassing, all that is over my friend. You may not like my methods, but they work. All talk and no action is meaningless. You have been saying that you don't care your entire adult life, but yet and still you run as soon as they call day or night. Vengeance is in the air."

"Vengeance? What or who rather am I, avenging? Manipulation is not my area of expertise. I can do, bad all by myself. The war is over!"

"No Joy, it has just begun. If you bothered to shut up for just a few moments at a time, you would be able to see how the individuals you call family and friends take advantage of your kindness and generosity. Has it ever occurred to you that if you weren't so busy paying off the debts of others you wouldn't have had to borrow the money from Darrin? Or did that small issue blow over your senses. I do believe you are lost in your own mind. Your defenses are down because you do not know how to defend yourself. Perhaps this is because you don't know who to defend yourself from. I bet apart of you is thinking that I am the enemy. That I need to be dealt with, that possibly I am a figment of your imagination. Well look in the mirror touch the contours of your face. Tell me what you see."

"Please just go away. I don't need any help taking care of my home or personal affairs. All I need is for everyone to simply leave me be. All of you keep volunteering your two cents in regards to my conscious ability to think and make healthy rational decisions. Well I can take care of myself, maybe I don't want to be careful or care about the outcome to all this mess."

"Then I'd have to say that you are continuing to lie to yourself," Which isn't going to do either of us any good. Humor me for about two minutes. Look at yourself. You need me. I am the one that can handle the harsh realities of this world."

"You can't be serious."

"Oh why not, I mean you have gone through life as clean as a whistle? I can count on my hand the times you were actually held responsible for some of the drama you have caused over the years? I mean look at you. You have managed to start an enormous amount of shit and here you are standing around weeping as if you are the victim. I find this whole act quite humorous. Being that I know you far more than I'd like to admit. You know now that I think about it, I can't seem to remember a time in your adult life that you took responsibility for your personal wrong doings. Sure you offer to take the heat for others often just so you will be viewed as the Good Samaritan. I mean really. When you were held accountable for your own selfish deeds? Isn't that what all these personal meetings in the bathroom are about, your personal counseling sessions, tears of remorse and confession? Is this truly your confession? We are the only ears that hear what we already know. Or are you suggesting that your frequent visits to the restroom are spent in counsel with God? Are you talking over your sins with Jesus himself?"

"I am not a shamed of who I am. You are merely a figment of my imagination, the evil side to my conscience. We both know that you are the cause of malice. So let's not place blame. I know how to shun away from your advances. The good in me will prevail. I know who you are and why you have come. Only I won't let you take over my soul no matter how unfair I feel my world of circumstance to be. I do use this time to conference with God. Instead, lately I am confronted by you, my ill thoughts of envy and hate. My insecurities about life and my ability to succeed, I used to think my reflection in the mirror was a force to be reckoned with. I could be lost in translation, admiring the beautiful characteristics of my face a face that at one time I hated because it was not my own. I even hated the good my siblings admired because if I was responsible, people would start to depend on me. You think I signed up for this role. It was birthed unto me. I tried out for other roles but I landed this one. You don't like me because I don't do for others to get to where I need to go, I peacefully surrender. I create my own venue and plan of action. So when are you going to get the picture that you are no longer needed?"

"When you show me independence, I see you glaring at me in passing. You purposely leave the door open to make sure you can peak and see that I have not left you. Your fear of abandonment has always left you vulnerable and susceptible to abuse. You are nothing but bait for those wishing to fish for the weak. I think that if we could just be honest about your neediness things would go a lot smoother."

"Really well maybe we can touch on that some

other time. Sam wants to talk. At least she seems to genuinely want to help me through this."

"Oh yea good luck with that, She is another problem, Joy. When are you going to cut the cord already? What!" Lilly laughed from deep within her stomach. "What's the meeting about this time? Oh wait, let me guess." Lillian placed her hand to her chin in wonder.

"I bet she is having issues with Charles and she would like you to mediate. Why with your psyche degree you are sure to have all the right answers. Why I bet you won't be able to get a word in edge wise with all the sniffling and harping about her and Charles. What about you? The two of you already have to share the same damn face. No wonder Charles is confused. I mean the only difference between you and Sam is that Sam has the balls to say no. You on the other hand scurry like a cat from water, when faced with confrontation. That's why I'm here Joy. You can cry now. After all that's what you do best. You cry while others get even."

"SHUT UP!" Joy yelled. She threw her hands up grabbing two handfuls of her curly mane and began to pull furiously. Joy was desperately trying to shake Lilly from her being. She was confused. The only way out seemed to be death. The pills were causing her psychotic breaks to become more frequent. In fact they were giving birth to more of her untamed personalities. Joy now physically fighting with her deranged mind was clawing at the skin on her face, yelling into her reflection in the mirror. Joy was frightened by the woman's flaming hair.

"Andrew's when did you get here?" Lilly directed her attention to the two faced woman. Joy was trying to run but her legs wouldn't move. She was so lost and confused she shook visibly. Her alternate personality had now split into two.

Andrew's held a gruesome mug as she shook her head at the two of them. Her arms were folded and she wore a smug grin on her bright red painted lips. "You rang remember?" Lillian stepped back into the shadows just behind Joy as she appeared to be intimidated by their seductive foe.

"You are a crazed individual. I don't know who you are but you and Lilly can both go. Your services are no longer needed." Joy tried to appear brave and under control as she spoke sternly to her evil twin who appeared to be aroused by the warm blood flowing from Joy's pores. Joy balled her fist, squeezing her hands tightly to watch the blood ooze from the cracks of her fingers. She felt an odd sense of liberation.

Joy shut her eyes tight in an effort to get rid of what she presumed to be a simple hallucination. She snuck a peek at her hands to see if she in fact had been dreaming of her sudden break of mental capacity. Whatever the matter with her, she was not coping well with the disappearance of her family. The demons were out to play and her mind and heart were wide open. Joy saw the blood as a reality leaking onto her floor and sink. She quickly looked at her reflection in the mirror, but nothing was there. Nothing, but her mangled hair and blood shot eyes. Her hands were clear of blood, her sink and floor as well. Joy breathed in deep and threw open the door to her medicine cabinet.

"There must be something here. I need help and fast." Joy searched high and low for some form of anxiety relief. She needed to get in to see Nurse Betty right away.

# ~23~

# MY SISTERS KEEPER

Sam's eyes welled with tears at her sister's obvious lost sense of reality. She was further gone than she had imagined. Sam had no idea that Joy thought her family was still alive. Daily she must have been performing her daily rituals, as if her family came home to her after school and work.

Sam just looked at Joy for a moment and turned to leave before the tears could hit her cheeks. She didn't want to acknowledge Joy's mental issues. Afraid that she would just stir the pot she left on a mission to seek medical attention for her sisters, psychotic break.

Sam slammed the door of her car and sped out of Joy's driveway. It was time to pay the doctor a visit. If Joy didn't get help soon, she was sure to be digging her own grave. The fact that Sam was left out of Joy's bout with depression angered her more. They were so close. Secrets were unheard of between the two of them. All their lives they shared every experience, they were married during the same month and pregnant at the same time twice.

Sam wasn't going to just let Joy go through such a tragic experience alone, even if she begged her to go home and attend to her own affairs. Just because Joy was the oldest didn't mean that she knew better all the time. Sam felt that it was detrimental that she found help for her sister before her depression worsened. She knew how bad it could get and she knew how Joy's blackouts could become murderous. She was a danger to herself and others. At least that is what she would go with. Sam's thin line between love and hate was nearing its peak. She too had frequent visits from the devil sitting upon her right shoulder. She had a rough childhood although she and Sam were twins, the girl's mother dotted on Joy. She was mom's pride and joy. Sam could never out right admit that she had deception lurking in the confines of her heart, but she was sure Joy had some clue. She was legally blind not dumb. Joy made a point to help Sam with whatever issue she had out of guilt.

Sam knew that it wasn't Joy's fault that their mother took to her more than she, but Joy was an easy target. Joy was the sweet one. She was always looking to help. Since Sam was deemed as the outcast and the unexpected baby, she decided to play up to the misfit persona. She was overall a good person, just misguided and misunderstood.

Charles was much to blame. They started dating when Sam was at an age where she couldn't begin to understand what commitment and love meant. She was in high school and while high school is the trial and error stage of adolescence, she spent her junior prom in the hospital giving birth.

Sam stopped just short of a red light in the middle of a busy intersection. Her thoughts were so clouded about her visit with her sister. Sam looked in her rear view mirror to catch a glimpse of herself. She had dark circles forming around her eyes. She had been up nights worried about her sister, afraid that she would receive a phone call in the middle of night. "Our parents are gone Joy, so are the rest of our brothers and sisters. I just wish you could give me a small break. I know you did everything you could for us, but I would just about die for an uninterrupted night of rest." Sam thought to herself wishing for a night of peace and tranquility, to possibly deal with her marriage. She and Charles were growing farther apart by the day. Sam didn't know how to console him with regards to Justin. Charles seemed lost in another world. He was secretive and up late at night checking the locks on the doors, as if he were afraid of something. Sam asked Charles about the phone calls, but he refused to divulge what they were about. Of course Sam was sure that Charles was cheating. She could only hope that the tramp wasn't pregnant. Sam was used to Charles and his other women, but she never had to worry about baby mama drama.

Sam was startled by a car honking behind her. She hadn't realized she was talking to herself in the mirror. She was lost in translation trying to make sense of her purpose. It doesn't seem like there is much left to do but have Joy committed for at least three months. Maybe with medication and close watch she could have some time to truly mourn her family and get back into the driver's seat of her life.

Sam could really use the time to get to the bottom of Charles mysterious attitude, with Joy out of the picture for a while. Patrice seemed to care about Joy, but Sam didn't trust her. Patrice seemed a bit too involved in the Anderson affairs. Sam was sure her sister would want a fresh mind and face to handle her affairs appropriately. Who more qualified to run the company than the younger twin sister that could run the business to Joy's liking if not better.

# ~24~

# GREY AREA

"Here! I want you to take two of these at night before you go to bed."

Nurse Betty looked up at Joy, "I mean it." she said pointing and shaking the pen as if waiting for an agreement. "Make sure you do not take your medication and decide you want to go out for a late night snack. You shouldn't be driving or operating heavy machinery. I would refrain from the use of a blender, iron, or stove on these babies. They are quite strong and they cause drowsiness."

"I guessed. Some of the precautions sound a bit scary. They will make me feel better though, right?"

"Not exactly it's going to take a few days for them to actually take effect. The medicine needs some time to get into your system."

"Okay, so am I going to be sick? I feel horrible as it is. I really don't want to be stuck on the toilet or hovering over it. I have a lot of work to do."

"Great! I'm glad you have decided to return to work. I think that would be a great idea actually. It will help keep your mind off of your loss. I know when I lost my son to cancer I buried myself into my work. I mourned my loss, but it was easier for me to work long hours. I couldn't stand coming home to an empty home. At least your home was destroyed in the storm."

Joy's forehead wrinkled. "I don't see how, I lost everything dear to me."

"I'm sure. I apologize for my candor. I didn't mean it like that. I meant that you don't have to be plagued with all the memories of your lost loved ones on a daily basis. The familiar smell, the empty bedrooms, or their belongings thrown about the home as you may so remember. I'm sorry." Nurse Betty apologized as she noticed Joy's lips pinching tightly as she continued her explanation for her lack of professionalism. "I don't exactly know how to use tact. I thought maybe a little humor would help to melt the ice a bit. I know how hard it must be to have to wake up daily to this madness. Seeing the humor and remembering the happy times helped me through my worst days while in mourning."

"Well Nurse Betty, thanks for the drugs. At least I can get some sleep out of the deal. I doubt it will do any good for my missing family." Joy jumped down off of the cold examining table and snatched the prescription from the doctor's manicured hands. "I better get going. I am going to meet Justin's mom and my sister, Sam, for dinner. They are making me go out tonight. I guess I spend too much time at home on my computer. I told them that I would meet for drinks at least, but don't worry."

Joy threw up her hands to stop her old friend and health care professional from going on a tangent about drinking and medication use. "I know. I won't be driving or taking any pills before driving. I have to find my family, remember?"

Nurse Betty looked up from her clipboard. She was busy writing out a prescription for her next patient. It had just dawned on her that Joy was delusional. Joy still had yet to come to terms with her family's passing. She would have to recommend her case be looked at by a group of psychologists. "I'm sure you will find them Joy and when you do you and your family will all be at peace."

Joy looked at the nurse with great admiration and hope. It was the first time in a long time she felt as if she could trust anyone with her feelings. Someone that truly understood the truth behind her family's disappearance, they were lost not dead. "I am going to find them." Joy smiled courageously.

"Well, promise me you will get better first. You need to make sure you can think clearly."

Joy smiled. She was confused by his sudden reference to the way she processed information. She could read people like a book and because Nurse Betty's smile was strained she could tell that she had been sarcastic in her support of the search for her family. "Thanks." Joy lowered her eyes long enough for Nurse Betty to notice. She glared back at her and folded her hands in front of her. As she rocked back and forth on her heels and toes her jawline flexed.

"Well Ms. Anderson." she said as she cleared her throat. "It is always a pleasure. I will see you out."

"Oh there's no need. I think I can manage. Should we schedule another visit to see just how these placebos you have prescribed are working out? Oh and please call me Mrs. Anderson."

"Yes, please see my receptionist on your way out." Nurse Betty ignored Joy's sudden attitude change. She started to wonder if Joy would even show up to her next appointment.

"Will do." Joy grabbed her purse and rushed out of the room towards the front desk. She quickly filled out the appropriate paperwork and left the building. She was in a hurry to get the dinner with her mother-n-law over with. It was sure to be a snore fest. Since, Justin's disappearance time with the family was a complete yawn.

# ~25~

# KISS AND TELL

Joy felt incredibly dizzy just moments after taking the pills Nurse Betty had given her. She decided to cancel dinner with her in-laws and Sam was suddenly M.I.A. She'd just rather curl up in bed and watch the, "House" marathon.

Dr. House was just one of her television boyfriends. His nonchalant attitude and 5 o'clock shadow, were his two sexiest traits. Joy had always had a tender spot for bad guys. She was infatuated with thugs and rogues. They were a true challenge. She vowed to make those that fell prey to her trap, gentlemen yet.

Justin however, stepped up to the challenge. He was cocky and ill mannered, yet soft and sensitive in his own way. His charm and bad boy sense of sensibility confused Joy. She'd met her match. Love came easy. She finally felt as if she could let her guard down.

Joy dazed and out of touch with reality stumbled into the bathroom. She turned the stainless steel knobs on her sink, until the water was an even flow. The cold water was sure to wake her from her confused state, she thought. Splashing her face with the cool fluid she arose from under a waterfall of relief and peered into her vanity mirror. The lights were gold, which provided a lovely glow to accentuate her natural beauty. Joy tried to focus her eyes as the water dripped from her eyelashes. Blinking hard and wiping her eyes gently she looked into the mirrors reflection.

Her face appeared to be distorted, like an abstract painting. Her countenance was split into two parts both filled with unpleasant emotion. Wiping the mirror in an attempt to clear her vision, she found no change in her likeness.

Joy became frantic as she started rubbing her face. She memorized the height of her cheekbone, the shape of her eyes and the fullness of her lips. Peering back into the mirror, her reflection had changed. The mirror reflected her true expression. Her eyes were red and puffy from crying. Spiraling curls escaped from her sloppy bun, tickling her brow and the nap of her neck.

Joy shook her head as she gripped the sink, trying desperately to hold herself up. She was suddenly filled with exhaustion. Joy grabbed her chest and checked for numbness in her arm. Feeling confident that she wasn't suffering from a heart attack she wet her face to snap herself out of her trance and back into the realities of her world. She dried her face gently with her hand towel and retreated from the bathroom. She made sure to turn out the lights behind her.

"Wow, Nurse Betty was right. These are some strong meds, I better lay down."

Joy threw back the covers to her king sized bed and jumped into the fluff of her feathery pillows. Suddenly, her doorbell rang. "Oh go away." Joy begged with a whining tone, hoping that if she were quiet her uninvited guest would go away. Again the doorbell sang three quick alarming chimes. Joy kicked wildly at her covers and flung her robe closed. She jumped out of bed and stomped down the hall towards the living room.

"Alright, alright, hold your damn horses."
"It's me Charles, open up."

"Charles?" Joy whispered to herself. Oh my God, it must be something wrong with Sam. Joy ran and unlocked her well-bolted door.

"Charles is everything alright?"

"Yes, Yes. I didn't mean to startle you." Charles

grabbed Joy by her shoulders and stepped inside the door.

"Then what's wrong?" Joy's forehead wrinkled as she closed and locked the door, behind them.

Charles sat down on the couch and put his head in his hands. "I just...I was just working late....just over the bridge...a client Justin and I worked with on a special project. The dude called to inform Justin that, he had been awarded the grant." Charles bit his lip and shook his head. "Hum, funny thing. I couldn't believe it. I was so excited I grabbed my cell and dialed his number. It had gone straight to voice mail before I had realized Justin was gone." Charles began to sob like a baby. He fell back into the cushions of Joy's couch to take solace. Joy was both stunned and filled with a strong desire to console him. Her loneliness overwhelmed her.

"I didn't even know he was working on a grant." Joy rubbed her sweat beading hands on the front of her robe. She was surprised and oddly nervous.

"Yes it was a surprise. He kept it a secret because he didn't want to jinx it by getting too excited. You know how superstitious he could be."

"Yeah I do. Too superstitious if you ask me. It often got into the way of his faith in himself and others."

Charles turned to Joy, with a sudden interest to converse about their lost loved one. "It was just hard for us growing up is all, down South it was God and Church. First and foremost we learned the ways of the land. Home remedies, old saying sand superstition. We held on to every word big mama and the rest of our elders spoke."

"Yeah I know he was always quoting something from the Anderson handbook of life. He ruled it to be just as valuable as the Bible." Joy laughed from deep in her gut. It felt good and scary at the same time. She stopped abruptly as the guilt surrounded her and spun her back to reality.

Charles noticed her discomfort and searched his

mind for something to say to clear the redness from Joy's cheeks.

"I'm sorry. I didn't mean to be disrespectful."

"No. It's quite alright." Joy smiled nervously, as her hands began to shake. "So what now, the grant I mean. Is there any way I can finish the project with you, in his absence of course?" Joy's voice trailed off as she headed for the kitchen. "Drink?" Joy called over her shoulder.

"What? Oh yes, please! I could use a nice stiff one right about now." Charles stood quickly and wiped his sweat beading hands on the lap of his slacks. He loosened his tie and unbuttoned his collar, on his way to the kitchen.

"The fund is entirely up to you, Joy." Charles uttered as he claimed his seat at the bar.

"What do you mean?" Joy looked up from her alcoholic concoction for clarity.

"The money is yours. That is the reason for my visit. I came to give you the check. It's for a million dollars." Charles nervously handed Joy the check. He was kicking himself for handing such a large amount of money over to someone, who had no idea it existed. "The money's yours." Charles didn't realize he was still gripping onto the check. He had to repeat the fact that it didn't belong to him, in order to understand.

Joy's eyes widened with both surprise and disbelief. "Wow! I had no idea."

"He was working on some government grants for your literary program."

Joy's eyes began to well with tears. She could no longer see Charles in full view. Her mind raced.

"Joy let me help. I'm sorry I didn't mean to upset you."

Joy was shaking so hard the drink no longer needed to be blended. She had shaken her toxic blend just perfectly.

Charles reached for Joy's arm carefully, as he took

his position behind her. He carefully removed the glass from her shaking hands and gently placed it on the counter. Charles couldn't help but smell the aroma of Vanilla and Shea Butter enticing him. He leaned forward into Joy's soft natural curls, to cure his temptations. Lingering for too long, he quickly retreated pulling his head back.

Joy was still in shock from the news. She hadn't noticed Charles slight slip in judgment. She couldn't be sure she was strong enough to ward off his advances, if in fact there were any. Charles cleared his throat, as he placed his hands gently on Joy's forearms. He still stood behind Joy rather close and as much as he knew his love was rising he couldn't find the strength to pull away. When Joy didn't respond, Charles squeezed her shoulders softly, in an attempt to massage the tension and stress from her neck.

"Joy can you hear me?"

Joy leaned her head back, as he felt the stress disseminating from her brow. She was overcome with comfort and relaxation. Charles noticed, wanting desperately to see her facial expression, he trailed his fingers seductively along the length of her neck. He removed the curls from his view.

Joy's mind drifted reminiscing about Justin, warmed her soul. She felt calm as Justin's arms wrapped around her. Closing her eyes she let nature take its course. Leaning against Justin, Charles welcomed her advances. He and Sam hadn't been sexually active in well over a month.

Joy's resemblance to her sister shocked both Justin and Charles when they first met. They got more than they bargained for. The two of them were head strong and stubborn as could be. A trait both Justin and Charles couldn't resist. They enjoyed the challenge. With the two sisters sharing the same genetic make-up, he was confused at how different the two of them were. Charles' mind drifted in and out of conscious awareness. He became conflicted by his natural temptation to flesh and salvation.

Charles could be found in confession bargaining with God. He knew that he was taking advantage of Joy, but continued to tell himself that she was of sound mind.

**\*\*\*\***

Joy shed her robe without being coached as she started to get into the motion of things. Charles didn't take his time his lust for Joy took control of his senses. Grabbing Joy around her slim waist he turned her quickly. He couldn't wait another moment to kiss her sweet lips. Taking control, as Joy spun into his arms he pulled her close and kissed her hungrily. Her lips were soft and melted between his own, she became like a drug to him hard to resist and illegal. He knew of his betrayal and couldn't blame Joy, for he knew she was vulnerable.

Joy felt Justin's strong hands caressing the small of her back, as she kissed him passionately. She moaned and relaxed in his arms. She drifted into a daze of hypnosis that she couldn't shake.

"Justin." she moaned as Charles lifted her from her feet and placed her on the kitchen counter. The cool granite singed, as her hot center warmed its surface. She begged for Justin to heal her burning desire. She yearned for his touch and longed to feel him inside her.

Charles now past point of mere arousal ignored Joy's obvious confusion and unbuckled his pants. He was having difficulty with the button on his slacks, so he ripped them open. Joy flew from under her nightgown. Her eyes were closed as Charles kissed her neck and moved down to her chest.

Again Joy called out to Justin now loud and clear as she was excited by his lustful foreplay. She had, had enough and was ready to receive him. Charles now fully aware of his indiscretion paused and pulled back from Joy as if startled.

"Joy, Oh My God." Charles spoke as if stunned he were in Joy's apartment. Joy looked dazed and confused as her medication was now in full effect.

"Justin what's wrong?" She responded as she noticed the look of hurt and deceit on his face. Charles could hardly muster a sound as he tried to clear his throat. He busied himself trying to fasten his pants and locate Joy's nightgown.

"I'm sorry Joy. I'm really sorry." Joy's eyes began to redden and fill with tears.

"Justin why are you doing this, what have I done wrong?"

Charles looked up from his solemn embarrassment and noticed the hurt and pain on Joy's face. Suddenly it dawned on him that Joy truly believed that he were Justin. Charles decided to play along, hoping that Joy would awake from her moment of psychotic break with no memory of his advances upon her.

"Its' nothing Joy." Charles responded hoping that his choice to follow along wouldn't come back to bite him on the ass. Hopefully she and Sam wouldn't speak of her romantic encounter with her dead husband Justin. Sam would be sure to get to the bottom of Joy's rendezvous, with her alleged mystery man.

"I just have to get back to work is all, you know! The project I'm working on. We have some loose ends to tie. After that I'm all yours sweetheart."

"Okay I understand." Joy sniffed as she slowly put her clothing back on. "Do you want me to make you something to eat before you go?"

"No thanks babe it's late. You should get some rest you have a job of your own to get to." Charles hurried towards the door to free himself from guilt. He didn't bother to look back at Joy. He couldn't bear to see the look of confusion on her face. The only thing he could do now was hurry home, to Sam and the kids. He nearly cheated on Sam with her sister. He felt like a crumb. "How could he stoop so low?" Charles spoke aloud as he smacked himself on the forehead.

He felt even worse about the money. Joy didn't even know about the fund. The things he could have done with that amount of cash would have been tremendous. She had no use for the money. Her business was going well.

Especially now since she had no responsibilities or children to feed, part of Charles ached for the loss of his close friend and blood. The other he envied.

Even in death, Justin was still the best thing since sliced bread. Just how long will he and Sam have to chase their dreams? Sam had spent so much time trying to live up to Joy's expectations she could never concentrate on her own affairs. At least that is the way Charles saw it. Joy could never do any wrong. The frustration of it all had seemed to be tearing him up the last few years.

He'd grown tired of his job and even more so tired of brushing the troubles of his marriage under the rug.

Charles knew that he was in trouble, but he knew he couldn't just out right go to Joy for help. However in her current state of mind, approaching her now would be his best bet.

# ~26~

# TWIN TELEPATHY

Joy felt dazed and dissimulated she couldn't understand nor explain the happenings of the last hour. She felt as if she were in a dream, but she knew full well that she were awake. Justin's presence made her feel alive again, as if she had, had a second chance at life and a family.

Joy was feeling sick to her stomach, perhaps all the drinking and motions of her near sex encounter jumbled her stomach. Before she knew it, she was running to the rest room before she vomited all over her Persian rug. Joy grabbed a towel from the towel rack to dry her face and mouth. Her throat instantly began to swell from all the vomiting. The medicine didn't aid in calming her stomach. It seemed that some of the side effects listed were nausea, vomiting, dizziness and possible delirium. The cautionary provisions to taking the medication were stifling.

Joy rinsed her mouth with Listerine and peered at her blushing cheeks in the mirror. She was thinking about what had just happened with Justin, reminiscing about how alive she felt. However, the medication begins to subside and her consciousness restores as she blinks the water from dripping from her eyelashes. Suddenly images of Charles appear in her mirror. They replay the events of the hour before haunting her wavering vision.

"Charles?" Joy became enraged and sick with emotion. She again flew to the toilet nearly missing it and vomited twice more. She was hurt and couldn't believe the betrayal she undecidedly participated in.

"How could he do this to me, to Sam? What am I to do?" Joy quickly dried her tears and washed her face again. Joy's mind quickly switched from the situation with Charles to finding her family. "Was this some ploy to get me to realize that something horrible happened to Justin and the kids?" Joy thought to herself speaking into her mirror, hoping for some sort of appearance or response.

"Joy I'm here, just waiting for your brilliant plan to unfold. What is your plan? You surely can't expect to go wondering off into the land without a destination or plan of action. I don't think you are thinking things through. More importantly how are you going to deal with Charles? You know you may be able to use this to your advantage." Joy's reflection sited the consequences of her actions as if it were her idea to screw her own in law.

"I haven't thought things through for a very long time. Why should I change now?"

"Maybe, because the lot of those that used to hang on to your every word question your sanity, possibly because this cushy town home isn't going to pay for itself. You need to take care to tend to the needs of your financial institution." Lilly reminded Joy with an evil arch of her eyebrow.

"I have money. The home is paid in full. The insurance from our home covered that. I have money from the life insurance policies on my children and husband as well. Policies I wish I didn't have to use."

"We have no say in our fate Joy. It's what you do with your hand that matters. The sooner you realize that the better off you will be. When are you going to tell them, Joy?"

"Tell them what?"

"That you have a gift. Your premonitions can help a lot of people. Do you know the amount of my money we could make? Joy you knew that the storm was coming. So tell me, why did you send your loved ones away?" Lilly sat back as she taunted Joy. She knew full well that Joy was unaware how her visions worked. She rarely knew when she was actually having one.

"You call this a gift? I saw a horrific accident happen, with no faces or dates, or place. The only thing I have is hate. Hate for myself for not being truthful to my family. I didn't know anything. I saw something happening in a dream, I didn't know when or how it was going to come about. I resent the fact that you are calling this a dream as if it, the storm, was something I conjured up with my secret powers." Joy shook her head dismissively angry at her evil twin's synopsis of the present state of affairs.

"You need to tell his mother, at least. If you don't want to let your family know that is your business. However this may be the only piece of her son she has left. You should tell her that you are pregnant. I can't believe you aren't busting from the seams by now anyhow. You have waited your entire life to announce that you are pregnant with twins."

"Really. I think it's hard to find joy in your children perishing in a storm. I feel like if I were to celebrate the life of my unborn children, I celebrate the loss of my children, lover and best friend. This is nothing to be happy about. These babies are a curse. When there is new life, the lives of others are taken, lives that meant the world to me. I refuse to deal with this right now. I want to find my family. Then I will tell everyone."

"If you go on this mission you run the risk of losing these babies? Do you really want to chance that? I am surprised with all the recent stress you haven't miscarried already. If you are going to go through with this pointless rescue mission, then tell Sam at least."

"What! No I can't. It's none of her concern. She has enough to deal with. Besides, what does this have to do with the present issue? What is Charles really up too? You don't think he is trying to prove me to be incompetent, perhaps to get his hands on the grant money, or Justin's company."

"She may be the only person that will understand why you are experiencing these emotional ups and downs. At least tell her about the pregnancy. She is your twin sister for God sakes. She should know, if you don't want to share this with his mother. That is if she hasn't already sensed it. She may think it's her that is pregnant."

"Well, you are the one who believes in this whole twin telepathy mambo jumbo. Shouldn't she tell me that I am pregnant?" Joy turned and looked at her reflection in the mirror over the sink in her bathroom. It's been awhile since she could muster the courage to really look at herself in the mirror. She hated herself so much it burned her throat every time she caught a glimpse of herself in a drinking glass or storefront window.

"I guess there is nothing more to say. If you don't tell her, I will."

"Over my dead body."

"It just may be."

Joy unfolded her arms and looked up at her reflection once again. "I'd really like to see how you plan to accomplish that. Especially since outside the mirror you don't fucking exist." Joy raised her eyebrow. Her reflection didn't respond.

"Oh I exist, Joy. It's time you realized just how influential I can be. I am trying to take care of you, but for some odd reason you want to continue to be played, by all these fools around you. You spend all your time rescuing and sponsoring all these projects that your loved ones as you say negotiate. What do you have to show for any of it? You are the one left holding the bag, each and every time. Well Joy! Maybe it's time Sam and the gang met Lillian Andrew's?

Joy shook Lilly's threats from her mind and went to her bedroom. She needed to get away a change of scenery will do her fine. The mountains seemed to call her. She took it as a sign. Perhaps Justin and the kids were there in the mountains waiting for her to meet them as planned. Joy grew anxious to embark on her adventure. She grabbed her duffle bag and began to throw the contents of her underwear drawer into the bag.

Joy had phoned Sam twice, but she had yet to answer. She was beginning to worry that something had gone down between her and Charles. Charles was in question for sure after the move he pulled earlier. She had to get in touch with Sam about the fiasco before he got to her. He would be sure to make it appear that she came on to him in some lonely desperate move to fill the void of her missing husband. Joy began to think further on that scenario. It was more than believable with all the ups and downs she had suffered in the last week. She would only have to trust that Sam knew her well enough to know the truth. Still, the fact that she wasn't answering her phone worried her.

****

"My sister needs help." Sam burst into Joy's Doctors office unannounced. She was furious with the care her sister was receiving or lack thereof. Sam walked fiercely towards the Doc's desk and slammed his pencil holder down onto the desk to get his full attention.

"I see you, there. It just so happens, that those persons I elect to speak with are announced by my secretary, they usually have appointments as well." Dr. Zimmerman looked up from his paper and peered over his glasses. Recognizing the face he immediately put down his wrinkled, coffee stained paper and looked at Sam with a look of surprise. "Joy's sister right? I have been hoping to get a visit from you. She talks endlessly about you in our talks. So what can I do for you?"

"For me, absolutely nothing, it's my sister that needs help. I would appreciate it if you would do your job and look into my sister's mental illness."

"There is nothing wrong with your sister. She has suffered a terrible loss. She needs to grieve."

"Doc, excuse me for over stepping my boundaries on your insightful professional opinion, but when is the last time you have spoken with my sister? Have you noticed any changes in her behavior, her presentation? She is not herself. My sister believes that her family is alive. She cooks and cleans for them, does their laundry and makes their beds as if they need to be tidied up. I don't know what else to do, short of having her committed. She even refuses to take her meds."

"I see. I thought she was dealing with the loss quite well. When she comes to see me she is very well dressed. She always talks about her work she is very excited about her writing career and her literary group for young writers."

Sam began to laugh hysterically. "Oh my God, this woman is playing you and you can't even see it. Joy hasn't been to work since the storm. She has yet to complete her book according to her publishing company. She is floating dangerously close to a breach in contract. She isn't strapped for cash though. She never is." Sam began to get angry and she couldn't stop her emotions from showing in her face. Dr. Zimmerman's forehead wrinkled as he noticed it clearly.

"I will see what I can do." Dr. Zimmerman needed to get in touch with Joy right away. He had uncovered a piece of the puzzle that made up a horribly confused Joy. "Sam I will talk with Joy, see if I can get her to take her meds. We are in the beginning stages of discussing the abuse and her febrile hallucinations that plague her dreams and have haunted her for the better part of her marriage. I don't want to rush. Now that she has lost her husband she has lost her best friend and her protector. To Joy, Justin was her savior. He came in and made her life worth living now, all that is gone. You must understand how that feels to be alone. Essentially that's what you are now. Right. Alone. You don't want to be alone, but you don't want to share your life or play second fiddle to your sister as well. This is a common issue with twins. I am also sure you feel some of her pain both physically and mentally. You can't possibly pretend as if you are not suffering. I know the strength of twin telepathy."

"I don't believe in twin telepathy. If you can't help her I will surely find a Doctor who can?" Sam tried to contain her anger. Her nose flared as she tried to shake the accuracy of the Doc's preliminary analysis. She couldn't believe Dr. Zimmerman had basically diagnosed her issues without her saying more than five words. She wanted to get out of there as quick as possible. "Just help her." Sam responded.

"I'd like to help you as well. I think you too, could benefit from a session in counsel."

"Just help my sister."

"Fine I will see you next week."

"For?" Sam was growing incredibly frustrated with the Doctor's forceful solicitation. His refusal to take no for an answer made her blood boil, she feared that perhaps her emotions were more accessible than she realized. Sam turned away from Dr. Zimmerman to search for an answer to her confusion.

Dr. Zimmerman noticed Sam's fear instantly. He was more intrigued to find out what was lurking in the confines of her mind. He was sure she was hiding something. Dr. Zimmerman paused briefly for the suspense rumbling in Sam's chest. He could sense her nervousness. Her forehead was perspiring visibly. "For my report." Dr. Zimmerman smiled a fake smile and looked over his glasses, as he did when he had a hidden agenda. Sam ushered her purse back onto her shoulder and left the office. She was not sure of the happenings of her visit, but she was certain that she was not ok.

Sam hustled onto the elevator as her phone rang for the third time. She was afraid it was Charles, wondering where she was and what she was up to. Rustling about her crowded purse she went in search for her phone. If she continued to ignore his phone calls, it would be hell when she arrived home.

"Hello." Sam finally managed to recover her phone before it went to voice mail.

"Hey." Joy greeted hoping that Sam wasn't upset with her. She wanted to apologize for earlier. She also wanted to let her know that she was planning on going out of town for a few days to get caught up with work. The home was lonely without Justin and the kids. The mountains were usually the place where she found comfort and came up with her best work.

"Um look. I'm sorry about earlier. I have been incredibly stressed lately I have a lot riding on this new project I'm working on and I think it may be getting to me. The research is quite extensive."

Sam sighed with relief. She really didn't want to get into it with Charles at the moment. She was thinking of somewhere to stop to grab something for dinner. Take out always lightened the mood. "Don't sweat it. I wasn't exactly ice cream and cake either."

"Ha! Nice come back. I like that one. I haven't laughed in what seems like forever. I think the corners of my lips may have split open. Joy's voice faded into a brief moment of silence as she reminisced about her and Charles laughing about Justin and their childhood. Joy felt the guilt hit her stomach as if she were punched. She became anxious, with a sudden urge to end her conversation as soon as possible. She didn't want Sam to detect anything wrong in her voice. "Listen, the reason for my call is to let you know that I am going to be going out of town for a few days."

"Oh yeah. Really! Where to? Wait before you answer. I hope you aren't planning on conducting some scavenger hunt to find Justin and the boys. I realize that you are hurting, but you really have to come to terms with this Joy. Patrice has a lovely service planned Saturday I hope you plan to attend. Hold off on this trip. At least until you can settle the issues with Justin and the kids. Lay them to rest."

"No Sam, I'm not planning on a rescue mission. I realize that I am just stressed. I think I just need a little vacation." Joy knew that she was lying and hoped to God Sam didn't catch wind of it. "I am going to take a drive down to yellow brook mountains. I think it will be nice to get out and see the snow."

"You sure Joy. Why would you be going out to the mountains? Isn't that where Justin was taking the kids?"

"Yes, Justin was on his way to the yellow brook mountains, but I'm not going on a wild goose chase. Justin and I had a cabin up there. I go there from time to time to work. It's peaceful. I do my best work on Mother Nature's home turf. I don't know. It must be something in the air."

"Joy I know. I also know how it is to experience tragedy and start to forget all the things God has done for you. You start to question and hate him for what he has put you through. I have come to know that with all these trials and tribulations, He has a plan. I may not understand it or want to hear it for that matter. But it's a plan just the same. You remember when I had my firstborn and we had that scare with him and his brain function. I cried every day for a month? My eyes were so swollen and filled with fluid I looked like a fish. Do you remember what you said to me?" Sam was digging deep at this point. She was good at pretending to care. She could cry on queue.

"Yes and no. That was a long time ago. Jr. is what seven now?"

"Yeah, but I doubt you would forget such a conversation. Think."

Joy shifted her feet as she paused on the phone to Sam's line of questioning. She scratched the tip of her nose the same way she always did to indicate irritation. "I do, but I hardly think this particular situation is comparable to that." Joy wasn't so sure she knew what Sam was getting at. It became obvious that she didn't fully believe Joy's story of traveling to cure her writer's block.

"That wasn't the question I am simply asking you if you remember what you told me." Sam's attitude changed.

"I do. I told you that sometimes we ask God for answers and/or direction. However, we have to find the time to settle and open our minds. He speaks, but we begin to question how, what, when and where. I said that God may give direction or perhaps an actual answer, but he isn't going to do the work for us. We have to embark upon our journey and believe in his word. We must step out on Faith. What does any of this have to do with anything?"

"It has everything to do with you and your current situation. Joy, you have to have faith that God will see you through. This happened for a reason. Please don't lose your faith in God. Perhaps all this happened because your faith is being tested."

Joy thought about Sam's lecture. She was growing incredibly upset, but she was in no mood to get into a heated discussion on religion and the realities of the world with Sam. Most of what she knew they learned together in their many nights, playing Bible trivia. She just didn't want to hear anything about God and his will at the present time. She wanted to vent and be angry. Joy sighed, "Ok, maybe you're right? I do have things I need to tend to. I will try and relax. I have been seeing a new mental health advocate about my recent issues. So perhaps this trial medication will work."

"Good. I hope this means that you will hold off on

your trip, perhaps attend the memorial service." Sam was hoping to hear that she would reconsider, her mind and body was tired after she had spent the better part of her afternoon trying to get information out of Dr. Zimmerman. What seemed to bother her most was his constant bantering about her and her personal involvement in the issues with her sister. Not to mention the issues of her personal life. Sam couldn't help but replay comments made by Dr. Zimmerman and his so called report. What could he be reporting on? Especially since he had yet to fully diagnose Joy. According to Dr. Zimmerman, Joy was merely suffering from the emotional strain of grief. It would all blow over.

Sam knew otherwise. Joy was taking medication. Medication she had retrieved from a number of medical professionals. They don't just hand psychotic drugs to anyone, so there must have been something going on with Joy. Sam said her goodbyes to Joy, as she pulled into the drive thru, at Popeye's. At least with chicken she could get a three course meal as if it were home cooked.

"Hey Joy! I will have to call you when I get home. I am rushing to get these boys of mine something to eat before they throw me in the dog house."

"Okay, talk to you soon." Joy hung up the phone a bit saddened that she had no one to cook for. In her lucid state of mind she knew of her illusions, although they were short lived. It was as though she forced her way back into a psychotic state so that she wouldn't have to deal with missing links.

Joy unpacked her bag of underwear and lingerie pieces. She didn't know where she was going and how she was going to survive in the snow without clothes, shaking her head at her obvious loss of sanity she ventured to the kitchen to make herself a late night snack. For the first time in a long time she was actually hungry. Fighting to put the incident with Charles out of her mind she cleaned the alcohol spills and blender from her countertop. The evidence of her near encounter was still afloat. It was obvious Sam had yet to be informed. So perhaps Charles was smarter than she thought.

Joy turned on her television in her kitchen as she grilled her steak and baby red potatoes. She poured herself a tall glass of red wine to set the mood and guzzled it down with a Percocet and a Sertraline, a mild anxiety pill to calm her nerves. It was amazing the amount of medication Joy could take without being the least bit affected. Although, her cognitive thinking was what suffered, her motor skills remained intact.

# ~27~

# WISHFUL THINKING

Charles hustled to get the kids in the car as he picked them up from Sharon's crib. She was rushed herself, afraid she would be late for work. It was unusual for Sam to be late picking up the kids and she was running late for her shift at work. Charles paid Sharon an extra twenty and sped down the road to pick up some pizza for dinner. The boys were agitated, but he did not mind. His mind was stuck in the confines of Joy's kitchen. He couldn't believe his slip in judgment. He forced thoughts of Sam to take the place of Joy. It was as if he didn't know Joy. She seemed different, free.

Growing more and more nervous, Charles phoned Sam once again, but her phone was busy. His stomach dropped as he waited for her to click over. It was no doubt in his mind that she was on the other line with Joy. Charles could barely think as he drove home. The boys were enticed by the smell of pepperoni and sausage. Charles could not eat if he wanted to, his stomach was too upset.

Charles pulled into the driveway of their four-bedroom home and noticed that Sam's car was not there. It was then, that his worry turned into anger. Where could she be at this hour? Charles ushered the kids into the home and instructed the kids to go get washed up for dinner. Charles slammed the pizzas on the stove and pulled his cell from his pocket. The battery was dangerously low his phone would not allow him to make an outgoing call. He grabbed the cordless phone and checked the fridge for Sam's work number. Charles found the contact phone number and dialed anxiously. As the phone rang, he cussed vibrantly loud. The second ring chimed as he heard Sam's keys rattling the door. Charles hung up the phone quickly. He pulled the dishes from the cabinet and began to set the table as if she were present as he continued to ignore her. Charles overlooked Sam as she walked through the door hauling the bags of chicken.

Jr. ran down the stairs just in time to catch a bag slipping from Sam's grasp.

"Wow, Pizza and chicken, what a night?" Sam looked puzzled and perturbed as she stared Charles down. He had yet to look at her and acknowledge her presence.

"Oh, you already got dinner?" Sam tried to ignore Charles obvious attitude and headed into the kitchen to help him set-up for dinner.

"Yeah, we hadn't heard from you so I thought I'd better grab something." Charles was still unable to look at Sam. It was more than her being late that bothered him. He was sweating under the collar and perspiring well through his baby blue button down. "Can you finish up here? I want to freshen and get out of these clothes." Charles sped by Sam without waiting for confirmation, as he passed Sam caught a glimpse of his pants and the familiar smell of cocoa and Shea butter. Sam's throat nearly closed when she recognized the smell. She suddenly felt sick to her stomach. She called for Jr. to come down and finish up while she followed Charles up stairs to freshen up. She knew something was up with him she just was not sure what that was as of yet.

Sam ran up the stairs two at a time in a panic. She could not believe, her own assumptions, but with Charles, her intuition was always correct. Ever since, her indiscretion with a co-worker he had taunted her about it. It was as if he were still punishing her for it.

Sam was tired, she felt as if he weren't ever going to forgive her and if that was the case he might as well just leave her and the kids alone. Sam froze just in front of the bedroom door. She didn't want to know what she would find behind the door. Perhaps more evidence indicating that he had been intimate with her sister. He was working late more than ever, not to mention he rarely answered his phone.

Sam barged into her bedroom door to find Charles hunched over the sink crying. He was shaking violently. It caught Sam completely off guard. The anger melted into concern for her husband's welfare. She stepped just behind him and wrapped her arms around his waist. Charles nervous, obviously in another place shook away from Sam's grasp. He put his hand up to warn her to stay away as he wiped the tears from his face.

"This is your fault. You know all I wanted was a family. A family I never had, a wife, children, homeland a nice job. I thought I had achieved all that, but somewhere down the line, I just ended up with a bunch of bills and heartache. I am drowning, Sam. I mean I can't trust you. I feel like I have to watch your every move. I'm doing both our jobs." Charles was feeling so much guilt he swallowed hard before he continued. The emotion overwhelmed him. He had other women within the realm of his marriage, but never had he stooped so low to seduce any of her family members. Even he, had boundaries.

Charles nearly spilled his guts about Joy and their close encounter. Sam just stood with her arms folded glaring at Charles. It wasn't the first time she had heard this little speech. It came whenever he had been unfaithful and he knew that the woman had been in touch with her. Her family used that approach well, they often "Got mad first," simply to weasel their way out of trouble. It was a scare tactic, which for the most part worked, unless you were hip to the shenanigans of the Andrew family.

Charles often forgot that Sam taught him how to use this form of mind manipulation.

"Who is she Charles? Furthermore, how long has it

been going on? I noticed the button from your slacks was missing. Your dreads are tangled and untidy. What is going on?" Sam waited for a response. She wanted him to admit to her that he had been unfaithful.

"I don't know what you are talking about. I don't have time for this mess either. The children are waiting for us to put dinner on the table and you are up here accusing me of sleeping around. Excuse me." Charles started to walk past Sam and into their bedroom area, but Sam caught his arm just as he was leaving.

"I know the smell, Charles, why her? What does she have that I don't? She is my sister for God Sakes."

Charles stopped dead in his tracks unsure of how to respond. He froze in time. He couldn't believe the accusations, however true they were. She had caught him red handed. Perhaps Joy had gotten to her first. How could he have been so stupid? What was he thinking? With the stress of hiding out all the time from loan sharks his judgment was beyond cloudy. "Nothing happened, Joy." Charles didn't bother to turn and face her and it wasn't until Joy's name flew out of his mouth that he realized he called Sam, Joy.

"Really!" Sam screamed, "Doesn't sound like nothing happened." Sam stomped out of the bathroom and screamed at the top of her lungs as she fell to her knees just beside the bed. "I can't take this anymore, Charles. Why are you continuously punishing me for a mistake I made over seven years ago?"

"Seven years ago, was just the first time." Charles was nasty in his tone. He showed no sympathy. It was as if he has switched into another person. He was all of a sudden angry and condescending. "I don't have to explain myself to you. I told you nothing happened. I stopped by her place to give her the grant check that Justin was working on. He was looking to get her new literary project funded. It went through. I gave her a hug. She got emotional about the whole thing is all, are you happy now?"

Sam continued to stare Charles down. She knew that there was much more to it than that. Joy was in a vulnerable state. Sam drifted into her own consciousness. She knew what it was like to be vulnerable and how easy it was to be taken advantage of. Standing to her feet she addressed Charles, ready and willing to smack him hard across his face at the slightest snobby response.

"What's even more shocking is how you would betray your own blood cousin. He has not been dead for a full month and you are already making a play for his wife. What is it not enough we share the same face and build? What else could there be? I am going to call her right now. No wonder she wanted to leave town, she was guilty and ole outspoken can never do no wrong Joy couldn't even be woman enough to tell me she had just boned my husband."

"We didn't."

"Save it!" Sam interjected. "I don't want to hear any of your sad excuses." Sam grabbed her head. She was so flustered her head began to pound. Her eyes began to blur and she felt extreme pressure at the back of her neck. She was afraid she was having a slight stroke. Sam was quiet. She couldn't think, worry quickly took the place of her anger.

"Sam, are you alright? You need to lie down."

Sam was so worried she couldn't even deny her needs. "No, I don't know what is happening. I came up here because I felt nauseated. Now I'm dizzy and I have this horrendous pain in the back of my neck." Sam began to panic, she couldn't see in front of her. Her vision went from blurry to black. "Help me." Sam crawled along the floor searching for Charles. Charles ran to her rescue and scooped Sam from the floor and carried her to the bed. She was hysterical. The boys ran into the room worried that something was going on with their mother. Charles had hit her before. Jr. was angry and ready to defend his mother if need be. He never asked any questions he just jumped right in swinging and flinging his arms in the air attacking his overgrown father from behind.

Charles instructed the children to go on downstairs. "Jr., get the boys a slice of pizza I will be down in a minute. Your mother isn't feeling well. Bring her a glass of water."

Jr. ran top speed down the stairs to the kitchen he threw the slices of pizza onto his two brother's plates and sped back upstairs with a glass of ice water without spilling a drop.

"Here Dad, Is mom going to be okay?"

"Yes, fine. Now go and look after your brothers."

Sam buried her head under one of her soft feathery pillows. She took the pills Charles had given her without looking to see what they were. She didn't trust Charles she admitted to herself after she'd swallow them down, but the pain in her head was far more important than to question his motives. Charles rinsed the glass and its contents down the sink. He was sure to put a sleeping solution in her water, to go along with the strong pain medication he had given Sam. She would be asleep within minutes. He needed time to think.

Charles jogged down the stairs to the kitchen with an uplifted spirit. He joined the boys in the den. They were watching cartoons, one his most favorite past times. It just made things go away for the time being. Charles busied himself shuffling food about his plate.

"Where's mom?" Jr. looked up from his glass of soda, which was more than his allotted amount.

"Sleeping, now eat up." Charles took a hearty bite of his Chicken and leaned back into his Lazy Boy. All he could think about was Joy and the money, even if he could get her to loan Sam the money under false pretenses that would do them just fine. With all the guilt of their recent encounter she would be sure to listen to Sam's plight and feel obligated to help. Charles' wheels were churning. He could barely finish his plate of food for planning his next move.

****

Joy cleared her plate, in the kitchen sink. She became infatuated with washing the countertops where some of the red wine had spilled into the granite. Pondering on the events of the night, she felt slightly relieved. The alcohol warmed her chest and she felt numb to pain.

"Joy."

Joy ignored the voice that beckoned her attention. She was not going to give in to it this time. She simply continued to wash the dishes and clean the countertops. Noticing a stain in the sterling silver knobs of her faucets, she scrubbed until her reflection was visible.

"So how long are you going to pretend that you didn't nearly fornicated with your sister's husband?"

Joy turned the water offend threw the towel into the sink in an effort to clear her thoughts. She ignored the question and put the remainder of her steak and potatoes into the fridge.

"I know the two of you didn't actually sleep together, but he is your sister's husband. I can't believe you would betray her this way."

Joy looked dazed as she starred at the distorted reflection, mirrored in her stainless steel refrigerator. "It wasn't Charles, it was Justin. He is my husband. Sam is just jealous, of my family and my relationship. She always has been. She and Charles have had so many issues, it's no wonder they haven't killed one another. I am not to blame. So if you don't mind I'd like to get to bed."

"You made out with Charles, Joy. Justin has been dead for over 3 weeks. The man came over to present you with a check for your literary fund. Do you remember the big project he and Justin were working on as a surprise to you? It is a shame that you would betray your dead husband by trying to sleep with his first cousin, damn near brother. It is sad how he went through such great lengths to provide for you and this is how you repay him? Some grieving wife you are. Its best you let me take control from here. You should take a few of those happy pills Nurse Betty gave you. I am starting to feel slightly light headed. I wouldn't want Sam to catch us off guard. I am sure she will be around soon to find out what's going on with you and her husband."

"What are you talking about?" Joy was confused. She grabbed her head in an effort to shake her thoughts.

"Don't stress yourself, just go and get the pills out of the medicine cabinet. Look, you and I both know that Charles isn't exactly Mr. Brains. He probably told Sam everything before he even made it home."

"I don't think so. I talked to Sam." Joy said confidently.

Joy ventured to the bathroom to brush her teeth before going to bed. She fought hard not to glance at her reflection in the mirror. She didn't want to conjure up Lilly. She knew that Lily would use any chance she could to encourage her to continue use of the medication. Joy could feel her sanity resurfacing. The last hour of her mania was dissipating. Joy thought about how she felt when she was under the influence of the pills. She could admit that they helped to calm her nervousness, but she wasn't at all in control of her thoughts and feelings in the way she felt comfortable. Joy slammed the mirror shut. Too hard, in fact it caused her to glance up at the mirror to ensure she hadn't cracked it. It was then, that she noticed a strange cloud of smoke in her reflection. It almost looked as if she were disappearing.

Afraid and discombobulated she took a few steps

back and retreated from the bathroom. Strutting fast to her sleeping area, she jumped in bed grabbing her remote. She then reached over to her bedside table to seize her glass of water and swallow the pills sitting next to her glass, without even thinking about it. Sadly the same pills she vowed to stay clear of, pills she didn't remember putting there.

# ~28~

# THE TRUTH AND NOTHING BUT

Joy awoke abruptly in the dark and unsure of her surroundings. Her phone was ringing just as her head. She couldn't figure which of the two were a reality. Painfully blinded by the piercing and stabbing twinge near the back of her head, she fought her way from under her blanketed cocoon.

The phone stopped ringing, but the bells in her head, still chimed. By the time Joy made it through her tunnel of blankets and fog, her head erupted into a full-blown migraine. Joy suffered from headaches from time to time but none as horrific as her most recent migraines, new breed to her current bout with tension and stress.

Joy crawled her way to the edge of her bed and slid onto the floor, making sure to keep her eyes protected from the light she shut them tightly and crawled into the bathroom. Joy pulled herself to her knees and rested briefly before pulling herself to her feet. Bravely opening her eye's she stood. The dim light of the bathroom was still a bit too bright for Joy's eyes. She closed them shut quickly as they burned, adding gas to the fires burning in her skull.

Joy panicked at the severity of pain she was enduring. She opened the medicine cabinet with an added force that said she meant business. Tossing the many pill bottles to the floor and about the sink she searched high and low for her Propranolol. It wouldn't do a thing for the pain, but as the doc said it worked to prevent the headaches. "Sure wish I could remember to take these damn things before the headaches hit it might do me some good yet."

Joy scolded herself.

Joy tossed a couple of Tylenol into her mouth, along with the preventative pills. She chased the pills down with half a cup of tap water and made her way to the kitchen for some breakfast. She was running about four hours behind schedule. The urge to jump back into bed overwhelmed her. She was under the weather anyhow. Joy turned over her omelet admiring its beauty. She had not eaten eggs her entire life until one day Justin asked her why she didn't eat them. She could make a mean omelet she had to admit they were enticing. Though she could never quite put her finger on why she didn't eat them.

Just as Joy was about to take a bite of her eggs the phone rang. She was hoping for peace, but honestly she knew that notion was farfetched. The only thing she could hope for was that Sam hadn't decided to call her on leaving town once more. She already told the woman she would stay. Of course, it didn't mean that she would attend the memorial services she had yet to hear from Patrice on the matter. Joy fell into a trance for a few moments as she pondered. "I should. Shouldn't I?" Joy questioned herself.

Joy's phone continued to ring. "I guess I'd better get that. It's not like they are going to leave me alone anyhow." Joy threw her fork back onto her plate and answered her phone slightly agitated.

"Hello." Joy's voice dragged on. She wanted to sound as if she weren't interested so that maybe the person on the other line would get the hint almost immediately and retreat off the line.

"Hey it's Nadine. You think you may want to come into the office today, I know you are like some hotshot literary analyst, but unless you hired me to watch the paint dry on your new office space, I could really use some direction. You have clients calling left and right asking about your reports on their work. Not to mention the funding officials asking if you are ok and if I think you are still sane enough to run the company."

Joy inherited an instant attitude. She could not place its origin. Her façade was sinking fast into a state of reality. "You mean my company. The agency I built from ground up. It's so funny how big wigs forget who had the ideas, when their money is involved."

Slightly offended by Joy's reaction, Nadine cleared her throat. "Well, I gotta tell ya, and I mean no disrespect, but could you blame them? You have been M.I.A., for almost three weeks now. Not, that under the circumstances anyone could blame you. I too, was a bit worried. You are a fighter. All the years I have known you, you have bounced back and shown such a fierce tenacity to succeed. I thought that this time, the blow has damaged your fighting spirit. Our funding partners and clients are worried about their investment. The competitors palms are itching, Joy, worried about their investment. Don't worry, I ensured them that you are still on the straight and narrow. You know everyone is just looking for something to put in the tabloids. It's nothing like a juicy story full of gossip and scandal. People flock, like moths to a flame, an irritating itch that folk can't seem to scratch."

"Drama, yeah I know. I have a little of that going on in my personal life that I would like to make sure is kept there as well." Joy sounded incredibly sad all of a sudden. She hated bad news, or any news that wasn't favorable that had her name scrolling in it. She called to her Grandmothers words.

"All you have is your name, hon. Take heed to take care of it. Material things have no matter in this world. If your name is tarnished, attached with scandal, slander, shady ventures and malice, its guaranteed people will refrain from going into business, socializing, or granting assistance. The first impression is very important it has a major effect on how people will see you."

Joy rolled her eyes up to the ceiling as she sighed.

"Grandma you were so right about that one."

"Huh?" Nadine interrupted Joy's thoughts about her grandmother.

"Nothing, sorry just thinking out loud."

"Oh ok. So, how are you holding up? Joy, seriously I have been worried sick." Nadine wanted to get to the bottom of Joy's issue on finding her family. Patrice was very concerned and talked her ear off about Joy's fascinations about the fact that she didn't believe her family was dead and gone. Patrice was trying to help, but she didn't know how to address the issue. Instead, she simply told the family to give her some space.

"I'm fine just tired lately. The headaches haven't let up either. In fact they are worse."

"Did you take the Vicodin I gave you?"

"Yeah thanks. I think I need to go in to my Doctor and tell them about this issue. I guess a part of me is scared that the doc will find something."

"Something like what, like cancer, a tumor, what? Nadine was frustrated with Joy. She became instantly serious. Her motherly voice chimed into full effect. "Come on Joy, you have to stop being such a hypochondriac. I realize you have been ill, but let's not forget I am a survivor of cancer as well. Nothing you say to me is blah, but I know what it is like to live in fear. You are just going to have to let that go and live your life. Catch my drift sister girl."

"Yeah I hear ya. I better get in the shower what time have you scheduled my meetings to begin?" Joy stifled herself to avoid continued discussion on the matter. She was in no mood to hear a lecture on topics she already knew about and/or had no plan of entertaining. She realized Nadine was her friend and trying to help. However, she had to admit that she didn't want help. She wanted the nightmare she was sure she was living, to end.

"Actually your day is clear from outside clients. We

~ 190 ~

need to meet and get this tour and project complete, so bring treats. I am starving. You're going to love your new office by the way, mine too." Nadine added with a quiet whisper as if she were talking under her clothes. Nadine laughed as she hung up the phone before she could be quizzed on the pricing of their new luxury home away from home.

Joy shook her head and hung up the phone she slithered out of her kitchen and retreated to the third floor. Joy turned on the shower in her master suite and took-a-look around her room. Her bed was a mess there were clothes on the floor of the closet. It was complete madness. Joy threw clothes every which way to locate herself a decent brand pair of underwear. She chose something to wear from the remaining articles of clothing that hung scarcely in her closet. It had been a while since she dressed professionally, wore make-up, or combed her hair for that matter.

Peering into the mirror at her finished product, she saw a flash of color that shaded in her black and white complexion. Joy touched her cheeks as she admired the color of her skin and the color of her shirt and pants. It was a step up from the dark, lifeless, world she lived in for the past year it was as if she were a Newborn baby seeing color for the first time.

**\*\*\*\***

Sam awoke groggy and disheveled. She had breakfast waiting for her at the foot of her bed. She smiled slightly at the single red rose left lying just above the plate. Sam wrinkled her brow and took a long sip of the orange juice and a hearty bite of her toast. She was beyond famished and extremely thirsty. Charles had since gone to work. He left early each morning, to drop the kids off and hit the freeway before the morning traffic. Charles worked a little under an hour away, but he didn't mind the drive. He worked in the heart of the city and enjoyed the view since he and Justin did most of the architectural designs and contracting out that way.

Sam threw back the covers and peered down at her attire. She didn't realize she had gone to bed fully dressed. The last thing she could fully remember was the migraine she'd fallen prey to. She felt bad about accusing Charles of sleeping with Joy. The argument with Charles was spotty. What did, come to mind was the fact that she talked to Joy and she sounded perfectly fine with the happenings of the previous night. She mentioned going out of town to work on some of her writing, but nothing about Charles coming on to her. Sam thought more about the situation with her sister and Charles. She pondered on the fact that Charles didn't deny seeing Joy that day and he acknowledged that he gave her a hug to console her. Sam bit hungrily into a strawberry and glared into space as she thought about the scandal that Joy perhaps conspired. "Why would she all of a sudden decide she was going to go out of town? Sounds extremely guilty to me." Sam popped up as if she had a grand idea and jumped down from her bed. Charles invested in these double thick mattresses for, "*mating season*," he called it. Sam laughed at the thought and quickly changed focus. She thought about the fact that he could have been frolicking about their living quarters with other women.

Sam was so confused she could barely think out her next move, her legs were incredibly weak. She felt as if she had been sick for days. She was groggy and slow. Sam limped into the bathroom area and turned on the shower. She was in a hurry to get to the salon. It was half past eleven already. Stepping into the shower she could hear her cell going off. The first time it rang she ignored it. "If it's important then they will leave a voicemail." Sam thought to herself as she embraced the warming sensation cascading over her body and tickling her scalp. Sam applied the shampoo into her thick curly mane. The smell of strawberries and cream was enticingly sweet. Just as she massaged a good lather into her hair, the phone rang once again. Startled, by the ring she dropped the shampoo and nearly bumped her head on the faucet in an attempt to pick it up.

"Shit!" Sam cursed into the wind. Sam quickly washed up and rinsed her hair. She towel dried her hair as best she could and applied gel to throw her hair into a silky bun. Twisting her ponytail into a Swiss roll, she searched for a hair tie. Her shower was so short the room hadn't had a chance to fully heat up. Sam ran about the room looking for her clothing to escape the chills of her frosty room. She threw on one of her favorite pair of jeans, a pair of pumps and a figure accentuating girl shirt.

Lastly, she added a pair of medium sized hoops, to add a little spice to her outfit and some lip-gloss. She and Joy rarely wore make-up, they were naturally beautiful. Their only flaw in their eyes was sharing their beauty. Because they shared their outer appearance, sibling rivalry existed in every other aspect in their lives, clothes, men, schooling, job, even their children. A rivalry unspoken, but they both knew it existed. To mention it would do nothing, but start a fistfight over who was jealous or not. Recently, however, Sam noticed a change in Joy's personality. She was nonchalant often. She usually wore her heart on her sleeve. She also took to wearing red lipstick and blue contacts. Although she thought it daring and fashionable, it was totally out of character.

Sam slathered a thick layer of clear lip-gloss across her full lips and smacked them to make sure it was evenly spread. Admiring her beauty, she stopped, as she noticed the lights flickering just above her head. One of the light bulbs was dying. It irritated her that the missing light was taking away from her natural beauty. Rushing from the bathroom area to check the linen closet for extra light bulbs, her cell rang once more. She ran to answer it. She had been waiting for a call from Joy. Perhaps she had thought about her wrong doing overnight and decided to come clean.

"Hello."

"Hello Mrs. Richardson, its Dr. Zimmerman. I wondered if you had time today to come by and take-a-look at the report, I drew up for Joy's condition. I wanted to set aside about a half hour to an hour to go over my report."

Sam smiled into the receiver. "You know what I will be right there." Sam was interested to know just what was going on with her sister. Maybe just maybe it would explain her less than savory attitude. Sam was not interested in giving Joy a pass for trying to come between her and Charles, but she was not the only party involved.

"Sure, sure, Dr. Zimmerman I will be right there." Sam hung up the phone and rushed to grab her purse and keys. She didn't want to waste another minute. After she found out what was supposedly wrong with Joy, she would be sure to pay her a visit at home or work. Sam was getting use to Joy's laziness. She was becoming the breadwinner of the family and she loved it. She could care less if Joy lost the business altogether. Maybe that would finally blow the lights from around the halo she had been wearing for so many years. It was high time someone else received some praise.

Sam was in no mood to talk to Dr. Zimmerman about anything involving her and Charles. The business of their marriage was none of his concern. "Joy is the one with the issues." Sam kept telling herself as she shook nervously trying to open the door of her car.

Sam walked into Dr. Zimmerman's office like a cool breeze. Her nose flared and her lips were pinched. She didn't want to hear Joy's name, let alone have an entire conversation about her. She was angry with the incident with Charles. There was no explanation or closure to the matter, which made things that much worse. She could only find comfort in finally finding physical evidence of Ms. Thing's, impurity. Mom's first born her pride and Joy, as she so named her, but not Sam the unexpected, unwanted twin.

Dr. Zimmerman greeted Sam with a hand gesture and directed her to have a seat, while he gathered his notes for their meeting.

"And how are you this morning, Sam?"

"I'm just fine thank you." Sam noticed the coffee pot brewing by the window and motioned for an ok, to partake. "I have just been under a lot of stress lately." Sam wiped her sweat beading hands on the front of her jeans and walked over to grab a cup of coffee.

"Oh? What about, is everything ok?" Dr. Zimmerman tilted his head he was very interested in hearing her story. He was interested to know more about Joy and Sam's relationship. He had a hunch that there was a lot going on with the two of them that played into some of the issues Joy was presently dealing with.

"I'm fine. Can we just get on with this report you wanted to see me about?"

"Sure, sure." Dr. Zimmerman adjusted his bifocals and shifted into his seat. "I believe your sister suffers from a series of issues that have made her mental dysfunctions rather hard to diagnosis. It has taken some time for me to get the report in order. However, I invited you here to discuss a little bit about the case, as well as ways in which you can help your sister through this difficult time. I just need you to be open-minded. Some of the suggestions I will make, may make you feel uncomfortable. Your honesty will be greatly appreciated."

"Sure Doc, anything. I want my sister to get well. I can't stand her like this." Sam looked down at her shoes as if she had to search for the right words. She didn't want to seem like she was interested in having her sister put away, but she felt that it wasn't the worse idea she had come up with. Especially since thoughts of her and Charles invaded her mind. She couldn't shake the sight of them making love. She suddenly felt sick. Sam sat up in her seat, as she was sinking into the leather couch. She became hot under the collar, her forehead sparkled with perspiration.

Doctor Zimmerman took his seat just across from Sam and began jotting down some notations before he had even begun his line of questioning. Noticing, Sam's slight discomfort he asked if she were ok, "Are you feeling alright Mrs. Richardson? Would you like some water?"

"Um yeah. I'm ok. No water, the coffee is fine. I just, I have been having some stomach issues lately. I think I may have a virus or something. You know with kids, it's no telling what kind of germs they have, with school and all. I have three boys, so you can just imagine how dirty and stinky they are." Sam was looking to distract the Doctor from her change in persona. She knew he was fishing for information.

"Well then. Shall I briefly describe some of my findings? I think it will behoove you to know exactly what you are up against."

"Ok." Sam breathed in deep as her stomach dropped to her feet.

"Joy suffers from hallucinations and exhibits some delusional behavior."

Sam looked dazed and with a puzzling frown upon her face. "What's the difference if any?"

"Hallucinations can involve any of the senses. For instance visual, she may see things. Joy suffers from aural. These hallucinations involve hearing sounds someone may believe that persons are speaking to them. Hallucinations can even involve taste? Though she has not demonstrated this aspect of hallucinogenic attributes, it doesn't mean that she will never experience it."

Sam's frown turned into a serious interest to get to the bottom of things. She put her hand under her chin and scooted to the edge of her seat. "Ok I understand and what about the delusions? Isn't that basically the same as her seeing things?"

"In a sense. They go hand in hand in a lot of situations. Delusional behavior differs in that delusions refer to the minds reasoning and thoughts. The onset could derive from many things, nightmares, vision changes, delirium, dementia and aura. For example Joy may be able to see clear as day at times, but in times of despair, changes in her stress levels, migraines, emotional strain she may be blind as a bat."

"Aura, I am still a bit confused, but as far as her eyesight this sounds unreal. I thought if you were legally blind it's just that?"

"Well, that's not true in every case. Joy exhibited signs of regaining sight during her stay at the hospital. She was able to see in black and white more so than anything. I think it's the color that really made her depressive state worse. I believe she is healing and may be in full recovery, but is afraid of that independence factor being that she has had to depend on her family for the past year. It can culture shock and be disabling.

These episodes of complete blindness often occur before a migraine or fainting spell. I understand that Joy suffers from very serious migraines. I placed her on a Beta-Blocker a few months back. The medication could also play a hand. There are a number of side-effects associated with medication. After the storm, did Joy see anyone for the head injury she suffered?"

"No she refused. She said she was fine, she was lucid in my opinion. More concerned about finding her family really, I don't know she seemed fine." Sam shook her head as she started to wonder whether she had made the right decision about leaving Joy to her own thought processes on the matter. Perhaps the latest incident with Joy's behavior was her fault. "She did say that she was out about 10-20 minutes, but she couldn't be sure. Other than that she was taking medication for anxiety, depression and sleep."

"You do realize that with all the medication she is on, this behavior could be a result of overdosing in meds? The toxicity level could be causing thoughts of suicide and furthering her depression."

"Dr. Zimmerman, I don't know what most of this means exactly, but I don't blame Joy for taking medication for her issues. I think I would be going crazy myself if my husband and children had been taken from me." Sam's eyes lit up as her lips began to tremble.

"That is exactly my point, Mrs. Richardson. She could be very well abusing those drugs."

"Wait, are you trying to accuse my sister of being a junky?"

"No! She could be abusing these drugs and not even know it. It is the prescribing Doctor's responsibility to ensure safety when prescribing medications, period. Whoever gave her such a hefty load of medications is responsible. Some of the medications Joy expressed having had some experience with can be used to treat the same symptoms. This incidence is very irresponsible on the prescribing doctor's part, downright illegal and grounds for dismissal on the basis of negligence. This is a malpractice suit easy. I have no doubt in my mind that Joy has seen more than one Dr., for this issue. My guess is each and every one of them simply gave her a pill and sent her on her way. Sam it doesn't take an M.D., to notice signs of drug abuse. Aside from the medication, does Joy have any alcohol problems?"

Sam looked around the room trying to hold back the tears burning her retinas. "Joy has had an issue with drinking." Sam breathed in deep and wiped her hands on the seat of her pants. She has a few drinks here and there, but not nearly as much as she did during college. She was diagnosed with Bipolar Disorder during her senior year of college. A lot was going on. She and her boyfriend at the time had been together since their junior year in High School. Things were getting hot and heavy, but she could never go all the way."

"I can see that, we have talked a bit about her childhood and the abuse she suffered."

"Yeah well, with the pressure her boyfriend began to place upon her about sex, the nightmares about what that bastard did to her as a child resurfaced. Her boyfriend started sleeping with her dorm mates. He couldn't deal with the fact that Joy couldn't be intimate. She found out he was sleeping around in class. A letter was being passed around. Some love note written to her roommate from dear ole Romeo himself. She flipped out. Started drinking heavily, missing classes and quit her job. It was her last semester of school she was in danger of missing out on her graduation." Sam grew quiet as she paced the floor of the office. She stopped and stared out into the grassy areas of the landscaped medical offices. She was drifting back to the college adventure she shared with her sister.

"Sounds like that was a very difficult time for Joy, it's amazing she was able to graduate. Summa Cum Laude, if I remember. I was looking through some of her file. With all the drinking and absence in class, it was a miracle, wouldn't you say?" Dr. Zimmerman removed his glasses and tapped the tip of them on the front of his teeth. He knew the answers. He just wanted to confirm his suspicions.

Sam cleared her throat and folded her arms. She continued to stare out into the open space just outside the Dr.'s window, "Yeah a real miracle." Sam was angered by the gloating Dr. Zimmerman continued to boast about the good deeds of dear old Joy. She was beginning to tire of hearing about how perfect she was. "Yeah, she is some piece of work, that Joy. Always coming out on top in the midst of the storm, but not this time, I guess this time she just couldn't get from under its wrath." Sam smiled slightly as she daydreamed.

Dr. Zimmerman noticed Sam's satisfaction and again scribbled into his notebook. "I don't think you are being completely honest with me. I don't think it was Joy that graduated the class. There is a lot more in that file that you don't seem to be aware of. I was hoping you would be more forthcoming about the issues with you and your sister, but I can tell that it is a sore subject." Dr. Zimmerman slammed his notepad on to the coffee table just in front of his chair and stood up. "If you plan on wasting my time then we can simply part company. I want to help your sister, but I can't effectively do my job if you are not honest about her history.

Sam was angry that Joy's shrink continued to fish for information. She wondered what else could be in her file, it worried her. "What do you need to know? You sound as if you are pretty abreast of the situation. It wasn't her that crossed the stage, but it was her that graduated. She did all the work. I was just a stand in. Much like I have always been, just Joy's shadow someone to pick up the slack, when she couldn't attend all of her obligated tasks. I didn't get to go to college. I got to stay home and take care of our grandmother. I did hair and don't get me wrong I loved it, but I didn't have a life of luxury.

Like I said Joy had issues after the breakup. Joy doesn't do well with confrontation. I love it. I love to argue. Our grandmother always said that I should have become a lawyer. I will argue you down, right or wrong. Joy did more than just flip-out after she caught Darrin cheating."

"Wait?" Dr. Zimmerman sat down in his chair and retrieved his notepad. "Darrin, Darrin, Darrin why does that name sound familiar?" Dr. Zimmerman asked as he combed through his notes on Joy.

"Darrin is Ashley's father. Sam rolled her eyes.

"Right." Dr. Zimmerman dragged on. "Ok continue."

"Well anyway, there was an incident at the college. Like I said, Joy flipped out. There was an incident with some girls in the dorm. A huge fight broke out. Joy wasn't herself. She confronted two of the girls during room check and destroyed their rooms. She threatened to kill them. It was nothing really. She was drunk as usual and hurting emotionally."

Dr. Zimmerman pinched his lips, as his brow creased. "So naturally you stepped in, while Joy cleaned herself up."

"Yeah, something like, that. I presented in her classes and I crossed the stage, but she did all of her work while in rehab. She couldn't attend any of her extra-curricular activities anymore, because she was under review by the disciplinary board."

"Why? Drinking is an issue, but if she were attending the meetings, why would she be placed on probation?"

Sam sighed, she felt as though she was snitching. Her sister privilege was being violated. She was in constant battle with her selfish heart. "The incident that took place on campus didn't end with the altercation in the dorm. The girls went missing about a week later. Because of some of the threats made by Joy to cause bodily harm, the school was forced to take action. She was never tried or anything. There was no evidence of foul play on her part."

"What about yours?"

"I can admit I can be a cold, calculated, conniving, gal of disastrous vengeance. However, I didn't kill those girls if that's what you're asking."

"No. I just wanted to know what your involvement was."

Sam was nervous, "Are we done here? I need to get to work. I think you have more than enough information, to properly diagnose my sister. I wish I could be of some actual help. Is there some sort of medication she should be on? I mean wondering around hearing voices and such can't be normal. I know she is in trouble. She cooks and cleans for her children, they are gone and she is clearly not registering that fact."

"I think your sister needs to vent about the ordeal. She is still blaming herself for being dishonest. She feels as if her family is still here, perhaps angry with her and taunting her because she sent them away, instead of revealing her illness. Your sister may actually be hearing things. The things I believe she hears are the voices of her lost loved ones and her conscious speaking to her. I am surprised you are not more so in tuned with these things, but as you said you know nothing nor do you believe in the power of twin telepathy. However, just by listening to some of your story, I beg to differ. You came to the aide of your sister because you too, felt her pain, her anger and her embarrassment. I can't prove anything, but I do believe that you were the one that handled the situation. While she crawled to a safe place, you took out the trash."

Sam grabbed her leather blazer and purse. "That is an interesting and intriguing thought. You are very creative. You should look into writing. You would have no problem getting a literary agent to back you. I am sure Joy would just eat all this up." Sam sped out of the doctor's office and nearly sprinted down the hall to get to the elevator. She wanted to get as far away as she could from that place. Sam was angry. Maybe Joy wasn't to blame for her encounter with Charles. She had to speak to her about it. Charles was as guilty as sin. She knew that fact and Charles did a very good job of making sure to place all the blame on Joy. As if he is the innocent one. She knew better, but she couldn't bear to face the truth. Sam slammed the door to her car. She put a call into Joy, but her phone went straight to voicemail. "Joy must have gone into the office," Sam thought to herself. That was the only time Joy's cell ever went straight to voicemail.

She was surprised that Joy had returned to work. Sam fired up her engine and set out to speak with her sister about the happenings of the night before. She needed to get to the bottom of the matter once and for all.

# ~29~

# THE CONFRONTATION

Sam swerved into the parking lot and snagged a slot right next to her sister's car. She threw her car door open violently with hopes of scratching the paint on Joy's black 2011 Denali. Joy loved that car. She enjoyed purchasing cars that were two times bigger than her small frame. It was a show of how powerful she was, a great boost to her ego.

Sam slammed her car door and raced to the entrance of the downtown building. She headed up to the penthouse suites. Her heels slapped the ceramic tiles of the floor with a vengeance. She was determined. She wore a frown as she chiseled her bottom lip. Anxious to hear what Joy could possibly have to say for herself she repeatedly pressed on the buttons of the elevator. For a moment she panicked, she thought that she may not be able to get out. Perhaps it was God punishing her, for the hate she brewed in her heart. It wasn't as if she hadn't made her share of mistakes. Yet she was so ready and willing to crucify her sister for what may have been a mere lapse in judgment

Sam nearly fell through the doors of the elevator when they opened un-expectantly. She leaned her back against them, in an effort to calm the panic attack stirring in the pit of her stomach. Roaring down the hall to reach Joy's office she barged in startling both Nadine and Joy.

Joy dropped her fork back into her foil tin plate and wiped her mouth. She was disturbed at the way her visitor interrupted a client meeting and without warning. Joy attempted to excuse herself from Nadine and Mr. William's.

Sam walked towards the table and took a huge gulp of Joy's lemonade and lowered her eyes. Joy was amused at her obvious effort to suggest a meeting. She became instantly irate at Sam's lack of respect for her place of business. She began to black out her coworker and client. Joy slipped deep into her consciousness. She was unable to decide her words as they were coming out without thought.

"What the hell is the matter with you? Have you lost your mind? Has something happened?" Joy stood up and made her way around the oval table to confront Sam. Nadine and Mr. Williams perked up, their eyes widened with excitement.

Nadine nudged Mr. Williams to give him a heads up. "This finna be good." Nadine winked at Mr. Williams. He was still in awe of her poor English.

"And you work for a literary agency?" Mr. Williams remarked as he smiled back at Nadine.

Turning their focus back onto Joy and Sam, Nadine adjusted her chair and plate of food in the direction of the show. Sam rolled her eyes at the two spectators as she began her interrogation.

"You know full well why I am here Joy. Don't play dumb with me. What happened between you and Charles last night?"

Joy felt guilty enough. She was angry for Sam barging into her office, but she knew that her reasoning was warranted. Still, she was handling business with a client. There is a time and place for everything. Joy was more than willing to talk about the situation, but not during her work hours. Joy wasn't so sure she even had an explanation for her actions. It was a mistake she wasn't herself. She missed Justin so much her mind played on those emotions. Sure, Charles came on to her, but she willingly accepted. No matter how clouded her vision. Joy sighed and placed her hand upon her hip. She was nervous about how her actions would affect her relationship with her sister.

"Please Sam, not now. I am behind schedule. I really need to get these chapters in order for my clients new book release." Joy started to explain the matters of the book contract. How it was a chance in a lifetime for her client and she wanted to make sure things were perfect.

Sam was not the least bit concerned about her work or her newest protégée. She wanted to know what exactly took place with her and her husband. "Please Joy spare me the details of your lavish life of imagery and fairy tale. I am much more interested in your relationship with my husband. What is the beginning and end to that Joy?"

"Sam, what the hell are you talking about?" Joy wrinkled her forehead and folded her arms across her chest in a bewildered state. It was as if she were someone completely different. All of a sudden the rewind button was pushed and Joy forgot Sam's reasoning for interrupting her meeting. Joy was defensive and ready for action. Joy didn't admit or deny anything related to Sam's visit. She downright refused to discuss the matter whole or in part.

"Joy cut the drama. When I returned home last night, Charles was acting beyond weird. His pants were missing buttons. He smelled of your shampoo and he admitted to being at your place last night. He said he stopped by to talk with you about some fund Justin was working on for you. I didn't believe a word of that mess. Then, he had the nerve to start sniveling like a baby when he realized he had been caught red handed. He said that you were emotional and he gave you a hug. Obviously, it was something far more to that story or he wouldn't have been so nervous. Besides, I can always tell when he has been unfaithful. The man starts crying and babbling about how I did him wrong and how I trapped him etc." Sam rolled her eyes and threw up her hands dismissing Charles and his excuses. "He even went on to call me Joy during his emotional breakdown. Now cut the bullshit and tell me how long you have been fucking my husband?"

Nadine's eyes bucked in surprise of Sam's accusations. She immediately flew from her seat to come to Joy's defense. "Uh, uh girl, how dare you come in here and accuse Joy of some mess like that, in her place of business as well. We all know of your indiscretions boo…boo it's no wonder he hasn't left you already. Now, Joy," Nadine turned her attention to her boss and friend. "I know this is your sister, but you need to put ole girl in her place. She has seriously lost her mind." Nadine blinked her artificial eyelashes bashfully, while smacking on her chewing game.

Nadine shimmied off. "Mr. Williams if you will come with me. I will show you some of the promotional packages we offer for your marketing and social networking strategies." Nadine whisked past Sam bumping her with her shoulder on purpose, as if to warn her to keep things cool.

It was amazing how ghettoized and professional Nadine could be. It was like an on and off switch. Joy enjoyed her tenacity and no nonsense sense of sensibility. Nadine was a stand up gal. She just wished that she could in good faith say that Sam's allegations were in fact a bunch of malarkey.

"Not to worry, Nadine. Sam and I will be fine." Joy raised an eyebrow at Sam. "Look Sam, I haven't been sleeping nor have I ever slept with your husband." Joy threw her hands in the air to warn Sam of her advances. She didn't have the time to deal with the insecurities, of her shattered relationship. She was tired of playing the mediator of Sam's quarrels with Charles. Perhaps now, that some obvious signs of cheating has surfaced, she can pack up and leave for good this time, even if it was her flesh and blood that caused a means to an end. Joy had bigger fish to fry. She was planning her book tour and she was going to get as far away from the Bay Area as she could, Mother Nature was calling. The hills were her favorite place. She still had yet to talk with Patrice about the pregnancy. She wouldn't dare tell Sam, not after her close encounter with Charles. She thought it best to just leave and start over.

Joy was growing more and more agitated as Sam stood her ground demanding answers to questions she already knew the answers too. Joy hadn't truly slept with Charles, but she could have if she wanted and Sam knew far before this incident that Charles was a no good cheating bastard. Who knew what other troubles Charles had lurking in his closet.

"Sam I'm warning you if you do not leave my office right away I will have to escort you out." Joy was serious. She couldn't believe she stood up for herself in such a way that she would actually do bodily harm to another human being, but she was being pushed to the edge.

Sam lowered her eyes at Joy as if she were inviting the challenge. "Joy, we will have this conversation. You are not going to just walk away from this one." Sam peered at Joy with an unwavering look of disdain and stood her ground. She was waiting for Joy to show some sign of admission, guilt or remorse. Joy didn't seem herself at all. She was strong and fearless. Her eyes were wide and focused. She never changed her position, as she spoke through her grinding teeth. Her irritation was obvious and she didn't mind showing her lack of interest. Something was different about the look in her eyes. She was more than confident. She was borderline arrogant.

"Fine." Joy responded. "Just get the hell out of my office."

Sam couldn't decide whether Joy's anger showed her innocence or proved her guilt. Sam grabbed her purse and turned to face Joy once more. "Talk to you later."

Joy didn't respond, she was curious to know what Charles told her. She was sure he thought of something to worm his way out of the line of fire. "What a coward." Joy thought to herself. She wanted desperately to finish with Mr. Williams, so she could track Charles down and give him a piece of her mind.

# ~30~

# DIRTY ROTTEN SCOUNDREL

Charles sat outside Joy's home for hours before he decided to make his way in. He wanted to search around and see if she had any cash lying around. He hoped she was under sedation. Those pills were a Godsend he had managed to get his hands on of a few of Joy's sleeping pills when he visited her laboratory before retreating home. Sam was out, in minutes and awoke, unaware of the hours before. A tired and confused Sam past out sleep in her clothing from the day before. They weren't talking much but, at least she hadn't mentioned divorce. He was in no way prepared to go through a divorce. He would surely be living in a box.

Nervous and confused as to what his plan of action was going to be, Charles turned the lights out in his car and walked down the block to Joy's house. He parked a ways down, so that if Sam decided to come by, she wouldn't easily spot his car. He just wanted to see if he could reason with Joy. He needed the money bad. The loan sharks were adamant about retrieving the monies owed to them, or they were going to pay a visit to his home. Joy had the money and he knew she would give it to Sam. The problem was he would have to tell Sam what he had been doing with all the money. She would surely leave him then. Charles couldn't think straight. He wanted to fall to Sam's feet, beg for her forgiveness and ask her to come to Joy herself for the money. It was bad enough he nearly slept with her. Now he was coming back unannounced and uninvited to steal money and beg for more.

Charles threw his sweating palms into his pants pockets and walked briskly down the block to Joy's place. He looked into the master bedroom window that faced the street and noticed the lights were out. Charles adjusted his stance and jogged up to the front door of the condo. He peered in the window, the blinds were cracked a bit and the curtains gave a sneak preview of the inside of her home, all was quiet.

Joy sat on her couch in the dark. She was so depressed about the events of the day she didn't know what to do. She begged for Justin to show face and comfort her. She knew for sure that he hated her. She hated herself. Joy wanted to get rid of all the pharmaceuticals that had lately assisted in her social demise. However she knew she couldn't survive without them.

Dr. Zimmerman may have been right to refuse her further refills on her prescriptions, but she had since, exercised other avenues to attain what she wanted. Nurse Betty was almost too, easy to manipulate. Joy knew she was using her as well. She needed a guinea pig to try out her theories and new drugs. Joy was very much obliged to do so. Joy sighed and scuffed to the kitchen to look for a bottle of wine. Her house slippers tapped the tile floor, as she switched from side to side.

Joy retrieved the last bottle of Vodka from the fridge and popped her open with little effort. Closing her fridge door she noticed a small glimpse of a man's shadow just in front of her bar. Slowly Joy closed her refrigerator and pulled a knife from her display on the counter.

"What are you doing here?" Joy addressed Charles with ease. She was surprisingly calm, as if she expected him.

"I'm home babe. What do you mean honey? It's Justin." Charles swallowed hard and cleared his throat. He couldn't believe he had tried to pull off such a scandalous act. It was his only defense, a desperate move to save himself Charles had to admit.

"Shut your lying lips. How pathetic of you to return." Lillian said enunciating every syllable.

"This stunt is amazingly atrocious of you, posing as Joy's husband. Her dead husband at that." Joy's mouth was moving, but it was clearly not her that had responded to Charles.

"Why are you here?" Who Charles presumed to be Joy asked once again, as she laid the knife on the countertop and switched on the light so he could see, just how serious the situation was.

"Look, I came to see you. We need to talk. How are you?"

Joy's reflection smiled, "Charles you and I both know that you don't give a damn about me, but I'll play for a while. I have nothing better to do at the present time. I'm fine, but Sam's a mess, thanks to you. What is your problem?" Joy licked her lips and lowered her eyes, as she was completely befuddled by the look of confidence Charles wore on his face. She wanted to reach across the bar and smack the taste from his mouth. "Are you allergic to being faithful? Does your dick just fall from your zipper on command? You sicken me. You tried to take advantage of Joy. Then you stroll on home and tell your wife that Joy fell off the little yellow bus and came on to you?"

"Really, Joy it's amazing how you can stand there with that stupid holier than though look, glistening in your angelic light, as if you weren't the other half to this mess. I don't recall whipping anything out. I do however, remember you shedding your clothes and hopping onto the counter top ready, willing and able. Until I came to my senses and pushed you away, we were both grieving. Things got out of hand."

Joy's image beamed at Charles as if he would catch fire right before her. With all the deceit and lies he spewed she was sure he'd die a slow gruesome death. "You are so creative. Your imagery and way with words is so convincing, but like you said, Joy is also to blame. We both know it was you that initiated the whole frolic and Joy was used and abused just as she always is. Now here you come pretending to care, when all you want is for poor Joy to validate your story. Continue to cover the lies you've told Sam. Does Sam know that you are here checking up on poor Joy? By the sound of it she played right into your story of quarrel and weakness, you are going to rot in hell."

"Yeah, ok Joy. I realize that you are hurting so I will just be going."

"I don't see the reason for your visit in the first place and its Lillian by the way, Joy is taking a nap." Quite proud of herself Lilly raised an eyebrow at a confused Charles.

Charles batted his eyes, twice and quickly covered his mouth to stifle his laughter. Puzzled and bewildered at Joy's new persona, Charles scratched is head, tussling his dreads to and fro, "Lillie? Who the hell is that? Oh I get it you're changing your name now. Is this the person that you claim to be taking over your mind? You know the whole family thinks you've gone crazy. Ever wonder why Sam stopped bringing the kids by?" Charles smiled as he noticed the heat coming from Joy's ears. He had hit a soft spot. He reveled in that. Hurting her were just his intentions.

"Get out while you still can, Charles. If you weren't my sister's husband..." Lilly's voice trailed off, she didn't want to say too much more. Her rage was building, she couldn't be sure she wouldn't act on it.

Charles smiled and turned on his heels. "Yeah ok Joy. Oh wait I mean Lillian. Oh would you tell your other personalities I said goodbye too?" Charles was full of smart banter, but inside he worried deeply about this new persona Joy took on. He was used to the vulnerable, needy Joy. So easy to convince and take advantage of. His entire visit was for naught. How was he going to get the money for these goons that were incessantly harassing him? His only hope was to either catch Joy at another time or reconcile with his wife and get her to ask Joy. Charles left and slammed the door unnecessarily.

"Sure will." Lilly, whispered silently and went back to sipping on her tall glass of brew.

Charles hopped in his car and started his engine. He popped in his CD and took one last look at the window of Joy's three-bedroom town home. "Come on Charles pull yourself together. The woman is crazy. Sam would be a fool to believe anything that falls from that Bitch's mouth." Charles thought to himself. He was worried. Who was he kidding? Sam was so gullible, she believed the lies he told willingly.

Hell, Joy could tell Sam the sky was red and Sam would either believe it, or research to find what truth was in the statement. Fabrication wasn't in Joy's genetic makeup, according to Sam. Well that was odd to Charles since there genetic makeup was identical and Sam could lie without moving her lips. She was good. It puzzled Charles how the sides of good and evil could reside so close together without overlapping. He was glad to finally see Joy exhibiting characteristics of the human race. For once she was scared, vulnerable and she didn't have an answer for everything. She even invented this personality to talk for her. All those hidden thoughts that now people would freak out about.

Charles had to admit those aspects of Joy's new personality turned him on. He couldn't stay away. He knew he had no regard to drop in on Joy unannounced especially after their recent indiscretions. Charles leaned his head back on his headrest as he reminisced, the foreplay he and Joy shared. He cursed aloud and slammed his fist into the steering wheel. "I better get out of here. You never can tell where Sam could be lurking around."

Charles took one last look up into Joy's apartment window and he made a point to drive down the block before he left for good. The lights were off. He glanced quickly and then again. He could have sworn to have caught sight of an image standing outside the windows edge. Looking up once again he saw an image or silhouette of a woman, standing on the ledge. Her hair was blowing in the wind. She was wearing a collegiate nightshirt. She looked down and caught his eyes. Charles was frightened by the woman. It was Joy's face and body, but her demeanor was not her own. She was cocky and fearless. She held a dominating swag as if taunting him. She looked him dead in his eyes. Charles was mesmerized by the crystal blue sparkles in her eyes that he couldn't tear his gaze from.

The temptress' swaying nightshirt flirtatiously blew in the wind, revealing her body's true form. She looked to be dancing. She ran her fingers through her hair and stepped closer to the edge of death. Charles froze, confused as to how to react to such a display. He shook his head in an attempt to refocus. He presumed his mind to be playing tricks on him.

Charles busied himself trying to put his car in gear. He was going to get the hell out of there. He didn't want Joy to jump, but if she did he didn't want to be the one to have found her. Sam would be sure to completely miss the foresight of her sister jumping to her death. She would be too busy trying to find out what he was doing at her home at such an hour. Charles put his foot on the gas without bothering to look up to see if Joy was still standing on the ledge. Turning his wheels he sped down the block, speeding down the road he took a quick right towards the freeway.

**\*\*\*\***

Lilly smiled as she enjoyed toying with the poor man. If he didn't fear her now he had better start. Joy sadly would be committed soon if she didn't stop all the horse playing around, but she couldn't help it. Lilly laughed as she retreated from the edge of her windows sill and went back into the home. Joy had rested long enough. It was high time for her to deal with the harsh realities of the world, for with each action lives consequence.

# ~31~

# TILL DEATH DO US PART

Staggering to the bathroom of her master bedroom Joy turned on the water to her tub. She'd drunk an entire bottle of wine and taken several pills. She was falling in and out of sleep as the tub filled with water. Stumbling about, Joy went to her bedroom to check her messages on her phone. She had thirty missed calls.

Fifteen of them were from Sam. Darrin had called a few times and surprisingly so had Patrice. She erased each and every call and voice mail without bothering to listen to them. She knew all they wanted to talk about was how she was holding up and if she was going to come to the memorial services in the morning. The funeral was a sore subject, she was not likely to attend. Joy had been very stern about her feelings in regards to conducting funeral services with no bodies.

Joy ran to the bathroom to turn the water off to her bath. She nearly overflowed the tub. Lazing about her room she decided that taking a bath would take far too much effort. She couldn't bear to undress, bathe and then get dressed all over again. Joy was suffering from a migraine and she was drunk. She feared that she were in need of medical attention. Unfortunately, there wasn't a hospital within a 50-mile radius that would see her unless an ambulance brought her in.

Joy could feel the depression settling. She turned on

her television. She flipped through the channels unable to find anything to erase her feelings of sadness. Joy searched for the Cartoon Network channel. Cartoons always seemed to help lighten the mood. She needed something to take her mind off things. The binge drinking had ceased to work the numbness fell into a heap of memories. The sadness began to hover over her and her sightings of Justin grew few. It was as if he were upset with her and refused to come and check on her. Joy sat still for a while. She wanted desperately to hear or feel a sign of her husband flowing upon her. Nothing happened. The still of the night remained. She was alone and she hated the feeling of loneliness and uncertainty. Joy turned to the, "Oxygen Channel," She smiled at the "Bad Girls Club," marathon. She and Justin often tuned in to check out the ridiculousness exploited on reality television. Joy often joked about developing a reality show, "Life with the Anderson's." With the pre-teen drama Ashley carried on and the boy's shenanigans, there was plenty to broadcast.

Joy lay down and drifted off to sleep instantaneously. The alcohol had taken its toll.

**\*\*\*\***

Sam rolled out of bed, with an unsettling feeling in her stomach. She'd spent most of the night trying to get in touch with Joy. She was beginning to get worried. She was angry with Joy about Charles, but she knew she hadn't acted alone. Due to the circumstances of the day she didn't want to upset Joy any worse than she already was. Joy had done a good job of avoiding the situation up until the day of the actual memorial service. Joy handed Patrice a 10,000 dollar check and left the planning up to her. She didn't agree on the idea of conducting a service for people that were still missing, but she didn't have the strength to continue on fighting with her about it.

Sam stood in the middle of her room twiddling her thumbs. She was having a hard time thinking of something to wear. She didn't want to wear the traditional black, but she didn't want to wear something inappropriate. Sam snatched a simple black dress from off its hanger and threw it onto the bed. She tried on a couple pairs of her black heels and made a quick decision. She still, had three boys to get ready as well. She had no time to waste.

Sam jogged downstairs to get the boys some bowls of cereal before getting them ready for the service. To her surprise Charles had already settled the kids down and was busy scrambling eggs and frying bacon. Sam was impressed. She liked the new Charles. He seemed to be sincere in his apology.

Charles greeted, Sam with a kiss on her cheek, as he asked if she were hungry.
"How did you sleep?"

"Not Bad. What time did you make it in last night? I noticed you hadn't come to bed?"

"I got in a little after 12. I slept in the boy's room I didn't want to wake you. I already ironed the kid's suits they are hanging next to the hall closet in the den. I figured you had enough stress with the service being today and all." He dare not mention Joy's name, but he knew that both her and Sam would be emotional wrecks. The one true thing he knew and understood about twins, was that they could sense and feel one another's pain. Charles looked at Sam to find her eyes focused on the fire underneath the eggs. He swallowed hard and against his better judgment he consulted her about Joy and had she been in touch with her.

Sam lowered her head. She hadn't been able to reach Joy all night. She was worried.

"I don't know, Charles. I'm worried about her. She is really acting strange. I think she may be abusing drugs and drinking again."

"What?" Charles busied himself dishing out eggs

onto the boys plates. "You can say that again." Charles snarled under his breath. His last encounter with her was quite an eye opener. Bug eyed, Charles hurriedly grabbed the hot sauce in the fridge hoping she didn't hear his last remark.

"Babe did you say something?"

"Oh no, I was just thinking that, drugs and alcohol could be the cause of all these strange behaviors." Charles cleared his throat as images of Joy in her nightshirt blinded his view of Sam and the kids. Charles bit his bottom lip. He was afraid he may have crossed the line.

"I don't know. I just hope that she can get past this. Somehow our fight seems unimportant. I mean sure we have problems, but I don't know what I would do if I lost you and the kids." Sam smiled and touched Charles' hand.

"I feel the same." Charles looked worried and sad. Something told him that it may be time to just sit down with Sam and tell her what was going on. If he truly loved her, he needed to trust her. Charles looked at Sam and smiled. "After all this, we need to sit down and talk, ok? I have something I want to talk to you about." Charles felt relieved just letting her know that there was something he wanted to get off his chest. He had taken the first step to fixing the communication problems in their marriage.

Sam agreed. She told the boys to quiet down and eat so that they could get ready to go. Sam just wanted to get the whole funeral business over with. She didn't care to stay for the re-pass or travel to the cemetery. Patrice was adamant about performing all the rituals of a memorial service and funeral bodies or not. She would make sure her son and grandchildren received proper burial. Sam kissed Charles on his cheek and gave him a reassured pat on the back before retreating upstairs to get dressed.

Sam dressed as quick as she could. She combed her hair into a sleek French roll and applied a thin layer of cover girl. With a touch of mascara and a clear lip gloss, she was all set to go. Charles and the kids met her down in the living room. Sam's eyes glistened as she looked over her boys. They were all so handsome. It saddened her that they were all dolled up for such a sad event. Sam scurried the boys to get into the car. She didn't want to be late.

Sam placed a call to Joy one more time before they got onto the freeway. She thought it may be a good idea to see if she needed a ride. They had to pass through her town to get to the church anyhow. Charles wasn't thrilled with the idea, but he didn't want to start another fight. So he kept quiet, secretly praying Joy didn't answer her phone.

Charles sped onto the freeway, as Sam hung up her phone, upset that she couldn't get a hold of her sister.

**\*\*\*\***

Sam ushered the children to the seating area of the social hall, while she took a quick tour of the church. She looked to find Joy tucked away in a corner, or hiding away in the ladies room, but there was no sign of her. Patrice ran up to Sam and gave her a huge hug. Sam was taken back. She was surprised and unsure if Patrice knew who she was. They had never been fond of one another. Sam figured that under the circumstances, some of the gripes were pointless.

"How have you been? Where is Joy? I have been trying to reach her for about a week now."

"I'm not sure. I am worried. I have been calling her all night. I am going to call her again in a few minutes. She hasn't been well lately. She did return to work. I was glad to hear of that. Her writing has always been something she could use as way of self-counsel. I visited her last week and she was just looking out into space with a blank notepad. She is so behind schedule with her publishing contract."

Patrice looked worried about Joy and her work. "You better call her. See if she is ok. I wish she would come to see me. We are family."

Sam excused herself to try and call Joy one last time before the service got started. She was hoping to hear that she was on the road. Sam pushed redial on her phone.

"Hello."

"Where are you?"

"Home…"

"So you really aren't coming?"

"Yes. What's it to you anyhow? He was my husband and they were my children or shall I say are because there are no body's present. I don't feel like talking about this right now Sam. I'm not feeling well. I am lying in bed. At any rate, didn't we have this conversation once before? I thought that I made myself clear the first time. I do not have any interest in participating in the glorification of my family's demise."

"You can't be serious Joy, glorifying death of a loved one. We are just trying to pay our respects to you and your family. Our family, Joy in case you have forgotten that we are sisters and Charles was his first cousin. This is equally as hard for us as it is you. Far be it for you to understand that."

"How dare you compare your loss to mine? Here you go again. I am not coming. Tell the coconspirators what you will." Joy hung up the phone without further ado and retreated to her bottle of wine. Joy surprised herself at how coy she was, due to the fact that her and Charles nearly slept together the night before. She was on a role. She felt liberated expressing her feelings freely.

Sam threw her phone into the bottomless pit she called a purse and went out to converse and greet with the guests. The memorial service was beautiful. Justin's mother was in good spirits and spoke about Justin and her grandchildren. Sam could barely speak as she said her goodbyes and Charles couldn't manage to speak at all. A number of Justin's friends and co-workers spoke of Justin and his fun loving spirit. Platters and bowls filled with delicious treats and entrées kept flowing about the social hall. Many asked of Joy's whereabouts. The chatter was loud beneath the clothes of women mainly, expressing how distasteful it was for Joy to be absent on such a day.

Patrice simply dismissed their inquiries by pinching her lips tightly together. The assumptions began almost immediately. Justin's friends and family speculated trouble in the marriage prior to the accident, possible infidelity or severe depression due to the loss of her children. Sam tried to clear up the matter as best she could. She made an announcement stating that Joy had taken the loss rather hard and had been ill for quite some time. She explained that with Joy's recent health issues and the death of her family, depression was inevitable and had in fact taken control. She went on to say that Joy was in need of prayer as she feared that she may be in fact a danger to herself and others.

Patrice's eyes were as wide as the sun as Sam spoke of Joy's condition. In mere minutes Joy Anderson of the Writers Group, had become a has-been.

Although Patrice did not agree upon Joy's blatant disregard for the families wishes to lay their lost loved ones to rest, she would never make Joy's mental condition public knowledge. Joy isn't feeling well and therefore is unable to attend today's service. Patrice commented to Sam as she slightly gripped her arm in passing as she left from the stages podium. She was livid. Sam smiled slightly at Patrice's show of aggression. She welcomed the confrontation.

"There is a right way and definitely a wrong way to convey a message Sam." Patrice lowered her eyes indicating her disgust at how things were handled. Sam didn't respond she simply looked down at Patrice's hand which held her arm rather snug. Patrice held her ground. She had mind to slap the grin from her glossed lips, right in front of the congregation. It took all that was Holy to keep her from hurling Sam into the standing flower arrangement just a foot away.

"Would you mind?" Sam looked down at her arm once again waiting for Patrice to release her. Sam lifted an eyebrow to indicate that she welcomed the challenge Patrice initiated.

"What's going on?" Charles ducked from around his circle of colleagues to break up the catfight.

"Nothing sweetie, Justin's mom and I were just having a heart to heart. We are just concerned about Joy and thought maybe she should see someone about this depression she is going through."

"Yeah, ok sweet heart," Charles' response was dry and he didn't buy the two girls explanations. Charles looked towards the ground. He was taking the reality of Justin's death quite hard, but there were other things on his mind as well. Sam was so busy running after Joy. She had little time to tend to their home and the children.

He hoped that their sit down would do them some good. Charles had begun to keep late hours at the office to keep the business he and Justin ran together a float, a change of lifestyle that he wasn't at all used to. It had become obvious that Justin was the true brains behind the business. Charles was simply lucky to have joined for the ride.

Charles was more concerned about the fund. It wasn't at all his issue to have worries about, but it was an extremely large amount of money. If it were up to him he would try to have the funds somehow funneled to Sam. Sam could take on the masses of Joy's project until her senses had returned. Only thing Sam knew nothing of Joy's work, She was both a writer and nonprofit director. The new literary group was something she had always wanted to do to help young authors become discovered. Joy's grass roots organization and magazine took flight just over two years ago. Both Justin and Joy built their empires together. They were a team. Charles only wished he and Sam could get along long enough to put their heads together to plan a simple family vacation.

Charles was in over his head in debt. He took out loans for Sam to go back to school, but she decided to drop out after she got pregnant again, more money wasted and gone down the drain. Charles took up betting to keep his mind off of the troubling issues of his home life, but soon found himself in more shit then he could handle. The gambling became a must. He was addicted. Entire paychecks were being bet on horses, basketball games and poker. Charles had to borrow money from Justin quite often to either cover a debt owed to some loan shark or pay a bill. He had done a great job hiding his gambling issues from Sam thus far, but with Justin gone he was sure to be revealed. Charles was in a complete daze as he thought of a way to get Joy to release the fund to San. Perhaps she would agree to a temporary change in shareholder, or executive director until she got back on her feet.

"Charles? Is everything ok? You seem lost."

Charles shook his head as if to snap out of a trance and addressed Patrice. "Yes I am fine."

Sam looked up at Charles as she tugged her arm from Patrice's grasp, "Charles Patrice wasn't talking to you. I was. Are you ok? Maybe we should go?" Patrice nodded in agreement.

Sam grabbed the arms of her boys and led them out to the car. She couldn't wait to get back on the road. She hoped that Joy was alright, but in a way she couldn't blame her for not attending that fiasco. Charles was beginning to worry about Sam. She didn't seem like herself.

The ride home was quiet. Charles had a lot on his mind. He wanted talk to Sam about everything. He just wanted to be sure that she was calm and relaxed. Under the circumstances he couldn't be sure that, a day of relaxation was in the near future. He was running out of time. Either they talk to Joy about borrowing the money, or they would have to sell their home to get the monies to cover his debt.

# ~32~

# I SAVED HER

Joy counted the hours down to the end of what she hoped was the memorial service. Patrice phoned and left her a message wishing her well. She said that Sam gave the audience an ear full about her mental dysfunction. Joy didn't care. She was just glad the whole ordeal was over. Joy twiddled her thumbs. She was alone and starting to feel like loneliness would soon be the death of her.

She sat down on her bed and felt around in the dark for her journal. Thoughts of Justin ran wild. Something she hadn't had in a while. She welcomed it. Her love for writing had been abandoned for nearly a month. Her feelings bottled up and masked by a fake smile.

Joy opened her leather bound journal and ran her hand across the pages. She could feel the rise of the ink on her pages tickle her fingers. She remembered how she felt when she wrote. It was her true calling. Joy missed writing just about as bad as she missed Justin and the children. She had no one left that she could truly trust with her feelings.

Feeling oddly polluted, she decided to take a bath. She wanted to be comfortable as she started to write her thoughts and feelings. Pulling off her robe, Joy walked into the bathroom to start herself a bath. Her girl t-shirt and jeans stuck to her from the sweat beading against her small frame, as her rob smothered her. Joy's bare feet smacked the floor of the bathroom. She playfully tapped around dancing in front of the mirror, as if warming up for a fight. Joy cracked her neck from side to side. Her natural curls bounced and tickled her eyes. "I'm back." Joy laughed into the mirror pumping her ego for the world and its wrath. She was ready to wage war for her sanity and independence.

"Wow! Don't we look confident," Lillian appeared in Joy's reflection, starring her down with a cocky glare.

"Yeah, I feel good. I think it's high time I take care of myself. I need to move on. I'm killing myself wondering, waiting all this bickering over spilled milk it's senseless. Moreover, it would be great if you too, would leave me alone. I know I am not perfect. In fact, many of my years I have allowed people to mistake my kindness for weakness. I do things only to appease others. I live for acceptance. Now I'm afraid I have no one to answer to. I have no one to please. I have nothing to lose."

"You sound as if you actually believe in yourself. You and I both know it is just a matter of time before you are ripping and running behind the next personality to ensure they are happy. I wish I could believe that you are ready to be independent. The truth is that you will never be happy, without being needed by someone else. You may as well join Justin and your children. Sam has Charles and Patrice has money, something you too, have but have no use for. You have the potential to be a very powerful woman. I know you don't have the balls however, to do what needs to be done. Charles and Sam, now they, they have the balls but lack the brains. You apparently are treading so close to ignorance that I frankly have become embarrassed of our connection. You my friend have dropped the ball. A blind person could see that Sam and Charles are playing you." Lilly laughed hard and loud about Joy's eyesight clouding her judgment.

"I'm not afraid of you Lilly. You don't exist. You are nothing to me."

"No Joy, you are nothing. You are afraid, because if

you weren't you wouldn't be in here discussing your next move with me." Joy's reflection tilted her head and threw her a huge smile. "I so love our talks."

Joy became frustrated. She was tired of being trapped in her emotional rollercoaster. She didn't know who to trust. Charles was clearly after Justin's money. Charles had Sam wrapped around his finger. Anything she told Sam in confidence was shared with Charles. Joy learned that, when Charles opened his mouth. She couldn't trust him as far as she could throw him.

Sam had always wanted a place in the driver's seat and Patrice had simply moved on with her small inheritance. She was alone Lilly was right she was afraid, very afraid. Joy opened the door to her medicine cabinet in search for a sedative of some type. Her head was swelling with pressure and what vision she retained became lost. Joy was welcomed by the many bottles of medicine that fell from the shelves of her medicine cabinet and into the sink.

"What are you looking for Joy? Can't you handle it? Or does the pain feel so horrific you can hardly breathe."

Joy ignored Lilly's constant chastising and searched for the correct pill to cure her anxious mind and horrendous headache. Joy combed through the medicine bottles frantically. Growing further agitated she busted open two of the pill bottles and took one of the pills from each. Joy could see her reflection in the knobs of her faucet. She looked deranged and untidy. Her eyes were red and wide, her lips were cracked and her hair was full and untamed.

"Would you look at yourself, you look like a damn crack addict. You don't even know what the two pills you took were for. Why don't you let me help? I can make this quick, easy and painless."

Joy took a look down in the sink. There was a shiny blade sparkling as if it were made of diamonds. The blade was beautiful its lustful shine glistened in the marbled pearl sink. Joy felt as if she could hear the blade calling out to her. She heard a voice that sounded so familiar to Justin's her heart jumped and her stomach fell to the floor. Joy was mesmerized. She was in love with the sight of light and the warm feelings of security. Joy picked up the blade and looked at her reflection. Her eyes now the lightest of browns, almost gold like honey with tiny flakes of emerald green that changed color with her mood. She became hypnotized by the dazzling beauty of her eyes. It was if they spoke and instructed her of what to do.

Joy moved towards the body of water that filled her tub. She knew that she was moving physically, but she didn't seem to have mental control over her motor skills. The anxiety pills worked to calm her nerves and the pain meds numbed her senses to pain. Joy could see outside of herself. She seemed to be having an outer body experience. She stepped into the warm waters, fully dressed. She was calm her face without countenance.

Sinking to the bottom of her oversized tub she wet her face and hair. There she sat underneath the water peacefully as long as she could stand it. As her body relaxed from the meds, she became paralyzed. Her body lay lifeless under the waters. She had to force herself subconsciously to rise from under the warmth of the water. Joy flew from the captivity of the soothing sensation and gasped for air. She was alive but felt as if she had died.

Drawing her attention to the blade she clenched ever so tightly into her palm she noticed the blood dripping into the clear waters, tainting them with her sorrowful, sinful, soul. She was ready to take on the wrath of her sin, own up to her many shortcomings and accept her fate. Joy looked into the blades eyes, which mirrored her own. She took the blade between her shaking fingers and slid the silver object across her wrist piercing her skin. The warmth of the blood flowing from her wrist warmed her soul. She felt weak, drugged and relaxed. Taking the blade into her other hand she performed the same procedure on her other wrist. Growing extremely tired and weak she fell into a deep sleep leaning back into the tubs head rest. She let her arms relax and fall over the tubs edge. Joy's arms and hands relaxed, as her fingers opened to the air, blood flowed as the blade escaped from her hands and fell onto the tile floor.

Joy stood looking at the sad sight of a woman fully clothed in the bathtub. Looking around she was joined by her three children and Justin. Joy was confused, but excited to see the faces of her family again. She had died and gone to heaven. Justin's smile froze and turned blank and the kid's faces were absent. She couldn't make them out. The emotions on their faces were unreadable.

Joy felt instantly uncomfortable and alone. She couldn't understand what she had done wrong. Justin looked at Joy and reached out to her.

"Why did you give up?" Justin was very disappointed in Joy. He couldn't understand her actions and he wanted answers.

"I don't understand what you mean. Why did God take you away from me? I don't want to live without you."

"I won't accept you like this. Go Back!" Justin was angry. Joy frowned and became hysterical.

Joy was confused about whether to go towards the light or find out what all the fuss was about in the real world. She could hear loud screams and a number of unfamiliar voices.

In mere seconds Justin was gone. He held the hands of their children as they waved goodbye. She cried as Justin's words pierced her soul, "Go Back!" Furiously he screamed at Joy, begging her to tear herself away from selfishness and live her life. Joy was confused. She couldn't decipher between reality and her imagination. Perhaps her sightings of Justin were all wrong? Maybe his visits were to let her know that he was in fact alive? Why else would he tell her to return?

"Go Back." Justin whispered into her ear once more before drifting completely away from her grasp. She was sure she was dreaming. All she could think about was saving the woman drowning in the tub. Completely, withdrawn from reality she felt herself being lifted, she screamed, frantically yelling for the woman to come back to life.

"I will save you." Joy screamed at the woman as she fought her way to consciousness. "I will save you."

****

Sam sat, at Joy's bedside nervous about what to say to Joy when she awoke. She was beyond worried at this point. The nursing staff was very adamant about Joy's condition. She was sure they were going to have her committed. Sam texted Charles her location as a heavily sedated Joy began to come to. She was surprised at her surroundings and even more surprised to see that Sam was at her side.

"Hey you"

"Hey." Sam smiled crookedly. "You know if you were trying to get my attention it worked. Just don't pull another stunt like that again."

Joy smiled and looked away from Sam briefly. "I was only trying to help. Nurse Betty came by to see me earlier. She was surprised to see me here as well. She wanted to make sure I was okay. No one will tell me how the girl is doing? I am very concerned. Have you heard anything? For the life of me I can't believe she came to my home. I was thinking that perhaps she lived there prior to my moving in. You know many people young and old who are dying, or plan to die retreat to their homes to leave this earth. It's where they find comfort."

Sam was confused about Joy's question, but she

didn't want to alarm or make her upset. So she just smiled and hoped for a new subject to come to mind.

"Hi. Excuse me, if I could have a moment of your time? I'd like to speak with you in private." The nurse walked in without knocking and drew back the curtain.

Sam was relieved and threw her eyes to the sky giving thanks and praise to God.

Joy sighed, she heard her fiddling with the lady in bed "A" she hoped that she would come in to give them some news about the girl, she saved.

"Um sure, that's no problem. I'm sure whatever you need to discuss can be discussed openly with Joy. We have no secrets." Sam quickly addressed the nurse and gave Joy a comforting pat on her shoulder. Joy looked at the nurse with confidence, waiting to hear what she had to say.

"Well, I know that the last month has been rough on her. So we at least try to keep things honest and out on the table." The nurse pinched her lips at Sam, as she took notice of her obvious fear of Joy and her reactions to the matter.

"She can take it." Sam reached for Joy's hand to comfort her. Sam's lips quivered slightly. "My sis is a trooper." Sam wasn't so sure she was prepared herself.

"OoooKaaay, Samantha." The nurse raised her eyebrow as she spoke with an obvious sarcastic tone. Joy took notice. She wanted desperately to reach over and smack her with her own clipboard, but she refrained from speaking.

"I need to ask you about the medications, Joy takes for the migraines, anxiety and stress related symptoms. How often and whether or not she was taking them under supervision?"

"Supervision. Joy interjected. I'm not a child. Or some drug addict." Joy was appalled and withdrew her hand from Sam's grasp. "What is this about?" Joy lay with her eyes wide and lips in a straight line.

"I am asking because there can be some adverse reactions to certain medications which may be the cause of Joy's suicide attempt."

"Suicide Sam, what is the Bitch talking about and why are you just standing there looking around as if what she has to say has some validation? Would you tell her, I found a woman lying in a pool of her own blood, fully clothed in the bathtub, my bathtub might I add? I don't know whether she was attacked or not. I just started CPR and called the paramedics."

Sam refrained from speaking at all. She thought it best to let the professionals do their job. She didn't know how to address her sister's illness and apparently it wasn't going to be an easy fix. Joy was in no way going to cooperate with these persons.

"Ma'am."

"Oh now you address me." Joy flared her nose, now angry and less than willing to hear what the nurse had to say. She was sure to ask for the supervisor shortly. Joy took a mental note of the nurse's name and staff number, so that she could report her unsavory bedside manner.

"You were the woman in the tub. Your sister found you and called the paramedics. We are very concerned about your mental state right now and would like to keep you, for a couple of days to run some tests." The nurse shook her head as she explained to Joy the situation and pinched her lips. She was a bit of an old fart. Her tone sounded as if she were a Southern Bell back in her day. She was old and therefore had very little tact. She dared anyone to question her authority. Sam noticed that her badge had a rusty 30-year valued employee button that was hanging on her laminated clip for dear life. Joy looked off into space. She was staring blankly at the woman.

"Sam what the hell is she talking about? I didn't... I thought...I was helping someone else. I merely fainted after all the trauma. Sis you have to get me out of here.

They are trying to keep me here. There is no way I can stay here. Take me to the girl. I know she is here. She told me the girl was doing well. Where is she?" Joy's blood was boiling. She searched Sam's face thoroughly to chime into her thoughts.

"Who told you? What did she tell you, Joy?" Sam looked puzzled as she searched the nurse's face for direction.

Joy looked into Sam's eyes. She started to answer, but she could see from the look in Sam's eyes that she didn't believe a word she was saying, "Never mind."

"Joy, I think you need to get some rest. You lost a great deal of blood."

"Yes Ms. Anderson. The reason you fainted was due to the loss of blood. I don't want to disturb you any further. I will get you something to help you get to sleep." The nurse looked solemnly at Sam and retreated from the room.

"Sam, do you think I'm crazy too? There must be some mistake."

"Joy. I don't want to upset you, but I need you to do something for me. I want you to think hard about last night and tell me what medications you remember taking. Just before…just before you rescued the girl from the tub."

Joy looked confused, as if she were deciding whether she could trust Sam's sudden belief in her turn table of events. "I…took a sleeping pill, my headache meds, my anxiety pill and I think the pain medication was a Percocet, I was all out of Vicodin. My head was pounding. I remember that much. I went up to my room with a glass of wine and turned on Law and Order. I watched one or two shows and that's when I heard the noise."

"What noise?"

"Help, there was a woman calling for help. I got up as quick as I could. I was a bit dizzy I admit. I walked into the bathroom. The water was running. The tub was overflowing. The water on the floor had turned pink, I panicked. I didn't know how she even got into the room. She was fully clothed. Mascara had run down her face and cheeks as if she had been crying. I couldn't tell whether she had been attacked or not. It all happened so fast." Sam wrinkled her forehead. Joy actually believed that a mysterious woman broke into her home to kill herself. Still she played along to see if Joy could help her get to the bottom of things. "What was she wearing?"

"Jeans and a girl tee nothing out of the ordinary."

"Tattoos?"

"Um No, I mean Yes. What does all this matter?"

"Did you get a look at the tattoos?"

"No not really."

"Ok! What about cuts, abrasions, bruises, did you notice anything of that nature?"

"Yes I did. Her arms were cut up pretty bad. Like glass had gut her wrists and arms. Nothing more like I said, she was fully clothed."

"Joy?"

"What?"

"Take a look at your arms."

Joy looked down at her bandaged arms and froze. She couldn't believe her eyes. Slowly she began to unravel the bandages to reveal, what was hidden underneath. She wasn't at all prepared for what she uncovered. The bandages were stuck to some of the cuts. The pus had crusted over and melded into the gauze. It was painful to remove. Joy's vision began to blur, the tears clouded her vision. She couldn't believe that she was the woman in the tub. She didn't know how she'd gotten there. She had no recollection of her suicide attempt. Joy looked up into Sam's face full of rage and determination.

"Where is she?"

Sam was confused all over again. Did Joy not understand what had occurred? "Who are you speaking of?

Joy you are her."

"I am not talking about me. Where is Lillian?" Joy froze and decided that she should keep her thoughts silent. If she kept on this way the hospital and Sam would be sure to have her committed to the insane asylum.

Although Joy knew how dangerous her thoughts were, she continued to think about how her so called friend left her to drown in the confines of a mental facility. "Where was Lilly now? She had some serious explaining to do. She promised she wouldn't abandon me in my time of need. Now, she was nowhere to be found. How long will I be forced to stay in this God awful place? Will they try to have me committed because of this suicide attempt? Oh God I have to convince Sam that I am not crazy. This woman is trying to kill me. Discredit me and take my life. What am I going to do? Joy looked up at Sam and finally let the tears expose themselves to the air. "I'm sorry Sam. I don't even remember what happened. I don't know what to do."

"Don't worry Joy. We are going to get you some help. The Doctor thinks that more than likely the medications were given in dangerous doses, which may have caused an adverse reaction. Your suicide attempt is not an uncommon side effect of at least 2 of the medications you are currently prescribed. I think you may just need someone to keep a closer eye on you. With me working and the kids, my husband, I don't think I will be able to do a 24-hour watch. I don't want you to have to stay here. I was thinking we could look into an acute nursing center."

"What?" Joy fondled around anxiously looking for her beds remote control to situate herself in a sitting position. "Sis I'm not crazy. Maybe they can tweak my meds."

"Before you say no, I really think you should consider the nursing home. You should think of all the perks. You will have your own room. Room service, medication on time and you will be watched for any change in behavior. I would really feel comfortable, if you at least tried the nursing home for a couple of weeks. The nurse and Dr. in charge of your care say that, "Shady Palms" is really a nice facility."

"Shady Palms. Really, sounds so inviting Sam." Joy was clearly being sarcastic. The name of the facility itself scared her. "With all the old people, are you kidding me?" Joy was nearing tears at this point, but she dare not let Sam see her. She wasn't sure just how much she could trust her either. With Charles close by, she could be in great danger.

"No, Joy. There are all kinds of people in this nursing home. It's an acute care center. It's for individuals who need short term care. Nobody stays there for longer than thirty days. Most have been in some sort of accident or something."

"Mental breakdown Sam, I believe that is the term you are afraid to say. As if I am going to reach for a sharp object and plunge it into my heart." Joy turned her head into her pillow with disgust. "That wouldn't be such a bad idea, right about now." she mumbled.

"I heard that Joy." Sam let out a frustrated cuss. "I don't feel comfortable about leaving you in some nursing home either, but I would feel a lot better knowing that someone is keeping an eye on you around the clock. I just don't think you should be left alone right now."

"I guess you're right. I know that you love me. I also know that I am getting to be a bit of a burden and causing a strain between you and your husband. I will try to control my life a little better. I just can't seem to let go."

Sam froze she didn't hear a word of Joy's sentiment. She pictured Joy and Charles frolicking about.

"Who could Joy? You lost everything. I will never be tired of you Joy. You took care of me when our parents couldn't. We are sisters remember?" Sam responded blankly and robotically starring straight through Joy.

"That's true. However you have a life and family of your own to tend to as well Sam. Go! I will be okay. The nurse says she will bring me something to help me sleep. I hope she brings a hamburger and fries with that." Joy managed to squeeze out a laugh. "Sleep is the best thing that happens to me nowadays."

"Oh really how so?" Sam questioned. As of late her sleep was scarce. When she did sleep she slept hard and long as if drug induced.

"I see them in my dreams." Joy's eyes became filled with tears once again. "It's like we are a family again. It's always the same. I wake up early to get Sunday breakfast underway. The pancakes and sausage are all done and it never fails. When I start scrambling the eggs I can hear the entire fleet running down the stairs. They are front and center awaiting breakfast as if they haven't eaten in days. I smile and ask baby Josh if he is ready to eat. He says, "Eat, Eat, I smile and wink… then I have to rush and get the eggs scrambled because I nearly forget I was still cooking. The children always get me in a forgetful way. I am intrigued by their presence and beauty. I used to just sit and stare at them when they were eating or playing."

Joy shook away her thoughts and turned her attention back to Sam who now was in tears herself. "Go don't worry about me I will be fine. I have my memories. Memories I hold dear to my heart." Joy flagged her hand to shoo her away. "I am fine, really."

Sam looked away and wiped the tears from her cheeks. "I brought you an overnight bag. It has a change of clothes, some more socks and underwear I know how you hate wearing hospital socks without your own underneath."

"Yeah thanks."

"I also brought you this." Sam reached down into the bottom of the duffle bag and pulled out at black cherry frame. It was a picture of Joy and her family, her two boys her husband and daughter. They were at the beach in Tampa Florida. A vacation the family took every summer. Sam handed the photo to Joy.

Joy reached for the framed photo slowly afraid to see their faces. "I..."Joy began but her throat felt as if it were closing. She was drowning. Panicking she searched her bed side table for fluids. Sam nervously fumbled for the cup and straw and quickly put it to Joy's lips.

Sam was unsure if she truly felt remorse. She was angry as hell at Joy for trying to sleep with her husband and she knew how fragile the issue was about her family. Deep inside she wanted Joy to be jealous of what she had. "I'm sorry. I didn't mean to get you all worked up. I just thought you might want a picture your Family to make you feel more comfortable here."

"No, its fine, I'm ok. Sometimes I feel as if this anguish will never go away. I still feel as if I am going to die when I look into their faces. I don't want this here. I know you meant well, but I can't have them here. I don't want them to see me like this. They will be here in spirit. I will keep them close to my heart in spirit."

Sam looked confused and understanding at the same time. She couldn't hide that she was befuddled about Joy's statement in regards to them. Seeing her in such a vulnerable state was uncomfortable, she wasn't used to Joy not being able to handle her own affairs. Part of her felt as if she were finally important. Another part of her was afraid to take on the responsibility. Sam brushed off her own insecurities for the time being. "Ok I will take it back to the house with me. I will keep it at my house until you get home. Is that ok?"

"Yes that's fine. I'm sure my nephews miss their cousins as well. It will be good for them to see a picture of them." Joy's eyes were getting heavy, although the nurse had yet to return with her meds. She could feel the start of a migraine surfacing as well. "Where is that damn call button?' Joy began looking around the rough material, they called blankets. "I need to get some pain meds in here right away. My headache is sure to be full blown in the next five minutes."

"I will get the nurse. Do you want me to stay until the nurse comes in to administer your meds?"

"No you go on home. You have been here long enough. I will be fine."

"Of course, you know I wouldn't just leave you here. I like to give the nurses a hard time just as much as you do. I will tell the nurse you are in need of some headache medication."

"Thanks sis. I appreciate it."

Joy buried her head into her pillows, in an attempt to relax and brace herself for the stifling pains of her headache. Sam left and nearly ran down the hall to get to the elevator. Charles was going to be furious. He was sure to pick a fight with her because yet again she skipped out to help her sister out of another bind. What was she to do? She couldn't just abandon her sister. Sam and everyone around knew that abandonment was one of Joy's biggest issues. After all she's blood. With Charles' recent indiscretions he couldn't exactly make too much of a fuss about her tending to her sister's needs. However, Sam knew her husband well. He would make an argument in his defense and blame Sam for the entire incident, without the least bit of remorse.

# ~33~

# SHE'S BLOOD

Sam practiced her line of defense the entire drive home. "Damn it!" Sam leaned her head against her steering wheel. "I don't know what to do for her anymore. I can't just abandon her, no matter what Charles say's. He knew when we married our family was all we had. Since mom left and dad died. Joy gave up her entire life to ensure they ate and finished school. What would I look like just leaving her to rot in some medical facility? She wasn't crazy. She was just going through something." Sam thought about how frazzled she would be if something happened to Charles and the kids.

Unsure of her own thought processes. Sam contemplated on the last few months of Joy's troubled life. She had suffered so much in the last year, her sickness and losing her family. Sam sighed heavily as she thought about the missing persons in her family tree. "In a way I don't blame the rest of our siblings for running and getting as far away as they possibly could. We are all so estranged now. However, now I am stuck to pick up the pieces, since Joy may have lost her mind."

Sam shook away her thoughts. "I'm sorry Joy." she whispered. "I didn't mean to say that. I'm just frustrated and tired. I think I am on the verge of checking myself into a hospital myself."

Sam inhaled deeply and turned the keys to her ignition. Exhaling she pulled her keys from the drivers station and opened the door. Smiling slightly to see her home, she pulled all herself together and started towards the front door. Her country porch was white as the snow in winter. The wind chimes blew slightly towards the west and her grass crunched beneath her feet as she stepped across her aging lawn.

She liked to think it was her father welcoming her home, safe and sound. He was funny like that. The signs of his arrival were always settle, but she knew it was his presence that guided and protected her. Joy always talked about that same presence. It was a calming spirit that always seemed to let her know everything was ok.

Sam's stomach jumped slightly as she pulled her key from her leather jacket pocket to unlock the front door. Before she could retrieve it, Charles opened the door. His face was plain. He didn't say a word just stepped from her way and allowed her to follow him inside. Charles locked the door behind them and walked just behind Sam. She stood just by the living room sofa startled by what she saw. Her boys were seated on the couch with jackets and hats on bundled up as if ready for a long trip. A lonely suitcase sat by the sofas edge. Sam turned to Charles.

"What was going on?"

Charles, looked at the boys and then back at Sam.

"We can't go on living like this, Sam."

Sam looked up from the suitcase and started to speak but no words came out.

"You don't have to say a word, Sam. I already know your commitments. You are not obligated to choose. I will make the choice for you. We are not leaving you forever. We are leaving so that you can have free range to look after your sister. I don't want us to get in the way of that. It's best we go and stay with my aunt for now. I sat and thought about a lot of the things you said earlier. I have been selfish. I know that you and your brothers and sisters have had nothing, but each other for a long time. I must admit they are all I have had for quite some time as well. I guess I was a bit envious of the relationship you all had. I never felt as if I had to compete for your love, until I married you." Charles put his hand up to keep Sam from interjecting. "I know I didn't have to compete.

I know that you love me and the kids unconditionally. We will be here. You need to do this for your sister, for us and yourself as well. Part of your continued connection to her is guilt, guilt because you feel as if she gave up her life for you. I'm sure she doesn't expect you to do the same. I know that she isn't like that Sam. But you need to do this to clear your conscience. You've never been one to owe anyone anything. You would be damned if someone else could hold a dime over your head. So I understand this is a rite of passage, you must endure to freely clear your mind. I love you."

Sam's throat burned and her eyes were frozen in time. She couldn't believe her ears. She knew that the decision Charles was making was best. She knew in her heart she wanted Joy to come and stay with them until she got better. In fact it was the first thing on her agenda to discuss with him, before the surprise of their departure.

"I...don't want you to go, but I do think that its best. She will need round the clock care for the next 3 or 4 weeks. I was going to talk to you about it but..."

"I know. It's ok. We will go."

Sam looked at Charles as he curled his lips together. It was almost in a sarcastic manner as if the entire scene were staged to see what she planned to do. Sam looked confused for a few seconds and regained her composure.

If this was some type of game she sure as hell didn't have time for it. She stood her ground. Her tears quickly dried. Sam turned to her kids and walked over to the couch to say her goodbyes. She held each of her boys for at least a minute and whispered her love into their ears. Charles Jr. was the toughest to say goodbye too. He was the little man of the house. He fought to hold back tears as he looked deep into his mom's eyes.

"Mom is Aunt Joy going to be okay. I think I should stay with you just in case she has another nervous breakdown."

"No, no sweetie. Aunt Joy isn't going to have another breakdown." Sam looked up at Charles to show her disgust with him. He had obviously had a lot to say, things that he chose to voice in the presence of their children, inappropriately expressed opinions that not only damage the children's opinions to their aunt, but showed a complete lack of respect for her family.

"How do you know mom?" Charles II, questioned he stood his ground blinking, irritated with his mother's lack of understanding. He wasn't so sure Aunt Joy was the safest person for his mother to be staying alone with. "The last time she was over she kept saying that I was her son and who knows something may happen she may think that you are some crazy person trying to kill her. I just don't think it's safe, mom."

"I know..., you and Justin Jr. looked a lot alike sweetie. I promise things will be just fine. I am going to see to it that Aunt Joy gets better and we are going to have a wonderful Thanks Giving and Christmas. I will see you on Halloween ok?"

"Ok mom." Charles Jr. agreed.

"You promise to be at school for the parade." Dominique yelled from beside his father.
"Yes Dom I will be there. Don't worry!"

"Come on kids we better get on the road. It's going to be dark soon." Charles glanced at Sam and gave her a fake smile. Sam did the same and planted a small peck on little Charles' forehead for reassurance.

"Go on I will see you soon." Sam patted Jr. on his back urging him to hurry before their father grew agitated.

Charles and the kids were gone within a minute. The events of the last hour were a blur. Sam paced the floors of her empty home and grew incredibly lonely. "What now Lord? What now?"

# ~34~

# GO AWAY

Joy threw back the covers on her hospital bed as the nurse tiptoed from her room. She pretended to be sleeping when the nurse came by to do her rounds. Though, she was experiencing great pain from the cuts on her arms, she didn't want to be sedated any longer. Whatever harm she had endured she wanted to be sure she could feel the effects of it. She was tired of being left in the dark. Samantha seemed to believe her but she couldn't be sure.

"Damn it!" Joy exclaimed. "Where are you?" Joy made her way to the vanity mirror over the small sink.

"I need help! What am I doing here? Why did you lie to me about the girl? There is no girl. The damn girl was me. I want out of this mess of a life. What are you trying to do to me?"

"I'm trying to help you. Aren't you tired of living this pitiful life? I mean how long are you going to mourn a family that was destined to be taken? Life is funny that way. When are you going to realize that God has a plan for you and it took you to lose something close to you, in order for you to be strong enough to endure his path? You may not like it. You may not understand, but it's all a part of something far greater than you. I am you, Joy the part of you that wants to be free, free from all the obligations of adhering to everyone else's dreams and goals. It's high time you look into the riches God has in store for you. If you have to die in order for you to regain life then so be it."

"I don't understand. I don't understand why you have put me through such humiliation?"

"Joy you did that to yourself. For so long you have refused to say no to people wishing for you to fail. You say yes. Yes to their will. Yes to their needs. Never have you paid any attention to the needs of your own. I told you the truth. I may have gone about things in a way in which you wouldn't have, but that is just it. It needed to be done this way. You aren't some rug that people should be able to walk all over. They need to recognize that your wishes and needs are just as important as theirs. It's up to you now Joy."

"You can't be me. You are a liar. You are vindictive. You are jealous and greedy."

"So is everyone around you sweet heart. Its time you woke up and I am not any of those things. I am actively pursuing my goals, regardless to what others wish of me. I am willingly pushing aside others that get in my way. I am making sure to call folk out for their conniving way of obtaining their worldly possessions. Just as they were trying to do you, by dragging you down, putting all of their cares and responsibility's on the weight of your shoulders. Stress will kill you and you are well on your way."

"I don't need you." Joy screamed louder than she'd planned. She had to look around to see had she drawn attention to herself. They would be sure to put a note in her folder about her delusional behavior.

"We shall see. Oh and Joy remember all those things you just listed, those traits you said that you hated about me? Why don't you take a look in the mirror? I am sure you will see some resemblance. The sooner you realize that I am nothing, but your conscience acting out the truths of your heart, the better off you will be."

"I will never be you." Joy bounced from bed and pulled her IV and trotted bravely to the vanity mirror of her patient room.

"You should have finished yourself off." Lillian murmured through clenched teeth. She was unnerved by Joy's blatant disregard for her subconscious and its views. "You are just a scared little soul. You won't amount to much. I guarantee you will always follow the likes of others and choose to please those around you in hopes to gain acceptance. You still won't be loved. You will just continue to be used and abused."

"Go away! GO AWAY!" Joy began to scream at the top of her lungs. She was yelling into the mirror. The nurse ran in from the hallway and yelled for help, in code to alert the staff on duty. Joy was irate by this time flinging her arms at the air. As she could swear she saw the girl laughing at her in the mirror. She was laughing and waving goodbye. The attendant grabbed Joy's arm. Joy broke free of the nurse before the assisting aide could restrain her. She grabbed the nearest cup and flung it at the mirror. When the water spilled down the face of the mirror her reflection was distorted. Joy could see her face for the first time. She could see that half of her face was burned. The other was perfect as if she were dipped half way into a bucket of acid. She was two faced a comical character. Joy began to scream as she bolted from the visitor's chair back towards the mirror for a closer look. The two women struggled trying to subdue Joy.

"My face! My face!"

"Ms. Anderson, please calm down. Please stay calm. What is the matter? What's going on?"
Joy was hysterical she couldn't calm herself. Joy continued to fling her arms in an attempt to shatter the glass of the mirror. Nurses began to pour into the room to restrain Joy and prevent her from yet another suicide attempt.

"What happened to my face? What's wrong with my face?"

The nurses worked busily around Joy's screams.

They were in a hurry to get her back into the bed and strapped down. Her arms were bleeding profusely. She was losing blood fast. If they didn't hurry she was sure to pass out. She had lost so much blood from her first attempt. Passing out wouldn't be such a bad idea on the nurses end. It would be much easier to sedate her.

Joy was flinging and yelling as if her body had been possessed. One of the nurses called for a psyche consult immediately. Joy heard her whispers and cursed her. "I'm not crazy, you Bitch. Tell me what happened to my fucking face. You people can't keep me here. I didn't commit a crime. Call my sister. I bet she doesn't know how you all are treating me."

"Strap her down. I will get the meds. Once we get her down, you write the report. She needs to be committed we don't have time for this."

"I will get right on it. I will have her transferred to the 3rd wing, right away." The nervous clerk grabbed Joy's chart and fled the room. She was sure that if Joy was able she would rip the skin from her bones. Her eyes burned a hole in her scrubs. She looked like she was a demon in disguise.

"You had better run." Joy yelled at the woman. "I will be out of here soon."

The nurses hurried to administer the meds into Joy's IV. She calmed as the fluid entered her blood stream.

"Thank God. I thought we she was going to kill herself this time. I am glad you got in here on time."

"I know. I hate to bother her sister about this break down, but she asked me to call her if anything changed. I don't know what she was yelling about, something about her face. It was a mystery to me."

"I don't know either. You just make sure to make a note of everything that happened here tonight. Explain very carefully that we had no choice but to sedate and restrain Ms. Anderson. She is a danger to herself and others."

"Will do."

# ~35~

# HONORABLE MENTION

Sam lay back in her bath of bubbles, trying to relax her mind. She had the house to herself but it was entirely too quiet. The talk with Charles was as romantic. They giggled and talked softly to one another. Charles was so cute, as he whispered sweet nothings into her ear. He was trying hard not to wake the boys with his playful flirtation with Sam. He called her Sammy. Sam blushed. She hadn't been Sammy for quite some time.

"I wish you were here." Sam exhaled as she ran her hands along the bubbles in the tub.

"Me too. What are you wearing?"

Sam laughed out loud. "How cute is that? A bubble bikini."

"What. Are you in the bathtub, without me? I'll be right there."

Sam giggled at his playful four-play. "You know you can't come home. I would love for you to see my bikini."

"Uh huh. So when does your patient get out of the crazy house?"

"She's not in a mental facility, Charles she's in the hospital. I'm supposed to pick her up tomorrow morning. The 24-hour watch will be over. All they need to see is that our home is suitable for Joy and that someone will be willing to watch over her for a few weeks." Sam thought about Joy having to stay with her. She wasn't all that thrilled, but at least she would be able to keep a close watch on her. Nadine would have no choice but to sign over the company's leadership role to her. Once that was complete she would have the funds to open her own salon. Sam thought about how she had treated Joy over the last few weeks. She knew that what she had done was wrong but she had dreams as well. She had no intention of physically hurting Joy. She just saw the opportunity to show Joy that she too could be vulnerable and need help.

The very fact that Joy was grieving left her open, if Charles hadn't developed a plan of his own, perhaps her plan to take over Joy's company could run smooth. One million dollars now lay in the balance. Joy's hands curled tightly around her pocket book when Charles showed face, in any regard. Sam knew that Joy didn't trust Charles. After all, she didn't trust him either and Charles was her husband.

Charles' willingness to go made things much easier, she could talk Joy into letting her handle the financial burdens of both the fund and business, until she got better. All the while she would make sure to set aside enough funds to get her business venture on the ground. Sam knew that most of her actions were unwarranted. She could simply ask Joy for the money.

She had no intention of going to Joy. She didn't want her to know that she helped her in the financing of her business. She wanted something to herself that she could mention from time to time. Something she wasn't sitting in Joy's shadow about. Sam shook herself from her thoughts to cause her attention to Charles and his playful seduction. He was noticeably trying hard to make Sam laugh and feel special, but she didn't want to say anything. She liked his attitude. His change in persona did however worry her. He seemed too, nice, nervous even.

Sam laughed at Charles' comment about Joy and her stay at the Richardson home.

"Yeah well, let's just pray that these few weeks don't turn into a permanent situation. I want to come home to my wife." Charles' voice trailed to a low silent whisper.

He was worried about the girls staying in the home alone. He felt a sense of relief that he was in a faraway place from his troubles and his children were safe. The only thought sitting in the confines of his mind, was the possibility that he was followed.

"I can't wait for you to come home." Sam smiled as she blushed. Again Sam felt as if butterflies were fluttering in her stomach. She had plans of stopping by the local mini mart to grab herself a pregnancy test. She'd been under the weather lately. A baby would be a wonderful gift to end her madness with Charles. Sam's other line chimed in. Frustrated she reluctantly checked her called identification. She was in no mood to talk with anyone, other than Charles.

Sam's stomach dropped. She became instantly nervous and sick to her stomach. Joy's sightings were becoming a reality to her she did in fact have a multiple personality. "Babe let me call you back. The hospital is on the line."

Charles huffed and puffed, as if he were upset about having to get off the phone with Sam, "Ok." Charles sadly dragged on. "Make sure you call me back. I want to hear your voice before I go to sleep."

"Awe ok. I gotta go." Sam clicked over to the hospital anxiously she was worried and couldn't imagine what the hospital could be calling about at such a late hour.

"Hello!"

"Yes is this Samantha Richardson?"

"Yes this is. How can I help you? Is Joy okay?"

"Um…, yes and no, Mrs. Richardson? I am calling in regards to your sister. I'm sorry to inform you that she has suffered some trauma this evening."

"Wait! What kind of trauma?" Sam got so nervous and shaky she nearly dropped the phone into her bath. Unable to ensure her device's safety she pulled herself from the tub and grabbed her towel. "Is she ok? What happened? Was there another attempt? Has her condition worsened in anyway?"

"Yes ma'am, well that is the reason for my call. Joy did experience another breakdown. It was very disturbing to both the staff and patients. A nurse found her yelling obscenities in her vanity mirror. We don't even know how she got out of bed. Apparently, she removed some of her IV tubing and her catheter. When the nurse confronted Joy she began to attack the nurse. The nurse called for help. When help arrived Joy began to throw objects about the room and broke the glass mirror over the sink."

"Okay... so is she ok?" Sam began to get frustrated with the reporters rendition of events. "Do I need to come down there or what?"

"Well Mrs. Richards is it?"

Sam ignored the nurse's question, but when she didn't respond the nurse simply sat on the phone breathing as if she were waiting for confirmation.

"It's Richard-son..." Sam annunciated.
"We had to sedate Joy. She has become a threat to both staff and herself. Putting restraints on our patients are the last resort. I wanted you to know that she will be transferred to the third floor within the next few hours."

"Third floor... What's on the third floor?" Sam was worried but yet glad that her case for proving Joy's mental capability was turning out to be a no-brainer.

"It is our Psychiatric wing. There, she will receive appropriate medications and the nurses are well prepared for out breaks of this sort. She will be watched carefully and put on a strict diet, as we are unsure if she will try to harm herself again."

"I don't think that Joy is suicidal Miss..." Sam was growing agitated with the woman's nonchalant tone and insensitive attitude.

"It's Jennings. I am one of the nursing clerks here. She has tried to commit suicide more than once correct?

Might I add there was one other thing that was a real big concern, she appeared to be talking to someone. It was very clear that she was angry with this somebody. This somebody was the reason for her mental illness, so she claimed. She also kept asking the nurses to tell her what happened to the right side of her face. She claimed that she saw her reflection and the right side of her face were completely burned. You and I are both aware that there is nothing wrong with Joy's face correct? I assure you that there is still nothing wrong with Joy's face. But in order to make Joy comfortable. After we sedated her we bandaged the right side of her face. This was the only way Joy would take her medications."

"What! Why would you go along with her hallucinations? That can't be healthy. You are no better than the doctors and nurses either handing her pills, or using her for test purposes, to merely advance in their career. You all are basically aiding her illness. I am not happy, this is unacceptable."

"We are doing what we must to help Ms. Anderson. I am just calling to inform you of the change, if you would like to speak with the supervisory staff on duty that is no problem?"

Sam laughed and hung up on the woman and her smug attitude. She had, had it with the nurses of St. Johns Medical Center. They were just peachy keen with torturing and neglecting the patient's real needs. Medication is all you here around there. "Ms. so and so… I have your meds. You rang? Do you need something for pain? It never fails. I have to get Joy out of there. She will be ruined for sure, if she has to stay another day in that hell hole."

Sam finished drying off from her bath and threw on her robe. "Damn it Joy! Well Lord. You know what's best. I pray that you lead me in the right direction. I am nothing without you." Sam threw on her worn jeans and her girl tee from earlier that evening. She spritzed her tight curls and

~

**FULL**

h an urge to gnaw away at
hands. The heat threatened
al like characteristics. She
effort to pull herself up to a
ted and falling fast into a
he opened her mouth to
from her mouth. She felt

ed. Her throat begged for
lled stale and stuffy. Joy
as she could and made an
of water on her bedside
to reach for the straw. If
e plastic stick she could
s to relieve some of the
Unsuccessful at reaching
ge to tip the pitcher of
o her blankets relieving
ts that were suffocating

k against the pillow to
ter soothed her burning
enjoy her new found air

l your nurse call button.

Joy was screaming from inside her sedated frame. She yelled for help. She squirmed to get free, but all she could muster was a blank stare, at the nurse asking what her needs were. Joy began to form tears. Her plain face didn't make a move or show a sign of emotion. Her only hope was for the nurse to recognize the tears in her eyes and know that something was wrong. Joy felt as if she was going to die from the burning itch climbing her hands and arms.

The nurse busied herself. She began to take Joy's vitals and get clean linens for her soaked bedding. Joy motioned towards her hands to see if she could get the nurse to offer a hand in the matter. The nurse understood and unraveled the bandages on her hands. Joy was oblivious to the fact that she couldn't speak. She had suffered from a nervous breakdown of some sort and had temporarily lost the ability to talk. The medication she was on was used to sedate her caused her emotions to be subdued. She could show no physical signs of human emotion at the present time.

Joy was as close to death as she'd ever been. Her suicide attempt had seemed far from reality, but she was forced to come to terms with the events of the previous night. The evidence was clear that she was the woman in the tub. Who had she seen? She wondered as the nurse took off her bandages and cleaned her crusted wounds.

Joy looked down at her hands and wrists as the aide nursed her sore arm. The pain of her cuts weren't as bad as the knowing that she herself had inflicted them. She was in and out of consciousness. Her understanding of reality was flawed by images of the past. She often saw Justin standing near her bedside. When she managed to drift off to sleep for a few minutes she would catch a glimpse of him when she opened her eyes for a second. She had to be reminded of her current place of residence. She often dreamed of opening her eyes to find herself snuggled in her own bed,

MIRROR OF DECEPTION

ija M.Butler

had to be sure to take her her volatile manic episodes. Sam hroom mirror and winked at her dbye and grabbed her keys.

back in her 3 bedroom condo. She missed her home. The home destroyed by the storm.

Sam and Charles were going through so many troublesome times at home Joy understood, full well why Sam couldn't risk taking an interest in Joy's condition. Sam was willing but Joy insisted she go home to her family. With her most recent episode she wouldn't be getting out. Her 24-hour surveillance turned into an automatic 72 hour hold, after she destroyed hospital property. The nursing unit all had to rush in and sedate her.

Joy was nodding and mumbling as the nurse cleaned her wounds with alcohol and saline. The burn startled her from her thoughts. Her mind was drifting away to the conversation she had with Lillian. Joy understood the many facets of Lilly's personality. After all she was a personality that she created. Joy was frustrated in that she couldn't speak on the matter. She needed and wanted to expose both Lillian and the demonic deeds of Andrew. Though, Lilly was the lesser evil of the two, she preferred to make her own decisions. She also couldn't let on that she was aware of the two extra people living in her brain.

"All done." The nurse said to Joy. "You should feel some relief from the burning and itching in a few minutes. I put some ointment on your cuts. I am going to go and get you some pain meds. That way you can sleep the rest of the night. The sedatives we gave you will wear off soon and your ability to talk and move will be restored. We are very sorry we had to use medication and restraints to subdue you, but you were exhibiting some dangerous behaviors. We didn't want you to hurt yourself, or anyone else for that matter."

Joy stared blankly at the nurse. Her blood was beginning to boil. She was growing tired of the nursing staff and their speeches. She wanted Andrew to come out at that moment and thrash the nurse, put them both out of their misery. Joy quickly shook her evil thoughts and searched her brain for a smile. She slowly managed to smile a bit, which alarmed the nurse slightly she couldn't be sure of Joy's thoughts or actions. Joy began to squeal she couldn't form words, just awkward sounds.

Joy's arms and legs were burning. Her stomach felt as if it were twisted in knots. "Nurse" Joy blurted uncertain of her ability's to convey her message. "Some…thing's…, wrong." Joy stuttered shaking violently with pain. She was falling into a panic, as the pains in her stomach swirled around to her back. "Nurse…"

Nurse Jennings inched over to Joy's side to check her vitals. She couldn't be sure of Joy's state of mind and she didn't want to be caught off guard. Joy grabbed hold to Nurse Jennings arm tightly and demanded her to unhook her restraints. Joy's voice was stern, deep and raspy. It was monstrous. She was a lot stronger than her frail frame suggested. It was as if some outer force of nature controlled her movement. Nurse Jennings was sure she had been trained in some sort of self- defense genre.

.      "Joy, I need you to calm down."

"It hurts, it hurts bad." Joy was confused by the pains in her lower abdomen. She needed help fast. She wanted medicine. "Where is Sam?" Joy was beginning to convulse, her blood pressure was dropping fast. The nurse hit Joy's panic button she needed assistance and a possible crash cart immediately.

"Joy can you hear me? Ms. Anderson?"

Joy was unresponsive. She had passed out cold from the pain.

**✳✳✳✳**

Sam checked her review mirror to ensure that her mascara was intact. She pinched some of the makeup from her lashes. Sam nervously batted her caked lashes trying desperately to flatten the clumps of mascara blinding her view.

"Shit!" Sam shrieked loudly as she noticed the pink tint on her fingernails. "Damn red dye is going to be the death of me." Sam fiddled with her fingernails trying to cleanse the fake blood from the tips of her fingers. Sam smiled at her theatrical play. It was too easy manipulating Joy into thinking she had tried to kill herself.

Sam looked at her reflection. Her eyes looked sad as if she were remorseful for her actions. Sam took a chance at cutting Joy's wrists, but she had to make things believable. Joy's toxic screen test would reveal that she had a number of sedatives in her blood. No one would question the validity of Joy's delusional thought processes'. As far as anyone was concerned, Joy had lost her mind. She was ill minded and it was only a matter of time before a violent incident would take place.

With the added fuss Joy was causing at the medical facility the verdict would be a no brainer. What she hadn't planned on was her husband's betrayal. Sure she knew of his many indiscretions with woman of all walks of life, but he knew how close her and her sister was and there was a line. At least one she thought existed. Sam was so angry it was hard for her to keep focus. Part of her hated both Charles and Joy but; Charles was the father of her children. He was also the bread winner. Her job at the salon depended on clientele and with the growing issues of the past month, Sam's roster was depleting fast.

Sam's stomach filled with butterflies. She was nervous about what the hospital had to say. Had Joy managed to remember the actual events of the night? Sam had to make sure Joy was heavily sedated. She hadn't planned on things going this far but she couldn't go to jail she had her children to think about.

Sam sped down the road to get to the hospital as fast as she could. There wasn't a car in sight, only her car speeding up and down the open highway like some mad woman. Sam took a quick right and nearly ran up onto the curb as she took her eyes off the road for a second to check her phones caller id. Before she could see who was phoning her phone stopped ringing.

"Damn it!" Sam was so nervous about getting to the hospital she was in danger of killing herself before she could get there. She came to a rolling stop at the street lights just a few blocks from the hospital. She quickly hit her redial button on her phone to see if she could return her missed phone call. It was Charles, but his phone went straight to voicemail. Sam decided she wouldn't call him back until she got to the hospital to check on Joy. She was excited about getting to a drug store for a home pregnancy test. She was still beaming with joy about her talk with her husband. She felt as if they were falling in love with him all over again. If it wasn't for Charles' inability to restrain from his lustful shortcomings and Joy's meddling, she wouldn't have had to take matters into her own hands. Sam was trailing on thin ice and stretching the line between love and hate.

Her betrayal in regards to her sister was done with good intention. She was only trying to save her marriage. Charles was having troubles with the finances of the home. So she figured that if she finally got off her rear and took care to open her salon things would get back on track. Owning her own salon had been on Sam's agenda for the past ten years. She was just busy with the children and learning how to become a wife. School wasn't her thing. She knew how to do hair and she was good at it. She didn't need a degree to do that. The business end of the company would be a cinch. She would just hire someone to manage the account aspects of her business.

Joy did and she was one of the hottest literary agents in the Northern parts of California. Sam found herself day dreaming as the light turned green. She wondered what her boys were up too. She knew Charles wasn't sleeping. It had been years since they spent a night a part from one another. Sam was glad to have something to do to take her mind off of her empty house. She was worried herself about how she was going to sleep alone.

**** 

Charles hung up his cell and threw his phone down on the passenger seat of his car. He made sure that the boys were all tucked in before he left to go out for a midnight run. He just wanted to hear Sam's voice. He didn't want her trying to call him while he was out. His forehead was beading with sweat. It was as if he couldn't go a day without placing a bet of some sort. The Casino strip was open all night. Gambling was just about as bad an addiction to drugs. He felt nauseous if he couldn't hear the roar of his fellow gamblers, cheering their bets.

Charles pulled into the "Salty Dog." and leaned his head back onto his seat. He pulled his wallet from his pocket and counted the twenty's he had neatly folded in the fold of his leather money protector. He counted five hundred dollars and inhaled the smell of the money as if it were a drug. Charles closed his eyes savoring the calm feeling and leapt from his car. He stood up straight and popped his collar as he entered the double doors of the gambling hall.

Charles strutted through the gambling palace with a cocky stance, as if he were the king, of the establishment. He took his seat at the bar an ordered himself a Hennessey with coke and a long island ice tea. Once he guzzled his shot of cognac, he scooped his long island and drifted to the card table situated in the back of the casino.

Charles threw two hundred dollars onto the table and asked the dealer to deal him in. The dealer laughed at Charles and his cocky mannerism. He was acquainted with Charles and his gambling debts. The dealer rose one of his eyebrows as he handed Charles two cards. He signaled the man to the left of the bar, to indicate that Charles had graced them with his presence.

The man came from behind the shadows of the bar and took a seat just next to Charles at the card table. Charles was so enthralled in his card playing he failed to notice the gentleman to the right of him was staring him down.

"What we got?"

Charles was immediately angered by the rudeness of the man and his line of questioning. It was a rule of thumb not to ask another man how he played his hand.

"Look man, I'm trying to concentrate here. Why don't you go get yourself a drink and take a gander at how a real man plays the game, of chance."

The man laughed and put his toothpick back into his mouth. "Oh yeah… Why don't you show me where my partner and I can collect our money? The money you owe. You know this is very interesting how you have two hundred dollars to bet at this card table when you owe us about fifty thousand."

Charles looked up from his cards and nervously took a swig of his long island ice tea. He was nervously trying to find the nearest exit out of the building. "Look man." Charles began with a nervous smile. "So much has gone on in the past few weeks. My cousin, my wife's sister's husband and children were killed in the storm. We have been trying to help them with the financings of the funeral. Man, Sam's sister hasn't been holding up too good, she has damn near lost her mind. Spending money frivolously and not giving a damn to take care of Justin's estate."

"Estate…." The man looked off as if slightly intrigued about the thought of possible monetary gain, but he knew better. The buff gangster wanted his money. He had played along with Charles and his shenanigans for far too long. He knew he couldn't trust Charles to pay the money and giving him a second chance to formulate a plan would only open a window for him to flee.

Charles looked straight through the man as he was talking. He was lying through his teeth. The woman he was describing was Sam. He blamed her for some of the financial troubles they had recently suffered but none of them amounted to how much damage he had caused with his gambling problem.

"I am trying to win you some of the money now. I haven't been able to sleep knowing that I owe you guys such a large amount of doe." Charles lowered his eyes hoping the heavy would go away peacefully.

"Well neither have I. When people have things that belong to me, I find it hard to concentrate. I too, have a family and things that cause for payment. Now tell me Charles, who is going tend to my mortgage and car payments? My wife gets her hair and nails done every Tuesday as well. How do you reckon I pay for those trips to the salon?"

Charles, first thought was to be snappy and offer his wife's services, but he quickly thought about it and decided to refrain.

"I'm working on it." Charles tried to end the conversation and continue on by asking the dealer to hit him. Instead the impatient gentleman pulled Charles up from his seat by his collar and slung him across the bar, knocking over a patrons table.

Charles, full of drinks and brassy as ever stood up and ransacked the over powering man. He tackled him down, hurling the massive thug onto the table just next to his gaming station. Charles' hair blew in the wind and his face was serious, as his eyes were crazed and reddened. Charles flung his arms in a murderous frenzy trying to protect his winnings and survive his near death experience.

"Hit me!" Charles boldly called out to the man at

the card table, once more.

The man refused and tossed the two hundred dollars Charles offered to bet into the wind. At that moment the owner of the Salty Dog, came from inside storage room heaving a bat into the wind.

Charles noticed the angered business owner and ran without a second thought. The man got up from the ground and fought his way through the crowd to get to his fleeing foe. Charles laughed as he weaved in and out of the crowd like he was the star quarterback. He ran hard and fast as he saw his life flashing before his eyes. He could see his car and in that moment he felt that he had won and survived the most horrific night of his life.

The large man staggered breathless after Charles into the parking lot. "Charles!" Charles' assailant's voice deep and loud barreled into the night. Charles ran like the wind only steps from his car. The man fired his weapon into the air. Charles felt the heat of the bullet enter his back. The crisp smell of gunpowder and the smoke from the gun blew into the wind like the calm after a blazing fire, soft crackles of singed flesh burned. Charles fell to his knees as the blood fell from his lips. The hit man stumbled drunkenly and exhausted after his run panting he shook his pistol into the night air. He stabilized his stance as he watched Charles struggle to get into a more respectable position to accept his fate.

"Any last words?"

"I'm sorry Sam." Charles whispered just before the heat of the gun pushed into his temple and the bullet entered his skull.

## ~37~

## SECRETS OF THE WOMB

Sam's chest began to hurt as she pulled into the hospital parking lot. She felt uneasy. She was worried that something horrible had happened to Joy. Sam slammed the car into park and buzzed the nursing station from in the emergency area of the hospital. It was after hours and only under special circumstances would they allow family members to visit during the night.

Sam ran to the elevator and nervously waited for the elevator to open. She was shaking and fidgeting around. She was trying to prepare herself for what she may find. Sam got to the third floor and pushed her way to the nurse's station to gather some preliminary information before entering into Joy's new room.

"Um... yeah hi, I'm Sam Richardson I am Joy Anderson's sister."

The head nurse looked up at Sam at first alarmed and then quieted by the woman's obvious dress and sense of sensibility. "Sorry, I wasn't expecting a twin." The nurse chuckled. "With all the ruckus Joy has been keeping up I couldn't be sure what her next move was. She suffered a mild attack of some sort. She was complaining of lower abdominal pains and burning of the arms and legs. I'm not sure if the nurse that phoned told you about the vanity mirror in her room or about the hallucinations. Apparently, she heard a women talking to her. She started in on the charge nurse screaming frantically about the burns on her face."

"Her face…?"

"She is calm now and I assure you there is nothing wrong with Joy's face. She is experiencing some side effects from the medications and the fact that she has been on so many anti-psychotic medications she will be experiencing some withdrawal. I am sure this is the cause of her hallucinations.

I do believe that she has more pressing issues we would like to keep an eye on. We explained to her that when you don't tend to the needs of your body you can sometimes suffer from heat stroke, dehydration and anemia. All these things are exceptionally important in Joy's case. She had better be lucky she was here when this episode took place. She could have lost her life as well as the life of her babies." The nurse looked back down at her paperwork and busied herself. "Oh she is in room 212, just at an angle from here."

Sam stood so still she was sure the slightest touch would knock her over. Her face grew pale and her lips as dry as her throat. She was stunned at the fact that Joy was pregnant. Sam wondered more so if the reason she had been experiencing so many symptoms of pregnancy was because of Joy's pregnancy and not her own.

Sam could hardly breathe. She gathered her senses and entered Joy's room. She was sleeping. Sam walked close to Joy and put her hand on her sister's shoulder. She didn't want to startle her but she wanted to wake her and get to the bottom of Joy's secret pregnancy. All kinds of thoughts plagued her mind. She wanted to know if Justin knew and if Charles had any recollection. Sam was deep in thought. She hadn't noticed Joy peering at her with a fierce look in her eyes. Sam felt so much guilt. Had her attempt to sabotage Joy and her mental health harmed her Joy's unborn children? She would never harm the children.

Sam's stomach became sick.

"So you know?"

"Yeah I know. How long have you known?"

"For quite some time I couldn't believe it, wasn't sure it was you."

"Yeah... Same here I thought that I myself was with child."

"I'm not talking about you being pregnant Sam, Joy either. I'm talking about you and Charles trying to steal Joy's money and take over Justin's company."

"What are you talking you about? Joy, are you raving mad? It must be the medicine." Sam was both livid and nervous. She didn't understand where all the accusations were coming from, but she knew full they were true. What made her even more so worried was the fact that Joy kept referring to herself in third person. Not to mention she was more interested in this mysterious pregnancy. Sam could hardly gather her thoughts.

"Joy you should really get some rest. I know that you may be going through some withdrawals and you must be heavily medicated. Just go back to sleep." Sam wasn't in the mood to play games. Part of her wanted to beat Joy about the head and shoulders, based on the notion that she had made a play for her husband. Even though Charles and Joy had not slept together they were still emotionally connected. She couldn't say in confidence that the fling was a onetime thing. Who knew how long Charles and Joy were deceitfully seeing one another behind she and Justin's back.

Sam was anxious to get Joy settled so that she could flag down one of the charge nurse's on duty to talk about the pregnancy. Sam seemed to cast away all the issues of Joy's mental state at the present time. Her mind and heart were at war. Her heart was trying to convince her mind that there was no way that Charles could have fathered Joy's baby. She could only hope that her babies were a blessing from God. She would be so lucky once again to have salvaged a piece of her deceased husband and have the chance to mother a child with the man she loved one last time.

Sam cursed her thoughts of envy. Even in death Justin was the hero and Joy was the Queen. Sam had to get to Charles and find out just how long he and Joy were seeing one another and whether the jump in her stomach were quickening's from her unborn child or was she experiencing symptoms of her sister's pregnancy.

Sam's thoughts were cut off by the sounds of the intercom, calling the nursing staff and doctors to the emergency area. Apparently a man was brought into the facility. He was shot twice. Sam's stomach dropped, she was knocked off balance by the blow to her stomach. She couldn't understand such a feeling.

"It's a shame how the world works. Pain and violence only creates more pain and violence just as lies and deceit. Poor Joy all she every wanted was to be accepted. Tried so hard to please you and the rest of them, but no you and dear old hubby had to have your cake and it eat too. Well it won't be long now. You will feel pain just as she has. Only with your evil natures I am sure you will find a way to get through. Joy on the other hand needs my help. She needs protecting from people like you. Justin was right about one thing he and Charles both couldn't understand how two people that looked and shared the same DNA could be so different. I bet you didn't know that she had a little secret of her own either did you. Maybe you and pretty little Joy weren't the only babies nestled in mommy dearest's little womb. It's Lillian I don't believe we've met."

Sam was startled and taken back by the woman's voice taunting her. The voice lingered into the air whispering into Sam's ear. Sam froze and her skin paled. Sam looked down at Joy, her eyes were starring back up at her but they looked lifeless. She was unable to move but her heart raced. She panicked motioning towards Joy's chest to make sure she was breathing. Sam yelled Joy's name once or twice hoping for a response. The woman's voice was gone and she demanded Joy to explain to her what the hell she was talking about. Sam was convinced that Joy was playing mind games on her, but she knew full well that Joy hadn't moved nor had her lips. Joy closed her eyes abruptly and slipped off into a deep sleep as if she were possessed and released.

Sam backed away slowly from Joy's bed. She had first mind to grab for her purse and get the hell out of there but suddenly she became incredibly worried about the man brought into the emergency room. She realized that she hadn't spoken to Charles in about two hours. She forgot about calling him as soon as she got to the hospital with the news she received at the nurse's station.

Joy looked at Sam and smiled slightly. She was watching her every move. It was clear that Lilly was calling the shots. Joy was too tired to fight her off. She couldn't understand the mixed feelings of joy, sadness, revenge and guilt she felt, but she couldn't control her emotions. For a second she managed to come out from within Lillian's grasp to try and reach out to Sam. Sam was busy combing through the contents of her purse in a desperate search for her phone.

"Sam, he's gone." She was fighting through her emotions fiercely. She had a smirk on her face but her eyes welled with tears. She looked deranged. Joy fell fast asleep once again without another word.

"Joy! Joy, wake up." Sam was violently shaking Joy in attempt to bring her back to conscious awareness. She didn't budge. The medication had her heavily sedated.

Sam walked slowly from Joy's bedside and out to the hall to see what all the commotion was about. She caught sight of Nurse Jennings whisking by the room with a bunch of charts in her arms, she threw them down at the nurse's station and picked up speed towards the elevator. Sam grabbed the nurses arm just before she broke out into a full fledge run down the hall.

"Hey, what's going on? Is everything alright? Is my sister safe here?"

"Yes ma'am trauma just brought someone into the hospital. You are welcome to stay with your sister if you like. The alarms just indicate that it is serious in nature and staff is needed to help contain the situation. It's okay Ms. Richardson."

"It's Mrs.!"

Nurse Jennings eyes grew wide, as the name rang a bell. "Oh." Nurse Jennings began to stutter and she was all of sudden hot under the collar. "A man..." Nurse Jennings began knowing full well it was against hospital policy to divulge information about patients in the hospital. He was still John Doe by hospital policy until further investigation.

"A man what?" Sam grew very concerned.

"I'm not supposed to say, but your last name matches the man's that was just brought into the E.R." Nurse Jennings touched Sam's shoulder briefly and ran down the hall to get to her station. Sam was unable to move. She was paralyzed from the neck down. She couldn't speak, she was going to faint.

"He's gone." were the only words she could hear, the words of her sister, just before she passed out from the medication. Sam fell to her knees on the third floor of the hospital. She buried her head into her hands and cried hysterically.

Sam's belly jumped with excitement. Charles' life line flattened. She was alone with three boys and another on the way. What was she going to do now? More importantly who was the woman inhabiting Joy's body. Sam was more confused and afraid than ever. The woman that spoke to her in that room was most definitely not Joy.

She was fearless and condescending as if she were challenging her. This woman knew of her plans to sabotage Joy and her company. These concerns began to weigh very heavily on Sam's heart. She was going to have to make a living for herself at this point. She needed Joy, the company and the monetary help. Problem was this new persona of Joy's wasn't someone that could be taken advantage of. She needed to find a common ground and fast. This chick was much smarter than the average bear.

Sam gathered herself scrambling to her feet. She hunched over her shoulders on the verge of a deliberate breakdown to set the mood. She was heartbroken over the loss of her husband but Lilly was right. She was a survivor. Sam set the stage to confront Joy with the news of Charles, assuming she didn't already know. She didn't know who she would encounter behind the curtain. Sam brushed past the medicine cart left sitting between the two beds in Joy's hospital room and slung back the privacy curtain to Joy's bed.

"Joy, he's gone. Charles is gone?" Sam's breakdown was right on queue and deserved an award. She put on quite a performance with such short notice. However, to Sam's surprise so was she. Joy's bedding was tossed to and fro and her gown lay haphazardly on the visitor's chair by her bed. Joy was missing in action.

# ~38~

# EMPTY

Joy walked slowly over the well-manicured grass. The cemetery was her last stop before heading out of town. She couldn't stand staying around all the city's monuments Justin and Charles worked so hard to create. Joy was headed to the hills. She needed to gain inspiration for her writing or her career would be sure to become a memory of her success. Traveling to the hills she would be sure to have the fresh start she needed to begin the process of healing.

She felt odd being there. It wasn't the way she had imagined her visit to be. In her dreams, there was a fog that hovered over the tombstones, like haunting ghosts in scary movies. Ice crystals covered the grass and had frozen the roses still. It would be oddly cold in the middle of spring and with each breath clouds of smoke would release from her parted lips.

Shuddering from the crunch of the grass, Joy stood just behind Justin's mother. She didn't want to disturb her so she didn't speak. "I didn't expect to see you here?" Patrice questioned. She could feel Joy's presence as she approached the gravesite. The winds blew in a frightfully cold whisper.

"I didn't either." Joy responded. She was more than uncomfortable considering the graves were empty. Joy twitched her nose at the irritation she felt in knowing that fact. Who was Patrice pouring her heart out to Joy was livid and cautious at the same time. She didn't understand Patrice's devotion to the memorial plaques of her family but she could never be disrespectful. Joy thought about the reasoning for her visit. She too, had come to at least explain herself if there were souls looking to be put to rest.

She however, would never give up. The fact that their names were etched in stone and simply forgotten burned her throat. Joy had every ounce of faith that her boy's and husband were out there missing. She had already lost her only daughter. She was not ready to grasp the fact that her boys were gone as well. Joy's eyes began to water she Patrice spoke of her beloved son.

She was singing and praying, weeping and humming. She had caught hold to the Holy Ghost. Joy shifted her feet as she was growing tired of holding her and the weight of her bundle hidden beneath her oversized parka. Joy muttered words of irritation under her breath about how the money could have been used to form some sort of search party instead of funding a funeral for empty caskets. She was more than disturbed at the family's lack of support and faith. She stepped alongside of Justin's mother and bent gently beside her to leave her a note of confessions.

Justin's mother looked up at Joy with obvious disdain and cleared her throat. "And what might this be?" She was referring to the small printed letter Joy casually left at his stone hedge.

"The truth." Joy responded and turned to head back towards her car.

"You know... you are not the only one hurting. You and I both lost someone very close to our hearts, not to mention you lost your children as well. It may do you some good to come around and talk to the family. We would love to have you. Its time like these that we as family should come together and embrace one another, living alone with all this guilt can drive a sane person crazy."

"I'm sorry. Is guilt what you presume I am feeling? Joy laughed aloud to herself and then looked seriously at Justin's mom. "What I feel is far from guilt and pain. There is a hole in my heart I have hate in my heart. For the life of me I can't understand why the family is so interested in having these dinners and family game nights when my husband and children may still be out there hurt and now dying.

Why come together now that he is gone…in any case? When he was here you were spread so thin we could barely get you to attend the children's birthday parties. So excuse me if I don't wasn't to join in on any of your reindeer games now. I happen to like being alone. At least now I know who truly has my back. My husband, lover and best-friend are gone, along with my children.

There isn't much else that links the two of us." Joy tugged at the collar of her coat to cover her chest from the angry cold and turned on her heels. The wind caught her jacket and blew her coat leaving her swollen belly exposed. Patrice focused on Joy's stomach and raised a hand to stop Joy from departing so quickly.

"My grandchildren. Assuming the baby you are carrying is my grandchild." Patrice never looked up to see whether Joy had bothered to turn around. She was fully aware that she had grabbed her attention by her statement and open assumption.

"Who in the hell do you think you are talking to? Surely, you can't be talking to me, I'm not Joy. My name is Lillian Andrews." Joy now Lilly stepped high and fast over the growing grasses of the cemetery to properly greet Patrice. Patrice looked as confused as ever but she dare not challenge the woman's identity crisis at the present time. After all the stories she had heard from both professionals and Sam she was looking for the fastest route back to her car. Alone in the fog was creepy enough. Patrice lifted an eyebrow and prayed Joy hadn't noticed her discomfort.

Lillian cleared her throat as she eyed Patrice, "Is everything okay, Patty dear? You seem out of whack all of a sudden." Lilly humped her shoulders and took a few steps towards Patrice. "You seem nervous."

"No just caught off guard. You and Joy look a lot alike."

Lillian laughed so hard she almost stumbled back in to an uneven patch of grass. "You're kidding me right? You expect me to believe that you are not the least bit befuddled by my presence?" Lilly closed her jacket tightly and fastened her scarf around her throat. Patrice simply stared at Lillian afraid the demon would attack her and ate her alive. She realized that her thought process on the manner was a bit overly exaggerated by so was the thought that Joy was essentially two different people. Patrice's mind ran wild. She began to think about Sam. If anything she would think that Sam suffered from some form of multiple personality disorder she too was quite the character.

Lilly appeared agitated that Patrice seemed to be untouchable she didn't have much of a bone to pick with her anyhow. Lillian called her attention for a brief moment to the head stone her eyes became red and began to fill with tears. Joy was resending back into her place of inhabitance. Patrice wrinkled her forehead and looked at Joy's eyes. They had changed back from an ocean blue to a hazel brown. This wasn't the first time she'd noticed a change in Joy's eye color. Though she never thought that it had to do with a split personality, she simply thought that the change was due to the accident and eye condition.

"Joy…" Patrice thought to call out to her to see if she could get Joy to respond."

Joy stood still as if she were paralyzed her legs so stiff and face plain. "I better get going. I have a long drive ahead." Joy's voice had very little emotion and she had her head down as if she didn't want to look Patrice in her face.

Patrice grew worried. "Joy... you ok?"

"I will be." Joy looked into the face of Patrice and blinked her eyes, before turning to depart. Patrice's eyes grew wide and her mouth flew open unable to tear her gaze away from Joy's eyes. Joy's left eye was a beautiful mix of brown and green and her right eye was a vibrant blue. The two different colors of Joy's eyes didn't bother her as much as what she say next. Her reflection mirrored the same image but she was clearly someone else. She stood with her arms folded and her eyebrow arched. She mimicked Joy's frightful stare and laughed loudly at how fearful she was. Patrice obviously alarmed at Joy's paralysis. She was cautious to ask Joy any questions. She merely stood quietly hoping that Joy was simply having a moment of silence to grieve her lost loved ones.

Joy gathered her senses and tried to speak confidently. "I'd better go." With that Joy moved as if she were possessed in a stagnated formation. She turned without a whisper of goodbye and marched her way through the frozen grass towards her car. Jumping into her car and starting her engine in one smooth gesture, Joy put her foot on the gas and sped down the road.

Joy looked into her rearview mirror and adjusted it so that she could check her reflection. She appeared normal, her eyesight wasn't blurred and her reflection showed little if any change in which she held her expression.

"So what now." Joy questioned her mirrored friend and foe. Joy paused at the red light dazed at her reflecting image waiting patiently for a response.

Lillian revived the red lipstick that had drowned into to a dull pink and put on her sunglasses.

"You live..." Lillian replied and she popped in her favorite traveling cd and cranked up the radio's volume. "You Live..."

# MY NEMESIS

## ~VOLUME 3~

## OUT FOR BLOOD THE RETURN

# ~39~

# DARRIN

"Darrin what are you doing up so late?" Marisola gripped the meat of Darrin's shoulders massaging slightly. Darrin pushed the tablet towards the back of his desk trying to hide what he knew Marisola suspected.

"Nothing babe, is everything okay? It's not the baby is it?"

"No! I just wanted you to come to bed. You have been out here for some time and I get lonely." Marisola seductively flirted with Darrin.

"I will be there in a few." Darrin responded short and dry as he was busy writing his thoughts. He missed Joy and He needed to speak with her. He needed to gain some closure on the matter. Sure He loved Marisola and his unborn child but there were many issues that still haunted him when it came to Joy. Darrin pondered as he watched Marisola switch back to his master bedroom. She was a hot number and her presence fulfilled the hole in his heart up until Ashley's death.

Marisola served as a great scapegoat she seemed to suppress his feelings of guilt and pain. During the hours of the day that is, the night owl plagued him nightly. He dreaded the moons presence. Marisola was a nice addition to his lifestyle, but her getting pregnant threw a wrench in his cozy stress free relations. He wasn't ready for Ashley twelve years prior and he admitted that fact to Joy. They were young and fresh out of college they knew nothing about the real world or where their careers would land or begin for that matter.

Darrin confessed to abandoning Ashley and Joy out of fear and he was admitting to himself that he was getting those same feelings of fear snapping him back into reality. He wasn't sure he was ready for fatherhood. The anxiety was taking its toll. Darrin felt guilty when he smiled at the thought of his newborn baby. He couldn't tell Joy anything regarding the child he just couldn't stand to see the look in her eyes.

Darrin stood up and decided he would take a stroll onto the balcony of his upstairs office. He was in awe of the nights beauty but fearful of it just the same. Darrin grabbed the bars of the balcony and looked down onto the bed of roses that lined his driveway. He was devastated and holding on to so much pain. It was a wonder he hadn't fallen to pieces. Darrin shook his head as he punched into the palms of his hands. He felt the release coming on. The quiet of the night would lead him to peace. Crying out to the moons stars he sobbed like a baby his shoulders violently shaking as the tears flowed heavily.

Marisola heard the ruckus she was snooping as usual creeping behind loitering about Darrin's desk. She peeked at his letter of solitude.

"What is this?" She yelled from across the room. Darrin was startled at her outburst and then astonished at her boldness.

"Darrin I am sick and tired of this shit. Are you still in love with this Bitch? Am I just here for show?" Marisola began speaking gibberish in Spanish harsh words Darrin knew.

"I don't know." he responded. "I just don't know. I do know that I love you and the baby you are carrying. I just have some unfinished issues to address. We just lost our child, Marisola."

"Yes a child you hadn't seen or been in contact with for more than ten years. Or did you forget that bit of information?"

~ 282 ~

"So…, I am not supposed to feel pain? I can't believe you would say that. I loved Ashley I just didn't know how to be a father. I was a young, stupid and selfish, man. If I had it to do it all over again, I would."

Darrin threw his hands to the sky and rubbed his head. Marisola was quiet she was saddened by the truths Darrin spoke. She was afraid of where she stood in the equation.

"So what is this some kind of front?"

"No babe, this WAS me trying to get over my past and make a future. A future with you, I thought…I won't lie to you about my feelings for Joy. I will say that I wouldn't act on them. I am just not that type of dude. I am committed to you. I am just worried about her. She hasn't answered any of my letters or phone calls. The only contact I have had with anyone is with Sam and she is such a liar, I know she wouldn't tell me anything if I paid her. She just said that she wasn't well."

"Wait!" Marisola was confused and enraged. Letter's… phone calls, what the fuck Darrin?" Marisola was so angry. She struggled to speak.

"Get out Darrin! Just go please."

Darrin grabbed his keys. He walked briskly towards the door then stopped dead in his tracks. He thought about the matter at hand. Darrin smiled at the thought of him leaving his own home. He could have been a real asshole and put her ass out, but he was sensitive to her pregnancy. Without a second glance he started towards the door with a dismissive hand. Chuckling he snickered, "I'll let you have this one." Darrin could taste the Hennessey and Corona miles away from the bar. He would make it there by ten he calculated. Just enough time to drink his troubles under a table and get him-self thrown out on his ass.

Marisola smashed the glass of water she gripped onto the top of Darrin's cherry desk.

"You pregnant and I get that but there's nothing protecting your face. You should be sure to remember that I am still in recovery."

Marisola was mad she just couldn't stop herself. "I can't understand why you even went to Joy in regards to Ashley in the first place. It's not like Ash ever asked to see you. Joy and her man weren't hurting for anything." Marisola was pushing buttons she knew were forbidden but the heat in her chest from the jealous rage had burst into a fiery flame. She was sick of the whole ordeal. She admitted she played along with Darrin and his shenanigans because she wanted him to be happy. However she too had needs. She hated to admit her glee about the dissipation of Ashley's commemoration into the family. She didn't think she could take looking at a child she knew Darrin Fathered with another woman. A woman she knew him to compare her to.

Marisola gritted her teeth at the smug look Darrin wore on his face. He didn't seem to be at all bothered about admitting his undying love for Joy, no matter how heartbroken she became in the process.

"I am going to leave, just as you asked." Darrin knew that his patience was growing thin. The very fact that he didn't have liquor on his breath saved her life. Turning his back he left, slamming the door behind him.

Sickened by Darrin's spiteful and hurtful remarks Marisola drifted her way into the master bedtime of her loves sweet. She was so frustrated. She knew that she could never be good enough for Darrin, not as long as Joy was still around. Sadly, she couldn't even blame Joy for Darrin's fascinations about reuniting with his first love. It was his own delusional mind that kept her from receiving all that she deserved from him. Marisola was desperate to show Darrin all that she was worth. She was deserving of love and she could no longer play second fiddle to his loves joy.

**\*\*\*\***

Darrin wasn't two blocks from his upscale condo before putting a call into Joy. She didn't answer as always. It worried him more in that he was afraid she blamed him for Ashley's death. He worried constantly that his relationship with Joy had completely dissipated. A friendship more than anything he wanted to be sure he kept in good standing. Pulling up to the bar he felt relieved to see the open lights flashing on the leather quilted door. With a sigh of relief he dropped his head back into his shoulders and bolted from his custom made 2012 Camaro and slammed his cars door.

# ~40~

# JOY

Joy jumped out of the driver's side of Justin's suburban and slammed the trucks door shut. She took in the view as she lifted her head towards the sky. She was in awe of nature's beauty. The change in scenery was long overdue. Joy felt a sense of peace. However her hopes disintegrated as the reality that Justin and the children, were not there waiting for her sunk in.

Joy inhaled the sweet smell of pine as she watched a few squirrels scurry up a tree and jump from branch to branch in play. She smiled at the thought of her children playing among the clouds. If only she had, had the chance to say goodbye, a small wish for peace of mind in perhaps a start towards healing her infected wounds.

Weeks had gone by and there was no sign of Lillian. Joy's belly had grown two sizes since leaving town. Her love for writing was slowly coming back to life. Nature was her most favorite place to be. The cabin in the hills was nice and warm, secluded from the city lights, smog and stress. There she felt she had finally started to cope with the loss of her family. She was happy to leave without a second glance. She hadn't heard from Sam and the children in over two months and for that she was grateful. She loved her sister, but the truth was she had never felt free. She was alone now in the world with an individual look and personality. At least in the hills of Merced County she was just plain ole Joy Anderson writer and convenient store owner.

The money wasn't an issue for her. It was just something she knew she had. Since Charles passing Joy thought about her nephew's a great deal. It wasn't Sam's fault that she was conniving. Joy set up a trust fund for the children and left the information in regards to the fund with Patrice. She was sure to send the check for her mortgage to the lending company so that the children had a place to live. She knew Justin would want the kids to be safe and cared for. She just couldn't bear dealing with her sister any longer. She would have to learn how to fend for herself.

Joy felt sorry for Sam and her loss, but she knew that with her current state of mind she could be of no real comfort to her. According to Lillian Sam wasn't to be trusted. Joy couldn't say she was wrong on that note because she had uncovered some truth to that notion. Rather than confront Sam on her inconsistency's she chose to flee the scene and try to get her life back in order. She knew that she could trust Nadine to take care of the business while she had her conference with God and his plans.

Patrice was just about the only person she could trust with monetary issues, so leaving the trust fund in her hands wasn't a concern. Patrice was controlling and old fashioned, but she wasn't money hungry, at least not in regards to bank accounts that were not related to her purse. She always said that to harp on others blessings is a waste of time and energy. It not only wastes your own worth and builds walls between you achieving your goals.

Joy dragged herself up the wooden steps to her cabin as she hauled the last bundle of firewood into the home. The summer months were like fall in the hills. The closer September came the colder the winds blew in. Joy plopped down in front of her fireplace and flipped through an old manuscript she had been working on since before the tragic storm. She finally decided to pull it out from the dust filled crates of storage to revisit the story line. She remembered how she used to read bits and pieces of her writing to Justin to get his opinion on things. She was often saddened that she didn't have him to bounce her ideas off of.

Plopping the manuscript down onto the coffee table Joy decided to take a break from her reading to ponder her plans for dinner. This too, was a task Joy would rather skip. She missed cooking dinner for her husband and children. She still found herself making entirely too much food for herself. Time after time Joy simply placed the remaining food into containers and took it down to the shelter when she went into town. Most of her work allowed for her to stay in the comforts of her own home.

The literary group back in town was doing well and her clients had since doubled. Joy decided that Nadine would do a wonderful job managing the company. She gave Nadine 24% of the shareholding vote and went on her merry way. Sam was out cold when she heard the news of Ghetto girl Nadine running the show. Sam said that she felt betrayed by Joy because she hadn't considered her for the position. After all she had just lost her husband and would need the supplemental income to help out with the expenses.

Lillian couldn't allow Joy to be sucked in any longer by Sam's manipulations. She chimed right in when Joy's wavering guilt was floating dangerously close to giving in to Sam's get rich quick scheme. The mortgage payment was more than enough help. Anything else would be up to Sam to take care of. Joy hadn't even stayed in town to say goodbye nor did she attend Charles' funeral. Sam thought that was the least she could do. She still blamed Joy for Charles' indiscretions with regards to their near sexual encounter. Sam believed or at least told herself that Joy manipulated Charles into fornicating with her by using her grief. Charles was just as good as Sam in manipulation. Joy couldn't contend with the two of them and their evil plots, but Lillian was one step ahead of the game each and every time.

By the time of Joy's departure from Oakland, she was conversing with Lillian about her every move. She had grown quite used to her new personality. She could count on her to be the heavy. She could remain sweet ole Joy in her eyes and let Lillian tend to all the dirty work. After all Joy and Lillian were two different people, they just shared the same bodily inhabitance.

Joy took off her work boots and set them down by her front door. She cleared the kitchen table of all her work and set her papers on to the computer desk in the living room. Exhaling loudly she blew the tendril from tickling her eyebrow as she canvased the area for edible treats. It hadn't dawned on her that perhaps she should go into town to pick up some groceries. An occasional visit to her store wouldn't be a bad idea since she was the owner.

Joy plopped down to the couch to reflect on her day. Her idea for dinner hadn't conjured up much of a creative meal a simple television dinner would suffice. Joy took comfort in the familiar smell of her husbands oversized lounge shirts it was just about all she could wear since the swell of her belly was overwhelming. Breathing was a task and as the minutes of the day went by Joy's prayers became a repetition of hopes towards having the children soon. She was begging for relief the heartburn was too much for her to bear as her gas was ghastly. Other times when the symptoms of pregnancy weren't hovering over her like a dark cloud, the feelings of loneliness and despair took its place. She missed her children and the love of her life. She couldn't imagine raising the children alone nor could she smile about her gift without harboring some feelings of guilt. She could barely stand to feel the presence of life in her belly. The indication of life living inside her made taste buds her sour. She longed for a family and pleaded with God to bring her loved ones back.

Feeling a faint chill of winter creep along her back, Joy wrapped tightly in her husband's down blanket. She felt closer to him that way. Flipping through the pages of her journal she jotted down the events of her day. She wrote to him daily. "Today was cold." she began and scribbled the words out from existence till close to putting holes in her paper. She started again uncertain of her thoughts. "I miss you." Joy paused and meditated on her words. Angry she threw her pen and pad across the room and began to scream. She was torn upset at her recent visit with Darrin. She felt as though she had cheated on Justin just by being in the same room. Possibly because now her thoughts began to wonder, she yearned for the touch of a man, one that loved her and would show her how deep his love was for her physically. Her hormones were raging and lately she felt big as two homes and unattractive. Getting around was beginning to be a bother and her trips to the convenient store were few.

# ~41~

## SAM

Sam was sick to her stomach with worry. All she could think about was whether the insurance company was going to clear the check for Charles' life insurance policy within the next week. Mike's bankroll lasted for the first few weeks but if drug lords weren't calling in to strike a deal with Mike the crocked bounty hunter neither was she. Sam was definitely in it for the money. After all she too had dreams and four mouths to feed. It was clear to Mike himself that his relationship with Sam was for monetary gain, but still he loved her. Guilt of Sam's wrongdoing only chimed in with pennies began to dwindle. Her over-zealous spending was taking a toll on Mike's pockets. She knew as much because he was beginning to slack up on his duties as her mate.

Sam walked down the road to Joy's condo and took a peak into the window. She searched her purse for the spare key she had made, while assisting her with the move in. Sam quickly unlocked the door bolted in slamming and locking the door behind her. She was sure someone was following her. Being downright vindictive was not her forte. She could be nasty and money hungry, but this was an all-time low.

Sam threw her large, "Bebe." Satchel on to the couch and ventured off into the bar area of the kitchen to search for a drink. She knew her sister well. There was no way she would be on empty in the wine and beverage area. Joy barely ate but she could drink. She drank like the end of the world was the following day, every day.

Sam found a nice bottle of wine and tall glass, she popped a few cubes of ice into her cup and went in search for a bottle opener, "Damn girl, you got a blender, top of the line cocktail shakers, shot glasses, but where is the damn corkscrew?" Sam began to get agitated bout the bottle. She felt the anger boiling in her chest once more. Unable to control her lashing of fury she broke the tip of the bottle against the thick marble counter top next to the sink. Sam laughed as she pour and rinsed off the small pieces of glass from the bottle, "Oh well." Sam sniffed as she looked down at Joy's staining countertop. "Someone should really clean that up!"

Sam peered into Joy's stainless steel Refrigerator and pointed her glass onto her reflection, "Cheers, to you girl." Sam rose her glass and took a long swig. After nearly choking on her beverage she threw the remnants of the expensive wine down the sink and ventured off to look through the files in Joy's office. She was sure that something was lying around, a bank statement/credit card or maybe the information on the house.

Joy's home was nearly finished. After the storm the insurance nearly covered the damages. Joy didn't have to take out a loan or anything to pay the portion uncovered by her insurance company. The insurance for the boys and Justin was more than enough to cover her living expenses for at least five years. If she had decided to do absolutely nothing she could. As Sam was completing her survey of monetary delight, she grew fierce with envy. She was hurt and cut deep to the core by Charles' death and his involvement with Joy. Although Joy told her the circumstances behind their passionate kiss, Sam felt as though both Joy and Charles thought she must have fallen off of the yellow bus. She could see Charles manipulating the situation, but she couldn't fathom Joy's inability to recognize Charles was not her dead husband Justin. Charles' time with loan sharks had run out and he was desperate to claim the million dollar check for Joy's company. Charles was a fool to have brought the check to her attention in the first place, a check for a million dollars without a name.

Sam felt that Joy had sunk to a low that she would never have expected from Joy. Mrs. Goody two shoes was actually giving her a run for her money. Charles she knew to be a bit of a hoe, but never with her flesh and blood.

Sam searched Joy's condo for anything she could use against her in obtaining the rights of her business. Once she could prove her inability to run the company she would force Nadine out. She still couldn't believe that Joy skipped town and left ghetto mouthed Nadine in charge of millions of dollars. Joy had truly lost her mind and she was going to see to it that the state saw things her way.

Charles left her with a sour taste in her mouth as well. The only good thing to come of his life and death was his insurance policy. The fact that he owed money vanished as well. Mike had come in handy, a chance meeting that left dollar signs dancing in her twinkling eyes. Soon his job would be complete and she would need to find a way to get rid of him as well. It wasn't in her nature to be tied down. The children were burden enough, she loved them but didn't know exactly have the maternal instinct needed to properly care for them.

# ~42~

## PATRICE

Patrice folded her linens carefully and placed them gently into the closet. She felt weary that evening. Her mind drifted to her son, she was in such great pain. She often thought about Joy's words. Joy had been so faithful and loyal to Justin she wondered why she ever had doubts about her motives. She realized she was over bearing. She just wanted the best for her son.

Thoughts hovered like a cloud over her small space. Her mind was filled with unanswered questions. She didn't know what lesson God had in store but she had to admit that lately she neglected His presence. She questioned God and his motives about taking her son and grandchildren. She cursed Him further about Joy and her moments of insanity. The accusations whispered into her ear nightly. Crazy as the notion she hoped Joy's outlandish plights were true.

What if Justin had found refuge during the storm? She would be so elated. A glimpse of hope spun her into hysterics tears welled into her eyes as reality resurfaced. She would surly ask Mike to search for Justin and the boys she knew the likes of them surviving was second to none. She didn't want to waste the time she had with Mike, chasing false hope. She would however look to see if he could put an alert out for Joy, looking for her would be enough waste miles time asking him to locate a woman he had never met was enough. She just wanted Joy home safely. She needed all the help she could get raising a new born and suffering from such grief, Post-Partum was inevitable.

Patrice smiled at the thought of Mike's return it had been at least four years since she'd seen her son. She took pride in both her son's accomplishments but just had constant worry over her brow, as he was always away. She couldn't wait to him but dreaded it just the same. She knew she would have to break the news about Justin and Charles.

Mike drove up the long driveway to his mom's home. He was anxious to tell her about his engagement. She hadn't met Sam but only because of how critical she was about the lady's he dated. Of course his life style was a complete blur to her as well. He couldn't possibly let her find out that he was a common thug. He was bounty hunter. His mother loved that her son was on the hunt for the criminals of the land. She always bragged about her son at her bingo games, often stating to the women that her son had put an end to their son's foolishness.

Mike bounced out of his pimped out Suburban and jogged up the walkway to meet his mom for breakfast. He could smell the eggs and bacon from the front porch. He was nervous about telling her about Sam. He felt guilty about how much in love he was with another man's wife and children, but he kept telling himself that it was the life he chose. Only he knew the rules. What goes around comes around. He believed highly in karma. The thought of his happiness with Sam depleting kept him on edge and it was beginning to affect his day job. He was a bounty hunter, by law, but in reality he was a thug among many. Ruthless as ever collecting bribes from the hunted, his riches came from his catch.

His selective memory paid for his mom's fancy country home and his penthouse suite. Things he couldn't bear to risk. Sam also benefited from his riches and he knew full well why he was still in good standing. Though he enjoyed the money however, he wished he could drift away from the drugs and gambling. He made a pretty good living off of his bounties and he wouldn't mind settling down and having a child or two of his own. Sam already had children four boys to be exact that he loved, but they lacked one thing. His blood, he yearned for that type of connection with Sam and prayed for God's forgiveness after having killed the father of her son's. He worried what would come of him if they ever found out. He dreamed of his murder often.

Walking up to his Mother's door he breathed in deep. He was almost 31 years old and he was still frightful of his mother's wrath. How she would react to him proposing marriage before she had the chance to interrogate her would be the topic of the conversation he was sure. Exhaling and wiping his hands on the front of his creased jeans he opened the screen.

"Mom." Mike yelled through the entrance of the home. He walked quietly tip toeing about. He wanted to surprise her with the bouquet of yellow roses he held behind his back.

"Well if it isn't my adopted son Mike. Mike, what took you so long to get here breakfast is nearly cold?" Patrice stepped close to her son and grabbed hold to his overgrown shoulders as she held him tight and long. She had longed to see him and had wondered how she was going to share the news about his brother. He was out of town during the storm and with the constant traveling his job required she could hardly keep up with him. "Come and sit down." Patrice managed to speak after swallowing the lump in her throat.

Mike handed his mother the roses and stepped a long side her trailing her path to the kitchen. Patrice was quiet. Mike took comfort in her calm tone he thought it may be fitting to speak to her about the matters of his heart while she was in good spirits.

"Mike." Patrice stopped in her tracks just in front of the breakfast nook in the kitchen. "I have some unfortunate news to tell you." Patrice smiled crookedly as she handed Mike a plate. Mike looked worried but now very anxious to tell his news as he could feel the mood souring.

Panicking Mike blurted his news just as Patrice spewed hers.

"I'm getting married."

"Your brother is dead."

Patrice stopped and stared at Mike as his brow folded with disbelief. Justin was Mike's adopted brother but he was blood in his eyes. They had, had a wonderful relationship up until he decided to become a bounty hunter. Justin wanted him to go into the design business with him but Mike knew he was more brawn than the artsy type. Justin was a trendsetter. Mike was the muscle. Justin had always thought that the two elements would make for an excellent business but Mike always held the fact that he was adopted in the back of his mind. It stifled his growth really. He couldn't see how a family could embrace an outsider so willingly and treat them like he was their own.

Still stunned at the news Mike dropped his plate on to the counter top and Patrice lowered her head. She couldn't imagine her son getting married to anyone. She was being selfish in her thoughts she knew but Mike was all she had left. She hadn't heard from Joy and that was bothering her as well. She wondered how she was doing and how her pregnancy was going. She loved Joy and she missed her. It was her conniving sister, Sam she could do without. Snapping out of her rage and disgust she decided to put her issues aside to comfort her son.

Mike was still staring at the tile floor of the kitchen. He didn't move. He didn't blink. He didn't cry. It was as if he were lost in translation. His heart was broken and in that very moment payback had hit him as hard as a ton of bricks. Mike bit his lip and looked into the face of his mother.

"I don't know what to say or what to do now, he was all I had aside from you, Mom." Mike tried to hold back tears. He hadn't cried since his biological mother was killed by his own father. He was used to tragedy but recently he had grown to love normality at least in his neck of the woods. Mike had somehow become immune to the facets of his job. He left the drugs, gambling and murder at the door when in the presence of his loved ones.

"We have each other." Patrice responded solemnly. "There's more."

Mike looked into the face of his mother and thought he would faint in the middle of the floor. His knees were so weak he thought that he would surely die if she told him that she was ill as well. "What is it mom? Just say it please."

"It's about your cousin, Justin's business partner."

"I'm not sure who that is I never met him."

"Oh you remember little Chucky. He used to come and play with you and Justin when you were boys."

Mikes brain continued to draw a blank. He looked about the kitchen and hallway for clues but the loss of his brother seemed to cover all of his memories. The pain was beginning to stifle his breathing. He was no longer interested in speaking to her about the matter.

"It was so long ago. I can understand if you don't remember you were about five years old. He and his mother moved away when he was eight so it's alright. I...." Patrice paused as she was afraid to continue. She had already upset Mike, but she couldn't see herself keeping anything from her children. She never had. "He was killed a few weeks after Justin died in the storm."

"What?" Mike lifted his head in disbelief. He was beginning to blame himself for all the hurt and pain his mother had suffered in the last few months. Playing the name back and forth in his brain he couldn't recollect who Chucky was. Mike's forehead held its crease as he placed a hand on his chin.

"Chucky, Chucky, Chucky." Mike repeated trying to jog his memory.

"Charles honey, his name was Charles, Charles Richardson."

Mike's breathing staggered, as he choked on his eggs. In a panic he grabbed his glass of milk and guzzled it down without coming up for air. Mike was so sick to his stomach he could feel the eggs and milk coming up his throat, but he quickly swallowed them down. He looked at his mom for fear she could see the guilt of what he had done all over his face. Visions of the night outside the bar played back. He could see Charles laughing at him as he threw the bar stool at him when he demanded the money for his gambling debt. He saw Charles in the rain on his knees and he could still smell the gun powder on his hands after viscously pulling the trigger, cowardly kill, shooting a man with his back turned. Mike nearly melted to the floor with guilt. He was in so much pain that he didn't know where to turn.

Patrice watched closely to Mike and his near death experience. She cleared her throat and began to tidy up his eating area. "I hope you are alright." Patrice blankly stated. Mike simply nodded. He had no words for his dastardly actions and without an excuse.

"So about this girl you are planning to marry, who is she? What's her name?"

Mike drifted deep into a depressive state of mind as he realized Sam was Charles' wife, the wife of his adopted cousin. He looked about the room looking for a name that he could supply his mother and an excuse to excuse himself from the room.

"Hello." Patrice called out to Mike. He was dazed and confused.

"I'm sorry mom. I guess I don't feel much up to discussing a marriage right now. I was hoping to have my brother standing by my side as my best man. I am sad that I haven't been around much. I am realizing now that I don't know anything about his life. I have missed so much."

"Well you are here now. I am so glad you are home. He was married and had two boys and his step-daughter Ashley they were all killed in the storm. Joy his wife has been missing for about four weeks now. She is pregnant with Justin's child and I am so worried about her. She was a sweet girl and she loved Justin more than anything. She took his death very hard, suffered a mental breakdown and was hospitalized for some time. I wondered if you could find her. That is if you could fit me into your busy schedule."

Mike looked up and sighed with relief. He was used to his mother prying further when he refused to explain himself. Locating someone for her was the least he could do. "I would be honored Mom. I would love to meet his wife as well and my niece or nephew." Mike cleared his throat and searched for a reason to exit. His mind raced and his ears burned. He would be sure to adhere to his mother's wishes. Locating Joy was the least he could do. Mike was filled with frustration. He had taken rides on plenty roads so dangerous there was no need for a seatbelt, death would come easy, but never had his heart been involved. Sam had played him for a fool and he was now willing to play the game, but by his rules and his rules alone.

# ~43~

# MIKE

Mike grabbed hold of his composure and adjusted his pants he tucked his gun into the back of his jeans and pulled his polo over to conceal his weapon. Jumping into his Suburban he buckled up and set his sights on touring some of his brother's architecture in the city. He thought perhaps to visit his office and take and look into Joy's company. Passing through town past old hangouts he inhaled the smell of the city and couldn't help but smile.

"So this is what you've been up too big bro." Mike chuckled to himself as he was in awe of his Brother's design. Justin had designed just about every office building and a five star hotel for upper class merchants in San Francisco. He was anxious to find out about the happenings of his business. Perhaps he could shine some shoes and clean up his act a bit. Justin would have wanted him to at least ensure his wife and mother, were well taken care of. Mike was sure the fish were biting hard. With Charles the board members must be chattering amongst the buyers.

Mike looked down at his navigational system to be sure he and his guide were on the right track. Patrice made sure to give Mike all the information about Joy she could remember. She did however neglect to mention one very crucial part of the matter that may be of some good to Mike, but she wouldn't dare suggest Mike question Sam. She was a dangerous poisonous snake and she couldn't risk

Sam slithering about trying to seduce her son. After all he was all she had left.

The fact that Joy and Sam were twins could be very helpful. The fact that she was a heartless Bitch may have helped as well. Still Patrice couldn't bear to even mention Sam's name without gurgling vomit.

Mike pulled up to Justin's office building and just sat there. He couldn't believe his brother was gone. Justin had always hoped the two of them could go into business together, but Mike knew it wasn't the life for him.

"You did good bro. You did good, real good. I am going to do my best to locate your wife and child." Mike buried his head down into the steering wheel as the tears began to blur his vision. He wiped his face quick and in a hurry realizing he was still in public. Never would he dare to show weakness while prying eyes were around. He looked over his shoulder constantly. Fear began to grow in his heart. Mike knew that any thug's day was numbered and lately his conscience tugged at the matters of his heart. Killing Charles he had to admit was his worse kill even before he found out he was family.

Mike questioned Sam's knowledge of it all at that point. He knew Sam was all about money. Her lifestyle was Prada and Lu Viton purchases on a fly by night Beautician's salary. Sam was nervous as all get out and as ruthless as ever. Ends weren't meeting and waiting on Charles to get the promotion was aging her literally.

Mike pulled his keys from the ignition. He wanted to go in and check things out, but he couldn't get his legs to move. He thought further on the matter of Charles and his place in the company. It dawned on him that Charles may have been just as trifling as Sam. He couldn't figure out who was pulling the strings although it was obviously Sam. After all she was still standing. Firing up the engine on the luxury car he sped off to take a look at Joy's place of business. At least there someone could perhaps answer some questions about her whereabouts.

Speeding down the quiet streets of Frisco was a first from what he could remember. It was Saturday so the business strip was mild in traffic, but plenty folk walking the outside malls and cafes. Stopping short of a light he noticed the buildings unique shape and silver logo just in front lined with crystals that resembled sparkling diamonds. Mike laughed to himself.

"Them can't be real diamonds or crystals blood, this woman must be finer than wine." Mike chuckled.

Pulling up to Joy's office building, He just about ran into the car in front of him when he noticed Sam walking up towards the entrance doors.

"What the fuck is she doing here?" Mike thought. Sam looked over her shoulder and back towards where his car was parked he quickly slid down his seat afraid she would see him.

Mike had to get to the bottom of Sam's visit to Joy's office what business would she have there? Mike at first thought to buckle out of his car and stop her dead in her tracks. After his visit with his mom he was furious with Sam and embarrassed of his own actions, embarrassed at his role in the entire fiasco made him feel as Bitch-made as they came. He vowed to change the scheme of things because he was ready to get out of the game and fall back for a spell, only now he couldn't trust Sam. The woman he was so willing to leave his cushy life and kill for, could possibly be the root of all evil. Mike thought about his new idea of freedom and family, but Sam wouldn't dare stay with a broke has-been. He would be next. Who knew her true motive?

# ~44~

# REMINISCE

Joy looked down at her cell phone to read the all so familiar number chiming in. She was happy to see that someone had cared for her enough to call and check in, but she could hardly stand the sight of Darrin. She knew in her heart that Ashley's death wasn't his fault, but the very fact that she was going to see him troubled her. It was a wonder she hadn't terminated the pregnancy. The guilt that weighed on her soul would have sent anyone into premature labor. Any reminder of her decision sent her back into depression. She was close to suicide often. Talking with therapists only angered her more. How could one speak on things that they had yet to experience?

Joy's mind wandered far off to a distant place, a time in her life when she could trust Darrin. Their relationship wasn't always bad. Getting pregnant wasn't in the cards, but neither was their breaking up or Darrin blowing his knee, which forfeited his chance in the NBA. The situation salted the relationship so much so, that Darrin took out his misfortune on Joy. He dropped out of school, but Joy stayed and seconds before graduation she found out she was with child. The occasional visits from her ex had left her struggling alone in the world. Hoping to embark on the career of her life it took a back seat until Ashley was able to go to school.

Still, things worked out. Things don't always go as planned. However this time she was glad that God stepped in and pulled rank. Joy and Darrin's break-up was nasty. He had cheated several times and had become verbally abusive. She didn't look back even when she found out she was pregnant. The relationship had gone sour as it was. It wasn't until three months she found out at any rate.

Joy herself couldn't believe how he acted. It was night and day with him caring and compassionate to evil and demented. Joy could remember the time when Darrin's love for her was genuine. His touch could simmer the heat of her burning eyes and lighten the mood when she was in her darkest of times. He was her first love, the love that set her mind to believe that it was possible to be loved and treated respectfully.

Only Darrin was human and as humans they all make mistakes. She was a handful she knew. She had a past that came back to haunt her in her dreams nightly and it killed Darrin to know that he couldn't heal her wounds. Joy was needy and had a fear of abandonment that drained the life out of Darrin. She trusted no one and no matter how hard he tried to make her happy he seemed to fall short.

Darrin could no longer live up to her demands of perfection. He pitied and envied Justin. He loved Joy just as much as the day he first laid eyes on her. He just couldn't take the challenge. Joy beat herself up about how hard she was on the people she loved. She felt like they would fail her sooner or later. So throwing up a wall she just assumed the worst in any given situation. Pushing people away was her claim to fame, an event she tried to shy away from, but her mind wouldn't let her. Her innocence had been stolen when she was a child and she vowed never to let anyone hurt her again.

When the dreams began to replay in her mind she regressed. It was a pitiful sight and it exhausted her to rebuild the trust she'd given away. She accused Darrin of happenings in her mind based on hear-say or misinterpretation. Lillian's first arrival in the mirror of his black and white marble bathroom, she denounced her existence. Though the visions played with such lucidity she could hardly stand the sight of Darrin. Joy's tongue was quick and hurtful, again Lillian stepping from inside Joy's conscious hoping to build Joy a backbone. By this time Darrin was staying out late at night drinking and returning without explanation. Joy couldn't handle the lashing Darrin spewed. He dribbled his drunken apologies and demanded she returned to bed. Only when Lillian peaked hell hath no fury. She was vengeful. The relationship turned physical and he welcomed her blows because apart of him hated her as well.

When Joy awoke from the fight Lillian and Darrin had, she wore the evidence of abuse. In these times she prayed. Her lapse of memory shunned the part she played in it all. Lillian was a figment of her imagination. She questioned God often, but her faith in him never wavered.

Lately Joy dreamed of Justin's voice. She longed to hear it once more. One word would do. She felt as though God had stolen him from her it just wasn't fair. To make matters worse Lillian had taken a sabbatical as well. She did so often after stirring the pot.

Joy was disillusioned about her life, the company and her unborn twins. The babies were just about the only thing she had to hold on to. She was lost in her emotions, still angered by Justin's family for calling off the search. She could only imagine the hurt and pain he must be feeling. Justin and Joy were so close they were far more than lovers. Justin was her best friend and without him she felt abandoned, close to tears with just the hardship of waking up in the morning. The empty space in her bed caused her depression to worsen. The pills Nurse Betty had given her were nearing the end. Though she couldn't say they were much help anymore.

Her writing did, however, blossom in that the heartache brought about stories of romance that she could ever imagine. Her journals were piled high on her Victorian desk nestled by a small fireplace. The cabin had been a Godsend. A quiet place she could go to find peace. The city was a constant reminder of her husband. Thoughts of him lost in the woods began to cloud her vision and dominate her thought process. She felt him. She could sense him out there somewhere looking for her, she just couldn't pinpoint where. Joy embraced her thoughts of finding Justin. She had yet to give up hope. The reality of him being gone forever was incredibly painful. Joy wondered how Justin would take the murder of Charles. She knew he could take it, but the loss of their daughter would just about kill him.

Joy looked deep into the burning flames of the fire as if lost in translation. The tears burned her retinas. The battle she fought to contain herself faulted. Unable to contain her flow of tears giving in to the pain she let them stream down her burning cheeks. Briefly she thought of Sam and the kids. She worried about how she was dealing with the loss of her husband. Joy could only imagine she herself was still suffering. According to Dr. Zimmerman her reality was out of sync. Doctor Zimmerman stated he felt as though she would never begin the healing process if she couldn't admit to his departure home. Joy smacked her lips and left his office on that note never to return. Betty and her experimental drugs took precedence. So far no life threatening side effects and the lung disease remained at bay.

## ~45~

## DARRIN'S DAMSEL IN DISTRESS

The entire time on the road Darrin thought about how stupid he was for coming after Joy. She hadn't answered any of his calls so it was evident she had no desires to see or hear from him. Still the worry in his belly wouldn't simmer, at least not until he was able to see her for himself.

Exiting the freeway the sun's glow was bright. He had since sobered since his drive out. Leaving the bar with such liberation he was determined to get to the bottom of his feelings for Joy. He needed to know if something was still there before giving up and moving forward with Marisola. She was right to want a man that was exclusive to her, but he could no longer lie to her about his feelings towards Joy. Every time he looked at the swell of Marisola's belly he was reminded of his daughter and how he wasn't a father to her. Now she was gone and he wasn't given a chance to make amends. Darrin couldn't be sure that he was just feeling guilty or he actually had unsolved feelings for her. Whatever the matter it was time to set things straight.

Darrin stopped at one of the café's on the strip of Joy's office building. He was sober but close to passing out from lack of sleep. He changed into a clean shirt and threw on his leather blazer before walking into the café. He always came prepared. It was the 'life of the streets' mentality he still held close to his heart. Darrin was never far from the hustle. He was still strapped, smoked weed heavily and drank like a fish. Somehow he remained forever on his toes. A true hustler he called himself. Leaving the game behind was the best decision he had made, it took the life of his brother of his brother to do so.

Stepping up onto the curb he adjusted his pants and walked briskly towards the café, he ordered impatiently and left without retrieving his change. He was anxious to see Joy. He couldn't waste time with greetings and such.

Darrin jogged down the street and into Joy's office building, he was anxious to surprise her. He had a few words for her ignoring his calls. He was worried and wouldn't be ignored no matter how angry she was with him.

Darrin popped out of the elevator with such force he nearly tripped over one of the receptionists.

"Joy's office please."

"To your right."

Darrin walked around the front desk and straight to the back office without first buzzing in. He was the only introduction he needed.

"I thought that was you, what brings you back over to the Northern Hemisphere?" Nadine spun around in Joy's seat with her legs crossed and hands folded. She was on cloud nine. Inheriting a seat in Joy's company hadn't swayed her from Joy's corner just given her a voice. She was arrogant as ever and much more protective of Joy and the company.

Darrin looked odd and nervous. His palms were sweaty, he had every intention to bust in and profess his love to Joy. Keep it short and simple and take the reaction as raw and uncut as it came and either head for the first exit or take her into his arms. He had no time for small chat. "I am doing ok."

"Those words don't quite fit the face. Are you alright?" Nadine switched her stance to her other leg and folded her arms across her chest.

"No. I'm not. I am worried about Joy. I didn't expect to see you here playing in her office either. Can you just tell me that everything is okay with Joy? She is ok right?" Nadine put her hand up in front of her to brace herself for the horrific news if need be.

"Oh no." Darrin interjected, his forehead was wrinkled and he was equally as confused, to see her reaction.

"No. I am here looking for Joy. I have something to say and I need to say it now. Please, help me find her. If I don't get this off of my chest I am afraid I will die."

Nadine calmed and made a long sigh of relief. She thought for sure he was there with bad news. Nadine pinched her lips and rolled her eyes. She knew all about Darrin and his fly by night way of parenting. Word on the street was that he was expecting a baby any day now from some Senorita down in the Los Angeles Mexico City district. Nadine couldn't wait for Darrin to finish pouring his heart out so that she could give him a piece of her mind. Yet again he was as selfish as he could be, showing no concern for Joy and her need to heal, but walking in like he was the knight and shining armor to profess a love that had long dissipated.

"Oh honey. Joy is long gone boo boo. What could you possibly want with her anyway?" Nadine put on her ghetto defense. Usually folk shied away immediately because she appeared ignorant and scary. She had on her 'I will cut you' voice and she stood with her hand on her blazer pocket like she was packing a razor blade for effect.

"Where did she go?" Darrin ignored her obvious protective tone. She must have forgotten he was from the streets of Compton born and breed.

Nadine humped her shoulders admitting her defeat and stared blankly towards the fountain in the center of the first floor lobby. "She is gone off on some retreat to gather her thoughts. I sure wish she had taken me along with. I realize that I have been with her in running this company from day one, but I am winded. Everyone is playing twenty questions about her state of mind and the future of this company."

Darrin had long stopped listening when Nadine said that she wasn't in town. All of the other, mambo jumbo was neither her or there. He needed to get to Joy immediately. "Nadine." Darrin interrupted her with his nose flared as if daring her to continue talking during his time to speak. "Where did she go? I need to speak with her."

"I am not at liberty to say. You know that, Darrin. She is off trying to settle the matters of her broken heart."

"I can mend that."

"That's funny I wasn't aware you were a factor. I don't think she wishes to be bothered, especially by you. Don't you have some, 'Chiquita Banana.' waiting for you back at home and a bambina on the way? It's bad enough she has lost her children, please don't start coming around rubbing your child in her face."

"First of all no one asked you to think. Secondly, I have no intention of hurting Joy. I love her. I always have. I am just sorry I allowed her to leave me and make a life without me. I am so proud of her success, but I won't just sit around and pretend as though I do not miss her and want her back."

"I can't get involved in this." Nadine said as she stepped back tucking her clipboard under her arm. She was looking for an exit from this uncomfortable conversation. She couldn't believe she was starting to feel sorry of Darrin. "Look." Nadine said as she backed her way into the elevator. "She's away in the mountains and you did not hear a word of that from me. I don't expect you to go out and find her anyhow. She is away working on some writing. At any rate as much as I need her home, I am not going to dare bother her with the matters of your visit, so she won't hear of this conversation from me, take care." Nadine watched Darrin with an evil eye as the doors of the elevator closed.

Darrin pouted a bit and turned on his heel in a flash. He was in a rush to get back to his car. He knew exactly where Joy had gone. "I bet dear old Justin thought he was the only one that knew about Joy's safe haven. The family cabin was her get away, but she hadn't always gone alone. Joy would never cheat on Justin, but she had, had a life before her knight and shining armor danced into the light. Darrin was envious of Justin. Not because Joy had actually married him, but because he knew that he could have walked her down the aisle just the same. He was just too cowardice to deal with the emotions of his recent bout with injury. He had the chance to provide everything he ever wanted for Joy and it had all gone to shit because of one foul move on a basketball court. "It is funny how life happens." Darrin chuckled sarcastically as he thought about his bullet riddled past. Both he and his mom thought he would surely die from gunshot wounds.

Sprinting back to his car he checked for a missed call from Marisola. Nothing yet, which meant he still had time to check on Joy without interruption. He knew if something were wrong Marisola and her mother would phone him right away.

# ~46~

# SHOWDOWN

"Sam." Nadine rolled her eyes. "Not again." she thought, my office is just raining with unexpected, unwanted guests. Nadine mugged Sam, as her eyebrows stood at attention.

"Nadine."

Nadine cleared her throat and swung her legs from behind her new desk. "I can't say I was expecting to see you here. I am sure you know Joy is out of town."

"That's correct. I'm not here to see Joy. I am here to relieve you. I know how you must feel. So overwhelmed with running a company you know absolutely nothing about. I'm sure Joy appreciates your standing in for her." Sam slapped the front of her jeans and smiled a fake smile to indicate just how sarcastic she was being on purpose. "You must be so confused. What you have maybe...a High School diploma, G.E.D., perhaps? You aren't qualified to take over my sister's company. Besides, we both know her mental state isn't at its best. Why else would she choose some old country ghettoized girl to act as the CEO of her establishment?

Nadine smiled at Sam's playful instigation. She was looking for a fight and she had come to the right place. Nadine knew that Sam too, was grieving, but she wasn't going to take any mess from Joy's identical foe.

"Look I realize you are in pain, so I am going to give you a pass. Why don't you go out, get your hair and nails done and do what you do best? You know the ole damsel in distress motif. I am right where I belong with my Bachelor of Science Degree in Business Management and minor in Art History. I can't say that I've seen or heard about any of your certifications. I think you should run along and play don't you? I wouldn't want you to get hurt."

"Hurt Nadine? I seriously doubt that. You do not want to try me on that one. I will be back, don't you worry about that. You may have my sister fooled, but I know that you are after her money and her business. I will be damned if I let you just come in and swindle your way into a seat that is rightfully mine." Sam grabbed her Coach hobo and turned on her heels nearly getting the heel of her stiletto stuck in the carpet in her attempt for a dramatic exit.

Sam was furious at Joy for not considering her to watch over the business. She had just lost her husband for God sakes. Sam felt as if she could use the work to pick up some of the slack on the mortgage and car payment. She had since given up on the hair salon for a while to get over the loss of her husband. Not to mention there were several incidences where she could have sworn she was being followed. She couldn't be sure, but the feeling of uneasiness never wavered. The suspicious cars pulling up alongside her vehicle and parked a few doors down from her home was enough to send her senses on alert.

Sure Joy sent the check for the mortgage every month, for that she felt grateful and belittled at the same time. She never got the check in her hand. Joy sent the payment directly to the company as if she couldn't be trusted to make the payments herself. Sam had every intention on calling Joy and giving her a piece of her mind in regards to her distrust, but she didn't want Joy to neglect to send the check due to something as petty as who gets to pay them. Her children were her priority for the first time in her young selfish life. Sam had always put her desires in front of the boys because she was the only female in the bunch. Well that was her take on things. She felt that she should be pampered and looked after. As if she hadn't given birth to the children. Charles was a stand in for normality. Sam loved Charles as best she could, she didn't truly love herself. She had a difficult time with self-worth, which ultimately caused her indiscretions in the years of Richardson Family Saga.

Sam stepped into the lobby of Joy's building and looked around at the architecture. It hurt her heart to see the art and design that both Charles and Justin put so much work into. The pain was overwhelming. Sam could feel the sting of tears itching, her retinas, as she read the dedication plaque on the wall. "To my darling wife and beautiful mother of my children, I built this building and designed its walls of eloquence to signify the love and uniqueness of you." Sam's eyes dried quick as she read the plaques signature over and over again. The heat filled her cheeks and burned her ears, as anger and resentment filled her heart.

Sam thought about how her salon could be a success and how Joy would have to make room for her glory and success. She was determined to get Joy to see just how big a factor she was. She couldn't help but feel as though Joy never took her seriously. As far as she could remember Joy never gave her the time of day when she wanted to discuss her plans of becoming an entrepreneur. She would smile and nod, but she wouldn't show true interest in any of her business ventures. Sam realized that a job of any kind would be hard with so many children, but Joy did it. Sam was tired of being made to feel as if she were less of a person because she got pregnant at a young age.

Sam jumped into the elevator as she gave the memorial plaque the middle finger and pressed for the bottom floor. She was anxious to get to her doctor's appointment. She was going for her first ultrasound of the baby. Sam smiled as she touched her swelling belly. She couldn't help but think that her being with child was a sign from Charles. She was so excited about having a final piece of him to carry along with her. She felt closer than ever to Charles. Sam's thoughts drifted to Joy once more as she thought about Joy with the twins on the way. She wasn't used to being away from Joy more than a few days and although she couldn't stand her at the present time, she yearned for her sisterly guidance on her pregnancy and welcomed the chance to sit in on her doctor's visits as well.

They were both alone, both husbands dying within a month apart what a tragic set of events. Sam's mind raced as she high tailed it through the dark parking lot to her car. She couldn't help but think there was something else behind her husband's murder. The police told her he was shot during an attempted robbery. They suspected him to be the victim of a car jacking, but the damn car was still in the parking lot. His keys were in his hand and all of his personal belongings remained on his person. Sam bit her lip. She froze just in front of her car before putting the key in to unlock the driver side door. "Wow!" Sam said to herself. Even the death of her husband sounds heroic and makes for a much better sob story. My husband was gunned down execution style in front of a gambling and titty bar. I wonder what that was all about.

Sam brushed off her curiosity and plopped down in her car. She was oddly exhausted in just the few moments she spent with Nadine. She couldn't be sure Nadine got her point nor did she seem to intimidate her. Nadine was the picture perfect example of turning nothing into something. Sam hadn't realized it before, but she was envious of Nadine as well. She was the better choice to run the company while Joy was away, but still she felt entitled to the position. After all blood is thicker than water so she thought.

It must be nice to just pack up and go. Joy just packed up her things, locked her home and drifted into the Garden of Eden. Her nature quest was a waste of time according to Sam. She didn't believe Joy was traveling to her cabin in Yosemite to regain her spark for writing anyhow. She knew Joy was in search for a family no matter how hard she pretended to come to terms with her loss.

Again, Sam couldn't imagine losing her boys. It was such a hurtful experience burying the children's Father. There were nights when she was unsure she would awake the next morning. None of what Joy was going through appeared to be out of the ordinary any longer. Sam felt as if she too were going crazy. The emotions of the pregnancy aided in her dive towards depression. Sam had long since stopped eating, but after Charles was murdered her size 3's and 4's swarmed her small withering frame.

Doing hair had always seemed to dumb down all the hustle and bustle of her life, but she was unable to go in and stand long hours at her work. Sam was tired of working under people, as a result her clients decided to try other stylists at the shop.

**** 

Nadine's call hadn't come at the best of times. She presently had no desire to return to the city. She was beginning to get used to the twigs crunching beneath her boots and the smell of pine. She could think clear, the water was fresh and people were a lot calmer. Nadine was right to be worried about her sister's motives. Joy knew full well that her accusations about Sam were more than warranted and quite accurate she just didn't care. As long as she paid the bills her guilt was at bay. There was only so much she could do. She couldn't bring Charles back no more than she could bring Justin. At least she still had her children.

Joy could admit the envy boiling deep in her belly. Her emotions fought about her glee and sadness towards her unborn seeds. Feeling guilty about the swell of her belly made her feel as though she were betraying her love for her children lost in the storm, she often feared that she would blame them for even existing.

# ~47~

## HOW SAM MET MIKE

Sam grabbed a pint of pineapple sherbet, raspberry sorbet and lemon custard. She was on an ice-cream binge, a family curse between her and her sister during hard times. The night hours were her worst. The guilt ate away at her soul. She missed Charles and she knew that her part in his untimely death would cause her great pain sooner or later. She believed heavily in Karma and the stars. As the children slept her thoughts wondered. She mourned the loss of her husband but she was frightfully dastardly about the happenings with him and Joy.

Sam pondered on her chance meeting with Mike. Something she regretted but couldn't stand to harbor on. Sam paused as her thoughts played. She closed the door of the stores freezer and slammed her grocery cart down the frozen foods isle.

"Excuse you." a tall buff man roared her way.

"Excuse you is right." Sam mimicked and continued on her way. The man stood still as he watched her leave. He knew exactly who Sam was and he was anxious to find out what she was up to these days. He couldn't believe his eyes. Mike thought that Sam was always the one that got away. In High School he cursed himself for his young and foolish ways. He just had to fit in with the other football players, dogging females and making out with the entire cheer squad.

They had a short fling in Los Angeles, while she was attending a hair show, but hadn't seen each other since. They were however, hot and heavy in online chat rooms and late night phone calls. Mike felt so sorry for Sam and her situation. His nose was so wide open he believed Sam's lies about the beatings drugs and not to mention the women her husband was sleeping with. Sam could have told Mike that the sky was red and he would have believed it.

Sam unpacked her shopping cart as she cursed the nerve of her overgrown stalker. Shaking her head back into reality, she anxiously paid for her groceries and she drove her bags to her car and popped the trunk.

"Need any help?" A man's voiced chimed into Sam's thoughts as she reached for one of her grocery bags.

"Umm." Sam responded unsure of the man intentions. "I'm married you know and I carry a gun." Sam tried to sound strong and fearless as she said the word gun.

"So do I." the man responded.

Sam smiled slightly, "So are you going to put these bags in the car or not. Mr. Mason." Sam teased as she jumped onto the passenger seat of Mikes black on black range rover. Mike threw the last bag in the car and jumped into the driver's seat.

Sam was lost in translation again thinking of Charles. The guilt kept her up at night. She and Mike were high school sweethearts. She had to admit, Mike was her first love, no matter how easy he was to take advantage of.

"I just needed the money is all." Sam kept saying to herself. The insurance was all she had left. Sam loved Charles, but manipulating Mike came easy. He was the same sad puppy just as he was in high school eager to please.

Sam was sick of waiting on Charles to win a seat at the dinner table. He was still waiting on his share of the company. He should have been on the board of directors, just as Justin promised. He was blood after all and his business partner. It was taking a century of Justin to pass the torch, or at least give Charles an equal slice of the pie.

When Justin passed, the entire company was awarded to Joy. Charles was left out cold, with a measly ten thousand dollar raise per year. To Sam, his slight increase was far from what he was owed. He should have held a seat on the board and shares in the company. Sam was vengeful when she found out that Charles wasn't one of the beneficiary's to the business. How could Joy possibly run both her own agency and Justin's design business? Sam wasn't going to stand idly by and allow her husband to be bought out. Joy would be easy to sway under duress. In the end Sam couldn't be sure that Joy would even allow Charles to keep his job based on her personal feelings for him.

Sam could bet money that Joy was just lying in wait, for a chance to punish Charles for mistreating her. She just couldn't help who she loved as she so told Joy often. Joy didn't believe a word Charles said and spoke uncanny about how Justin needed to be sure to protect himself and the company. She knew that they were family but Charles was a manipulative bastard. He was no stranger to cheating and he didn't mind hitting Sam either. He'd hit her quite a few times and was known around town for sexually harassing women.

Still she loved him but the lifestyle took precedence to all of her morals and values with regards to love and family. She never felt secure in any regard. The love for materials helped to curve her desire to be truly loved. Charles was busy with his newfound love for gambling. Between her and Charles the bills suffered. Sam's shopping sprees were cancelled. She went back to what she knew the hustle, at any cost.

Sam was quiet the entire drive back to her home. The guilt was eating her alive. She and Sam hadn't spoken for weeks. It was just as well they both were in great pain. Sam couldn't help but blame Joy for her misfortune. After all it would be completely out of character to admit things she was responsible for. Sam's eyes burned but she dare not show weakness in front of Mike his days were numbered as well she was nearly through with his presence.

## ~48~

# LOVE ME TO DEATH

Marisola was so pissed she slammed her fists into the mirror of the medicine cabinet. Smashing the glass, the door of the cabinet swung open there she was met with a remedy to her problems. She found the pill bottle glistening against the dim lighting, fascinatingly delicious and tempting rescue. Marisola thought about what could happen if she took the pills, but she was in great pain both physically and mentally. She would only take two of the Cytotec and a few Vicodin for the pain.

Marisola looked at her reflection in the mirror. She barely recognized herself. The tears streamed down and smeared her mascara over her blushing red cheeks. Her stomach hurt as it was filled with a nervous anxiety. She was tired of being hurt and ignored. Marisola thought if she could just get her labor to start Darrin would be forced to return home, from his drinking binge and tend to her and her needs. She was sick of playing second fiddle to Joy and her many issues.

Tossing the pills back and guzzling a half a cup of water, she smiled at her blossoming love and drifted to the nursery to wait for her man to return to her. Sitting in her baby's nursery she looked at the life she wanted to build with Darrin. She would be damned if Joy messed that up. Marisola scooted out of her over-sized lazy boy and walked about the condo. She was in deep thought. She was excited to see her new baby and worried at the same time. What if the baby didn't bring the two of them together? What if it only made Darrin run back to Joy to try and prove his love for her and their deceased daughter? The guilt was eating him alive. Sadly, she couldn't tell whether it was just the guilt of abandoning Joy when she was pregnant with Ashley or if he was still in love with her.

Marisola trotted into the kitchen to heat up a few pieces of pizza from the night before. She was famished. She wasn't two bites into her supersized late night snack before the contractions began to stifle her breathing. She wasn't at all prepared for the amount of pain she was enduring. Marisola began to panic as she thought that the pills may have possibly done something to her baby. Running towards the bedroom she retrieved her cell and placed a call to Darrin.

Marisola's blood pressure was beginning to rise with each call she made to Darrin. He wasn't picking up and she was beginning to grow more and more agitated by the moment. The baby had stopped moving and set off an alarm as well. Four phone calls later Marisola decided that the pain was too great, so she called her mother to come over.

Marisola by this time could barely make out words as soon as her mother picked up the line she let out a horrific scream for help and passed out. No time for much explanation Marisola's mother Theresa simply texted, "Emergency." in all caps to let Darrin know it was time to get to the hospital. Theresa was so nervous driving to meet Marisola at the hospital she could barely see straight. Running several stop lights and breaking nearly most of the rules of the road she grew furious wondering where Darrin had gone in the first place with her daughter so close to her due date. Theresa knew all too well how Darrin treated Marisola. She was always crying about how Darrin said this or that to her about Joy and his hope for some sort of reconciliation.

Theresa was busy planning her attack as soon as Darrin walked through the hospital doors. She was sure he would show up drunk dribbling his pathetic apologies. This time there would be nothing he could say to fix the mess he made of her daughter's life. He would pay dearly if something were to go wrong with Marisola and the baby.

Theresa pulled into the hospital parking lot haphazardly and ran towards the maternity wing. It was a wonder she remembered to put the car in park and grab her keys she was so nervous. It was her daughter's first pregnancy and her first grandchild, she was ecstatic.

Yelling for help as if she herself had brought Marisola into the emergency room she high tailed down the wings of the hospital looking for her daughter. By then her patience was thin and her English was turning into a Spanish whirlwind of terror. When one of the nurses approached her to tell her to calm down she immediately put her in her place in both English and Spanish.

"Where is my daughter? Her name is Marisola Santiago. Theresa stood still waiting for a reply.

"Yes, are you a relative of Ms. Santiago?"

"I am her mother."

"Right this way, we were able to get her stabilized for now. The cuts on her hands are severe and she was in a lot of pain. We gave her some meds to calm her in hopes it would aid in getting her blood pressure down. This is our biggest concern as far as the health of the baby. We are confident she will be having this baby today. We just need to be sure that she is stable enough to go through the birthing process. Other than that we will perform an emergency cesarean. Do you follow?"

"Yes but I am concerned about the cuts etc., what do you mean cuts? Was she attacked? Did she fall? I am extremely confused. When my daughter phoned she was frantic and simply yelled out for help. I assumed she was just in great pain from labor pains. This is my daughter's first pregnancy."

"Oh I see." The nurse practitioner looked down at her clipboard in search for a respectable way to ask her next question.

"Does your daughter have any mental problems? Was she having a hard time with the pregnancy, was she being abused by perhaps the father of the baby? Was she happy to be pregnant even?" The nurse looked onto the face of Marisola's mother. She was disgusted by her line of questioning and looked as though she were about to pounce on her. "I am sorry I have to ask these questions, but due to the nature of this case, I have to ask."

"Nature of the case, the girl is pregnant. Is there something you are not telling me? What happened?"

"Your daughter came in presenting signs of possible abuse, physical abuse to be exact, her hands, legs and feet were cut badly from broken glass in the home. We had an officer look over the place, while the medics tended to her wounds. Although we found nothing out of place we still feel as though something happened in the home. My guess is the father of the baby. I do also need to tell you that we found traces of medication that is used to induce labor. I didn't see in the chart where this medication was prescribed to Marisola. Her blood pressure was dangerously high for her and the baby so we will be keeping a close eye on that issue. "

Theresa stood in awe of what the nurse had to say about Marisola's case. In that very moment she knew that it was time for her to step in Marisola and the baby would be leaving the hospital with her. Darrin would just have to cut his losses because she was not willing to let Darrin upset or mistreat her daughter any longer.

Theresa was well aware of Marisola's issue with men, but her grandchild would not be a victim of such madness.   Theresa and the nurse stopped short of the entrance to Marisola's room. All of sudden Theresa afraid to go into the room, she couldn't be sure but she was certain that the nurse believed that either Marisola was attacked by Darrin or she did these things to herself. The medication use made absolute no sense to her. Why would she try to induce her own labor at home? More importantly where in the hell did she get the medication?

## ~49~

# TORCH

Darrin couldn't wait to see Joy. He had a bone to pick with her. He was worried sick and although he knew they weren't together and she owed him no explanation, he was still equally as worried. He considered himself a permanent fixture in her life with or without the presence of a bloodline.

Joy was presently sick to her stomach thinking about Ashley and her missing children and husband. She missed them dearly and wondered how she would face the folk at home. It was a constant worry and with Darrin phoning every five or so minutes she could hardly think. He was beginning to resemble that of a stalker. She knew it was just guilt eating away at his selfish soul. Joy knew better than to fall for Darrin's sentiments. She fell and she usually fell hard, only to find that he was lost in love with some other woman. He was a two faced gorilla the perfect depiction of a thoroughbred Gemini.

Joy took a walk around her cabin thinking about the times she had with her daughter. "My child gone at 12." Joy whispered to herself as she stroked a picture of her on her mantle above the fire. Joy stumbled back saddened by the thoughts of her daughter's passing. She tortured herself on the day's events. Trying to put the pieces together of how the crash came about and how fast she died. Joy became physically ill with thoughts of her daughter and the amount of pain she suffered during the crash.

Joy rubbed her face furiously. It burned as it became raw from her repeated self-mutilation. The pain of her constant scrubbing soothed her heart. She could forget about her emotional strain and concentrate on the burn of her skin. Joy stayed still for hours just staring at the many pictures of her family. She couldn't move, she was paralyzed by its view. Part of her was unsure she could move if she wanted. Her belly was big she would have to somehow roll over to her knees and pray her way to her feet.

The door of her oversized two-bedroom cabin cracked open and in it fell the trail of a pair of size fifteens. He cleared his throat, but the silence remained still. Joy was fully aware of her company, but she was so much in daze she couldn't lift her eyes from her delusion. She often found comfort in her memories. However lately, as her thoughts wavered to her return to the city, where her life ended, the memories were a blur. The sadness weighed heavy and she barely ate.

Darrin walked in quietly unannounced, partly to surprise Joy, but also to prepare himself for the worse. He was worried about her as usual, but this time he decided to place action behind his words. Marisola was devastated about his departure, but she couldn't keep him there if she wanted. She knew him well and though he may have said he was going to get a drink, Joy could easily sway him to the Northern parts of California with one phone call.

Darrin could be a horrible person. The very reason why he and Joy's relationship dissipated so many years before, why he bothered as of late was a great mystery to her. However she was so lost in her own emotions. She was too lost to pay attention to Darrin and his issues.

"Joy." Darrin called out lurking about what seemed to be an abandoned cabin.

Joy didn't speak. She didn't ask for help. She barely breathed. Darrin made his way to the top of the stairs and looked down the hall. It seemed to last for miles. All he could see was a shadow of a pregnant woman slumped over in the hall. Darrin ran down the hall as soon as his brain fully registered that Joy was on the floor. He didn't know whether she had fallen or simply had a breakdown. Rushing to her side he fell to his knees just beside her. He grabbed her up into his arms and picked her up. Joy fell softly into his arms.

"Why do you do this to me?" Darrin whispered. He was so in love with Joy he couldn't stand it. He couldn't stand his place in the manner. A position he signed up for. He couldn't abandon Joy even after their break-up. He was her guardian angel. If she fell he would always be there to pick her up. His back was worn, but he didn't care much. Not until the responsibilities of his life knocked him out on his ass. Marisola was his soon to be wife. He did love her and she fit his needs of companionship, but she was too easy. He could walk out and she would throw a vase or lamp, cry and stomp about, but that was the worse it got. He was never fearful of her leaving. Darrin knew it was wrong of him to think of this small fact to be an upper hand. He knew that Marisola loved him more than anything, but he couldn't give his complete heart to her. He had only loved one woman in his life and she was lying right next to him.

Joy snuggled closer to Darrin and smiled slightly. She was dreaming again. Justin had come home and she was back into the fold of his arms. Nothing would come in between them again. She vowed to be honest about every facet of her life. She swore by the swell of her belly. They had another chance to be parents. Joy's throat became dry and the lump that began to form started to choke her. Abruptly she was shaken back into reality. As if startled by her whereabouts she sat up suddenly gasping for air. Darrin arose shocked and afraid that something was going on with her pregnancy.

"Joy is something wrong?"

"No, I just think that you should go. I know you were concerned about me, but you shouldn't have come."

"I was worried about you. You didn't answer any of my phone calls so I came." Darrin grabbed hold to Joy's shoulders desperately fighting the urge to take her in his arms and have his way with her. The swell of her belly enticed him further. He never got a chance to see her pregnant with Ashley. Somehow seeing her in her present state caused his mind to drift. He daydreamed about the baby in her tummy. He thought about what she was having and secretly wished that she was carrying his son. Thoughts of Marisola played as well. His reality was waiting for him back in Los Angeles. How he could leave a woman that so desperately wanted to make a life with him puzzled even him. He knew how Joy's mind worked and how demanding she was. He could never satisfy her, but he knew in his heart that he could spend the rest of his life trying.

Joy sat up and stared Darrin down. She wasn't impressed. She just wanted him to leave her be.

Darrin was angry by Joy's nonchalance. He was pouring his heart out and it was though she was stone, her face numb and her touch cold.

"I'm getting married, Joy. She is pregnant also due any minute now. I just couldn't go through with everything without at least telling you how much I still loved you. I know I messed up, but I have never stopped loving you. I need you. We need each other. I am worried about you and your pregnancy. Sitting out here in this cabin isolated from civilization what if something happens to you. The medics would have hell getting out here to you."

Joy's eyes burned. She was near tears. Her belly was tight from stretching beyond her arms reach. She was hurt by Darrin having this baby with a woman she knew

~ 331 ~

nothing about. The events of their conversation played back when he asked for Ashley to come down to Los Angeles and stay with him in the first place. He was going to have that woman around her daughter without her knowledge or her permission. She could only imagine how uncomfortable Ash would have been. Meeting his whore of a girlfriend, not to mention the fact that she was pregnant and her own father abandoned her. It was a complete slap in the face really. "How dare you." Joy snapped into rage.

Darrin's phone rang for the fifth time. He purposely had it on vibrate. "Damn it, what now?" he thought as he slide it from his jean pocket to take a glance. A text that said, "EMERGENCY." spread across his big face touchscreen. Darrin ignored Joy's outburst and immediately pulled his phone into plain view.

"Shit! Joy I have to take this call it's about Marisola."

Joy looked as if she were in a daze feeling both abandoned and ashamed at the same time. She couldn't place her irritation with this miscellaneous woman but it was definitely penetrating a nerve.

"No problem its fine, handle your business, we have no ties." Joy rolled over and scooted towards the edge of the bed to gather her composure. She was on edge and confident her feelings were much too strong for Darrin at this point. Chalking her feelings to mere emotions of pregnancy she ran her fingers through her hair and jumped to her feet.

"Go to her, she needs you." Joy turned her back as she knew tears that she could not explain stung her eyes. She folded her hands above her belly and smiled as her children danced in her belly.

Darrin got up slow and stopped just behind her. She closed her eyes. She wanted him to take her and make love to her, but she knew that the feelings she was having were for Justin.  Darrin raised his hands and placed them gently on Joy's shoulders.

"I am sorry for everything Joy. I need you to know that. I need you to forgive me. I still love you very much. I just want to do right by you."

"Then leave." Joy said as strong as she could muster acknowledging she was close to a breakdown.

Darrin spun around fast and sped from the room. He wanted to stay with Joy to make things right but he couldn't help but replay the text message that read, "EMERGENCY." on his phone. When Darrin got to the airport he tried to phone Theresa four or five times, but there was still no answer. Darrin walked down the winding path to catch a trolley to Yosemite Village there he flagged down a taxi to escort him to the airport. He couldn't bear to leave his car parked at some airport. After all, his car was his right hand man.

# ~50~

## LIFE AND DEATH

Darrin bolted into the doors of the Los Angeles county hospital nearly falling head first into the glass doors. He was nervous and excited about the arrival of his new baby girl. Pressing the elevator buttons frantically he jogged in place as he wiped the sweat from his palms. His overgrown hands were full, hoarding stuffed animals and a bouquet of flowers for Marisola. He was excited to see his little girl. He had hoped for a caramel complexion, green eyes and coffee colored hair. A perfect mix to his brown skinned Chicana and his African American heritage.

However he was nervous about the nature of the call, "EMERGENCY." in all caps made his stomach quiver. He hopped on the first thing smoking leaving his precious car with Joy. Another argument full of excuses and explanations he was surely in for.

Darrin couldn't bear to tell Joy about Marisola and his new baby after Ashley had passed. She just wasn't the same, but who could blame her. Though, he knew that it was the right thing to do. She seldom returned his calls and according to Sam she had lost her mind completely. The last thing Darrin wanted to do was make things worse. He cared for Joy deeply, but time was running out. Little Tatiana would be born shortly.

The fact that she pretended as though the feelings they once had for one another were completely gone disappointed him. He loved Marisola, yes. At least that is what he kept saying to himself. However he couldn't help how he felt when he entered into the same room as Joy. Somehow seeing her pregnant, her full breasts and bright skin tone left him in a daze. He had to refrain from taking her whether she wanted him or not.

Darrin felt guilty as ever. Hoarding his love from Marisola he harvested dreams of reuniting with Joy. It was for not. He knew it to be true. He was making steps to move forward with his life but he also knew that it would be hard to let go of Joy completely.

Upon Ashley's arrival he and Marisola had plans to sit Ashley down and talk to her about the new baby. He couldn't wait to share with her the news and how wonderful it would be for her to be a big sister. Darrin hung his head as his thoughts drifted to Ashley. He often wondered if she suffered great pain during the accident. He was selfish to think that if she hadn't stopped to save another would she have perished during the storm.

"My daughter the hero." Darrin whispered ringing the neck of one of the stuffed bears he brought for his daughters arrival. The tension and guilt was so thick he could hardly stand it. He too, questioned his sanity at times. Mulling over the same issues soured his spirits. The very fact that he was lost in love with another woman while waiting on his child to be born from another was trifling enough. The hurt was devastating. He realized that his anguish was based on fear. He ran down a list faults and failure he held close in regards to Ashley.

He and Joy's break up was bitter he thought it best to simply stay away. He had to admit that he blamed Justin for many of their arguments. He was sure Justin was behind

Ashley's sore attitude towards him. Inside he knew that wasn't true. Ashley was an old spirit. She had a sassy, straight forward mind of her own, often calling others out for their mischievous acts. He just wasn't ready to be a father. Quite frankly he still wasn't sure.

Darrin took a deep breath as the doors of the elevator slowly screeched open. His eyes brightened and filled with tears before he could get close to the nurse's station. The birthing center was busy as usual nurses flying up and down the corridor with their badges and clipboards flying in the wind.

The screams of horror resounded as his Timberlands smacked the waxed floors of the hospital. It was a scary walk to the nurse's station. Announcement balloons and solemn husbands filled the hall. Darrin shook his head as he bit his lip in an effort to keep from laughing out loud.

As Darrin plopped his goods onto the counter of the reception desk he heard a familiar voice followed by a scream for help. It was Marisola, screaming at the top of her lungs. She was complaining of pressure and pain in her lower abdomen.

"Help I am bleeding, please help."

Darrin was startled at the very mention of blood. Without a second thought Darrin zoomed towards the horrific screams leaving his welcome home baby package behind. His chest was heaving visibly threw his Roca wear shirt as he panted approaching the bedside.

Theresa was screaming trying to push her way past the attending nurse. Darrin shook the shock from his weary shoulders and grabbed Theresa trying to calm her still. Unable to subdue her, Darrin blacked out completely zoning as if he were standing on a live movie set. Theresa fell to her knees begging the nursing staff and doctors to help her daughter.

The alarm buzzed and cold blue was announced throughout the maternity wing. Darrin froze as he couldn't believe what was happening. He couldn't bear the possibility of losing Marisola and the baby. His knees grew weak and his stomach dropped at least two or three floors.

Nurses filled his path instantaneously pushing him aside as Marisola began to seize Darrin was afraid. He didn't know what was happening. The Dr. ordered the nurse to prep Marisola.

"What the FUCK is going on?" Darrin finally chimed in. "Is she going to be okay, what about my daughter?"

"Sir, please calm down or I am going to have to ask you to leave. The baby is my priority." he exclaimed.

Darrin set out a loud sound of anguish as he searched for words that would indicate his demand for attention. One of the nurses noticed his plea and asked Darrin to come with her to the waiting area until they were able to stabilize Marisola.

Darrin refused, panting heavily trying to catch his breath as he noticed the desperation surrounding Marisola.

"She's hemorrhaging." the nurse yelped.

The doctor called for a crash cart. Darrin couldn't believe his eyes as he watched Marisola's chest rise from the heat of the machines jolt. He saw her soul pass. He was in complete denial as the machine chimed in a flat line. The Dr. called the time of death as he called for his surgical knife.

"What's happening Darrin yelled at the doctor's and nurse's all attending to Marisola. They were whispering directions one another's way as they worked diligently. There was no response to Darrin's inquiries. The Dr. began to cut Marisola's stomach. He quickly grabbed Tatiana from Marisola's belly and cut the umbilical cord. Tapping and suctioning the baby, the doctor's and nurse's waited for signs of life.

Darrin and Theresa's eyes filled with tears as they too waited earnestly for a miracle. Just as Darrin was nearing his breaking point, Tatiana let out a loud scream. Her head was full of hair, her skin a soft mocha and her eyes were big and bright. Darrin thanked God for saving his daughter, his only thoughts now that she was ok was getting her out from under Theresa's grasp.

He knew Theresa would be on the same hype. She didn't like him and he couldn't stand the sight of her, but under the circumstances he'd hoped they could work together.

Darrin was having a hard time grasping the loss of Marisola, as the nurse prepped Tatiana for the nursery. He was vengeful at that point; ready to pounce on anyone in his path. Sickened by his latest actions his disrespect and doggish ways he nearly vomited on the floor of the disheveled room. He stood far from Marisola's bed looking at her lifeless body. Noticing he was standing in a pull of blood he had to close his eyes and swallow the lump protruding into his jaws.

Theresa was staring at Darrin with fierce eyes. She had switched into some sort of beast. Lunging over to Darrin she tried to tear Darrin from limb to limb as she pounded on his chest. The mental pain had drifted into the physical driving his terror into reality.

Theresa was screaming in both English and Spanish. All Darrin could do was watch Marisola's lifeless body as it lay there in a pool of blood. The nurses continued to scurry about tending to his daughter who was screaming for dear life. Her lungs were strong as her breathing. She had a fight in her from the start. As the doctor approached Darrin and Theresa, Darrin could see that he too was visibly shaken. He had never lost a patient in such a manner. He was solemn and wanted answers to rule out some of the thoughts that plagued his subconscious.

"I am so very sorry." the doctor finally spoke and nodded his head looking directly behind him.

Theresa spun around and demanded the silent officer to arrest Darrin.

"Officer I am so glad you are here arrest this man."

Darrin didn't fight or respond to Theresa's allegations. He just looked up at the officer and held out his hands.

"Ms. If you would just calm down, no one is under arrest here. I just have a few questions and would like to talk to you is all."

Darrin motioned towards the exit as Theresa kept on in her ranting.

"I want full custody of my daughter." Darrin stated immediately. "I will be taking her with me today after she is ok for check out." Darrin's face was plain. He left no room for argument or question.

"Over my dead body!" Theresa exclaimed. "You didn't give a damn about my daughter, not to mention that innocent baby in there."

Darrin could feel his hands curling into a tight fist but he quickly changed his composure. "I will be sure to pay for any medical bills and funeral expenses for Marisola."

"We don't need your fucking money. You are the reason my daughter is dead. You practically drove her to taking those pills. You were always running after that woman. What's her name....your first baby's mama? Joy is it? She didn't want his ass either." Theresa directed her attention the confused looking officer. He had yet to start his line of questioning but he was getting an ear full already. "Why don't you tell this nice officer what happened to your first child. She's dead too, you know. Killed in a train crash during the storm, storm not his fault maybe. But the fact that she was even coming down was entirely his fault. He hadn't seen or done a thing for the girl in ten years. I guess the guilt was eating up at him. Yet and still he didn't think of the stress that he put upon Marisola. She was worried sick that the girl wouldn't like take to her. She was going to be a new mother for God sakes."

Darrin by now was full of rage. He wanted to slap the taste out of Theresa's mouth but stifled his urges.

"Okay, I think I get the picture here." The officer interrupted. "I only have one question. Where did your daughter get the pills?"

"What pills..."Darrin interjected calling his attention to the previous mention of them.

Theresa looked at Darrin with a surprised look on her face and then back to the officer. Nervous and shaken she thought twice about making a motion to flee. She grabbed her throat as if she were trying to soothe her voice back into play. Clearing her throat she responded with a guilty brow and quivering lips. "Me."

# ~51~

# THE BOUNTY

Mike jumped out of his small sports car once he was sure the coast was clear. He never thought that he would have to tail his soon to be wife but after seeing her at Joy's office he was puzzled about what sort of dealings she was into. Mike knew she was beyond money hungry but he was sure she wouldn't sink so low as to try and convince Joy of relinquishing Justin's company to her.

He couldn't be sure of how scandalous Sam was after all they planned and killed her own husband. Mike knew he would be next or at least the pawn in her next plain for material gain. Still, he couldn't put the pieces together with her relation to Joy. Who would be so bold enough to come to someone's place of business demanding a seat at the round table? Sure he was speculating her visitation agenda but he knew enough about Sam to know she wasn't going around giving out her condolences. It worried him that she had yet to shed a tear for her lost beloved Charles. Regardless to the circumstances of his untimely death he was still the Father of her children.

Mike had to admit that looking into the faces of Charles' children drew him to tears. The guilt was eating away at his soul so fiercely he was sure to develop an ulcer. Mike followed Sam to the San Francisco strip where all the latest fashions were displayed in an outside mall. Confident she would be occupied he sped off to visit Joy's office building once more. He was anxious to see what business Sam had with Joy and what was said. He was also anxious to meet the beauty Justin had chosen for his wife. He was sure she was as beautiful as the sun.

Feeling a jump in his groin and a butterfly in his stomach or two he couldn't be certain of his interest in Joy. Patrice had spoken so highly of her he had unintentionally fantasized about sweeping her off her feet and saving her from her bereavement.

Mike shook thoughts of lust and heroism from his confused head as he pulled up to Joy's office once more. He still couldn't believe how beautiful the office building was and the diamond studded emblem out front. Mike adjusted himself as he got out of the car and grabbed his gun and holster. It wasn't in his nature to suit up in broad day but he had a badge so he felt liberated to do so. He wanted to be sure that whoever he came in contact with they knew that he was legit and about business.

Hoping to catch Joy before she left for the day was a whisper to God, Mike knew that would just be too easy of a bounty. He loved the chase, so to find her now would ruin his taste for the hunt. He was a sweet giant, but a savage when the street lights came on. He did his best work at night, as most crooks do.

Mike walked into the glass doors of the building looking for a sign of some sort to point him into the direction of Joy. Walking swiftly down the hall of the lobby he noticed his fly was open. Wrestling to get himself all prepped for his first introduction to Joy he paused just in front of a woman walking briskly with a stack of papers and a Mocha Frappuccino.

Nadine was in such a rush to get to her last meeting of the day she hadn't noticed the fine specimen holding up traffic. She walked straight into his brick wall of a chest spilling her coffee all over Mike's shirt and dropping her paperwork about the floor of the lobby. Nadine was so startled and nervous she began to shake nervously.

"Shit." Mike yelled. "Can't you see?" Mike was furious about his clothing, especially since he had plans on meeting his brother's wife for the first time.

"Um, excuse you as well. Mr. I am made out of glass and I can just post up in the middle of the walk way." Nadine scurried about picking up the papers that were in danger of coffee stains.

Mike looked down at the woman whose caramel breasts pulsated through her blue satin blouse. It was a nice compliment to her skin tone. Her short hair was a sexy addition to her small frame and long legs. He was impressed.

"Sorry I am just in a rush. I didn't mean to be disrespectful. I am looking for my brother's wife maybe you've seen her." Mike thought that maybe he had just had the luck of running into her. She was beautiful, a bit clumsy but the accident wasn't entirely her fault. She was in a rush.

"Sorry, I don't have time for small talk. I need to get to this meeting the entire business is counting on these projection sheets to reach the appropriate hands. Oh my God." Nadine became flustered and dizzy as she was scurrying about the floor on all fours trying to make sense of the mess she had landed herself into. She was frantically putting the papers back in order in hopes that she wouldn't have to run back up to the office to reprint them all. "Joy is going to kill me." she whispered fighting back tears.

Mike's attention was grabbed at that point. "Here let me help." Part of him was relieved that she wasn't Joy. He was having entirely too good of a time watching her crawl about the floor.

"So this Joy, she is who I am looking for. Do you work for her or something?"

"Look if you are a spy from one of our competing companies or a corporate buyer looking for her to sell Justin's company then the answer is no. We are not interested. We are not selling, sharing, or open for negotiations. Joy would never give up her company or his. She is just in mourning right now, but she's strong and when she gets back things will be in order. So go run and tell that." Nadine was irritated she could hardly stand. So many unwelcome guests were floating about the office it was a wonder she could get any work done.

"I'm not any of those things. My name is Mike. I am Justin's brother."

Nadine's mouth dropped to the floor as she looked up from her wrinkled presentation. Nadine swallowed hard as she stood and took in how awesome looking the man was. Slightly, taken back she offered her hand. "I apologize, glad to meet you. You must be Mike, the bounty hunter right?"

Mike blushed a bit. He was happy to hear that Justin had told his family and business partners about him. It gave him a sense of acceptance and he felt as though he wasn't forgotten.

"Yeah that's me. I was looking for Joy. Mom is really worried about her. She hasn't answered any of her phone calls and she just wants her to come home so that she can help her with the baby."

"Yeah I can understand that. Joy is headstrong. She doesn't accept help very well. She is on some mission to find the spark again. If it were up to me she would be here sorting out all this mess." Nadine caught her composure so that she could swallow the lump molding in her throat. She was sad for Joy and near tears, but frustrated that she was left holding the bag. Sure she had Joy's back to the fullest however it was times as of late where she realized that Joy was the heart of the company and she could use all the help she could get.

"I guess it's true. The assistant tends to do all the work." Mike chimed in as he offered his hand to Nadine.

"Don't get me wrong." Nadine realized that her comment may have sounded a bit downgraded in Joy's capabilities towards running the company. "I just meant that we are both busting our humps and while she is gone taking care of the business is an over load at times for me. Now I see and appreciate all the work she does."

"I get it. Don't worry, it's okay to vent sometimes. So do you happen to know where Joy is? I am not here to bother her or anything. Mom's just wants to make sure she is okay. After all it is her grandchild and she feels as though that child is the only thing she has left of Justin. I am sure you can understand that."

"I feel it. I know where you are coming from. Pardon me if I am a bit dry on the issue. So many of her folk have come by asking questions about her whereabouts I have just been at a loss for words. I don't see how she can get any work done or mourn her loss with so many people chiming in all the time. I think you should know that Darrin is here and he is out to profess his love as though he was around from day one."

Mike looked puzzled. "What the fuck? Well I will deal with him when the time comes, Ashley's dad right?" Mike shook his head as his memory was jogged. "Yeah I remember that cat? Justin told me that he was a bit of a pest. I've never met him and I am sad I never got to meet Joy and the kids either. I am looking forward to meeting her and my new niece or nephew."

"Well I am glad. She will need all the support she can get. She is lucky to have had Justin and a family that loves and supports her. Her family hasn't been the best of supportive circles, which is why she chose to distance herself. She is in the hills, the cabin…do you know where it is."

"No, I can't say I do."

"It's in Yosemite Valley. The family took trips there every winter and summer. She often goes to the cabin when she is writing or just needs to clear her head. As far as I know the pregnancy is going well, there are no complications with the twins."

"Twins, wow. I didn't know. I am sure mom will be so excited to hear about this. Thank you Nadine, I really appreciate this. I just want to make sure she is ok so that my mom can rest."

"Understandable."

"It was nice to have met you as well Nadine. I hope to see you again." Mike commented flirtatiously forgetting that he had been chasing his wife to be all over town in searching to fill the holes in her story.

"You too, if you see her before she returns my message could you be so kind as to tell her we have some business that needs her immediate presence. I spoke to her briefly and left her a message but I need her to understand I was actually serious this time. I need her and I am worried about her just the same. She needs to be around her family."

"Will do." Mike dumped the stack of papers he retrieved from the floor into her overflowing arms and jogged his way out of the lobby and back to his car."

# ~52~

## LOOK WHO'S COMING TO TOWN

Joy packed her bags slowly, dragging her feet about her warm cabin. She would miss her nights by the fire just watching the flames flicker about the burning logs. "Time will heal all wounds, is what they say, I have yet to feel soothed of this ache however." Joy sank down into her cozy chair and wrapped up tightly in one of her faux fur throws. She loved her winter look in summer. She was finally in a place where winter, her favorite part of the year was three fourths of the climate.

Sickened by the thought of coming in contact with her sister and Justin's mother made her lag even further. It was like pulling teeth. Joy struggled with the thought of having to do business of any sort in relation to the literary group she was building with Justin and Nadine, nor his private design company. With Charles gone there was no one left to step in but her, sure she couldn't stand the way he treated Sam but the truth of the matter was he knew the business. Justin wouldn't have kept him under his wing if he wasn't worth the trouble.

Joy was frustrated with how long it was taking her to pack a simple bag. She wasn't planning on staying in town very long and she had high hopes that Nadine was simply being herself, an over dramatic diva. Sadly, because she knew her sister well she thought twice about just simply sweeping the issues of the company under the rug if she wanted something to return to.

Overwhelmed wasn't the half of it when Joy thought about entering back into the busy streets of Oakland and San Francisco. Sure she missed her hot latte' before work and the sound of her heels hitting the pavement, but she was far from ready to go back to work and face the fact that her husband was gone forever.

The kick of the babies started her back into reality. She would be a fool to think that she could just go back to town full blown pregnant and not catch the eyes of the public. Questions would be in plain view across her colleague's foreheads. She was faithful to Justin that wasn't a doubt. Just the very mention of the babies and the sad looks on their faces would send her to tears.

****

Darrin was anxious to get to the nursery to formally greet his newborn baby. He couldn't believe Theresa was trying to sabotage him and Marisola's relationship. Actually he could, he just didn't expect her stoop as low. She would pay for it with the rest of her life. In jail is where she landed herself, giving pills that weren't even legal in the United States to a depressed pregnant woman. The jail time wouldn't be the issue however; she would be let out on probation. It was living with having a hand in her daughter's death that would ultimately kill her. Darrin got inches from the nursery window and suddenly felt as if his knees were going to buckle. He was nervous and scared that he wouldn't be able to take on raising his daughter alone. Still he wouldn't miss out on the chance.

Darrin placed his hands on the glass; he used it to hold him up. He was sure he were going to faint. Pressing his forehead against his cold reflection he prayed a small prayer. He hoped that he would be able to take the walk around the corner to meet baby Tatiana. One of the nurses that were tending to baby Tatiana came out to greet him. She could smell the fear from inside the nursery's walls.

"Come with me, you will be fine. Let's just get you cleaned up."

Darrin took the nurses hand quivering with fear, as he walked slowly around to the entrance of the nursery.

"I don't know if I can do this." Darrin looked at the nurse with tear-filled eyes. "I just lost my firstborn in a storm a few months ago, now Marisola is dead. I don't seem to have the best luck around women."

"It's normal to be afraid. I am a new mother myself about a year ago. Sure I look after them in a hospital setting but with your own, it's different. You will be fine I will be here to help you if you need anything. Trust me once you hold your daughter in your arms you will fall in love with her instantly."

Darrin smiled and stood up straight as if regaining his composure. Wiping his sweaty palms on the lap of his jeans he walked tall and headed straight for acrylic basinet marked baby Santiago.

**** 

Still in awe of Nadine's beauty Mike was finding it hard to concentrate on the road. He was looking to get to Joy and possibly have a sit down before her arrival back to town. Joy and her wellbeing over shadowed his thoughts of distrust with Sam. Only time would tell. He knew that once he got to Joy the missing pieces would link right up. Mike shook the thoughts of Nadine and Joy when his phone interrupted his thoughts. It was Sam. Mike decided to ignore her phone call. He was in no mood to hear her whining about the insurance policy she was expecting her she had bills that needed to be paid. Most of his monetary aide was due to his guilt in killing the boy's father. He felt like such a fool listening to Sam and her allegations of abuse. The children adored their father and hadn't directly seen their father hit Sam.

Mike was a complete fool he had been two seconds from knocking the taste of Sam's mouth a number of times. It was the abuse of the children that sent him over the edge. Once again he had fallen for a skirt. Mike had, had enough of playing, "Captain save a Hoe." Mom always said a woman would be the death of him. As of late he was looking towards disproving that notion.

Mike didn't realize how fast he was driving but he was high tailing it down the highway up towards the hills. Yosemite National Park was a wonderful place to hide. He already dug her style. Speeding around the turns in his Land Rover he thought about his introduction. He wasn't sure how receptive she would be and by no means did he want to come across as an insensitive over grown thug. After all he knew full well how over bearing his moms could be. She was surprised she even liked Joy. So she had to have been a diamond in the rough.

Whispering a few goodbyes to her peace and tranquility Joy locked her cozy cabin and through her bags into the car. She wasn't going to take the trip in her own car. Darrin was in such a rush she would take his car. What a way to reenter the Bay; give the haters something to talk about? She knew it would turn heads. More questions left to answer, but that didn't matter to her much. Folk were talking already.

Her disappearing act lifted a few eyebrows and her size 12 belly would add fuel to the fire. It was her hopes Marisola would catch her driving around in Darrin's vehicle, the scandal it would create. She needed something to keep her mind off of the usual madness. She was tired of being the innocent one.

Joy looked at her reflection in the glass of Darrin's custom design and realized she didn't recognize who she was. She could feel bits and pieces of her past floating across her mind and disappearing as if they were pieces of someone else's past. Lillian's eyes peered back at her. She greeted her with a smile. Jumping into her brand new car she applied her make-up rolled down her window and sped off to Beyoncé's, "Sweet Dreams."

~53~

## IDENTITY THEFT

After about a 6-hour drive, Mike pulled up into the lodge where Joy's cabin was nestled, it was in a pretty secluded area. It would take at least a half hour to reach her if she needed medical attention. Mike wrinkled his forehead at the thought of what he may come across upon entry into the cabin. He swallowed hard and parked his car. Jumping out among the bark he nearly trampled two squirrels hustling their grub back their home in the trees. He smiled and inhaled the sweet smell of pine as he slammed his car door.

He was happy to see Justin's truck parked next to the cabin, it was a sign that someone was home and he could finally get some answers. He wanted more than anything to make sure that Joy was okay and to do whatever he could to help out with the babies. He realized she had no need for money. She was brilliant herself, but nothing could take the place of love and support. He could feel the urge to lay into Darrin upon crossing his path as well. The fact that he would even show face after being an absent deadbeat dad for twelve years was beyond his understanding. Almost as if he showed up to stir up trouble.

"It's all good." Mike told himself as he made sure to straighten his clothing before approaching the cabin's front door.

Mike jogged up the cabin stairs feeling a bit nervous. He still had a few butterflies fluttering about in his stomach. He didn't want to alarm her and he had to make sure to prepare himself for what type of mood she was in. He realized that he himself was an emotional wreck. He'd been on the road ever since his visit with Patrice. He hadn't truly processed the death of his brother. He had adamantly put all thoughts of Charles out of his head, at least for the time being. He knew that he would have to come clean about his killing him.

Mike knocked on the door of Joy's cabin several times before he realized that there weren't any lights or signs of life around the entire premises. Panicking Mike searched the front porch for a clue or perhaps a spare key. He tried to peer in the window's to see if he could see Joy lying on the floor or slumped over. Frustrated Mike grabbed his head. He couldn't understand his urgency. Perhaps the panic stemmed from this being the only way of gaining some redemption from his previous evil deeds.

"Damn it." Mike cursed. Mike took two steps back and then one quick leaping hurl towards the door with his foot. "Joy!" Mike called out as he stumbled about the cabin searching for a light switch. Mike nearly tripped over the sofa but the corner of a table caught his attention.

"Fuck." Mike yelled. It hurt like a bitch but he quickly recovered hoping Joy didn't walk in to find him buckled over nursing his wounds as though he were some pansy. Massaging the wall to find a switch of some sort he finally flicked it on. Mikes eyes widened at first sight of the cabin. It was beautiful yes, but that wasn't the half of what caught his attention. Pictures of Justin and the children were hung about the cabin. He had photos of every book

Joy had written and every magazine cover he'd been on. There over the fireplace was the picture that took his breath way in more ways than one.

It was a huge picture of who he knew to be Sam, but it was clearly Joy. Her face was identical to Sam's but her face was softer. Her eyes were kind and her hair was long and black like Sam's but it was vibrantly styled. She had the cutest smile. His urgency to meet Joy had become dyer. Sam had failed to mention she had a sister a twin sister at that. She was married to Charles, his cousin and tricked into killing him over domestic and child abuse that didn't exist. Charles owed money to some of the same bookies he had made deals with. So the hunt for him was easy, but the kill wasn't. Now he had to face the music of it all. His only relief was that Justin wasn't around to see how bad he had loused things up.

Mike fell back onto the couch in awe of his findings. He buried his head in his hands and began to sob like a baby it began with feelings of regret and sentiment for all the pain he had caused and ended with a fire in him that was sure to burst into flames. Sam played him from the start, but she wasn't going to get away with it. First, he would make sure that Joy and the babies were ok then he would deal with Sam. Mike jumped to his feet and cleaned himself up in the sink of the small kitchenette.

"Darrin had better make sure to stay out of my damn way." Mike uttered to himself as he fixed the door to Joy's cabin. "Damn door." Mike cursed as he nearly hammered the nail straight through his overgrown hand. His nerves were so bad he couldn't imagine making the drive back to the city. The long drive had taken its toll.

Mike finally got the door back in order. He double-checked that the door was opening and closing properly before locking up and jogging back to his car. He decided that he was much too tired to drive back up to the Oakland Hills so he would find the nearest rest stop and just pay for a night's stay. He thought about Sam for a brief moment. As much as he wanted to curse her, he couldn't fight his feelings. He was in love with her no matter her trifling ways. Just couldn't understand what she needed so badly that she couldn't be satisfied.

Mike did hope that once she was able to get the insurance money for Charles' death she would settle down. He knew that her son's may one day find out his true identity and decide to get revenge, but he still felt as though it was his duty to care for them. He didn't plan on leaving them behind whether Sam wanted to marry him or not. It became evident to him after his short stay that she didn't care too much for the boy's in the first place. They were more of her possessions. Charles Jr. cared for most of the boy's himself. He was an old soul and hard to get close to. His swag was commendable. Mike couldn't help but respect that. Mike did however want to make Charles Jr. understand that he was a young man and deserved to do things young men did. He was given another chance, after his birth mother was killed in front of him.

Mike laid his head onto the steering wheel for a few moments. All of a sudden he couldn't breathe. He just wanted the whole mess to be over. He felt so helpless. It was times like these when he could go to Justin and tell him what was wrong. Justin was the level head in the bunch. When Mike was on some set it off shit, Justin brought up the jailhouse and a more lucrative way of getting even. He was right. His job paid off and left criminals at his mercy. Wrong yes, but he was taking from the rich and crooked. He wasn't stealing from old ladies and banks.

No matter how he danced around the issue he was guilty of murder. He had murdered his soul and his family. Now he could barely stand to look at himself in the rearview mirror. Again he thanked God that Justin hadn't bear witness to his poor judgment. He vowed however that he would do all in his power to fix things.

~ 355 ~

Mike popped the hood of his car to check the fluids before his attempt to find shelter for the night. After checking the oil he slammed his hood and jumped into the driver seat just in time for Sam's call. He hadn't realized it but she had called him at least ten times. He had been preoccupied with his thoughts. Mike thought about it before answering her phone call. He wanted to talk to her about their relationship and the secrets she kept from him, but he wanted to speak with her face to face. Why hadn't she told him that she was a twin? Thoughts still clouded his mind. Had Sam knew, all along who he was in relation to Charles and Justin for that matter? Could she be that malicious? Question's he'd asked before in regards to her visit to Joy's office but now that he knew of her relation, he knew that Sam couldn't be up to any good at all. How he was going to live with loving such a malicious Bitch was still his biggest issue?

In the end Mike ignored Sam's phone calls. He decided that it would be best to talk with her once he got back to town. It was his hope to get both Joy and Sam in the same room with one another. Maybe the truth would come out. Mike punched his steering wheel in frustration. He had a few things to hide as well. Both he and Sam were in the hot seat. Sam encouraged and manipulated the hit, but it was Mike that carried it out, a sucker for love.

## ~54~

## DADDY'S HOME

Sam tried Mike's phone one last time before deciding she would turn in for the night. She was furious in that he was refusing to answer his phone calls. She couldn't believe the nerve of Mike so she was sure to let him have it via text messaging. Realizing she had a big day ahead she stifled herself. She needed her rest.

Sure Charles' check would clear the following day she busied herself. She had a long list of things to do and buy. Mike wasn't in the cards for the long haul. She did enjoy his company but his job had him on the road so often he couldn't possibly think they could be anything more than friends with benefits.

Sam carefully washed the make-up from her face and brushed her hair, as she thought about her day's events.

****

Darrin couldn't stop looking at Tatiana. She was so beautiful. She had her mother's eyes. Her hair was soft and thick full of curls. She was attentive at two days old and ready to enter into the world. Darrin couldn't wait to take her home. He was still confused about Marisola's death but he thought that it was a true sign from God. Maybe it was a blessing from him, a sign that he and Joy were supposed to be together. Darrin sat and rocked Tatiana while he waited for the discharge papers. He was anxious to get on the road. He had every intention of sweeping Joy off her feet and taking her and the baby home to his Los Angeles condo. He realized it was a long shot since Joy had her and Justin's company to think about but he was sure that a change of scenery is what she needed. Besides she was going to be a new mother all over again and she would need the support.

Darrin smiled as he caressed his daughter's hair. His only worry was that she would resent baby Tatiana since they had lost the daughter they had, had together. Darrin somehow thought that bringing Tatiana to Joy would make up for their loss. It hadn't worked thus far for him but it did shade some of the pain.

Darrin lucked out when it came to fighting with Theresa. For that he was grateful. He knew she wouldn't do any jail time for her negligence. It was her first offense. She would get a few months of community service and probation at best. The good thing was that no court in the state would grant her custody of a child due to the type of crime she had played a hand in. Darrin was just saddened that she would have to live with the fact that she aided in her daughter's death. Her hate for him burned so deep she was willing to use her daughter's loss of sensibility to trap him.

Darrin was contemplating on calling Joy to let her know what had gone down, but he thought it best to just face her. He didn't know how she would take him bringing another women's child into her life but he had accepted her children just as if they were his own. Darrin had to revamp his last thought. Striking it from the record he checked himself on that. He knew full well he was giving himself too much credit. He stayed away all together. He accepted the children because he didn't have to be responsible for anything anymore. He admitted to himself as he sat watching Tatiana sleep that he reveled in the fact that he had this baby mama that wasn't a pest. Joy rarely contacted Darrin for anything unless it was just out of her reach in all aspects of the notion.

If left up to her there would have been no contact. Not because she just couldn't stand Darrin, but just so Ashley wasn't confused or expecting something from Darrin she just wasn't going to receive. Darrin didn't have to call, check in, or send a dime and he wouldn't hear a word from Joy on the matter whether he did show support or did nothing at all. After pondering over his behavior he began to feel like a sap. What kind of man defaults on his responsibilities?

"A scared one." Darrin's sense of sensibility chimed in but the common sense of his brain told him that he was just making excuses for his selfishness.

Darrin laid his head back on the wooden hump of the rocking chair and closed his eyes for a brief moment. He wanted to take in the smell of peace and tranquility. He knew he had better savor the moment. There were many sleepless nights to come.

"Sir." the discharge nurse tried to get Darrin's attention. "Sir." the nurse repeated and added a slight nudge to Darrin's shoulder. Darrin awoke a bit startled and taken back as if he had forgotten in those few moments where he was. He still held tight however, to his precious bundle in his arms. Darrin would never lose sight of Tatiana. Darrin told himself she was all he had left to live for her and Joy. He just hoped she would take him back. He knew that she still loved him. Although Joy often said that she had moved on. It was still this look in her eyes that had held a spot for him. He just knew it.

Darrin high tailed his thoughts back to reality as the nurse asked for his attention once more. "Yes." Darrin finally managed. "I dozed off a bit, I apologize."

"No worries." the nurse smirked. "Every little bit counts. You are going to have your hands full with this little beauty." the nurse smiled then became solemn. "I am so sorry for your loss." The nurse looked down at the floor and then tried to quickly change the subject realizing that her comment may have been inappropriate.

Darrin didn't know how to respond so he simply nodded. All he wanted to do was sign the paperwork and get on about his day. He wasn't sure where to begin but he was certain that putting his family back together again was first on his agenda.

Darrin bundled baby Tatiana in her car seat and waved a goodbye to the nursing staff. "Thank you." Darrin chattered and sped out of the doors to the hospital with hopes of putting the night's horrific ventures to rest.

Darrin shuffled his package to the car and buckled her safely in the seatbelt. He was beginning to get a sense of peace as he blushed at the sight of his love's joy snuggling under her pink and cheetah faux fur. He was anxious to get on the road to see Joy, but first he would spend the night meeting is daughter and start fresh in the morning.

## ~55~

## THE MEETING

Joy arrived home in what seemed like mere minutes. Her mind drifted along with the passing of trees as she traveled back to the congestion and fog of The San Francisco Bay Area. The cold winds blew a slight chill but she refused to turn on the heat. She didn't want to use anything in Darrin's car. It was bad enough she stole it. Lillian would take care of his spitfire tongue he would be sure to have something smart to say. It wasn't however like he didn't have four and five cars. It was the principle of course.

Joy cleaned up her already tidy home frantically as if she were expecting guests. She was so nervous and couldn't pin point why. The doors down her hall on the third floor of her condo were slammed shut. She still decorated and designed rooms for her children even though in reality they had gone to glory.

Joy walked slowly down the hall in hopes of confronting her demons. She felt like the only way to heal would be to confront the issue head on. She thought about hosting a little get together to announce her arrival. She was thinking of shedding her good girl image to start taking some names. She would make Lillian proud of her yet. It was high time she start standing up for herself.

Joy crept down the hall trying to get close enough to the door without hyperventilating. Stopping just in front of the door she placed her hand on the knob and tried with all her mite to open the door. Suddenly, it was as though she was paralyzed. She couldn't move nor speak. Her thoughts ran, but no force towards opening the door and placing some closure to the hole in her heart came about.

Finally remembering that breathing was essential to her survival, she exhaled and turned the knob of the door. Joy stopped for a second and closed her eyes tightly. Slowly, she opened her eyes to reveal the purple and pink stripes on her daughter's wall.

Joy couldn't breath the kick in her belly startled her and sent her into devastation. She began to shake violently, tears streamed down her face and she bellowed out a horrific scream. She was finding it hard to stand. Her chest heaved heavily. She was getting dizzier by the moment.

Darrin pulled up in front of Joy's condo excited to see his car parked out front. He smiled at the idea of Joy speeding around in his car. "Uh Huh." Darrin smirked as he scooped Tatiana up and flew towards Joy's front door. Darrin knocked on the door softly at first then like the police the second and third time. There was still no answer. Alarmed that something was terribly wrong Darrin checked the front door to see if it were unlocked. He was relieved to find it was open.

"Joy." Darrin called out. He was beginning to panic. "Joy, its Darrin, where are you?"

Joy could hear Darrin calling for her. She was sick to her stomach and she felt great pain but her speech was slurred. Her mouth was suddenly filled with so much saliva she was nearly choking to death.

Darrin ran up the steps towards the muffled sounds leaving baby Tatiana safe in her car seat by the stairs below. "Joy..., you alright?" Darrin called out once more as he began to feel tears burning his retinas.

Darrin reached the top of the stairs. He was nervous but he could see that Joy was still standing. The moment she saw Darrin she began a long fall to the floor. Darrin ran to her and nearly dropped her. He hadn't gauged her weight very well. Darrin caught Joy in mid-air and guided her to the floor. Joy was whispering something over and over again, a faint whisper about the pain in her stomach, lower abdomen and legs.

Darrin was instantly concerned about the nature of Joy's pain. He tried to coach her to her feet but she seemed to be out of it. Darrin sat Joy up as best he could, with intentions of going to fetch Joy a glass of water.

"What are you doing here?" Joy opened her eyes. Startling Darrin, Darrin noticed that her eyes were a lighter shade of brown, hazel with speck of emerald green.

He was more confused than ever. Joy's eyes were different. Not only in color, but they were cold, as though she had no true memory of their past together.

"What did you think Joy was going to welcome you with open arms?"

Darrin nearly dropped Joy's body to the floor as he realized that the woman he was talking to couldn't have been his lost love. She was speaking from within Joy' body but it wasn't Joy.

"GET AWAY FROM YOU ME YOU SON OF A BITCH!" Lillian began to gain her composure as she pulled away from Darrin's grasp.


****

Sam awoke startled out of her sleep. She thought she was dreaming about the phone ringing. Stumbling from her bed she trampled about the clothing and bags of goods she had splurged on for the past few weeks. Her bank accounts were beyond empty and her credit cards were maxed out. All she could really count on was for Joy to pay her mortgage. She was grateful for that now.

"Hello...?" Sam answered the phone frazzled and discombobulated. She nearly dropped her phone into the sink as she washed her face.

"Mrs. Richardson is that you, you don't sound well? Is everything all right?"

"Yes it is. I'm sorry if I sound a bit out of it the phone startled me is all?"

"So have we closed the deal on the insurance policy?" Sam asked her lawyer with a hint of bass in her voice.

"Well that is what I am calling about."

Sam was instantly standing at attention she was, concerned with her lawyers tone. "What's going on with the funds?"

"I am sorry, there is no money. Your husband depleted all of the finances from the policy. With his constant refinancing of your home and borrowing against it, he just..." Sam's lawyer was almost as choked up as she was. He couldn't believe how negligent Charles was with is finances, not to mention the funds for his children's college. All Mr. Samson could do was shake his head and keep apologizing to Sam about the devastating news.

After Sam came to, she decided that the only thing left to do was to ask just how bad she was in the whole. She just knew that she could at least get a couple hundred grand. It was a 5.5 million dollar insurance policy. "So how much is depleted? I can't cry over spilled milk. How much am I looking to collect and how soon can the check be processed?

"Mrs. Richardson, I am sorry I don't think you quite understand. There is no money." Mr. Samson tried to enunciate his words carefully without sounding as if he were being funny about the situation, but it was obvious to him that she was experiencing some denial in regards to the situation.

"Are you fucking kidding me? How are my children supposed to live? How am I going to pay for food and shelter? You mean this man has left me with absolutely nothing?" Sam was beyond irate. "Okay, okay, so what about the business. He was business partners with Justin. I am sure that there is a clause somewhere indicating his shares in the company and how much he stands to gain if the company is sold. What's going on with that?"

"Samantha, that is entirely up to Joy. The company belongs to her now. She is the sole owner and stock holder of the company."

Sam could feel the smoke billowing from both her ears. Her fist curled into a tight ball. She could have sworn she was going to blow. "Well I will just have to see about that." Sam hung up the phone while Mr. Samson was still talking. She could hardly think straight. Sam skipped the shower and threw on a pair of jeans and a girl tee. She didn't know if Joy had made it back to town yet but she had every intention of using her spare key to wait on the Bitch to arrive.

**\*\*\*\***

Mike wasn't too far from the city and it had just turned 10am. He was speeding but he was determined to put his nerves at rest. He couldn't be sure of Joy's condition. All he wanted to do was make sure she was safe, his last good deed before fleeing town for good. Mike was furious with Sam he didn't know how he was going to approach the situation but he was surly going to have a sit down with her. His life of crime had come to an end. The matters of his recent indiscretions made things much worse than his usual shenanigans "I'm sorry bro." mike whispered as he sped into the busy streets of Oakland.

## ~56~

## ACE'S WILD

Darrin couldn't believe how insensitive Joy was being about Marisola's death. He knew that it would be hard for her to take on raising another child, being that she had just lost her own but somehow he thought that it would make things better. He was sadly mistaken. He couldn't understand Joy's new persona the speaking in third person really threw him for a loop and the eye contacts weren't necessary. He liked Joy just the way she was.

Darrin looked at Joy with sad eyes once he helped her to the couch in her living room and grabbed his daughter. He was sure he would pass out from a broken heart. Lillian had asked Darrin to leave several times, but he'd refused. Darrin just thought that perhaps she was delusional. She kept calling herself Lillian and referring to Joy as the weak on.

Darrin trotted Tatiana to the car and slammed the door. He thought to just drive back to Los Angeles but he wasn't going to just give up on Joy that easy. He could tell that something was bothering her. So he just sat in his car to let her blow off some steam.

Joy was busy ranting and raving as she mellowed out. She and Lillian were having a discussion about how to deal with the rest of the perpetual liars and scammers in her family. She was setting up for her biggest fight ever. It was only a matter of time before Sam slithered her ass to her door begging as usual.

Joy washed her face as she recovered from Lillian's outburst. She was coming back into her own. Joy still couldn't believe her eyes. What was Darrin thinking showing up with that woman's baby? She felt for him and his loss, but she was in no way prepared to take on the care of another child. She was carrying twins for God sakes. Again, she thought about how cruel Lillian was to Darrin. She couldn't come out to show remorse if she wanted to, because those were her thoughts and feelings. She was bitter and hurt that he had, had another child with someone else as if she hadn't had a family of her own. It hurt more in that he hadn't thought enough of Ashley to take care of his firstborn. Now that she was gone, it seemed unfair that he was all into the birth of Tatiana.

The look on Darrin's face puzzled her even more. He seemed to be convinced that there were unresolved issues with their relationship. He was right she admitted but the unresolved issues were those in concern with their deceased daughter. Joy blamed him for most of what happened and it took a toll on her conscience as well. She was constantly reviewing her decision to send them away. Now all she had going was the ailments that came along with pregnancy as though one canceled out the other.

Joy felt relaxed after her encounter with Darrin, Lillian had showed up just in time. She didn't think she couldn't handle the emotional tirade with Darrin at the moment. Joy could feel the heat brewing in her chest that was fueled by Lillian it was the first time she was actually present during an attack.

Most of the time Lillian would just show-up without warning. She would come to without any recollection of prior events. She felt liberated and somewhat in control of Lillian now that she could bear witness to her sidekick's wrath.

Darrin on the other hand had never seen Joy in such a way. It startled him to think that she had literally lost her mind. He jogged back to his car with Tatiana in tow. Disappointed and dangerously close to tears he just sat in his vehicle for a full thirty minutes before he noticed Sam pulling up. At first thought he had mind to warn Sam of Joy's change in persona, but he knew she deserved whatever Joy had to dish out. She was as ruthless as they came, a coldhearted full-blooded sister of Joy's with the looks to match.

Sam noticed Darrin sitting in his car before she even pulled up to Joy's condo good, but she didn't care. She had a bone to pick with Joy. She was left with absolutely nothing. All she literally had was a pot to piss in. Charles' no good ass had depleted his insurance. He even took out the kid's college funds, after he had refinanced the home as much as he possibly could.

Sam had no choice, but to come crawling back to Joy for any assistance she could give. She had her sights on a few sentiments, but a slice of the company would do. Mike had turned out to be a waste of time. He was sure to ignore her phone calls after her angry load of text messages through the night. "Coward." Sam whispered.

She couldn't tell which was worse out of the two men. Sam could smell fear and weakness from a mile away and could tell that Mike's finest hour had long since drifted away. His guts were soft. Sam knew that she would have to reveal what she knew about Charles murder soon, if nothing but to clear her name. It would be his word against hers. He was expendable he had no relation to the family just some cat she fooled around with a couple of times over the years that caught feelings.

Sam opened the door of Joy's home without an invitation. She found Joy mixing herself a smoothie in the kitchen on the second floor of her tri-story palace. Joy didn't acknowledge her she was busy and didn't have time for small talk. Darrin had set her on fire and she was ready and waiting for the next round.

"Joy."

"Hey Sam." Joy was somewhat dry in her response. Her mind was still with Darrin and his daughter.

"Joy, don't hey me. I'm sure you know why I'm here." Sam placed a hand on her hips as she noticed how big Joy had gotten over the last few months. She looked as though she were going to pop any second.

"Actually. No, I don't. I thought that you were here to welcome me home, but I know that's too good to be true. Are you here to thank me for covering your mortgage payments? Maybe that's too farfetched as well?" Joy still had yet to look onto Sam's face. She wasn't interested in looking at the gritty look on her face. She wore the same countenance as well. She was just ready to get all the formalities out of the way and get to the bottom of her trifling ways.

Sam started to walk around the den looking at all of Joy's artwork and décor as if she hadn't been in her apartment before while she was gone. Joy still went about her business making herself a smoothie. She didn't bother to even offer Sam one.

"So what can I do for you sis?" Joy sat down in the den and grabbed the remote.

"You can give me what is rightfully mine." Sam stopped just in front of Joy and stood over her as though she were standing on guard.

Joy's forehead wrinkled as she sipped slowly on her strawberry banana smoothie. There was no fear present and she was just lying in wait for her sister to feel bold enough to either swing or step within her breathing room. Pregnant or not she had so much anger and frustration built in she would surely knock Sam on her ass with one blow.

Sam could sense her sisters urge for violence and backed down slightly but her fierce need for material gain would give her just enough courage to try her sister in any regard. "Where is my husband's cut from Justin's business?"

"He doesn't have one." Joy answered simply. She didn't have to explain a damn thing to Sam. She was doing just as her husband would have wanted her to do in regards to Sam and the children. She was paying the mortgage making sure they had a roof over their heads. What more could you ask for from a business owner that knew his partner was swindling funds from the company to pay for his gambling debts. Sam wasn't innocent in the matter either. She had her issues with over spending and traveling to supposed hair shows that turned up as just escapades with her latest lover. Joy was no fool and if she was Lillian wasn't going to let anyone else get wind of it.

Sam looked at Joy with such fierce eyes she herself was having an outer body experience. She envisioned several fighting moves she could have easily performed on Joy without her even having the chance to defend herself.

"Is there anything else?' Joy asked. She herself couldn't tell whether it was her speaking or Lillian.

Sam was so out done she just rolled her eyes and retreated to the kitchen to make herself a smoothie. Joy smacked her lips and grunted as she changed the channel on her television. She still couldn't believe Darrin's ass showing up to her doorstep.

Sam was still mumbling shit under her breath as the blender was working overtime mixing her fruity blend with a touch of Bacardi. "I see that Darrin has been here. What did he want?"

"Oh." Joy responded nonchalantly. "He brought his ass over here with his girl's baby, hoping that I would take care of it and open my home to him. I believe the man thought that there was still something left to salvage between he and I." Joy didn't take her eyes off the television as she ranted on about Darrin's visit.

Sam was shocked she didn't take him back and take care of the man's baby. Joy was always the type to accept and please. Hell she was brilliant, but her soft heart made her weak and easy to manipulate. She had to admit this new persona was one to be reckoned with. Sam had no words.

~ 370 ~

"Well I guess he is having a hard time understanding no and leave the premises because he was sitting out in his car like some sad puppy when I pulled up. He almost looked as though he were going to speak. I knew something was wrong then. I just pretended like I didn't see him and came on in."

"Well it's just as well. I don't own the complex. So if he wants to sit outside and enjoy the scenery then have at it." Joy was serious as all get out. She had, had just about enough of everyone's expectations of her. It was time she took charge of her own life.

## ~57~

## BLOODLINES

Joy was lost in her mind as she was sitting flipping through the channels on her television. Sam was chattering about something, but she couldn't understand a word she was saying. Her thoughts were clouded and she couldn't decipher why Darrin was still lingering about her home. It was bothering her more than it should.

Mike was instantly aggravated when he saw Sam's car parked in front of Joy's home. Mike hopped out of his car without hesitation, ready to defend his honor at any cost. He was on a mission to salvage whatever reputation he had left. He was tired of running scared so he used his night of solidarity to repent for his many sins and prepare to face his guilty pleasures head on.

Darrin placed baby Tatiana back into her car seat and took a peak at the tall beefy man walking from his truck. Darrin lowered his eyes as he thought for a split second that he recognized him.

"Damn." Darrin hit his steering wheel with a closed fist, hitting his horn and alarming the man walking briskly across the street. Darrin waved a hand of dismissal, but the question mark on his head was still visible. He didn't want to cause too much attention to the seemingly familiar man because he had no idea of who he was visiting.

"There were at least 100 condos around." Darrin told himself as the man kept walking towards Joy's home.

Darrin became alarmed as Mike stepped onto the front porch of Joy's condo. He jumped from the front seat of his ride in hot pursuit. With a quick glance at his daughter to ensure she was still asleep, he fell into a brisk stride.

"Aye bro!" Darrin yelled across the street at Mike as he grabbed the front of his belt. "You must have the wrong house broody, I am pretty sure you have no business here."

Mike turned at full attention and addressed the man hustling across the street in his direct path. "Nah, I'm at the right address. It's you that's out of place. This is Joy's spot right? My girl is here." Mike looked into the face and realized that he recognized dude standing posed as if he was ready to pounce.

Darrin looked hard onto Mike's face as well, wrinkling his forehead. He more than recognized him. Darrin reached for his 45 from his back and pulled it on Mike without hesitation. Mike responded just the same.

"No, I know you, you that Bitch Ass Nigga from Compton that played ma boy outta his club."

Mike laughed at Darrin so hard he nearly lost his grasp on his piece. "Nah, I'm that cat that took his club. Cuz he owed me money, Cuz." Mike enunciated his gang term so that there was no question of his gang affiliation.

Darrin's eyes turned a blood red when he realized Mike was a Crip. "Nah blood." Darrin responded. "This is ma girl house."

Mike was unsure of just who, he was referring to but knowing Sam it had to be her. Joy wasn't the type even in his dreams. Mike had never met the woman yet he knew better. Mike was as heated as the sun. "You might want to back up and get back in your whip and slide on about your business, before things get real out here."

Both Mike and Darrin didn't seem to notice the show they were putting on for the entire neighborhood.

Both had guns drawn. The quiet suburban area had turned into the Gangland streets of Compton and South Central.

**\*\*\*\***

With the blender going and the television blaring Joy and Sam couldn't hear the ruckus going on just outside her door. Joy was busy trying to scoot her way off the couch when she heard a few extra voices screaming alongside the television. It caught her attention, so she muted the sound to make sure it was just her mind playing tricks on her.

"Sam did you hear that?" Joy called her attention to Sam as she was busy dancing to the imaginary music in her head as she was sipping her alcoholic smoothie. Joy hustled to her feet as she could have sworn she heard Darrin's voice amongst the scuffle.

Sam dropped her glass into the sink as she too recognized the male's voice outside. She couldn't understand it nor could she fathom why Mike would be at her sister's place but at first thought she thought she had better pretend as if she didn't know who he was. Hustling down the stairs to the front door both Joy and Sam raced to find out what was going on. Joy was breathing hard as she bust through her front door, landing smack dab in the middle of a war zone. Darrin's eyes grew wide when he realized Joy had stepped right outside her home screaming for the two of them to put their guns down.

Mike started to yell at Joy instructing her to get her ass inside the house. Joy was instantly angered and felt disrespected.

"Who the hell are you? Darrin put down your gun. Sam, call the police." Joy was barking orders every which way.

Mike noticed Sam standing at the door in silence as though she was just some innocent by stander. Mike immediately directed his attention to Sam and demanded some answers. "Who is this cat Sam? Why is he here looking for you? He say he's your man. If my memory serves me correctly I was your dude." Mike completely ignored his previous issue with Sam and the secret she kept about having a twin.

Joy's mouth flew open with such force her jaws began to ache. "What the fuck is he talking about Sam and who the fuck is this Sam?" Joy badgered her sister almost driving her finger into Sam's face.

"I'm Justin's Brother." Mike yelled as he was trying to hold his eye's steady on Darrin and his wavering conscience. He knew Darrin was getting antsy.

Sam still stood without saying a word to confirm the story or at least set the record straight. She couldn't say anything especially since her face had fallen to the floor in about a million pieces at the news that Mike was Justin's brother and Charles' cousin.

"You bastard." Sam finally interjected as she saw her road of escape open before her. Mike obviously hadn't known beforehand that he was related to Charles and neither had she, but she knew that it was her only way out. "You murdered Charles."

"What!" Joy flew off the handle and lunged over at Mike with such force she nearly fell face first onto the pavement. Something Sam should have been doing. Darrin screamed for Joy as he dropped his gun and went to catch Joy before she fell to the ground.

All of a sudden a gunshot went off as Mike tried to prevent Joy from falling onto her stomach. Sam let out a scream of horror as she saw the blood flowing from Joy's white maternity blouse. Mike frantically searched Joy to see where she was hit as Darrin fell to his knees to grab and take Joy in his arms. Darrin's guilt flowed into rage, as the sirens culminated the streets of Oakland.

The blood stained the pavement of Joy Anderson's front porch, her lifeline was faint, her breathing shallow. They say a life lost brings forth a life anew. Will there be a trade, much like the trade Marisola endured with the birth of her daughter? Or will all lives drift in the winds turning a fires rage to ash. Karma, living life in the fast lane…

www.ingramcontent.com/pod-product-compliance
Lightning Source LLC
Chambersburg PA
CBHW062003170626
46813CB00001B/19